The Aviatrix

VIOLET MARSH

Published by Montlake, Seattle

www.apub.com

ISBN-13: 9781542027618
ISBN-10: 1542027616

Cover design by Caroline Teagle Johnson

Printed in the United States of America

Dedicated to my own Milly (Dottie) and her Planey (Rhododendron) and all little girls who dream of big futures and adventures

Chapter One

Early June 1923
North of Saint Louis, Missouri

"What do you mean, you're canceling *our* family's flying circus this year?" The words tore from Mattie McAdams like shrapnel ripping through the canvas wing of a biplane.

"We're out of cash." Her brother Jake looked uncharacteristically sheepish as he helplessly shrugged.

Mattie squeezed her eyes shut as she painstakingly gathered her patience to deal with not one but *three* older brothers. In her younger years, she would have just exploded. Now, she at least tried for a bit of calm.

"I knew we were having money troubles, but I didn't know it was that bad," Mattie finally managed to grind out with an evenness she didn't feel. Her other two siblings shifted uncomfortably in their hard straight-backed chairs. Beside them sat their family's star performer, Leo Ward. The flying ace kept his posture rigid, his boyish features as incongruously stoic as always. Yet Mattie thought she caught a hint of guilt in her former friend's cobalt-blue eyes. Her father, Walt McAdams, attempted a comforting smile, but even with the bill of his ever-present flatcap obscuring half his face, he couldn't hide his weariness.

"We didn't want to worry you, Swift," her father admitted. The old nickname triggered a poignant ache.

Mattie drummed her fingers against the rough wood. Her father had built the dining set from a hickory tree that he'd felled to clear the original airstrip. Normally touching the solid slab gave her a sense of comfort. The furniture was as stout and steady as the man who'd created it. Mattie had expected her pa's current overprotective behavior from her brothers but not from him.

"We thought we could turn it around, and we didn't want you to fret," Otto, her middle brother, admitted ruefully. Like Mattie, he had their mother's red hair. He tried to smooth his wavy locks with petroleum jelly, but the stubborn strands always escaped. Today, one curl looped over the middle of his forehead, giving him a comically earnest air. Unfortunately, Mattie was not in the mood to be amused.

"Fret!" Mattie burst out, crossing her arms over her hand-me-down shirt that used to belong to her brother Will. "I don't fret! It's the lot of you who act like a bunch of mother hens, always worrying about *me*."

Her brothers exchanged looks among themselves and then glanced toward Leo. Mattie groaned and beat out an even faster tattoo along a gouge in the hickory wood.

"If we'd told you about the difficulties, you would have tried to fly crazy stunts to bring in an audience." Will leaned back in his chair, as if his statement explained everything.

In a way, it did. But not how he'd intended.

"Of course I would have!" Mattie jumped to her feet with such force the heavy hickory chair toppled backward. "Flying circuses aren't as rare as they used to be before the war! We need more dramatic stunts, not less. This was Alfred's dream. We can't let it die too."

Almost unthinkingly, she stopped by her twin's old chair. The empty one. The one nobody ever used. The one they even avoided looking at. Instead it sat as a dusty, silent monument to their loss. Rarely acknowledged but always there.

A lump swelled in Mattie's larynx. Swallowing hard against the physical pain, she gripped the back of Alfred's seat, wishing once again that her twin were still here. He'd understood her. He'd supported her. And he never would have allowed the circus that had permitted both of them to soar through the skies to flop over into financial ruin.

"Mattie," Leo's voice came, soft and steady. He rarely spoke during the McAdamses' discussions, especially the heated ones. The fact that he did so now shocked Mattie as much as it disheartened her. This Leo, this shell of her former friend, would never again champion her desire to perform stunts like he had before the Great War.

"Yes, Leo?" Mattie spoke more sharply than she'd intended, but her frustrations had collided with her old grief, making her raw.

He did not react to her tone—at least not outwardly. But Mattie sensed his momentary pause. As a flight instructor, she'd learned to detect her students' masked misgivings. Leo had always hidden his trepidations the best, yet somehow, she could still read him the easiest.

When he spoke, his voice was steady, neutral, perfectly balanced despite its hollow ring. "Alfred wouldn't put you at risk to save his circus."

A sizzle of rage blazed through Mattie. She was tired, so tired, of being mollycoddled. "I seem to remember Alfred *helping* me sneak into the hangar so I could take one of the planes out when Jake, Otto, and Will said no. In fact, I also recall *you* being the designated lookout."

Leo rubbed the back of his head—the only outward indication that her words had meant anything to him. "We were just kids, Mattie. We didn't fully understand the risks."

Mattie started striding up and down the room again, feeling trapped inside the wooden structure, as if the thick overhead beams were prison bars. "My comprehension of physics is just the same as it was then. You forget that *I* was the one who taught *you* how to fly."

Leo moved his hand even more vigorously against his scalp, causing the chestnut-brown strands to stand up. Fortunately, he didn't use the popular brilliantine, or his hair would always look an unruly mess.

"I'm not denying your skills as a pilot, Mattie, or that you showed me how to make a bird soar. I still admire what you can do in the air. That hasn't changed. But I'm not the same fellow who used to pull pranks with you and Alfred before the war."

No. Leo wasn't. Very little of the handsome, athletic man before her now reminded her of the scrawny, rawboned kid who'd turned up one day at the flight school offering to do odd jobs in return for her teaching him how to fly. But he'd filled out during his time overseas and now had the muscles to complement his height. But the greatest change hadn't been physical. Although Leo had always been quiet, he'd returned even more withdrawn. His rare laughter had become a mere wisp of a memory, and worse, he seemed to have assigned himself as her personal protector.

"No," Mattie said, her voice as jagged as her emotions. Long-buried angry words bubbled forth from Mattie, brought to the surface with the pain of watching her twin's dream die too. "You're not the boy I taught to fly, Leo. *That* boy would have allowed me to properly honor my brother in the airplane procession dedicated to Alfred's memory. *He* wouldn't have ratted me out and got me grounded from the flight."

"Swift, it was Jake who made the decision not to let you take the stick that day, not Leo." Mattie's father broke into the conversation. He rubbed one finger against his chin, his expression more haggard as he once again assumed the role of peacekeeper for their rowdy family.

"Leo was right to tell me that you intended to do a stall maneuver during the memorial service." Jake folded his arms over his broad chest, ever the oldest sibling.

"But it was Alfred's signature move and his favorite one!" And it was Mattie's too. She loved pitching the nose of her plane toward the sun and climbing ever skyward until the magnificent machine slowed to the point where it no longer had sufficient air moving over the wings to maintain control. The craft would stop midair, flop to its side, and begin a glorious, mad spin toward the earth, like a maple seed caught in a tornado.

"It's a dangerous stunt, even for a man," Otto said. He was the sibling who looked the most like Alfred, but he had even fairer skin, which tended to flush at the slightest provocation. Right now, he looked redder than a fresh tomato straight from the garden. "You're our sister, and we don't want to see you hurt."

Mattie stopped midpace. "Why is it that if I want to do something, it is nonsense, but if you boys do the same thing, it is bravery?"

"Mattie, you're a girl." Will sank his hands into the front of his scraped-back locks, causing the strands to break loose from the petroleum jelly holding them in place. He'd be rearranging his coiffure as soon as he caught sight of himself in the mirror.

She placed her arms akimbo. "So?"

"You should be doing girl things, not purposely stalling your Jenny." Will tugged on his forelock again, making it even more bedraggled.

Mattie held back a frustrated cry and instead channeled her disgust into a particularly cutting look that she first leveled at the youngest of her surviving brothers and then the older two. "The three of you always say you don't want me risking *my* neck, but when it comes to performing your own tricks, you have no problems risking your *manly* ones."

"Stalling a plane is disorienting to every pilot." Leo spoke quietly, unlike her hotheaded brothers, his voice so annoyingly *reasonable.* "I saw more than one ace crash that way during the war when he used the maneuver to fool the enemy into thinking that he'd been hit."

Mattie threw her hands into the air as she returned to striding through the room. "I always maintain my focus. If you all planned more stunts like that for me, we wouldn't have the problem drawing crowds. Think of the publicity we could get with a female headliner! I could take over Alfred's old role instead of Leo."

Will scratched his temple, breaking more strands of red hair free from their greased confines. "I don't reckon that a girl flyer would have more draw than a war hero, especially one with Leo's popularity."

At the reference to his fame as a daring balloon-busting pilot, Leo cleared his throat uncomfortably and went back to rubbing the back of his head. Mattie knew that he didn't like the attention he still received from his exploits in the Great War. Even the national papers covered his career. Only her knowledge of Leo's patent discomfort kept Mattie from angrily striking back at Will's comment.

"Children," Mattie's father interjected, his voice calm yet unyielding as he pushed back on his cap. "This bickering isn't doing anything but stirring up ill will. It's not going to fix the matter at hand."

"I am *trying* to offer a solution to make the circus more popular so that we *can* save it," Mattie protested.

"Mattie, we don't have enough funds to pay for the fuel to get to our second tour stop," her father admitted as he removed his hat entirely and molded it in his hands. "If we don't find sources of steadier income, we're going to lose the flight school too. We're about to default on the loan."

Not the flight school. Not the place that held so many memories, where sometimes she swore she could still hear Alfred's voice when she worked by herself repairing an engine. Not the airfield where she'd first taken to the skies and later executed her first loop. Not the home her father had built himself, where they'd received the news of Alfred's fatal crash. Not the hangar where the best photograph of her twin hung beside his war medals.

"We can't let that happen." Mattie forced the words through suddenly numb lips.

"That's why I am going to take a job with the US Airmail Service designing mail routes," Otto said, his skin now flushed in fierce resolution. "It'll bring in steady dough."

"I've signed on to be an airmail pilot," Will added as he patted his hair in an attempt to fix the mess he'd made. "Jake is going to be a mechanic on the ground like he was during the war."

"I'm looking for a job as a test pilot," Leo said. "I'll make sure to send money back to help keep the flight school afloat."

An incongruous mix of frustration and gratitude filled Mattie. Of course Leo would have chosen the most dangerous option, even if it also was the most lucrative.

"Where does that leave me?" Mattie asked, pausing between Leo's chair and her father's.

Her father reached up to pat her hand reassuringly. "You and I will run the flight school. It's about time we started offering classes in the summers again."

Of course she would be stuck here in Missouri! Just like she'd been during the war. Oh, she'd tried to join as a pilot, first in the French Lafayette Escadrille and then in the US Army Air Corps, but neither country had wanted a female aviator, no matter how talented.

"You can work on your radio designs," Leo offered.

Tinkering with gadgets and engines was Mattie's second love. Lately, she'd been trying to figure out how to harness radio signals to improve communications. But too much frustration pumped through her to allow her to concentrate on anything engineering related.

"Just so I can receive another rejection letter from a manufacturer?" Mattie bit out. "No one is interested in a woman's designs, and they are even less inclined to hire me."

That was the crux of it. Unlike her brothers and Leo with their military backgrounds and sheer *maleness*, she was unemployable in the professions that she excelled at.

Suddenly, the pressure of everything—losing the business, losing her main opportunity to dance through the skies, losing her tight-knit family, losing *Alfred*'s dream—became too much for her. She needed to escape.

"But perhaps you are right," Mattie added. "Perhaps my designs will produce the miracle we need. It is, at least, one thing that I can try. I need time to think things over, and I do my best considering when I'm tinkering."

Mustering a smile that she didn't feel, Mattie nodded toward the assembled McAdamses and Leo and then ducked out the door. She had just started down the long covered passage that connected the main house to the hangar when she heard her name—soft and low, but no less intense for all its quietness. Even if Mattie hadn't recognized Leo's voice, she would have known who had followed her. They'd always been able to anticipate each other's moves.

"Don't do anything foolish, Mattie," Leo said as soon as she turned toward him. At first, he looked as stiff and impassive as ever, except for the slightest tightening of the muscles around his mouth. Mattie opened her mouth to lambast him, but then she saw it: a flicker of concern in the blue depths of his eyes and maybe, just maybe, the slightest tinge of fear.

He knew she wasn't going to tinker, but to fly. It appeared, though, that he didn't intend to peach on her to her brothers for once. She appreciated his discretion but not his concern.

"I won't, Leo," Mattie said wearily. "I might not be like you and lay out my flight path as if I were General Pershing planning troop movements, but I know what I'm doing. One of these days, I'm going to prove that to you."

Leo nodded stiffly. His Adam's apple jerked as he visibly swallowed. He'd spread his feet apart, his hands clasped behind his back, his muscular chest puffed out. She'd dubbed it his *war-monument pose*, and she knew he assumed it whenever he felt uncomfortable. Eons ago, before the War to End All Wars, she would have teased a laugh out of him. But she hadn't tried for years, and she doubted that she could even coax a slight smile.

"Thanks for keeping my secret this time, Leo," Mattie told him softly just before she turned and opened the door to the hangar.

Mattie breathed in the familiar scent of Rockol engine oil, grease, and gasoline. The clink of gears, the rattle of chains, and the pump of pistons had been the background sounds of Mattie's childhood. She still loved watching cold, motionless pieces of metal suddenly transform into something almost alive. But even those marvels could not compare to taking flight. She'd never forgotten the rush she'd felt the first time the wheels had left the ground and the plane had pitched its nose straight into the wide blue sky. She'd begged her father to stay up longer, and he'd managed to hold the old-fashioned, kitelike bird aloft as long as he could. Ever since that day, she'd been absolutely air mad.

Walking past the worktable tucked away in the back of the hangar, Mattie headed instead to the Shaker peg rack that held their gear. Alfred's still hung next to hers where he'd placed it after his last flight before leaving for France. Mattie could still remember Alfred laughing as he'd flung the leather strap of his goggles over the cylindrical piece of wood. He'd promised to write home to her about all his adventures. *"I won't leave anything out, Matt. I promise. Gosh, I wish you could come with Leo and me. With us three flying in formation, we could chase the Jagdstaffeln back to Germany in no time."*

But she hadn't been there at her brother's side on the Western Front. Even now when she woke in the middle of the night or when things got too quiet in the workshop, she'd wonder if her presence could have made a difference. Maybe she would have managed to waggle her wings to signal to her brother that he was going the wrong way. Even if she'd just been a ground mechanic, perhaps she might have developed a better navigation or communications system that would have alerted her brother to his fatal confusion before it was too late.

Mattie reached up with one finger and gently stroked the leather cap that her brother had worn. "I won't let you be forgotten, Alfred. I'll keep your dreams alive."

The leather felt rough and dry under her fingertips. It was time for her to clean it again with saddle soap when no one was looking. After giving the helmet one last touch, she straightened her shoulders and headed toward her own gear. She shoved her helmet down over her red hair and stuffed the rest of her long braid under her flight jacket. She planned on doing stunts, and she didn't want any auburn strands whipping about her face and causing problems.

Huffing out a sigh of pent-up frustration, Mattie headed toward her Curtiss JN-4, or "Jenny." The aircraft's buttercup-yellow nose and wingtips normally made her smile, but even the sight of the sunshine-bright highlights on her baby-blue plane failed to penetrate the heaviness settling inside her. Only taking to the air would accomplish that.

She stepped on the wing, hoisted herself into the cockpit, and started the routine preflight checks. When she flicked the switch to check the spark that ignited the fuel, she frowned as she realized the first magneto wasn't working. She'd modified all their planes to include a backup magneto, which had become a safety standard after the war. The Jenny, being an older, cheaper design, hadn't originally had such a safety net.

Thankfully, Mattie's second magneto worked. She eased back in the cockpit for a moment, debating if she should take the time to fix the first one. But the pressure inside her threatened to fissure the seams of her control. She wanted in the air. She *needed* to be in the air.

Her decision made, Mattie hopped down and yanked on the Jenny's propeller, starting the noisy motor. Leaping into the cockpit again, she pulled back on the throttle. The responding roar of the engine pounded through her heart, breaking through the suffocating pressure encasing it.

Mattie maneuvered the aircraft into the bright, late-spring Missouri day, and more of the smothering vexation inside her dissipated. Her brothers and father must have still been crowded around the table, since no one had rushed to stop her. She spied Leo on the porch, his eyes shaded as he followed her progress across the clay landing strip. It wouldn't surprise her if he planned to take out his own plane and follow. Sometimes she swore that he thought he was still a squadron leader like he'd been during the war, constantly burdened with the safety of the new pilots. At least Leo was letting her soar today.

As Mattie buzzed farther down the runway and picked up speed, the nearby stand of hickory, cedar, and black walnut trees melded into a blur of pure green. By the time her wheels lifted from the ground, she forgot about Leo and her brothers in her delight at rising with the grace of a phoenix. Like the mythical bird, she felt rejuvenated, reborn even, every time she soared. It never got old, this wild, freeing ascent. As the whitewashed walls of the flight school grew smaller and smaller, so did the pain. Up in the air with only swifts, hawks, and swallows for company, Mattie could think of Alfred without a sharp sting of bittersweetness.

She set her course for the nearby town. Despite living near an airstrip, the residents still loved when the planes flew overhead. The grocer and the druggist sold postcards of Leo and his stunts, a sight that always sent him into his monument pose as he rubbed the back of his head. All summer long, local sweethearts would spread out blankets on the hillside by the airfield and eat a picnic lunch just for a chance to watch one of the Jennies take off. Mattie had even spied more than one young fellow proposing to his gal.

Reaching Main Street, Mattie let out a whoop as she flew her biplane low and woke up the formerly sleepy midwestern town. Folks puttering down the road in their Model Ts paused to watch her flight. Girls abandoned their jump ropes, and boys looked up from their games of marbles. Storekeepers wandered out of their shops as they shaded their eyes to track her progress. Some people waved enthusiastically. Others watched unabashedly openmouthed. Everyone—young and old—smiled.

The maneuver looked deceptively simple, but buzzing so close to the buildings took skill . . . and nerves. With the wind buffeting her, the engine roaring in front, and the landscape rushing below, Mattie couldn't tamp down the wild excitement begging for release. She wanted—no, she *craved*—the exhilarating freedom only soaring could bring. Flinging away her remaining caution, she whooped again and did a roll, letting her Jenny skim perilously close to the dirt road leading away from town. In the inverted position, her leather-clad head dangling downward, she could see patchworks of farmland and remaining stands of trees from ancient forests. Young stalks of corn blurred into a sea of green, and the wind from the propeller caused the field to form magnificent, undulating waves.

Feeling on top of the world even as she hung upside down near its surface, Mattie grinned. Other than her, only Leo would dare try this trick. Her brothers would never risk it, except for . . . Mattie's smile slipped. *Except for Alfred.*

The return of the old memories threatened to suck away the bliss of flying. Resolutely, Mattie rolled the plane upright and yanked the stick backward to shoot into the sky, letting the thrill once again chase the pain away. When she executed a swooping figure eight, her joy rekindled. She could make airplanes dance. She *lived* to make airplanes dance.

Unable to stop herself, Mattie flew low again, banking the Curtiss JN-4 hard on its side, enjoying watching the patchwork of fields from a perpendicular position. Just as she began to right the plane, she caught sight of a cherry-red Duesenberg convertible coupe. Despite the Jenny's height and speed, Mattie recognized the sleek outline of the unique car immediately. The Duesenberg brothers had earned a name for themselves in the racing circuit, and anyone who knew anything about automobiles dreamed of owning one of the sleek, prohibitively expensive motorcars.

To Mattie's surprise, a fashionably dressed woman drove the coupe with no male companion in sight. The driver wore no hat, and the wind caught the black curls of her bob, her bright-red scarf trailing out behind her. She looked just like a magazine model or a movie star. Mattie normally didn't give a fig about women's fashion, but something about the flapper's flamboyant elegance drew her attention. Grinning, Mattie waved as she finished straightening the plane. The stranger lifted one gloved hand, the fabric dyed to match the car's gleaming paint job.

Intrigued, Mattie looped back. On her second pass, she spotted a small spaniel perched in the passenger seat, its ridiculously long ears flapping in the wind. To Mattie's shock, she thought she spotted a flash of a red scarf around the dog's neck that matched its owner's. As Mattie started pulling away, she knew the woman was laughing merrily, even though the Jenny's engine drowned out any sound.

Mattie started to whoop again, but the mirth turned into an expulsion of air when she felt an odd prickle run down her neck. Turning slightly, she squinted and searched the airspace around her. The bright spring rays made her eyes water beneath her goggles just as she spotted a flash of white and navy blue. Leo's Curtiss. He'd approached her with the sun directly behind him, a stealth maneuver he'd learned during the war.

Hell's bells and buckets of blood. It wasn't easy for anyone to get the drop on her. Leave it to Leo the Flying Lion to manage it.

Deliberately ignoring her unwanted tail, Mattie had begun to pull the plane farther skyward for another barrel roll when, with a sudden puff and splutter, her engine died. Utterly and completely.

Instead of panic, the energy that shot through her was sharp, focused, and precise. Mattie didn't have a backup magneto. She had one—*one*—chance to restart the engine. And that would require plenty of nerve. Luckily, she had that in abundance.

Mattie dived like an osprey toward the ground. It was the only way to pick up enough speed to spin the propeller and give her the opportunity—the only opportunity—to try to restart the engine. The cornfields transformed into an angry sea of swirling green, threatening to swallow her up and drag her under. The effect of the sharp plummet was dizzying, but she let the spinning sensation fuel her rather than disorient her. If this was to be her last dive, she was going to make it one heck of a spectacle.

Just as the nose of her plane seemed destined to crash into the field, the propeller began to spin. Mattie flicked the control to the magneto. The temperamental mechanism sparked back to life, and the engine roared. She did, too, whooping and hollering as she steadied out the deadly descent and skimmed over the farmland. As she shot high into the air, joy, excitement, and pure release mixed inside her. Yelling out her triumph, she spun her bird madly through the atmosphere.

This. *This* was the best way to celebrate being alive.

Chapter Two

Horror exploded inside Leo with the force of an artillery shell. The past and the present meshed. Flames licked the edge of his vision. Alfred had died in a ball of fire, and Leo swore he could feel the lethal heat crackling over his own skin. His breath grew harsh and staccato as memories of Alfred's fatal dogfight crashed into Leo's mind. The sharp whine of bullets exploded in his ears, amplified to such an unholy degree he thought his eardrums would burst.

Guilt and helpless terror plowed into him. Mattie dived her plane straight toward the unforgiving Missouri dirt. He retained enough sense to realize that she intended to gain speed to turn the propeller. Yet the sight of her plunging Jenny flickered in and out with Alfred's Nieuport until Leo could barely discern the real versus the remembered. At times, it seemed that her tail was aflame, too, with tongues of fire scorching toward the fuselage.

Somehow, Leo gathered the presence of mind to fly toward her, as if he could somehow lift her plane with his own. He'd trade places with her, just as he would have with Alfred. If any of them should die, it should be *him*.

Then, just when he felt he would rip in two, Mattie managed to restart the engine and take back control. She zoomed skyward. Back among the clouds, she twisted her plane in tight barrel rolls, as if her near-death experience was something to *celebrate*. Leo's spark of frustration at Mattie's cavalier attitude toward her own demise cracked through the husk of horror encasing him. Slowly, the sensations of being in a dogfight receded, and his body sagged as he sucked up the air that he'd forgotten to breathe. But he had no time to allow relief to flood him. Not at four thousand feet. Instead he dug into his aggravation.

Still feeling shaky, he watched as Mattie deftly landed the plane. A few seconds after her Jenny rolled to a stop, Leo touched down beside her. Wingtips only a yard apart, they cut their engines at the same time. Mattie whipped off her leather helmet and sent her red hair flying. Almost all of it had escaped her ever-present braid, and it hung around her face like a curtain of fire. The goggles fell off next, revealing her eyes, which had turned a warm golden color, the green-blue hues almost swallowed up in her excitement. Her pale cheeks were flushed a faint pink, complementing the smattering of freckles across her nose. She jumped from the cockpit, not waiting for anyone to help her down. She had so much spring in her step she practically bounced like a rubber ball. She was a walking personification of exhilaration, and he desperately wanted to gather her into his arms . . . to try to capture that wonderful energy, to assure himself that his eyes hadn't deceived him and she really had pulled out of the seemingly deadly spiral.

Anger and relief mixed with desire, creating an unholy brew. Fortunately, he was accustomed to dealing with the potent cocktail of emotion he felt toward Mattie. If he had one talent other than flying, it was masking his feelings. Hell, sometimes, he could even hide them from himself.

Leo leaped from the cockpit and stalked toward Mattie as he tore off his goggles and helmet. Clenching the leather in his fist, he tried to measure his approach as she stood, her shoulders thrown back, her defiant posture reminding him of a stylized hood ornament on a fancy car—ready to face any obstacle impudent enough to stand in her way.

"What happened up there?" Somehow, he managed to keep his voice calm, but Mattie still crossed her arms, her unique hazel eyes sparking a greenish gold.

"My magneto didn't fire properly," Mattie explained.

Leo shoved his hand into his hair as a sick feeling twisted through him. "What about the backup?"

Mattie's lips tightened. She still met his gaze, but he could see the flicker of sheepishness. He squeezed his eyes shut as he realized that she'd purposely gone up in the sky knowing she only had one working spark. And no one understood the inner workings of an engine better than Mattie. She'd comprehended the risk and recklessly accepted it.

A fresh surge of anger burned through his habitual numbness. Leo's next words blazed from him before he could think of a less inflammatory delivery. "That was beyond foolish."

Mattie flicked her long hair behind her back. She always managed to look like adventure, even after she'd nearly terrified his soul into leaving his body.

"You're not exactly in the position to give lectures on caution." Mattie's words hung in the air, a gauntlet thrown down by the damsel. For a moment, Leo almost spoke the truth—that when he'd watched his best friend's reckless heroics end in a horrific, fiery crash behind enemy lines, he'd sworn on Alfred's memory, and to himself, that he'd protect the rest of the McAdamses.

"Mattie, you just knowingly took a malfunctioning plane into the air and performed tricks with it."

She bent slightly at the waist, placing her upper body closer to his in a clear challenge. "I'm not the one with the reputation for utter fearlessness."

Leo didn't know if he'd ever really experienced an absence of fear. He'd lived with dread for so long that he'd become numb to the constant thrum of it. He felt no anxiousness at the idea of his own passing. When he'd lived as a runaway on the streets, a premature demise had been a foregone conclusion long before the Great War. But after he'd trained with the McAdamses and discovered a home with them, he'd registered the sharp bite of fear again. His own end might not concern him, but the deaths of any members of his newfound family did. Mattie's most of all.

"I don't make spontaneous decisions when I execute stunts." He spoke the half truth. True, he wasn't the hothead Alfred had been and Mattie still was. But that wasn't why he insisted on performing the most dangerous tricks. He didn't have kin who cared about him or even close friends outside of the McAdams Family Flying Circus. But if he mentioned that to Mattie, she'd protest and start fretting over him. She'd make it her mission to convince him otherwise, but he knew the truth. To survive, all unclaimed foundlings had to recognize at some point that they were alone.

"Well, I'm sorry I can't be as mechanical as you are about flying."

Leo suppressed a wry, humorless smile that he knew Mattie would read only too well. He used to love the thrill of soaring as much as she did, maybe even more. It had been one of the first true pleasures in his life. He'd felt powerful, *unstoppable*, as he'd charged through the sky—cities and their inhabitants mere specks below. The freedom he'd found hurtling through the air had damn near intoxicated him. But dogfight after dogfight had drummed that joy right out of him. He didn't care if he never stepped into a cockpit again. But even if he hadn't given himself a mission to protect a family who currently made its living running a flight school, he'd still be working as a pilot. After all, it was the one thing, the only thing, he knew how to do.

"Flying is risky enough, Mattie, without taking a single-magneto plane out for a joyride."

Mattie waved her hand dismissively, the movement causing her red curls to bounce. "We all used to fly them."

Leo pinched the bridge of his nose as he kept rubbing the back of his head with the other hand. "Because there were no other options. There's a reason you modified the engines so that we have two."

"It's not like you've never made the decision to fly with only one working magneto," Mattie pointed out as she stepped closer to him.

Leo froze as he realized that Alfred must have written to her about that particular exploit of his. It had become a legendary story—not only in his squadron but in the entire US Army Air Service—of how he'd restarted the dead engine in midair with two Fokkers on his tail. He'd managed to loop back over his trackers, placing himself in the chase position before shooting both German fighters down.

"That was war, Mattie. This isn't."

"But there were plenty of other pilots and planes who could have flown instead. You could have taken the time to get the problem fixed."

But he'd been the one in command of his squadron. "Mattie, the two circumstances are not at all alike. You need to be more careful."

Mattie lifted her eyes toward the heavens. He followed her gaze as she tracked the swallows flitting in the bright afternoon light, dark shadows against the endless blue spring sky. He'd been watching her gather patience with her brothers like this for years. More and more, she'd begun employing it with him.

When she leveled a look in his direction, her remarkable hazel eyes had turned more green than brown, a clear sign that something had upset her. He could detect anger, but it was the hurt that sliced him.

"You're not going to be happy, Leo, until I give up flying altogether, are you?"

The softly spoken words, unlike her normally bold statements, caused his throat to swell closed. He shook his head.

"Not that," he managed to force out. *Never that.* He didn't wish to take soaring away from Mattie. She loved it too much. At night, when he had trouble sleeping, he'd think of her laughter as she sat in the cockpit and he in the passenger seat. Somehow the sound perfectly echoed the sensation he used to get when flying—light, buoyant, and utterly thrilling.

And Mattie was *good*, maybe even better than him . . . *hell*, probably better than him. Definitely better than any man he'd seen, Allied or German. No, he didn't want to curtail her flying.

"I don't want you risking your life just to chase a thrill or to impress a bunch of spectators," Leo said.

Mattie stomped toward him, jabbing her finger in the direction of his chest. "It is my life to lose, Leo Ward. They're my risks to take, not yours. I am tired of you, of my brothers, of my father, of any *man* deciding what's best for me. You judge for yourself what stunts to try, and so do Jake, Otto, and Will. It should be my decision, and *my* decision alone, how I fly."

Enthusiastic clapping echoed through the air. Leo spun to discover a vaguely familiar woman lounging against Mattie's plane. At her feet stood a small floppy-eared dog wearing a ridiculous red scarf that matched the woman's. Although Leo understood little about fashion, even he could recognize that the interloper's attire wasn't typical.

The woman, however, ignored him, her gaze entirely on Mattie as she continued her applause. "I couldn't have said it better myself, darling."

Dropping her hands to her sides, the stranger sauntered across the runway with the air of a monarch. Beside her, the little spaniel trotted jauntily, its white fan-shaped tail wagging enthusiastically.

"I'm Vera Jones," the woman announced, extending her hand to Mattie. The name caused a flicker of recognition to spark to life in Leo's mind. An heiress, the avant-garde flapper dominated the gossip columns. He never read the society pages, but even he'd spotted photographs of her.

"Mattie McAdams." As she took Vera's hand, the dog plopped down politely beside the two women. Its tail thumped insistently on the ground, its dark-brown eyes huge as it stared longingly up at Mattie. Leo could empathize.

Mattie made an *aww* sound as she bent and rubbed the spaniel's ears. The animal emitted a small happy sigh as it leaned into her hand. Evidently a life of luxury had given the bit of black-and-white fluff excellent taste.

"And who is this?" Mattie asked, her voice sweeter and higher than usual as she stared down at the pup. Her capacity for affection had always fascinated Leo, drawing him toward her like a magnet.

"Ruby," Vera answered with the patent pride of an adoring pet owner.

"Pleased to meet you, Ruby." Mattie scratched down the spaniel's spine, and the dog wriggled her back end in excitement. The enthusiastic movement caused the animal's collar to glint from underneath her dapper scarf. It looked suspiciously like rubies and diamonds. On most pets, Leo would assume glass or paste, but given Vera Jones's reputation for flamboyant excess, Leo rather thought the gemstones real.

When Mattie straightened, Vera held her palm out to Leo. "You must be the famous Flying Lion."

Leo delivered one of his practiced, affable smiles—the one that he'd learned to make while being interviewed during his war days. Mattie called it his *press face*, and silently he agreed. The grin always felt like a stiff facsimile of what people expected of a daring aviator.

"Yes, ma'am."

The dog padded over to Leo and situated herself close to his feet. He glanced down. Having grown up in New York City, he wasn't accustomed to animals. He'd encountered a few dogs and plenty of cats while living in dark, dank alleys, but they'd been as feral as him—all snarls and distrust. This carefully groomed dog with her bejeweled collar and perfectly brushed fur belonged to a different stratum where food appeared in porcelain dishes and soft bedding provided a cocoon of warmth.

Ruby's ears drooped slightly, and her round eyes grew even larger. Leo bent down and patted her awkwardly on the head. Even with the clumsiness of his gesture, the pup seemed enthralled by his attention.

Her pink tongue darted out as she eagerly licked the side of his hand. Despite himself, he was charmed.

"Ruby likes everyone," Vera said, "but she seems particularly taken with you."

"Really?" Leo said in surprise. He straightened and shoved his hands into his bomber jacket, his feet spread into his *war-monument pose*.

"So what brings you to the home of the McAdams Family Flying Circus, Miss Jones?" Mattie asked quickly.

Leo sent her a grateful look. Of course Mattie noticed his discomfort.

"Call me Vera," the fashionable woman told Mattie with a wide smile. "And I am here to talk to you."

"Me?" Mattie made an atypical squeak.

"Why are you looking for Mattie?" Leo shoved his hands farther into his leather coat as suspicion snaked through him.

Vera didn't answer him directly and instead turned to Mattie. Her violet-blue eyes twinkled with a mix of mischievousness and determination. "In the spirit of my maternal grandparents, who operated a circus, I'm starting my own flying one. It will be called the Flying Flappers and feature primarily female daredevils. I will, of course, be the headliner. I'll wing-walk and do other stunts outside the cockpit. I need female pilots, though, and from what I've just seen, you're one of the best."

Vera paused theatrically, and trepidation thudded through Leo. When the heiress continued, her next words proved that his talent for predicting peril hadn't dimmed.

"Mattie McAdams, do you want to fly with me?"

Her emotions already bouncing around faster than a Ping-Pong ball at a table tennis match, Mattie temporarily froze. She—who did everything fast—actually needed to stay completely still as she replayed the words just spoken by *the* Vera Jones. *"Do you want to fly with me?"*

Yes. *Yes!* She *had* heard the infamous heiress's question accurately.

Excitement roared through Mattie like an eight-cylinder engine rumbling to life, but she knew better than to fully release its power. Although Leo and her brothers might accuse her of flying recklessly, life had taught her caution in all other areas. Folks didn't cotton well to the idea of female pilots. She'd had too many hopes smashed. She would not allow this woman, no matter how famous or fabulously dressed or spirited, to play her for a fool. Unless under drastic circumstances, Mattie would never jump into an unknown plane without checking its engine first, and she certainly wouldn't accept this offer without question. But it could—just *could*—be her chance. To save her family's business. To even resurrect Alfred's dream. To achieve her own. To fly *how* she wanted, *when* she wanted, *where* she wanted. She'd never achieve it stuck at the flight school or under the watch of her brothers.

"Why do you want me in your troupe?" Mattie asked skeptically. "It's not like I'm as famous as the Flying Schoolgirl or Brave Bessie." Modern-day princesses like Vera didn't just show up in middle-of-nowhere Missouri and offer a chance at a fairy-tale life, especially to someone like Mattie.

Vera Jones's painted lips, however, quirked into a decidedly pleased smile. "I do appreciate a skeptical woman."

Flattery clearly worked on Mattie, more than she'd suspected it would. Yet she ignored the delighted flutter. Everyone knew Vera Jones's father was one of the most successful businessmen in the world. It only made sense that his daughter had picked up a negotiating skill or two.

"But that doesn't really answer why you want me to fly." Mattie moved her arms akimbo, just as she did when dealing with one of the boys. Leo moved beside her and crossed his arms, as if to punctuate her words. Mattie rather wished he'd let her handle this entirely on her own, but at least he stayed quiet.

Instead of looking offended by Mattie's insistence, Vera tilted her head, causing the diamond, flower-shaped brooch on her cloche hat to wink in the sunlight. "I like your spirit, Mattie McAdams. You and I are going to go far. As to why I'm asking you to join, it is rather simple. One, there aren't too many licensed female pilots, although there are more than folks think. Two, news from Saint Louis does travel to Chicago, where I live, and when I started asking around about fly girls, your name came up more than once. So I thought I'd pop down here and see for myself. I planned on asking you for a demonstration, but you've already provided me with a magnificent one. Which leads me to my third and final point. I would be an utter chump if I didn't hire a bear cat who not only can successfully restart a motor midair but who has the presence of mind and derring-do to execute a series of barrel rolls after a nearly fatal malfunction."

Finally. Someone who recognized Mattie. Fully recognized her. Not just her flying skills but her courage. For once, someone was cheering her on and not hypocritically pointing out the alleged rashness of her behavior.

But even if Vera was saying precisely what Mattie longed to hear, she had no intention of being a patsy swayed by pretty words. "How much does it pay?"

"Oh, handsomely, of course." Vera waved a hand covered by cherry-red silk that matched her dress perfectly.

"How handsome is handsome?" Mattie asked.

An intense light crackled in Vera's violet-blue eyes. "You are an excellent pilot, but I see you might just have the workings of a businesswoman too. Females are too often taught not to discuss finances. I find it refreshing that you do. I plan to pay five thousand dollars a year."

Wariness and excitement flickered through Mattie in equal measure. At that stunning amount, she'd be making more than her brothers and even Leo. But Mattie's father had taught her the old adage that if something seemed too good to be true, it most likely was. "Why would you be so generous?"

Vera shrugged, causing the silk chiffon of her cherry-red dress to flutter. The movement caught her spaniel's attention, and the little dog licked her mistress's ankle. "The simple answer is that I can afford to be. I don't need to make a profit, and I won't be surprised if I lose money on this venture."

"Then why are you doing it?" Leo asked. The confusion in his voice echoed Mattie's own.

Vera lifted her shoulders nonchalantly once again. "For the fun. The excitement. The chance to prove women can be just as talented and courageous as men. To show the world women can fly."

"But to pay five *thousand* dollars a year?" Mattie repeated.

"Darling, I have a sinful amount of money, and there is only so much frippery a gal can buy. I get joy out of helping other women thumb their noses at society's absurd restrictions on our sex. And I want my circus to shock and amaze. I plan on doing tricks that no one is trying yet. It'll be dangerous—exciting, but not without peril. If I'm asking you to risk life and limb, the least I can do is compensate you."

Danger. A word designed to intimidate. But for Mattie, it was utterly thrilling and beyond tempting.

"Mattie," Leo said softly, "don't be reckless. This is like haring off with only one functioning magneto."

Don't be reckless. How many times had she heard that phrase? From him? From her brothers? Even from complete strangers?

Mattie whirled on Leo, forgetting Vera momentarily in her anger. "Don't be reckless. Don't be *reckless*? Aren't you the one who is planning to look for a job as a test pilot? How is *that* not reckless? At least I'll be in a machine that I know and have maintained myself."

"It's completely different." Leo assumed his monument pose.

"How?" Mattie tossed both her hands into the air. "How is it different? Do you think you can fly better than me? Safer than me? *Smarter* than me?"

"Mattie, I never said—"

"You forget that it was *me* who taught you, the Flying Lion. If I hadn't, you'd still be a harmless, clawless kitten." She stalked toward Leo until only inches remained between their bodies.

Leo's mouth twitched, but Mattie couldn't tell if it was from amusement over being compared to a baby feline or from irritation.

"I'm only trying to keep you safe, Mattie, and I was never harmless. My claws have always been plenty sharp." He moved closer, too, his muscular chest puffed out.

"Well, my talons are sharper." Caught up in the wild maelstrom of emotions stirred up first by the wild plane ride and then by Vera's offer, Mattie gave Leo a poke for good measure. His strong pectoral muscles barely depressed under her fingertip.

"You forget that the student can surpass the master." He stepped into her jab, his breath hot against her face.

"Not the cocky ones. You're like Icarus, who flew too close to the sun and melted the wax holding his feathers together, causing him to fall to the ground." Mattie leaned forward too. This close she could see the starburst pattern in Leo's blue irises.

"You're the one who's going to melt her wax wings." Leo gently grabbed her finger, which was still pressed against his chest. The warmth of his hand mixed with her blazing outrage and wild exhilaration, making her burn like a wildfire. She permitted him to move her hand down to her side, but only because that allowed her to shift even closer.

"I have wings of steel," Mattie said. The argument barely made sense anymore, but she couldn't think properly.

"So do I." He dropped her hand, but it still felt scorched from their mutual heat. He inched closer so that only a sliver of space remained between them. If either took too deep of a breath, their bodies would brush against each other. Mattie's already overexercised heart stuttered and then slammed against her rib cage like the flooded engine of an old airplane pulling out of a loop. She swore the starburst pattern in Leo's eyes grew brighter as his chin dipped ever so slowly. She watched the descent, fascinated and unable to move.

Clapping echoed around them, and all Mattie's other senses came flooding back. Once again, she could smell the nearby grove of cedar trees mixed with the last blooms on the lilac bush outside the hangar. She could hear the birds singing and the faint chatter of industrious fox squirrels instead of just the beat of her own heart and the fast breaths of Leo.

With an aborted gasp, Mattie leaped back. Leo moved so quickly he stumbled despite his legendary reflexes.

"You two are fabulous together. I can't get enough." Vera was staring at them with unabashed interest.

"Pardon?" Leo asked.

"You may be my favorite couple. Sparks. Humor. Both daredevils. I love it!"

"We're not a couple," Mattie corrected quickly as she sidled farther away from Leo. "We're not even friends . . . at least not anymore."

"I am not a believer in long-term romantic entanglements myself. They are quite a nuisance to a modern woman. But it *is* a pity to let such delightful sexual sparks go to utter waste."

An odd bolt of energy shot through Mattie, igniting her already charged nerves. She felt on the edge of something grand. Beside her, Leo spluttered out a cough. His tanned face had turned a peculiar shade of purplish red. He was rubbing the back of his head with such vigor Mattie actually feared he might create a temporary bald spot.

Vera laid her gloved hand on the sleeve of his bomber jacket. "Oh, don't mind me. I say outrageous things all the time. It is part of my charm."

Mattie glanced at Leo, and a peculiar sort of awareness bloomed through her. She felt . . . different. Electrified. Light, yet somehow fuller. What had Vera spied that had triggered her outrageous observation? Could—

"Whatever the reason, you both produce the wildest sparks," Vera said, addressing Leo. "The audience will eat it up. Which is why I've just decided to offer you a job too. Same terms as Mattie."

"Me?" Leo asked, and at the same time Mattie said, *"Him?"*

"I've read all about your exploits as the Flying Lion, so I know you're an excellent aviator. Then there are your marvelous interactions with Mattie. I'm not planning on hiring many male performers, but you would have your uses."

"My . . . uses?" Leo asked, his voice a little nonplussed. Mattie herself felt a bit unsettled by the idea of Leo joining her if she accepted Vera's offer. Embarking on her own sounded much more adventurous. Besides, what did *she* have to do with *Leo* being hired?

"Conflict. Tension. Drama. Everything you need to draw an audience into a story."

"What story?" Mattie asked as she and Leo shared a look. It was the first wordless, companionable exchange that they'd had in years.

Vera began to pace, the loyal Ruby happily tripping after her. "I can see it now. It would start out with you two arguing—just as you are now. Mattie as the New Woman—trousers, shirt, boots—all very tailored and tight fitting. Leo in a handlebar mustache . . ."

"You want me to grow a mustache?" Leo asked, looking slightly horrified. He'd always chosen a clean-shaven look, even before the Great War, when facial hair had been popular.

"Oh, you can use a fake one." Vera flicked her wrist as she pivoted elegantly on one foot. "But we need something evocative of the last century. Victorian, if you will. Something that looks like times gone by. You'll be characters, you see—Miss Modernity and Mr. Yesteryear. Will the future or the past win? Audience members will instinctually pick a side to root for during your flight duel."

"Flight duel?" Mattie asked, her interest piqued. Perhaps Leo joining Vera's circus wouldn't be such an awful idea. She'd love an opportunity to show up the stiff-rumped hypocrite.

"Of course. It's absolutely perfect for an aerial show. You each will try to one-up the other's stunts. It will be part scripted, part real competition."

"You want me to challenge Mattie?" Leo asked, his voice as tight as a wire stretched to the limits of its tensile strength.

"I can always find another male pilot willing to fly with her if you're not."

The hand buried in Leo's hair sped up even more as he scrubbed his scalp. "And you'll pay me five thousand dollars too."

"Yes. Same as Mattie."

Leo stared off unseeingly in the direction of the cedars. Unlike him, Mattie didn't need to mull over her decision any longer. She wouldn't let his concerns—or anyone's—hold her back.

"I'm in," Mattie said.

"How about a ladies' handshake? I find them ever so much more binding than a gentlemen's." Vera extended her hand. Mattie wiped hers on her trousers first. She never knew when she might have grease on them, and she didn't want to spoil her new employer's silk gloves.

With a sense of satisfied anticipation, Mattie closed her fingers around Vera's. The exchange was as firm and confident as any man's.

"If Mattie's joining, then so am I," Leo announced, holding out his palm.

To Mattie's surprise, she didn't experience a wave of frustration at Leo's decision. Instead of feeling trapped, she found it rather exciting.

"I am going to thrash you, Mister." Mattie kept her voice mostly light and teasing, but she made sure no one could miss her underlying conviction as she jabbed a finger in Leo's direction.

He leaned toward her. "Not if I thrash you first."

And for a moment, Mattie spotted a flash of her old partner in crime. She didn't back up but instead jammed her face near Leo's, her lips less than an inch away from his. "Challenge accepted."

Chapter Three

Mattie heard the male footsteps in the hallway outside her room—Jake's, judging by the heaviness of the tread. Her brothers weren't always attuned to subtlety, but even they sensed something was awry after she'd retreated to her room for three hours. Mattie had made Leo promise that she'd be the one to break the news to her family.

Mattie, however, found herself stalling . . . something she never did. But she was still struggling to find the right words. It had always been her siblings and Leo going off. Now she was the one who had to tell Pa that she was leaving. Over the years, her father had become more than just a parent; he'd become a friend. When her brothers had all been deployed, she'd helped him run the flight school. They'd grown even closer when they'd comforted each other after they'd received news of Alfred's death. Now he would be on his own.

And pains that they were, she'd miss her knuckleheaded brothers. They'd always cared for her in their own boisterous, overprotective, teasing manner. They showed it in little ways, like now as they took turns checking on her. None of them dared to knock. Her room with a big window overlooking the landing strip had always been her sanctuary. It wasn't girlie or filled with frilly things, but it was hers all the same. She didn't have many possessions—a toy plane her father had carved for her, the crazy quilt her mother had sewn before her death, a silver brush that had been her mother's mother's, a beat-up music box Alfred had bought for her on their tenth birthday, and a single dress for church, weddings, or other fancy occasions. Other than that, she had her brothers' cast-offs. It never bothered her, not having bric-a-brac lying about. She had engines to tinker with and planes to fly. That was what she loved, not motionless, functionless objects.

If she wanted her independence so badly, she needed to stop avoiding the hardest part about it. After throwing her shoulders back, she opened the door.

Jake popped his head out from the larger bunk room that he shared with the rest of the boys and Leo. "How are you feeling, Mattie?"

"Just fine," she told him. "Where's everyone?"

"Doing maintenance," Jake said. "Leo insisted. Something about a dead magneto and needing to get ready for us all departing."

An odd mix of annoyance and something akin to affection swirled inside Mattie. Leo was checking up on her *again*, but he was also keeping another secret. If her brothers knew about her near crash, it would make the latest news all the harder to tell.

"So the whole family is outside the hangar, then?" Mattie asked as she moved forward and pushed open the door that led to the yard.

"Yup." Jake slanted her a look. "Why? Are you planning to make a big announcement or something? Is that why you and Leo are acting all jumpy? Don't tell me that you two are in cahoots like you used to be."

Were she and Leo in cahoots? Her brother's attempt at a joke was oddly searing. In some ways it was like old times, Leo covering for her again. But it wasn't the same and maybe never would be.

"We're not in cahoots. At least, not exactly."

"What is that supposed to mean?" Jake stopped short.

Mattie ignored him and kept on walking. "You're going to find out in two shakes."

"Find out what?" Otto asked, lifting his head from the engine he was tinkering with. Even though he was perched on a ladder, he was the closest to Mattie and Jake.

"Mattie has some sort of announcement," Jake hollered, causing all the male McAdamses to swivel in her direction like a group of marionettes on the same string.

"What is it?" Will asked.

"She won't tell me." Jake crossed his sizable arms over his barrel-shaped chest.

"Does this have something to do with the ritzy car I spied a few hours ago?" Her father put down a wrench and walked toward Mattie, his eyes dark and solemn without their usual ever-present twinkle. Bittersweetness swept through Mattie. One of her earliest memories was of her father picking her up and comforting her after she'd fallen and scraped her knee while trying to keep up with her older brothers. After her mother had passed, her father had read a story every night to her and her siblings—daring tales like *Treasure Island*, *The Count of Monte Cristo*, *White Fang*, and *Around the World in Eighty Days*.

"You saw it? Why didn't you say anything?" Mattie asked.

"I figured you'd let me know in your own time, Swift."

"What ritzy vehicle?" Will asked. Out of all of them, he was the most obsessed with race cars. "What did I miss?"

Mattie disregarded Will's rapid-fire questions while she watched her father as she made her revelation. "I received an offer today to fly in a mostly female circus."

Her father's eyes, normally so expressive, seemed shuttered, but not angry or upset, just . . . unreadable. Around her, her brothers broke into a chorus of concerns, their voices raised like squawking jays fighting over a nut. For the moment, she ignored them. She'd anticipated their reactions, but what she hadn't known was what her father would feel. She still didn't as she tried to study his schooled expression.

Will gently tugged at her arm. "Surely you told her no."

"Mattie, I don't think it is a good idea for you to go traipsing off on your own with a bunch of other women." Jake had lowered his voice a little, using the tone he always assumed when he acted as the financial head of the business.

"It's not safe," Otto said. "Not for lone females."

When she ignored them, they turned to their father, clearly intent on telling him to make Mattie see reason. *Their* reason, of course.

Leo, for his part, had returned his attention to checking fluid levels in the engines. Although Mattie always regularly inspected her Jenny, Leo cared for the planes like a stable master protecting the champion stallions. It hadn't escaped her notice, though, that he spent the most time on *her* aircraft, as if she couldn't check it herself.

Quickly, Mattie looked away from Leo. She didn't want to feel any more frustrated than she already did. This conversation required delicacy, not anger. It didn't help that her brothers had encircled their father.

"One at a time, boys. One at a time," Walt growled out, his voice weary.

"She's going to get herself killed," Otto barked.

Jake refolded his arms over his chest. "I told you that it was high time that we all stopped encouraging her nonsense."

"Exactly," Will seconded.

"What's your decision, Swift?" her father asked quietly as he ignored his sons. Guilt stabbed her. She hadn't meant to tell him amid such chaos.

"Let's go to the hangar," Mattie said quietly.

"This should be a family discussion," Jake said. Although he ultimately deferred to their father, Jake liked to think himself the second-in-command. The rest of the siblings disagreed, but no one more than Mattie.

"Let them have their privacy." Leo's quiet voice somehow managed to rip through the tensions surrounding them. When the family argued, he'd usually hover on the fringes. If asked his opinion, normally by a McAdams on the losing side of the argument, he'd generally evade the question. Mattie hadn't expected him to come to her aid, especially when he obviously didn't approve of her decision to join Vera's circus.

Shock prevented her brothers from immediately protesting. Taking advantage of their momentary silence, Mattie lightly grabbed her father's arm and led him in the direction of the hangar. As soon as they entered the building, Mattie dragged the door shut.

Her father leaned against the scarred wooden workbench. Quieter than his offspring, he didn't speak. Instead, he waited. Normally she found his willingness to simply listen comforting. Right now, it had the opposite effect. Resisting the urge to pace, she bounced once on her heels.

"I've agreed to take the offer." Mattie paused, her throat dry but *not* from the heat of the closed-up building.

"I assumed as much, Swift," her father said, his voice kind but still neutral, not betraying a single thought.

"The flying circus is run by Vera Jones." Mattie didn't know why she said that. It wasn't one of the most important details in this particular conversation, but it was one of the easiest.

Her father's gray eyebrows lifted, his first sign of emotion since she'd closed the door. "The granddaughter of Peter Harrelson, the famous circus owner?"

Mattie nodded and then spoke so quickly her tongue almost tangled. "I'd get to design my own tricks, Pa. Not like here."

Her father rubbed his chin. "I know your brothers have clipped your wings more than you'd like, but is this really what you want?"

This time Mattie rocked forward on her toes. "Yes, Pa. I'm sure. I'll miss you. I'll even miss the boys, but I *need* to do this."

Her father sighed, deep and long. His hazel eyes flitted over her face, as if cataloging its details. "Your mother would have my hide if she knew you were set on traveling the country on your own."

Mattie gave a grin she didn't feel. "I would've worn her down."

Her father's eyes twinkled in the dim light, but he didn't laugh. "That is probably true."

"Pa, all I have ever wanted to do is fly. This is *my* chance. My brothers have had so many. This is my only one. And I'll make good money."

Walt studied the dirt floor for a moment. When he glanced up, he looked solemn. "Your mama's sister wanted to take you in. Said I had no business raising a little girl on my own. Maybe she was right. Maybe if I had listened to her, you'd be living in a nice house with a good man and a passel of babies and not worrying about my money problems."

Mattie snorted. If her brothers or Leo had said something like this, she would have been livid. But she understood her father spoke from guilt. He'd always supported her dreams of flying, but that didn't mean he hadn't occasionally expressed a worry that he'd denied her a normal girlhood by treating her as one of the boys.

"I have no desire or need for any of that domestic poppycock. Not when I can own the sky and help out the family."

A true smile curved her father's lips, his mustache drawing up too. "You have my ability to dream combined with your mother's passion."

"Then you understand why I'm leaving?" Mattie asked hurriedly.

"You weren't meant for just helping out at the flight school. I saw your raw talent the moment you took the controls, Swift. There's a reason I nicknamed you after a wild bird and not a domestic one. You're meant to fly freely."

Mattie threw her arms around him. When he folded her into an embrace, she knew he supported her decision just as he had her brothers' to find work elsewhere.

When they stepped back from each other, her father cleared his throat as he returned to the workbench. "Is Leo trying to wrangle his way into joining this female circus?"

Mattie blinked in surprise. Why had her father thought to ask about *that*?

"He will be joining as well."

Her father gave a nod, as if he'd expected her answer. "How did he manage to convince Vera Jones to hire him if she's looking for female pilots?"

Mattie sighed as she perched on the worktable next to her father. "Vera plans on hiring male performers, too, and she has this grand idea of Leo and I engaging in a semimock flight duel during each show."

Her father raised both his silver-brown eyebrows. "Flight duel?"

Mattie tapped her fingers against the rough wood. Although her father let her do more tricks than her brothers, he didn't like the more dangerous ones. But he'd also yelled at Alfred for doing the same.

"I am supposed to be Miss Modernity, and Leo will be Mr. Yesteryear. We stage an argument about whether a woman can fly better than a man. Then we have a competition where we each try to outdo the other's stunts," Mattie said.

Her father's eyebrows rose even farther until they were almost obscured by his cap. "*Leo* agreed to challenge you?"

Mattie shook her head. "Not exactly. Vera sort of cornered him. She said if Leo didn't, she'd find another, more willing male pilot. When I agreed to join her circus, Leo quickly said he would too."

Her father let out a knowing *huh*, as if he'd again predicted something of that nature. Mattie pushed off her makeshift seat to pace.

"I hope he won't fuss over me like a mother hen," Mattie said. "Leo has all the opportunities in the world to fly the way he wants. Like I said before, this is my only one."

"I wouldn't be so hard on him." Her father spoke slowly, as if first considering his words.

"Hard on *him*? He's the one who's hard on *me*! I swear he's getting worse than the boys."

"Leo has his reasons for protecting you, Swift."

Mattie snorted. "He's just being a typical man. He can risk his neck, but heaven forbid if a silly female tries to do the same."

Her father leaned even farther back, an odd expression on his face. "Leo's more complicated than he lets on, Mattie."

"That I highly doubt." Mattie emphatically crossed her arms to punctuate her skepticism.

Her father's knowing grin deepened for a moment before his expression flattened into seriousness. He stood, then stepped toward her.

"I'll miss the both of you, but I'm glad you're pursuing your dreams and that Leo's going with you."

The little trickle of guilt returned. "I'm sorry we're leaving, Pa. I only meant it to be me, not the two of us. But we'll both be making a lot of cash, which we'll send back to you to pay off the debts—"

Her father pulled her into his arms again. "I'll be fine, Swift. I can manage to find my way out of this financial difficulty. I have in the past."

"You're not mad that I'm striking out on my own?"

"Not in the slightest. Just promise that you'll write."

"I'll send you a letter every week."

Her father gave her a squeeze. "You take care of yourself and Leo."

Mattie sniffed at the idea of Leo allowing that. "He thinks *he*'s the one watching over *me*."

Her father patted her shoulder. "I have a feeling that you're both going to discover something about each other."

"Why are you supporting her harebrained ideas, Leo?" Otto and his brothers were following Leo as he checked the propellers for pitting. Leo was doing his best to ignore the gaggle of McAdamses . . . and the guilt chewing at his gut, but succeeded at neither.

"Back up," Leo barked out before he yanked the uninspected blade downward. He'd never liked conflict much, and arguing with a McAdams never led to any good.

"Surely you don't approve of what she's doing?" Otto demanded.

"Mattie can soar as well as any male pilot—probably better," Leo said quietly as he reached up to touch the belly of the plane. Luckily what he'd thought was a tear was merely a shadow.

"See," Jake said. "You *are* encouraging her."

Leo sighed as he cocked his head to scan the plane's canvas skin for any rips. He wished the problems in life could be so easy to spot and repair. Luckily, before any McAdams brother could raise another complaint, Mattie stepped out from the hangar. Her brothers instantly headed in her direction. Leo debated about intercepting them, but Mattie had always been able to hold her own. And he wanted a chance to talk to her father alone.

Slipping past the debating siblings, he headed into the barn, where he found Walt McAdams waiting for him. The man nodded at his entrance. "I figured you'd be in here next."

More remorse flooded Leo. He'd always held a deep admiration for the soft-spoken man, so different than the rest of the raucous clan. He kept the group together—the soft yet strong mortar between a bunch of hard bricks.

"I'm sorry, sir."

A wisp of a smile pulled at the man's thin lips. "No reason to be, son. This has Mattie's stamp all over it."

Son. Walt had always called him that. It both warmed him and made him uncomfortable, especially now.

Leo rubbed the back of his head. "That's not *all* that I have to apologize for."

Walt placed his hand on Leo's shoulder. There used to be a time when Leo would have flinched at the contact, but the McAdamses were a physically demonstrative lot. After all these years, he'd mostly learned to accept their embraces, just as he'd learned the mechanics of airplanes.

"You're not responsible for that man's actions, Leo."

"But he is *my* father," Leo pointed out, unable to keep the bitter frustration from creeping into his voice, "and you paid him off to protect *me*."

The lines in Walt's face deepened, but his broad shoulders didn't sag. "That was my decision, Leo. I didn't even want you knowing about it."

But Leo had walked into Walt's office that day. He'd heard the awful story the bastard planned to take to the press unless Walt coughed up dough. And over Leo's protests, Walt had.

"You've protected me," Leo choked out, "even from your own family. You haven't once hinted why the flight school is in arrears."

"I won't, because it is not your fault. You need to forget about the money, Leo."

But I can't. Leo wanted so badly to keep on arguing, as if words could somehow fix the turmoil he'd once again brought down on the McAdamses. But he'd never done well talking about feelings. He was good with discussing SPADs, Nieuports, and Sopwith Camels—mechanical things, orderly things, *predictable* things. And this was as messy as it got.

Walt studied him closely. "Has your father tried contacting you again?"

Leo never lied to the man who had given him so much . . . except about this. "No. He hasn't."

Walt's gaze, though, stayed on him for a few beats, and Leo barely kept from shifting. The experienced aviator likely recognized the falsehood. After all, Walt knew that the money Leo gave him each month to bolster the school didn't match the income from Leo's endorsement deals, and Leo obviously wasn't spending it on himself.

Walt didn't press the issue, but his next words made Leo nearly as uncomfortable. "Try and see this new opportunity as the adventure that it is."

Leo glanced at Walt in surprise. Did his old mentor suspect that he'd long lost the pleasure of flying?

"You're not disappointed we're all leaving?" Leo asked, not able to shake the layers of guilt smothering him.

"Children grow up," Walt continued. "They leave home and seek their own opportunities. The boys will be fine. This is right for Mattie, and it's right for you. I'm just glad you'll be together."

"I'll make sure to inspect Mattie's plane."

Walt grinned and gave his head a slight shake. "Don't try to protect her too much. Be her partner, not her keeper."

Partner. The word tantalized Leo before embarrassment flooded him at his foolish response. Mattie's father had clearly only meant *partner* in the platonic sense.

"And, Leo?" Walt said.

Leo jerked, wondering if the man had divined his thoughts. But Walt's expression remained open, kind. He certainly didn't wear the scowl of a protective father.

"Have some fun too. Use this opportunity. Let yourself soar again."

Leo frowned, not sure if he understood Walt's advice. "I fly every day."

Walt placed his hand on Leo's shoulder again, this time keeping it there. "You go up in the air, and you maneuver the plane, Leo, but you don't soar. It's high time you started feeling the joy of it again."

Chapter Four

"Are you ready?" Leo asked Mattie as he swung his knapsack into the passenger seat. He'd never had many possessions. At the orphanage, he hadn't even owned a second set of clothes. But his most prized belonging was the bundle of letters that Mattie had sent him during his deployment. He had them practically memorized, but he still opened them up and slowly read them on nights he couldn't sleep.

Mattie swallowed, casting one last glance at her brothers and father. The McAdams men stood like soldiers at muster, shoulders back, chests puffed out, arms down at their thighs. Leo thought he might have caught the faintest hint of mist in Walt's eyes when he'd hugged his daughter, but Leo hadn't wanted to look too hard. Unlike Mattie, he hadn't gone down the line embracing the people he considered his family. They'd just shaken hands as they'd nodded at each other—stiff, economical movements that betrayed no emotion.

"Yeah, I guess I am." Mattie gave another wave. The row of McAdamses acknowledged her gesture with another jerk of their chins.

"Having second thoughts?" Leo asked, hoping his voice didn't sound too eager. "It isn't too late to change your mind."

Evidently, he hadn't picked the right tone or words. Mattie shot him a rather withering glare. "No, I am not. Even if I was, I have a ladies' agreement with Vera. I'm just going to miss Pa and the boys. That's all. Aren't you?"

Leo grunted, not wanting to admit how much he would. He'd survived all these years by shutting himself off, not by wallowing in things that couldn't be helped. "They'll miss you, too, even if they don't say it."

"I know." Mattie sighed. "Sometimes I wish this family was more open about how they felt instead of being so *manly* all the time."

Leo emitted another noncommittal sound. "Maybe they aren't trying to be tough—it's just their way of dealing with things." Or self-preservation, like it was for him.

Mattie shrugged as she lifted her own bundle of possessions into her Jenny. It wasn't a big bag, but it was nearly double his. Life had taught them both to travel light. "I suppose, but I still think it would be best to talk about it. Alfred would've."

"He was one for chatting," Leo said, his voice feeling as rough as a splintered piece of wood with dry rot. He didn't like discussing his friend in the best of times and especially not now, when he was already feeling more raw than numb.

"Anyway." Mattie whipped her braid over her shoulder as she started to shove her helmet over her head. "I'll feel better once we're in the air. There's nothing like soaring, is there?"

It was Leo's turn to lift his shoulders. "It gets the job done."

Mattie stopped with her helmet still bunched around her ears. Her hazel eyes had grown wide, her pink lips slack. "It *gets* the job done!"

Leo cleared his throat as he wondered if he'd made a serious misstep. "Well, it does. Gets a body from point A to point B faster than anything else."

Mattie's mouth pursed into a circle as she slid her finger under the leather encasing her head in order to straighten the hide. "Is that what you think of flying nowadays? Don't you feel that thrill? That excitement? That wonder?"

Leo rubbed his neck, wishing he hadn't triggered this line of inquiry. Heck, he and Mattie hadn't talked this much since he'd ratted her out to her brothers on the day of Alfred's memorial service. Leo needed to turn Mattie's focus away from him and back to herself. "Every flight is like the first with you?"

Mattie hesitated for a moment before buckling her chin strap. "I suppose it is. Isn't it for you?"

Leo had already jammed his helmet on his head, but he snapped down his goggles. Maybe if his eyes were obscured, the conversation would veer away from his personal feelings.

"Hold on to that sensation, Mattie. It's a great one to have," Leo said, purposely skirting her inquiry.

"Aren't you excited about this new gig? Just a little?" Mattie cocked her head, as if she could penetrate the thick glass stretching from his cheekbones to his forehead.

He wasn't, not really, at least not in the way she meant. It would pay a lot and help him work off what he owed the McAdamses. And he'd be with Mattie, something that shouldn't have pleased him as much as it did. But the actual flying? It was just another job.

"Miss Jones is offering us a good opportunity, Mattie. One we should be getting to. The sun is over the horizon now, and our new employer is expecting us."

"But—" Mattie began to protest.

The McAdamses began to shift, probably wondering what Mattie and he were nattering on about. Leo tilted his head meaningfully in their direction.

"We'd best head out now unless you want to go through another round of goodbyes." Leo really hoped that Mattie did not. This conversation was making him itchier than a heavy wool sweater in summertime, and he didn't want to endure more of the awkward discomfort that always accompanied a departure.

Mattie sighed. "You're right. Plus, the sky is calling. It's been a while since I flew into a sunrise. I always love soaring through pinks and oranges. If I were designing a movie poster for an epic, those are the colors that I'd use."

"Humph," Leo said. He used to love it, too, but now it just reminded him of the Great War, when he'd rise early to fly east over the lines in hopes of catching and bringing down a German observation balloon. Tension pulled inside him, making his chest tighten as he prepared for a threat that no longer existed.

Mattie leaned closer, peering at him again. Avoiding another inspection, Leo swiveled on one foot and climbed into the cockpit. Unlike Mattie, he did it without flourish. If circumstances didn't require him to catapult inside to save time or thrill an audience, he didn't.

Whistling jauntily, Mattie headed over to her Jenny. She bounced onto the wing and popped like a reverse champagne cork into her seat behind the stick. She gave him a salute, and Leo returned the gesture. Walt stepped forward to turn Mattie's propeller, and Jake yanked on Leo's. Their engines rumbled to life almost simultaneously, but Leo waved for Mattie to take off first. She blazed forward, the yellow wingtips of her Jenny shining bright in the early light.

When he reached altitude beside her, she wigwagged her wings. The cheerful little welcome caused a smile to bloom across his face, but it didn't last. The old numbness returned, but at least blankness was better than the turmoil he'd felt on the ground. Glancing over his shoulder to his right, he cast his gaze on the pastel streaks of daybreak. He tried to summon the joy Mattie had described, but he just found himself calculating their position in the sky based on the direction of the rising sun.

"That was glorious." Mattie ripped off her goggles, in part to punctuate her words and in part to see Leo better. "Didn't you get a thrill when we flew near the Railway Exchange in Chicago?"

The glazed-terra-cotta edifice had gleamed a bright pearly white as they'd swooped over the blue waters of Lake Michigan. Beside it, the beginnings of the Metropolitan Tower were taking shape. When finished, the skyscraper would rise like a behemoth over the shoreline and stretch over *thirty* stories high.

Leo removed his helmet and immediately began to pat down the unruly chestnut strands that stood up in spiky clumps. "It's a good landmark, I guess."

Mattie yanked off her helmet. Half of her hair had once again slipped from her braid, but instead of fixing it, she whipped it around, letting the air fluff it even more.

Did anything give Leo a sense of wonder anymore?

Mattie jumped out of her Jenny to move nearer to him. "What about the lake itself? Wasn't the light hitting it just perfectly? It looked like it was made of diamonds and sapphires, it was sparkling so much."

"There was a lot of shipping traffic," Leo offered with the air of someone who really wasn't interested but was desperately trying to make conversation. With almost palpable reluctance, he climbed from his Jenny to join her on the ground. He seemed cagey and uncomfortable as he scanned the flat field. His gaze didn't pause on the sedges, the sandy white strip of beach, or even the deep-blue lake. He even ignored Vera's grand home situated on a gentle bluff above them. Considering the heiress lived in a towering pink castle with a blue-gray slate roof, the fact that Leo paid it no notice was almost as extraordinary as the building itself. Instead he focused on a supply shed with a ladder leaning against it.

"It seems wonderful here." Mattie tried one last time to elicit *something* from her old friend as she gently laid her hand on his arm. In his blue eyes, she thought she saw the faintest flicker, like a flame in an old kerosene lamp slowly coming to life. But before it could catch hold, Leo banked it. And Mattie felt . . . odd—both closer to Leo than she'd been a moment ago and also more distant.

Leo shrugged as he stepped away from her touch and toward the stepladder. After dragging it beside her Jenny, he climbed up to inspect the motor. "It's not half-bad here."

"Not half-bad! It's like we've stepped into a fairy tale." She stood at the base of the ladder, steadying it. She'd helped Leo like this a million times before, but for some reason, today, it felt different.

"Don't those fairy tales normally include lurking monsters?" Leo's voice sounded muffled as he leaned inside the engine bay to check the coolant and oil levels. The position placed his rear precisely in front of Mattie's eyes. An alien awareness kindled inside her, and she realized she'd never really noticed his posterior before. But old friends, even former ones, didn't ogle each other. Quickly, she glanced away. Yet something . . . something pulled her back.

"I refuse to let you dampen this moment." Mattie lightly bopped Leo's shoe, which was one of the few places she could easily and safely reach. She couldn't stop her need to touch him again. Could another caress retrigger that brief hint of sentiment that she'd witnessed in Leo's eyes? Would it ignite this time?

To her surprise, he paused to grin down at her. No scowl. No flat expression. No annoying "press face." But his real smile. The shy, sweet one that she hadn't spotted in years. The one she hadn't known just how much she'd missed until now.

An odd brilliance burst to life inside her. It was as if her heart had become a fairy-floss machine, madly spinning sugar into a soft confectionary. The emotions she felt certainly seemed as light and airy as the cotton candy her family hawked at their air shows . . . and just as sinfully delicious.

His blue eyes widened slightly, as if she'd spoken her thoughts aloud. Then they darkened marvelously. His gaze set off a flare within her like a spark plug igniting the gas in its cylinder. Her breathing changed . . . and so did his. Transfixed, she watched the increasingly deep rise and fall of his muscular chest beneath his white cable-knit jersey. His solid-black oxfords moved a rung down and then another until he stood before her, his intensity sweeping over her like a wave of hot vapor.

"Are you certain you two aren't lovers?" Vera's cheerful call obliterated the marvelous, wholly unexpected tension. Mattie jumped back, but not as far as Leo. He bumped into the ladder and would have sent it clattering to the ground if he hadn't possessed such quick reflexes. Somehow, he managed to steady it before it hit the dirt.

Vera sauntered over. She wore a poppy-red tube dress with three-quarter-length sleeves and a boatneck collar. The simple yet fashionable silk garment draped over her tall thin figure, the shockingly short hemline exposing most of her elegant calves. Her cloche hat matched the hue of her shift, and a beautifully beaded flower bloomed against its wide white band. Ruby trotted beside her mistress, pausing only to sniff into the wind before dutifully catching up.

"Don't worry about scandalizing me with the truth. I'm certainly not a prude." Vera flashed a brilliant smile, her latest lipstick containing the same warm hint of orange as her ensemble. "Quite the opposite, I assure you. In fact, some might call me a downright hedonist."

She paused and winked one kohl-lined eye. "They'd be right, of course. I firmly believe you shouldn't have to suffer for pleasure, especially when it comes to the trials and tribulations of getting hitched."

"We're not lovers." Mattie laughed at Vera's blatant boldness, glad for the humor to fully chase away the lingering attraction she'd experienced.

Leo made an odd, half-strangled sound in the back of his throat. He seemed rooted to the spot, his hand jammed in his hair, a faint flush under his tanned skin.

"It was kind of you to meet us," Mattie said to Vera. She wanted to turn the conversation away from intimacy for Leo's sake, but she meant her words. She hadn't expected the heiress to play hostess. When on the road, Mattie was used to being regarded with the suspicion shown to itinerant folks. Her status as a female barnstormer had only made her even more of an oddity.

"You are my honored guests." Vera spread open her arms, her poppy gloves bright splashes against the grassy-green airfield. "When I heard your planes whiz past the castle, I just had to drive out to meet you. The coupe will be tight, but the three of us can squeeze."

"You brought the Duesenberg!" Mattie scanned over the sedges until she spotted a flash of cherry red.

"Of course." Vera linked her arm with Mattie's. "I use *any* excuse to take a spin in it."

"I would absolutely do the same." Even to her own ears, Mattie sounded reverent. She didn't know what thrilled her more: the marvelous vehicle or the fact she'd found another woman with a deep appreciation for machines.

"Would you like to drive back?"

Mattie stopped walking so quickly that Leo bumped her from behind. He wrapped his arms about her to steady both of them. The contact was brief, but gee whiz, the absolute chill it sent through her. And then there was the *heat* from his hands and the *feel* of his muscular chest.

Don't lean into him, Mattie. Do. Not. Lean. In. You didn't join Vera's circus to spend your time starry eyed over a man. If you have to choose between a marvelous machine or romance, pick the contraption.

"I'd love to see how your coupe rides," Mattie told Vera quickly.

"I assume you know how to handle an automobile." The flapper made a sweeping motion with her gloved hand toward the steering wheel.

"If it has gears, a motor, and a gasoline tank, Mattie can operate it." Leo's voice sounded rough—almost as if from affection. "But be warned, she drives just as she flies—like one of the horsemen of the Apocalypse."

Vera laughed brightly. "My kind of driver."

"Yeah," Leo said, his voice full of resignation. "I figured that."

Mattie sucked in her breath as they got closer to the sleek torpedo-shaped Duesy. "Are you sure you don't mind me driving it?"

Vera opened the door and gestured for Mattie to sit down. Mattie didn't need any more encouragement. With a sigh somewhere between a gasp and a squeak, Mattie sank into the buttery-soft leather cushion. It felt like luxury and power even before she turned the ignition. She placed her hands on the narrow steering wheel, and she might . . . just might . . . have groaned. Softly, of course. And hopefully under her breath. But a groan nonetheless.

Mattie appreciated machines like a connoisseur did stunning art, aged whiskey, or decadent chocolate. Watching her slide into the driver's seat as her hands opened and closed over the steering wheel in a gentle massage, he felt . . .

Hell.

A hollow darkness lived inside Leo that he didn't want touching Mattie. Ever.

"Come on." Vera waved to him as she stood holding open the passenger door with her other hand. "Hop in."

Under normal circumstances, Leo would have gestured for Vera to enter first. It was the gentlemanly thing to do. Plus, as the tallest and broadest member of their little group, he would have the hardest time cramming himself into the middle space.

They seemed totally oblivious to his discomfort, or at least Mattie was. Vera sent him a rather knowing look as she settled back in her seat.

The engine rumbled to life: the beautiful, smooth sound of a well-tuned machine. Leo had dreamed about riding in a Duesy but had never thought it would happen. Although he'd flown with a few sons of millionaires during the war, in peacetime he didn't run in circles with people who could afford the masterpieces of engineering. But instead of enjoying the ride, he only registered Mattie's nearness.

"Feel free to drive like an apocalyptic horseman." Vera spoke to Mattie, but she sent Leo a wink when she referenced his previous statement. "I certainly do."

"Are you sure?" Mattie asked, showing uncharacteristic hesitation. "I wouldn't want to hurt your car."

Vera gave one of her trademark elegant shrugs. "That's why I employ a personal mechanic."

Mattie's grin stretched wide, and Leo thought his overworked heart might actually stop this time. She looked so alive, so confident, so darn wonderful.

"You asked for it." Mattie shot the car forward and laughed as the wind blew the fiery tendrils of hair that had escaped from her braid. Beside him, Vera's dog snorted and then stuck her short muzzle into the air. Vera patted the spaniel's back as Ruby's ears fluttered behind her like two curly pennants.

The Duesenberg raced along the path, the grass and sedges flipping by like photos in a zoetrope. Mattie drove like she did everything else—fearlessly . . . and with little regard to the consequences. Even when the road climbed upward along the edge of the bluff, she still didn't slow. She sped up.

Suddenly, the gravel road curved away from the lake, bolting toward the looming pink turrets of the huge house built in the Scottish Baronial style. Mattie entered the turn with a whoop. Gravel sprayed out behind them, but still Mattie maintained control. She had an uncanny knack for immediately recognizing distances and understanding angles and speed. Good thing, because she rarely took time to think through a maneuver before executing it.

Vera held on to her hat and laughed brightly. "You are a magnificent driver. Have you ever thought about racing?"

Mattie shook her head as she shifted gears. "Nope. I like soaring too much, although your Duesenberg is tempting."

"We need to get you in a real race car," Vera promised.

Leo lifted one of the hands he was using to brace himself and jammed it in his hair. "Don't you think we should master our new flying stunts first?"

"Is he always such a wurp?" Vera asked, using the popular word for a wet blanket as she peered around him to address Mattie. Another common term was *bluenose*, and Leo figured he'd be hearing that one next.

"This is actually him being mildly optimistic." Mattie sent him a grin to soften her words.

"Well, Mr. Bluenose," Vera said, "race cars are going to be part of the act."

Leo froze. Although he'd predicted the first part of her sentence, he hadn't prepared for the latter half. He should have.

"Are you planning to jump onto a plane from your Duesenberg or another roadster?" Mattie asked, her voice slightly higher than normal. Leo recognized the excited tone from when they were adolescents and had been about to embark on some madcap exploit with Alfred.

"Most definitely the Duesy." Vera leaned back against the leather upholstery, as if soaking up the sun and the wind.

"I'll be happy to be your pilot for that." Leo made the offer as quickly as he could. If he didn't, Mattie would volunteer instead.

"Actually, I had Mattie in mind." In a gesture of pure freedom, Vera lifted her hands into the air, allowing the breeze stirred up by Mattie's driving to whirl past her fingertips. "She flies absolutely divinely, and I want the first stunt focused on the women. It's going to be the bee's knees."

"I'd love to do it," Mattie said as she skidded to an impressive stop in front of the castle. It took everything for Leo not to bury his head in his hands. Vera and Mattie were just the fuel-and-fire combination that he'd feared.

"I knew you would, darling." Vera climbed out of the car and bent to let Ruby down. Vera joined Mattie, and the two linked arms. Together they ascended one of the dual sweeping staircases that led to an intricately designed door. Instead of a forbidding medieval iron portcullis, the oxidized-copper art piece formed sweeping loops and lines to create two butterflies perching on intertwined roses. Additional stonework flowers bloomed over the lintel above. It was showy and theatrical . . . and entirely Vera.

"Welcome to my home, Fete Castle." Vera gestured around the foyer with a flourish. Although Leo had seen art nouveau buildings when stationed in France, he'd never been inside a private residence of that style. Opposite the door and above the connecting balcony of another dual staircase was a large stained glass window of a dragonfly skimming above an azure lake. Green and blue light reflected on the shined, polished wood floor below. The staircases had a wrought iron railing, the metal forming delicate vines and flowers. But the true pièce de résistance was the lamp hanging below the skylight in the middle of the three-story atrium. More than a light fixture, it was a piece of art. Cast in fluid lines of bronze, a woman hung from a trapeze bar by her long bent legs. In her coppery hands, she held an illuminated piece of glass with a swirled emerald-and-cerulean pattern.

"My grandmother." Vera jerked her chin in the direction of the stylized statue. "My grandfather had it commissioned for her on their fiftieth wedding anniversary. He first saw her when she was flying under the big top, and he said he instantly fell in love. He was always the romantic. They both were. This castle was built by them thirty-odd years ago, and they left it to me."

"It is absolutely beautiful!" As usual, Mattie did nothing to hide the kaleidoscope of emotions flitting across her face. She'd tilted her head back to fully absorb the majesty of the entrance hall as she stared in unabashed wonder, her pink lips parted slightly. A flush of excitement glowed under her smattering of freckles, adding more color to her creamy complexion.

"Thank you!" Vera smiled. "It was very state of the art when built. It has running water and electricity. I've kept it up too. You'll find every modern convenience at your disposal."

Leo rubbed the back of his head. The first and only time he'd been in a grand home was when his squadron had been stationed in one during the war . . . and it was during that time period that Alfred had made his last, fatal flight. Leo jerked his head to the side as he tried to force the old memories away.

Mattie's wonder, however, had only increased. And Leo focused on her face, wishing he could catch the excitement rolling off her.

"Does that mean you have your own power station?" Mattie asked excitedly. "This house was built over thirty years ago, so it must have had some way of generating energy if it was wired."

Vera clapped her poppy-colored silk gloves together. "Oh, this troupe is just going to be perfect for each other! You know, you are now the third member to ask me that, and the question rarely comes up nowadays. We do have a generator next to the workshop that runs the lights and the servants' call box."

"I'm not the first to ask?" Mattie sounded surprised and cautiously excited. Her other brothers were never as mechanically minded as Alfred, and Leo suspected she'd missed talking to her sibling about articles she'd read in *Popular Mechanics*. Heck, *he'd* missed those old debates, and he'd never had the vision that Mattie possessed.

"No, darling. Both Carrie and Sadie inquired about it. You'll get to meet them and the rest of the team in about an hour. That will give you time to freshen up. I've put you both in the north turret. It has wonderful views of the lake and the field where we'll be practicing. Mrs. Lewis will show you to your rooms."

As if conjured by magic, a tall middle-aged woman appeared from one of the arched doorways. She wore a neatly tailored black dress with an apron around the middle. Smiling warmly, she greeted them and then led them through the house. As they walked, Mrs. Lewis told them about the history and architecture of the castle. Mattie, being Mattie, chatted amicably with their guide. Leo, though, hung back, feeling like an invader. He observed the small details as they walked—carved wooden scrollwork on doorframes, whimsical woodland creatures peeking out from banisters, and peacock sconces with each feather illuminated. Every turn and twist of the hallway revealed another stained glass window depicting frogs, grapevines, goldfish, or birds.

Finally, they entered a tight circular staircase. As they climbed, Mrs. Lewis kept talking. "Miss McAdams, you will have the top floor. Mr. Ward, you'll have the one directly below."

"I have a floor?" Leo asked before he could think better of the question. He'd rarely had a room to himself and never an entire apartment. Even as an adult, he typically bunked with one of the other male employees of the McAdams Family Flying Circus.

Mrs. Lewis glanced over her shoulder. Her blue eyes were kind, not judging. "The tower isn't too big, so the rooms are generous but not oversize."

Leo grunted and scratched the back of his head. Any bed that wasn't a bunk would feel spacious. He had no idea why Vera hadn't put them in the servant quarters. He would have felt more comfortable there, but Mattie would enjoy living in a turret. No one enjoyed a view more than her.

"Here are your rooms, sir." Mrs. Lewis paused on a landing and pushed open a wooden door. "Miss McAdams's apartment is identical to yours. The Misses Lenhart will also be staying in this tower."

Leo stepped inside with Mattie close behind. If Mrs. Lewis was surprised that Mattie boldly entered a man's room, she didn't show it. But then again, the housekeeper's employer was the legendary Vera Jones.

Leo's cheeks burned, and he hoped his tan hid the flush. Already, Mattie's mere presence in his assigned apartment caused his heart to chug like a late express train trying to make up lost time. Mattie, of course, remained oblivious as she ran to the big round glass window that overlooked the lake. She gasped in utter delight as she leaned forward, her fingers clutching the deep sill, her forehead nearly pressed against the glass. Excitedly, she waved for Leo to join her, obviously eager for him to take in the scenery and not realizing that he'd much rather watch her delight than gaze upon the bright-blue lake below.

Mattie thought no more of entering his assigned bedchamber than she would one of her siblings'. Despite her odd heated looks after they'd landed in Vera's field, she just saw him as another annoying brother. Nothing more. Nothing romantic. And he should want to keep it that way. He *needed* to keep it that way. For her sake. For his.

Chapter Five

"Well, isn't this the berries! Just when we need a hero, the Flying Lion appears." The breathy voice seemed to float up the circular staircase like floral perfume. Mattie peered over Leo's shoulder to catch a glance at the speaker. With large Clara Bow eyes, the blonde woman stared up at Leo. Her makeup mirrored that of a movie star, her mouth painted into a perfect Cupid's bow. Soft short curls completed an innocent, sweet look that sent an incongruous whisper of awkward unease through Mattie. She felt like a schoolgirl again, wearing her brothers' hand-me-downs while her female peers in their big bows and frilly pinafore dresses regarded her like an unwanted toad who dared to approach songbirds.

The starlet in training somehow managed to make her doe eyes even bigger as she continued to regard Leo through her thick black eyelashes—a look clearly obtained by applying powdered coal mixed with petroleum jelly and *not* through nature. "I've followed stories about you since the war. Why, you're even more handsome in person than in your photographs! Those grainy black-and-white shots do *not* do you full justice."

Although vamps always crowded around Leo before and after his aerial performances, their attention always made him visibly uncomfortable. Oh, he hid it well, but Mattie could always detect the strain at the edge of his politeness, just as she could now. Evidently, the newcomer was unwittingly making him feel even more ill at ease than Mattie felt in this woman's presence.

"Why are you in need of a hero?" Mattie asked.

The woman's blue gaze swept over Leo's shoulder to land upon Mattie. Although the flirtatious gleam dissipated, the blonde's seeming good cheer did not, much to Mattie's surprise. "Oh, you must be Miss McAdams! I'm Lily Lenhart, by the way, wing-walker in training. My sister, Sadie, is going to be another pilot in Vera's circus. We're originally farm girls from Western Pennsylvania, so we have a lot to learn."

Despite the husky quality of her voice, Lily delivered each detail in rapid succession. She did *not*, however, answer Mattie's actual question.

"Is there some kind of problem that I can assist with?" Leo asked, his quiet voice laced with concern.

"Oh yes!" Lily said as she pivoted and started to lead them down the staircase. "It is so handy that I ran into you. I know we were all going to meet in the pink parlor, but when Sadie and I were looking out the window, we spied Miss Aida Sanchez-Espinosa arriving. She is an heiress too! Not Sadie, of course, but Aida. She's from California, but she and Vera roomed together at a boarding school in Switzerland. Can you imagine? I would have absolutely thought I'd died and gone to heaven if I'd been able to live in such a ritzy place, although I guess I'm staying in a castle right now."

"But what's wrong?" Mattie prodded, trying to keep the frustration from her tone. She didn't even try to parse through the details. She figured she'd meet the other women soon enough.

"Aida's car, of course. Steam was pouring out of it like a teakettle. Sadie—who always insists on poking around tractors—went running out to help. I stayed behind for a few minutes. My makeup wasn't done yet, and I am next to useless when it comes to machinery. When I glanced out before I left, I spied Vera."

"Is Leo's help really needed if your sister is good with motors?" Mattie asked, her patience starting to fray.

"Well, it's always good to have a hero around." Lily wiggled her gloved fingers, as if that explained everything. They'd reached the bottom of the steps, and the blonde led them through a set of french doors out onto a terrace. In the section of the driveway situated behind the castle, a black Dodge sedan stood with vapor hissing out from it. A short gal with her brunette hair pulled back in a simple braid leaned over the open hood. Dressed in practical trousers and a shirt that, like Mattie's, were a little too big for her slender frame, she eyed the steaming radiator. Although the tanned, freckle-faced farm girl looked nothing like the bubbly, Hollywood-style Lily, Mattie still assumed she was the aforementioned sister.

"You overheated the engine, Aida," Sadie called out as she started to pull on long leather gloves to protect her hands before working on the hot radiator.

"I'm afraid I'm not accustomed to a Dodge. I must have pushed the poor thing too hard. I was treating it like my parents' Rolls." A woman whom Mattie assumed was Miss Sanchez-Espinosa, the California heiress, lifted her head from the notebook she'd been scrawling in. Aida's cream boatneck dress was just as elegant as Vera's, but hers had a more tailored, polished look, and the hemline hit lower on the calf. Her Dutch-bobbed dark-brown hair gave her wire-rimmed spectacles a jaunty flair. Like their hostess, she had perfectly applied lipstick, although it was a richer burgundy shade, which complemented the warm undertones of her light-brown skin.

Vera patted her boarding school chum's arm. "I don't know why you didn't just borrow an automobile from me. I have a whole carriage house full of them. The least you could have done was buy a Packard, Lincoln, or Cadillac."

"The Dodge looks like it's a good-quality vehicle," Sadie called out. "It just wouldn't have the ability to cruise all day under a hot sun like the Rolls."

"I wanted something durable to take on the road with us," Aida explained. "It's practical."

Vera bumped her friend's arm. "Are you insinuating that I'm not practical?"

Aida shot the flapper an exceedingly dry look before returning to writing in her little bound book. Lily stood on her tiptoes to glance over the Californian's shoulder.

"Whatever are you scribbling?" Lily asked.

Aida did not lift her fountain pen from the page. "I am taking notes for my thesis about the upending of traditional gender expectations. Anecdotes like this will keep my essays quite lively and will help me turn the project into a book."

Mattie stared at the heiress, almost as interested in her as in the Dodge engine. She definitely understood Aida's words less than she did the machine, but they fascinated her nonetheless. *Upending of traditional gender expectations.* What a delightful, tantalizing turn of phrase. Mattie wanted to take it apart as much as she did the machinery a few yards away.

"Aida is pursuing a doctorate in sociology," Vera said. "She'll be with us just this summer, since she'll return to classes in the fall."

Mattie had never met anyone with a PhD, let alone a woman. The thought of a female pursuing a higher education in a scientific field fascinated her.

"Sociology?" Lily asked, wrinkling her slightly upturned nose.

Aida laughed brightly. "Rooming with Vera for over half a decade at a Swiss boarding school made me keenly interested in how people behave and react to social strictures."

"I always strive to be a source of inspiration." Vera's coral-painted lips curved in amused satisfaction.

"It was also due to that misspent youth that I acquired acrobatic skills from Vera," Aida said.

"They are so handy when it comes to sneaking out of the upper stories of dormitories, even formidable, fortresslike ones." Vera paused for a beat. "In fact, *especially* the fortresslike ones. They always have such useful decorations to support one's footing. I am quite fond of grotesques and gargoyles."

Aida winked mischievously. "Much to my parents' chagrin, aerialist skills are quite handy for sneaking out of California haciendas too."

"Aida, it looks like the relief valve's gummed up. I'm going to unscrew the radiator cap to relieve the pressure," Sadie called out as she tucked her long braid into a rather ragged flatcap.

Interested to see the result, Mattie hurried closer to the Dodge but stood far enough back to avoid being caught in the release of steam. All pilots knew to respect an engine almost as much as they feared a fiery death from leaking fuel.

Lily, however, took no such precautions. Without warning, she flounced over to her sister just as Sadie began to carefully unscrew the metal cap.

"Lily, step back," Mattie cried just as Leo called, "Watch out, Miss Lenhart!" Unfortunately, their warnings came too late. A gout of scalding steam shot into the air. Lily cried out, pinwheeling backward, her hands fluttering. The vapor immediately caused her makeup to run and flushed her face a bright pink, but thankfully she hadn't gotten close enough to catch any more than the edge of the cloud, and she didn't appear to be burned.

"Lily!" Sadie cried out in horror as she dropped her wrench and rushed over to her sibling. "What were you thinking! Are you injured?"

"My makeup!" Lily cried out, holding up a finger covered in black, greasy soot. Between the dark drips around her luminous eyes and the red running from her painted lips, the flaxen-haired beauty looked a bit like a melted circus clown.

"Hell's bells and buckets of blood," Sadie called out, using one of Mattie's own favorite phrases. "Stop worrying whether you have Mae Murray's bee-stung lips. Did you get scalded?"

"I . . . I don't think so," Lily said as she reached a shaking hand to her hair. When she touched the limp wet locks, her pixie-like face crumpled. "My curls are utterly ruined, though!"

"Hey, stop!" a new female voice called out. "Somebody stop that man! He was taking photographs!"

Two women stood on the back veranda. The taller one, with her dramatically white skin, reminded Mattie a bit of Vera, but it was the second newcomer who drew her attention—and not because she was raising the alarm.

Recognition slammed into Mattie as she realized she was in the presence of another pioneering aviatrix, Miss Carrie Wilcox. She looked just as she did in the newspaper—her short bob arranged in perfect rows of finger curls, her dark-brown skin smooth and flawless, her features strikingly confident. But she didn't wear a smile this time as she took off running in the direction of a fleeing figure. The man was moving quickly despite the large camera clutched in his arms.

Realizing an image of a bedraggled Lily foolishly caught in the spray from the radiator would not be good press for the circus, Mattie joined the chase, and she heard Leo's shoes slapping against the ground. The three of them had almost reached the man when he jumped into a Chrysler half-hidden in the trees. Within seconds, he was speeding through the sedges to reach the main road leading away from Fete Castle.

Still in the lead, Carrie skidded to a halt. Bracing her hands against her knees, she gasped for breath. Mattie stopped beside her, just as winded. Leo seemed in the best shape, but he, too, was gulping more air than normal.

"Chickenhearted cad! Two-faced muckraker!" Vera yelled out, shaking her fist in the air as she and Aida finally caught up to the rest of them. With their heeled shoes, the two heiresses hadn't been able to run very fast and had only managed a brisk trot.

"You know him?" Aida asked.

"Unfortunately, I may have let him escort me about town once or twice. His name is Benji Pringle, and he's become the worst kind of scandalmongering reporter. After he saw me on the arm of one of his numerous pilot friends, he began to write the most mean-spirited articles about me. I'd thought he'd grown past his petty revenge, but clearly, I've misjudged him yet again. Although I do have to admit I was always more attracted to his deep-set dimples than to his character. I can never resist a chiseled jaw and an indentation in a man's cheeks when he smiles."

"It *is* her Achilles' heel," Aida confirmed. "That and a clover club or a bee's knees or a mint julep or a—"

"Speaking of cocktails, we should all get a good stiff drink. Did you happen to bring any wine?" Vera asked her former school chum. Then she turned to the rest of the group and added, "Aida's parents own a fabulous vineyard, which is tragically producing its delectable products mostly for sacramental uses due to Prohibition."

"We *do* also have rather extensive orchards, including almond, fig, and apricot trees," Aida said, "but Vera is, of course, focused on the grapes."

"Not the fruit, darling, but its fermented juices. That reminds me that I must thank your older sister for sending me a large shipment of wine blocks—and the handy warning of how *not* to ferment them."

"All in compliance with the law." The left side of Aida's lips turned up. "It is certainly not our fault if some of our customers choose to ignore the cautions and inadvertently turn our blocks of concentrated grapes into wine."

"Yes. Inadvertently." Vera arched one of her sculpted eyebrows. "It is amazing how one can continue to do something inadvertently on such a regular basis."

"Indeed," said Aida, a little too gravely. Mattie couldn't help but be impressed by the grape growers' innovation to circumvent the draconian antiliquor laws prohibiting the sale of spirits.

"Although 'accidental' wine is not the tastiest," Aida added rather wistfully.

"Yes, but it *is* so deliciously subversive." Vera winked.

"Well, lucky for you, I brought another block of grapes with me during the trip. A railroad porter loaded the crate in the back of my Dodge at the station."

"Are you telling me that you left wine-making supplies in the trunk at the mercy of this heat!" Vera pivoted on the heel of her right pump.

"I'm not really sure how that would make it taste any worse," Aida said, but she headed after her friend, who was striding quickly back to the Dodge in a clear rescue mission. Lily was still being consoled by the tall Vera look-alike while her sister, Sadie, had returned to inspecting the exposed engine.

Mattie took the momentary reprieve from the chaos to introduce herself to the legendary aviatrix beside her. "Miss Carrie Wilcox?"

"Yes?" Carrie looked at her and Leo expectantly.

"I thought I recognized you from an article I read about how you and Bessie Coleman flew in an amazing loop formation in tandem," Mattie said, mentioning the famous Black Cherokee barnstormer who was considered one of the best stunt aviators in the country.

"We spent weeks practicing that."

"What's it like actually being inside a craft with Brave Bessie?" Leo asked quietly.

A wide smile spread over Carrie's face. "Like nothing else in the world. She's the one who taught me how to fly. She's hoping to one day open a flight school for Black people. That way Black folks like Bessie and me won't have to travel to Europe to learn to fly."

"Didn't Bessie go overseas twice?" Mattie asked.

Carrie nodded as the three of them began to walk back to the Dodge. "First to France for her initial license, then later to the Netherlands and also to Germany, where she met Anthony Fokker and trained under one of his best test pilots."

"Brave Bessie knows Anthony Fokker?" Leo asked.

"You're familiar with him?" Carrie asked.

"Well, I know his work," Leo said. "I tangled with more than one of Fokker's planes during the war."

"Leo was an ace and a balloon buster," Mattie said, knowing that he'd never mention his heroics.

"Oh yes!" Carrie's brown eyes glinted with recognition as she glanced at Leo. "You're the Flying Lion!" Her gaze turned next to Mattie. "And you must be one of the McAdams siblings."

"Yup," Mattie said, and then before Carrie could ask Leo anything about his war record, she quickly added, "How did Vera convince you to join her troupe?"

"She promised to start a scholarship program for Black women who want to attend a university like I did," Carrie explained. "With all the prejudice thrown our way, it's hard enough to get accepted to a school, no matter how qualified we are, and I'd love to help any way that I can."

Mattie had never met so many college-educated women. In fact, she'd never encountered more than two people with a degree in a single day. Considering Vera also had one, Mattie had just talked to three graduates in the space of half an hour. And, as Carrie had stated, racial prejudice would have presented even more obstacles for her and Aida, making their success even more impressive. Mattie began to wonder if someday she, too, should pursue higher education, such as some sort of engineering degree. Of course, that would require money that she simply didn't have. Any she earned would go directly to saving the flight school.

Mattie was just about to heave out a sigh when Lily's shrill shriek drew her attention. The blonde had wiped off most of the makeup, and her hair had started to dry, but she looked even more upset than before.

"What do you mean, a *newspaperman* took *my* picture! I'm an utter fright. You don't think he'll *publish* it, do you?" Lily practically collapsed against the woman who looked like Vera.

Vera exchanged a look with Aida. Instead of answering Lily, the flapper turned to the servant carrying the crate of grape blocks into the mansion. "Samuel, could you please tell Mrs. Lewis to set up drinks?"

The young man nodded and hurried into the house. Vera moved to sling her arm around Lily's shoulders. "Why don't we all retire to the veranda and have a nice clover club cocktail?"

"I'll just have a club soda," Leo said quickly.

"Me too," Mattie chimed in. She'd only tried strong liquor once or twice when Alfred had managed to secret some away. Although she wouldn't mind experimenting, she certainly didn't wish to start in front of brand-new compatriots. Leo, for his part, had always avoided alcohol, even before the war. Part of his serious nature, Mattie supposed. Alfred had written to her that his squadron called Leo "the Reverend" due to his natural tendency toward sobriety in all matters.

As they walked onto the veranda, Lily glanced up at Leo through her considerably shorter and blonder lashes. Even without her Hollywood makeup, she still managed to look like a beautiful ingenue. "You know, I would feel so much better if the Flying Lion sat next to me after the day I've had. After all, if a balloon buster couldn't protect me, who could?"

Leo stiffened noticeably. Without thinking, Mattie reached out and squeezed his hand, as if she could relieve some of the pressure he felt. As his warm fingers curled about hers, she realized how long she'd yearned to offer him any small gesture of comfort. After the war they'd never been close enough, physically or emotionally. Leo had dug himself into a trench that she couldn't overtake. But now, as she pulled him down next to her on a white bench, she didn't feel as terribly separated from him.

"Leave the poor man alone." Sadie jabbed her sister, Lily, with her elbow. "You're embarrassing him."

Undeterred, her sister only fluttered her eyelashes at Leo as she picked a chair closest to him. "Given his war record I bet nothing flusters him. Am I right, gorgeous?"

Vera paused in fixing herself a frothy pink cocktail. Holding a cut glass stopper above the decanter, she arched an eyebrow in Leo's direction. "Are you absolutely *certain* you wouldn't care for a drink?"

To Mattie's shock, the notorious teetotaler looked rather longingly at the gin. Slowly and with a surprising amount of reluctance, Leo shook his head.

"Oh, do stop tormenting the poor man." The Vera look-alike headed to the table of bottles. Choosing whiskey, she mixed up an old-fashioned and then turned to address the rest of the group. "I'm Alice Kunkle, by the way, and Vera's cousin."

"Always the mother hen looking out for everyone, Alice." Vera bussed her relative's cheek before she draped herself onto a chaise longue.

"Well, someone must cluck over all of you." Alice swirled her drink. "And, Leo, don't worry that you are to be entirely besieged by females. My husband, John, will be joining us in a few days. He and I are both trapeze artists and will be wing-walkers along with Vera, Aida, and Lily."

Mattie glanced around the group crowded on the veranda and realized with startling clarity that she found herself surrounded by women. In fact, Leo was the sole male occupant—a sharp reversal of their normal roles in their male-dominated flying team.

"Alice's grandmother was a sister to mine," Vera explained. "We come from a long line of aerialists."

"And of course, Vera recruited my husband and me to perform for her new enterprise," Alice said. "I must warn you that he will be bringing our three children with him—two girls and a boy. Some might call them *wild*, but I prefer *precocious*. They range in age from four to ten. They are accustomed to life on the road and are thrilled that Mama and Papa will be flying in air-o-planes, as my youngest calls them."

"Milly, who's the baby, takes the wooden model airplane that I gave her to bed with her," Vera explained. "She also dresses it up in doll clothes. It may be the cutest thing I have ever witnessed."

"She calls it Planey and gets very upset if you do not refer to it as a girl."

This announcement was met with a chorus of *awww*s from everyone, except for Leo. He did, however, issue a rather sentimental-sounding grunt.

Mattie's heart simply melted at the idea of a little child falling in such love with her aircraft. She also adored that Vera had gifted the girl with a toy most would relegate to the world of boys' playthings. Glancing around at the women, Mattie realized that each one was bold in her own unique way—even Lily for all her outward silliness. Mattie felt a sense of comradery fall over her that she'd never experienced—never even thought possible. She had not fit in before, not entirely. She'd been deemed too girlish by the boys and too boyish by the girls. But here, she didn't feel like she straddled two spheres. Among these women—who fixed automobiles, chased after trespassers, and embraced little girls who treated their airplanes like dolls—Mattie might just have finally found her place.

Unease rippled through Leo, making his guts tighten. He recognized the sensation of his body gearing up for a danger that no longer existed. But no matter how many times Leo told himself that the Great War had drawn to a close almost five years ago, he had moments when the rest of him refused to believe that peace had been achieved. Sometimes

Leo understood what triggered the old now-unnecessary battle readiness; other times, it reared up like a striking rattler without reason or warning.

Tonight, he had no problem identifying the root of it. His palatial rooms in Vera's turret reminded him too keenly of the château in France. He remembered staring at the old plush furnishings, ancient woodwork, and thick mullioned glass windows and wondering how the world could hold such beauty, such grandeur, as Alfred's body lay somewhere over enemy lines. The Germans had respectfully buried him, but Leo only had received that confirmation after the armistice. During Leo's endless nights at the exquisite former residence of the aristocracy, he'd been plagued with the urge to borrow a motorcycle and begin a suicidal dash over No Man's Land in an attempt to retrieve the remains of his best friend. The desperate need to bring home Alfred's body had lessened somewhat when their squadron had been transferred to another aerodrome with standard barracks. Being back in a military setting had made the loss of Alfred less immediately raw, the spartan living conditions mirroring the harshness and emptiness of war instead of offering a cruel, luxurious contrast to the suffering.

It was odd, though, how the exterior of another, older château had been one of Leo's favorite landmarks to confirm his flight path. The proud, ancient stone had reminded Leo of the continuity of life through all the horrors of history and had given him a sense of comfort whenever he'd flown over the tall, unyielding fortress.

Yet being inside a castle—inside the opulence—made him uncomfortable. And Vera's house affected him the same way, stirring up his normally tightly sealed emotions like wind from propeller blades aggravating a thatch of tall weeds and dispersing the unwanted but tenacious seeds.

Realizing he wouldn't get to sleep for hours, if at all, Leo rose from his bed. Stretching did little to relieve either his physical or internal tension. He didn't bother to turn on a light. Fresh air would help better than illumination. Striding quickly, he headed directly to the open window, where the gauzy curtains fluttered in the breeze. Unfortunately, in the darkness, he didn't notice the writing desk. Ornate and delicate like the rest of Vera's fairy-tale decor, the furniture had no bulk to counter the force of the collision. The dainty table clattered to the ground, creating a surprisingly loud, resounding bang. Leo cringed, hoping he hadn't woken anyone.

This time he did head toward the nightstand, wanting to turn on a lamp to assess any damage he might have done to the functional art piece. Unfortunately, in his rush, he did something he rarely did. He miscalculated the distance. He knocked his shin against the table with another loud thwack. The corner of the nightstand gouged him in the exact same spot that the writing desk had. Before he could stop himself, he emitted a rather loud grunt. He managed to cut it off in a rather strangled "Ermph," but it still echoed through the massive room.

Leo heard the floorboards creak above him. He jammed his hand into his hair as he realized that he must have woken Mattie. Sure enough, he heard her pad across her room and then tread down the stairs. When her knock came, even though he'd realized her intent, he still stood frozen, staring at the space where he remembered the door being.

"Leo?" Mattie's voice came soft and quiet . . . and definitely concerned. "Are you all right?"

"Yeah, I'm okay," Leo said as he belatedly flipped on the light. The Louis Tiffany dragonfly lamp didn't add a lot of illumination, but it was better than the previous darkness.

"Can I come in?" Mattie called again.

Leo glanced down at his sleeveless union suit. Although it covered everything important, his body heated at the thought of Mattie seeing him like this. "Ah, just a moment."

Hastily, he pulled his shirt over his head. It took him a little longer to yank up his trousers, but he moved as quickly as he could. "I'm ready now."

The door inched open, revealing a rather wild-haired Mattie. She, too, had taken time to throw on clothes, but she still looked like she'd just tumbled from bed.

Hell, he really should not think about *tumbled* and *bed* in conjunction with Mattie.

Unlike him, she didn't seem at all embarrassed by this midnight encounter. She stepped into his room like it was broad daylight, apparently oblivious to how the low glow shining through the art glass cast an intimate warmth over the richly appointed apartment. Years ago, Leo had sneaked out at night with Mattie, but Alfred had always been with them. Now it was just the two of them . . . and they weren't youths any longer.

"I heard a crash and a thud." Mattie peered around his room.

"Yeah." Leo awkwardly stepped back as he rubbed the back of his head. "I was trying to get some air and ended up tripping over the writing desk. Then I bumped into the nightstand."

Mattie glanced over at the fallen piece of furniture, and Leo belatedly remembered that he hadn't inspected the carved wood to make sure he hadn't broken or chipped anything. He hurried over, and Mattie joined him.

"It looks fine to me." She ran her finger over one of the fragile-looking decorative loops.

"Thank goodness. I have a feeling this costs more than everything I've ever owned. With the trouble the flight school is in, it would be hard to even repay Vera in installments." Leo started to lift the writing desk. Although it was light and he could have easily carried it with one hand, Mattie helped him move it back to where it belonged. It felt good, working together with her again.

"You know you're not obligated to help my family out of debt." Mattie rubbed her thumb over the highly polished wood, her gaze focused on the grain before she lifted her eyes toward his face. Her irises looked just as golden as the honey-colored hard maple.

He swallowed. Hard. His heart felt even more swollen than his throat. He didn't want to confess that he was the reason for the flight school's financial difficulties. Nor did he wish her to know the shame surrounding his birth.

"Your father said the same thing," Leo managed. It wasn't really an affirmative answer, but it seemed to satisfy Mattie all the same. Glad she wasn't about to dig into his reasoning, Leo relaxed his shoulders. Unfortunately, her next question sent them practically up to his ears again.

"Were you having trouble sleeping?"

"Some. New place." It wasn't entirely true, but it wasn't completely false either. He often had trouble bedding down in new places—a vestige not just from his war days but from his time on the streets, when every nap had meant leaving himself vulnerable to danger.

"Would you like to go for a stroll?" Mattie asked.

"Together?" Leo asked, glad his voice didn't crack in surprise. It would've if she'd asked him a question like that in the middle of the night when they were adolescents.

"You mentioned that you wanted air, and I thought maybe you'd like some company. You used to take walks, didn't you?"

He had a lot after his return from the war. The McAdams brothers slept deeply as they snored away like freight locomotives chugging up a hill. No one had ever heard him slip away . . . or at least he'd *thought* no one had.

"You heard?" Leo asked.

"One of my windows faced the door to the bunkhouse," Mattie answered. "I always figured that you wanted to be left alone, but now I think that maybe you could use the company. I know I could."

Leo instantly forgot his own awkwardness as sudden concern spiked through him. He instinctually stepped toward her and then stopped. "Is something bothering you?"

Mattie hesitated and then slowly jerked her chin. "This evening when I started to write the weekly letter that I'm planning to send to Pa, I got thinking about the financial mess again."

"It'll get sorted in time," Leo said with a confidence he didn't feel as fresh guilt stabbed at the already gaping wound.

"Even with us and the boys all pooling our resources, the numbers are still coming up short." Mattie flexed her fingers as she talked, the movement reflecting Leo's own frustration over the situation.

"There's always your idea about using radios to make flying safer," Leo said. "It could earn a mint."

As if she could no longer contain her energy, Mattie began to pace the room. "If only I could figure out how to make it workable. I feel the answer is there, but it keeps slipping away, taunting me even."

"Maybe you're trying too hard?" Leo suggested. "You always say that you do your best thinking when you're tinkering."

Mattie jerked her head. "That's why exercise would help. I don't have a workbench or tools here, and I need to do something active."

It could be dangerous, strolling under the stars with Mattie, hearing her gentle breathing as they moved through the grasses and sedges. But he yearned for this release, this escape, just like he'd needed the fresh air. And Mattie needed it too. That detail alone would have directed his decision.

"Okay."

By unspoken agreement, they didn't say anything more. Noiselessly, they crept down the turret stairs and then through the main house. Luckily, they both possessed an uncanny sense of direction, which helped them find their way to the back garden with relative ease. They quietly shut the french doors and slipped out into the cool night.

"Isn't it magical here?" Mattie asked as she gave a little twirl. The sight of her whirling about, her face turned toward the sliver of the moon, caused Leo to smile. He'd missed being with her like this. She'd always exuded so much zest that her delight was infectious even for someone like him. Although *she* made him feel spellbound, he still didn't understand how she could derive so much pleasure from simply stepping into the inky darkness.

Leo lifted his head as he'd done so many years ago when he'd tried to envision the world as Mattie saw it. But his mind only took in the important details. "Lots of stars are out. It seems like it'll be a clear day tomorrow. Good visibility."

"Leo?" Mattie asked, her voice oddly soft and a little uncertain.

Accustomed to her boldness, Leo immediately whipped his head in her direction. She didn't look worried . . . just contemplative and earnest.

"What?" he asked.

"Would you indulge me? There is something I'd like to try even if it might sound a little silly. Would you shut your peepers? Just for a moment?"

If anyone else had asked Leo to close his eyes, he would have balked. But this . . . this was Mattie. He trusted her not to harm him. So he did as she asked.

"What do you smell?" Mattie asked.

He inhaled deeply, trying to detect what she wanted him to notice. For the first time, he paid attention to the perfumed air buffeting his skin. A part of him had already recognized and dismissed the smell, as it contained no vital information to his or Mattie's well-being, but now the sweetness filled his nostrils.

"Roses," Leo said.

"How many?" Mattie asked.

He breathed in again, noticing how heavily the scent hung in the air. "Lots of them."

"Full bloom?"

"Probably," Leo said.

"What do you hear?" Mattie asked.

He listened carefully. "The lake. Some birdsong. It's nice. Pleasant, I suppose." The lapping current had a quiet, rhythmic quality to it. Peaceful. And the avian calls reminded him of the roses, honeyed and pleasing.

"Open your eyes," Mattie instructed. "Now what do you see?"

Her. Mattie stood amid a patch of cream-colored roses, fireflies twinkling about her. The pale, dim light from the moon illuminated the white of her cotton shirt and the petals of the flowers surrounding her. He thought about how he'd gone with her and the rest of the McAdams siblings to see the film version of *The Secret Garden* shortly after the war. He'd never completely understood why all the characters found the walled-in, forgotten plot of land so darn intriguing. In fact, he'd fallen asleep in the middle of the picture show. But now . . . now he wondered if he should have paid more attention to the message it had been trying to convey.

"Maybe I spy just a bit of that magic you were talking about," Leo admitted gruffly.

Mattie rewarded him with a bright smile that, to him, outshone any pretty posy. "There's always a bit of enchantment in the world as long as you know how to look for it."

Leo had no idea why he decided to blurt out the next words. Perhaps because he felt so oddly comfortable in a way he hadn't felt since before the war. Possibly because Mattie's eyes looked so kind. Or maybe because he needed to say it. To someone. To *Mattie.*

"The last time Alfred and I were stationed together, it was at a fancy house like this one." The words rushed from Leo's mouth before he could dam them up.

Mattie instantly froze. Although he could not see the color that her eyes turned, they grew wider. She obviously hadn't expected him to mention her twin. Heck, *he* hadn't expected to blurt it out either. He jammed his hand in his hair and spread his feet as a new guilt gnawed at him. Had he ruined Mattie's enjoyment of Vera's estate with his thoughtlessness?

But then . . . then her lips formed another smile. A tremulous one. A soft one. But a *real* one. "I remember him describing the château in letters he sent home. He was so excited to be in a place like that and living shoulder to shoulder with millionaire flyboys."

Alfred hadn't minded that most of their fellow aviators had been from rich, privileged backgrounds, but then Alfred had always been able to get along with anyone. It hadn't been that way at all for Leo. He'd always felt like an interloper.

"I'm sorry I mentioned it," Leo said quickly.

Mattie gave her head a firm, emphatic shake. "No. I'm glad you did. I want to talk about Alfred. I *like* to speak of him. But sometimes I feel like I'm the only one."

Leo had tried, and failed, to push away his memories of his best friend. The good ones. The bad ones. Even the seemingly trivial ones. But despite all the years of trying to shove those feelings aside, it struck Leo that it felt *good*, right even, to discuss his fallen comrade.

"He would have thought this place was the bee's knees," Leo admitted, and it felt like something—another little something—broke loose inside him again.

"Oh, would he have *ever*," Mattie agreed. "And can you imagine how he would have flirted with Vera? Those two would have been shameless, each trying to upstage the other with outrageous flatteries."

Leo's lips did something that they hadn't for a very long time during discussions of his best friend. They stretched upward into the barest hint of a grin. And he *felt* the smile too. A touch of bittersweetness bursting through all the layers of numbness, guilt, and remorse.

It was—as Mattie was beginning to discover—very difficult to conduct a private conversation at the foot of a staircase, even in a mansion. The phone at the flight school was also in a high-traffic position, but she rarely had any need to use it.

Mattie did *not* appreciate being pulled from a rather scrumptious breakfast spread to talk to her eldest brother . . . or rather to *soothe* his worries for her.

"No, Jake." Mattie tapped her well-worn oxford against the marble floor. "I am not going to drag Leo from his bacon, pancakes, and spiced peaches just to confirm I haven't been trying any harebrained stunts."

"Why not?" Jake asked grumpily.

"One, Leo is *not* my keeper." Mattie wanted to grab the receiver in both hands and shake it in frustration. "Two, this call is expensive."

"Then will you tell me if you have?"

"Nope." Mattie rather delighted in saying that word. In reality, they weren't going to start flying until late morning, but she didn't want to give Jake the satisfaction of knowing that. Let *him* stew.

"But . . ."

"Are you going to give me detailed updates on Will, Otto, and your adventures with the postal service?" Mattie asked sweetly. "What if you go to any disreputable speakeasies? That could be dangerous. Will you give me reports on that?"

Jake, thankfully, fell silent. Mattie took the opportunity to bring up the subject that she *actually* wanted to discuss. "Jake, I've been thinking about how we need to earn more money, and I swear I'm close to an idea about taking advantage of radio communication. If I come up with a workable design, would you float it around to your bosses at the Airmail Service?"

This time, Mattie didn't appreciate her brother's long pause. Her stomach clenched, and her hand tightened around the conical Bakelite receiver. "Jake?"

"You know I think you're brilliant when it comes to mechanical and electrical things, right?" Jake's voice sounded soft, gentle. That was *not* a good sign.

"Yeees." Mattie dragged out the word. Her brothers had at least always encouraged her puttering around in the workshop. The first Christmas after the prohibition on civilian use of radio had been lifted after the Great War, her siblings had put their money together, along with Leo, to buy her everything she needed to build a crystal set.

"Anyone who can hobble together an entire backup spark system for a JN-3 is definitely capable of coming up with something brilliant with radio," Jake continued.

"All this flattery is beginning to concern me." Mattie wanted to pace, but she needed to speak into the mouthpiece, and she wasn't about to trot around with Vera's entire candlestick phone in her hand.

"The thing is, Mattie, it's hard to convince people to try any new technology, and when they hear that a girl—"

Anger and frustration tightened the muscles of Mattie's throat, and for a moment, she couldn't speak. At just that moment, Sadie—the brunette sister from Pennsylvania—started down one side of the dual staircase. Mattie doubted that the woman had seen her. This time she did grab the entire phone, stand and all, as she tried to duck farther into the alcove between the two sets of steps. She really did not want one of her new compatriots to see her this upset.

"Mattie?" Jake asked. "Are you still there?"

"Uh-huh." She forced out the sound, glancing furtively over her shoulder to make sure that she didn't attract Sadie's notice.

"You're not upset, right?" Jake sounded nervous now. Her brothers were forever worried about making her cry, which was complete nonsense since she never did.

"Nah," Mattie squeezed out. She *was* disappointed and irritated at the whole situation, but if she said anything more, Sadie would definitely hear. The new flyer's feet were just about level with Mattie's head.

She could see the woman's shoes and khaki pants between the railing's decorative ironwork.

"Mattie, I would use anything that you invent, and I'll do my darndest to convince my new superiors at the Airmail Service to do the same, but I just don't want you to get your hopes up," her brother said.

"Mm-hmm." Mattie made the noncommittal sound, knowing in this instance Jake was at least *trying* to encourage her.

He huffed out a relieved sigh. "Now that we have that out of the way, would you please get Leo? I really do want to know what you've been up to."

Mattie whipped her head back around in the direction of the mouthpiece. "Jake, for the *last* time, Leo is not responsible for me and neither are *you*. I am going to fly how I want and when I want, just like you and the boys all do. This time none of you can stop me."

Mattie would have jammed the handset back into place, but she retained enough sense to realize she was using someone else's property. Instead she gave Jake the crispest of goodbyes and gently but firmly ended the connection. Still infuriated, she whirled and found herself face to face with Sadie. Mortification now mixed with aggravation.

Sadie, however, fixed Mattie with an understanding smile. "Let me guess. That happened to be your brother."

Slightly more at ease, but still self-conscious, Mattie responded with a weak grin. "I currently have three of them—all older, all convinced it is their most solemn duty to protect me."

"You poor thing. Luckily, I only have to contend with two." Sadie shook her head in patent sympathy. "And I have Lily, so we are evenly matched against the male members of our family."

"I'm the only girl," Mattie said. "My mom died when I was pretty young, so it's always been me and the fellows for about as long as I can remember."

"That's rough." Sadie studied Mattie closely and seemed to come to a decision. "Whenever my brothers start acting all absurdly manly, I always sneak off to the barn and work on fixing a piece of equipment. Luckily, when you live on a farm, there's always something that needs repaired."

A pleased surprise rushed through Mattie. "If flying isn't an option, that's exactly what *I* do too!"

"Most people think it's a crazy thing for a girl," Sadie said. "But for me it is the most sensible and natural thing. Gears work the way you want them to work, the way they're supposed to *work*. Why wouldn't I want to tinker with them when everything else has gone amok."

"I couldn't have said it better myself!" Mattie had read all about kindred spirits in L. M. Montgomery novels, but she'd always dismissed the concept as nonsense. But here, in this world of daredevil women, she felt a hint of connection, perhaps a homecoming even.

"We still have over an hour before Vera wants us all to congregate on the training field, and I've already had breakfast." Sadie glanced over at the ornately carved grandfather clock that looked like two cranes holding the timepiece under their intertwined beaks. "Would you like to see the dynamo that helps power the building? Vera showed it to me when Lily and I arrived four days ago. There is a machine shop next door to the power station that Vera said we could use at our leisure if we were so inclined. Carrie's father is the owner of a bicycle boutique in Chicago. He was one of the first who started offering motorized ones, so she grew up around machines too."

"Truly?" Mattie said as her heart kicked up a beat.

Sadie dipped her chin in confirmation. "So are you ready to see the engine that powers this place?"

"Am I ever," Mattie said as she followed Sadie to a nondescript door tucked away in an alcove near the grand foyer. Decorative vine-like scrollwork helped obscure the entranceway to an entirely new world. Unlike the grandeur of the main house, the hidden hallway was narrow and utilitarian. But despite its unfussy appearance, it was clean and brightly lit with electric bulbs.

Just as curious as she'd been about the display portion of the castle, Mattie scanned the servants' corridor. She wondered what it would be like to work in a big house, hurrying unseen behind the walls. How often did she feel like that? Her work concealed, unnoticed.

The stairs down to the subbasement were equally simple but well maintained. As they descended past the kitchen and the laundry, Mattie didn't envy the servants who had to make this steep trip multiple times a day as they lugged trays of food and freshly pressed linens. Although gas ovens with enameled tops, electric washing machines, and newfangled electric-powered vacuum machines made the business of running a household easier, it didn't mean all manual labor had disappeared, especially in a mansion of this size.

Even before they reached the power room, Mattie could hear the steady *lub lub lub* of the motor. The rhythmic sound had a way of both soothing and thrilling her.

"My dad says that the steady thump of a thresher used to put me to sleep," Sadie said, as if she'd heard Mattie's thoughts. "My mom would put me under a tree on a blanket, and I'd drift right off. Lily, though, used to howl something terrible. It's funny how folks think twins should be so similar. My sister and I have always been as different as oil and water, but thankfully we get along a lot better than that."

Twins. Mattie hadn't realized until now that the sisters were fraternal ones. Yet somehow the revelation didn't cut as deep as she'd thought it would. It gave her yet another connection to this woman who seemed to echo her own internal thoughts. Maybe Sadie would understand emotions Mattie felt about Alfred when no one else ever had.

"It's funny," Mattie replied as a rush of sad fondness flowed through her. "My twin and I were the classic peas in a pod. We always liked the same things—flying, machines, even the same food. None of the rest of the family can abide braunschweiger, but Alfred loved it just like me."

"I didn't know you were a twin too! I've never met another set," Sadie said excitedly as she went to push open the door to what sounded like the power room, given the intensity of the steady sounds emanating from behind the wood. "I take it he's an aviator too?"

"He was." The words were still hard to say, even after all these years, but there was comfort in talking about him. "He died in France. Fighter pilot. Same squadron as Leo. They were best friends too."

"Oh," Sadie said softly, her hand frozen on the partially open door. "I'm so sorry. I shouldn't have brought up the twin thing."

"It's okay," Mattie assured her and then realized that it was. "You didn't know."

Sadie gnawed at her lip. "Does it bother you? I mean me and Lily being . . ."

"Twins?" Mattie finished as the other woman trailed off, as if unsure if her words were doing harm or good. When Sadie nodded affirmatively, Mattie waited a beat before speaking, trying to figure out the answer for herself.

"In my family, it's like Alfred is just on a trip, ready to return—his belongings still waiting for him. But we don't talk about him, and it creates this emptiness. I think it's good for me to see you and Lily together, to think of the good times, to fill in that hollowness with memories."

"If you ever need to talk about your brother, both Lily and I would be more than willing to listen. If I lost Lily, I'd probably natter on about her all the time and keep a little bit of her alive with me."

Something akin to relief washed over Mattie. "That is exactly how I feel. I just said something similar to Leo. Being on this grand adventure makes me feel oddly closer to Alfred than I ever did when eating at the same table as his empty chair. I just keep on imagining how much he'd enjoy all this."

"What do you think he would have thought of this room?" Sadie asked as she finally pushed the door open, revealing a massive masterpiece of machinery. The two-cylinder motor and the Crocker-Wheeler generator whirled madly. The rhythmic pounding of the pistons overwhelmed the senses, but Mattie could almost feel the flow of power running from the engine, through the driveshaft, and into the generator, where it sparked to life, lighting and putting into motion the entire mansion.

"Oh! Alfred would have loved it!" Mattie shouted as she walked toward the equipment, drawn in by its power.

"It was designed by Dr. Cyprien O'Dillon Mailloux, the same man who's responsible for the electrical systems in the Astoria Hotel and the Biltmore House."

"I've read some articles written by him!" Mattie leaned closer to the motors as she watched the valve rods pop up and down in time with the firing of the cylinders.

"Vera has his original plans." Sadie bent down.

"Does she?" Thrilled, Mattie glanced over at her new compatriot, who was now critically eyeing the carbon brush on the generator's armature.

"Oh yes." Sadie didn't turn her attention from the apparatus. "She lent them to me to read. I'm sure she'll let you borrow them too."

"Oh, that would be just the berries!"

"Do you need any assistance, ladies?" a male voice intoned—pleasant enough but definitely confused.

Mattie spun with Sadie to find a man dressed in clothes that were too fancy to be those of a mere laborer but too casual to be those of a businessman. His noncommittal grin matched his tone. "I am Mr. Berkley. I oversee the operations of the power system here at Fete Castle."

Sadie, who had radiated confidence around Mattie and the other women, seemed quieter now, less sure of herself. "Right, um, Miss Jones mentioned, uh, that you were. She said to tell you if you, um, asked that she said we could take a look around. I'm, uh, Miss Sadie Lenhart, and this is Miss McAdams."

"Oh yes, Miss Jones did mention that guests might be stopping by," Mr. Berkley said kindly—perhaps a little *too* kindly—as if he was trying too hard to be welcoming. "Would you like me to explain how it all works? I shall try to use words that you can comprehend."

"Oh, no bother." Mattie gave a wave of her hand, just like she'd seen Vera do. "Miss Lenhart seems well versed in this machine."

"Well, if you are certain." Mr. Berkley dragged out the last word, indicating that he definitely doubted Sadie's capabilities.

Mattie glanced over at Sadie, who seemed to have clammed up entirely. Mattie, however, had no problems defending her new friend. "We are positive."

Unconvinced and seemingly slightly put out, Mr. Berkley gestured toward a smaller, movable generator system that Mattie recognized from trade journal articles. "Would you not wish to know more about this booster, which is—"

"Used to increase and decrease voltage, as designed by Dr. O'Dillon Mailloux," Mattie answered. "For example, it can help give an extra boost to the longer feeder wires. Due to the vertical construction of Fete Castle, I would think this advance is rather useful."

Mr. Berkley cleared his throat, obviously not expecting *that* response. Beside Mattie, Sadie restraightened. She even took a small step toward the engineer. When she spoke, her voice was back to its normal strength. "Yes. And the booster is also used to charge the batteries and to make sure that not too much amperage is sent through the circuits, which could damage the light fixtures."

The man at least appeared contrite instead of digging a trench around his notion that females couldn't understand electricity. "I shall leave you two to your explorations, then. Just be careful not to touch anything."

"We're not foolhardy enough to tamper with our host's power system," Mattie promised, although part of her wanted to deliver a flippant answer about how she planned on playing with all the controls embedded in the marvelously complex marble switchboard.

After dipping his head in acknowledgment, Mr. Berkley crossed his hands behind his back and finally retreated. As soon as he disappeared into another room, Sadie exhaled a whoosh of air. "Thanks. I normally get tongue tied around strangers, especially men. There's just something about the troupe that Vera put together that puts me at ease."

"Me too," Mattie admitted, surprised by how fiercely she agreed with Sadie's statement.

"You know a lot about currents." Sadie walked over to the massive switchboard and stared up at the contraption that controlled so many facets of the castle towering above them.

"So do you," Mattie pointed out as she moved to stand shoulder to shoulder with Sadie. "Electricity fascinates me. Radio waves as well."

"Me too!" Sadie agreed. "That and the technology behind moving pictures. Not just the projectors and the film, but the special effects too. Lily goes for the gowns, the jewelry, and the romantic leading men, but I'm all for the fan-created waves, the fake blood, and the monsters."

"I have to admit I watch for the stories, the momentary escape from reality," Mattie said.

"Lily wants to go to California someday and make it big in the movies. All that glitz doesn't tempt me, but sometimes the technology does. It's sort of like being a modern-day wizard, don't you think?"

"Radio is like that for me. How it can carry voices and music over incredible distances, through the air to boot! I have an . . ." Mattie drifted off, catching herself. She didn't know if she should reveal to this woman her dream of making airplanes safer by using radio signals.

"Do you have some sort of advancement in mind?" Sadie's voice crackled with an excitement that mirrored Mattie's own. And Mattie couldn't help but share just a little. After all, the entire concept wasn't a novel idea.

"I don't know what exactly, but it seems with radio growing so much, especially in the last year, that there is some way to take advantage of it to improve airplane safety, especially when it comes to solo flights, night flying, and the Airmail Service. I've thought about working with radio communication, but the technology just isn't developed enough to use in planes. Transmitters are too big, and receivers are too finicky for a pilot to operate without a navigator."

Sadie thoughtfully tapped her finger against her lips. "When I have a problem trying to find a solution, it is normally that I'm overcomplicating it."

"Do you see a way to simplify my plans so that I wouldn't have to develop more compact transmitters?" Mattie asked as she turned back to the generator.

"Maybe start with what technology is available, and figure out what to do with it," Sadie suggested.

A spark like lightning flashed through Mattie. Sadie was right. There was elegance in simplicity, and it was best to always start at the beginning of things. "You're brilliant, Sadie! Instead of trying to work backward from a dream product, I need to look at the realities of what is available *now*. Just like when I tinker with a motor—I start with the materials that I have on hand."

"Precisely!" Sadie said. "That's how I do it!"

They shared a grin then, in the bowels of the castle, the machinery whumping behind them, the smell of grease permeating the air. This was a world Mattie enjoyed, and for the first time, she'd found a female friend with whom to share it.

Chapter Six

> A reasonable observer needs only to glance at the photograph of Miss Lily Lenhart caught in the steam from an unscrewed radiator cap to fully comprehend the perils of petticoat flyers. Women with their delicate sensibilities and even more delicate constitutions are not meant to handle dangerous machinery even on the ground. It is clear that they should not be attempting to take to the skies in our modern mechanical beasts of the air. Anyone who attends a Flying Flapper performance is only encouraging travesty . . . and certain tragedy.
>
> —Benjamin Pringle, *Chicago Advance Leader*

Chaos. Leo had entered pure chaos.

"I look dreadful!" Lily wailed as she clutched the news article in her hand, her face scrunched up in an expression of horror worthy of a screen star. They had just taken a break from practicing their stunts outside to read the afternoon paper. "The second picture is even worse! I look downright hideous with my makeup dripping over me. How will I ever be discovered with press like this? My life is *over*. Fini. Fait accompli."

Leo saw Mattie and Sadie share a look as Lily draped her hand over her forehead and swayed backward slightly, as if she was about to faint. Vera's cousin, Alice, however, stepped forward to wrap her arm around Lily's shoulder.

"It is not as drastic as that." Alice gave the blonde's bicep a pat. "All performers get bad pictures taken of them. It happens to me all the time."

"You mean I'll have more of these!" Lily's voice climbed even higher. Leo fought against the urge to wince as he tried to drift farther away from the center of the scene.

"Yes, but you'll have plenty of wonderful ones too," Alice said.

"And the best way of doing that is to come up with a routine that puts you in the spotlight in the way you want to be seen," Vera advised.

Lily sniffled. "Should I practice my dance routine some more?"

"You're a wonderful artist." Sadie grabbed her sister's hands. "You're sure to wow the crowd."

Lily squared her thin shoulders and looked surprisingly resolute. "Alice? Aida? Will you help me again?"

"Certainly!" Aida closed the notebook she'd been scrawling in. Together the three wing-walkers marched to an elevated board where they'd been practicing earlier. One of them would stand on the piece of wood while the other two pulled ropes attached to either end of the lumber in an attempt to simulate the movement of an airplane wing. As far as Leo could tell, the women had just made this exercise up out of whole cloth. Although they'd hung a net under the "training equipment," he doubted they'd put much science behind their madness.

"This really is a setback for the circus," Vera said quietly, her voice pitched low enough so that it would not reach Lily's ears. "We *must* create stellar acts. We can't allow folks to view us as a bunch of incompetent amateurs. If we do, we'll never attract audiences, and this enterprise will end before it even has a chance to begin."

"We can't let that happen!" Mattie spoke emphatically, and Leo could hear her unspoken fear. Both of them needed the money from this gig.

"I'm sure we can come up with something." Carrie tapped her finger against her cheek thoughtfully. "Mattie and I are both skilled barnstormers. It won't take much to think of something visually impressive from the ground without taking unnecessary risks."

Finally, a sensible thought.

Leo was about to second Carrie's statement when the blare of fast-paced jazz music drew his attention. Standing on the elevated board, Lily waved her arms and kicked up her legs. She was a lithe and energetic dancer, but the sight of her routine caused nervousness to skitter through him. On the surface, the quick steps didn't look particularly dangerous until one considered the fact that Lily clearly intended to try them on the wing of a moving *airplane*.

Mattie's voice suddenly broke into Leo's concentration on the wing-walkers' practice. "And then you could climb from Carrie's plane holding a spare landing wheel . . ."

With a snap that literally cracked his neck, Leo spun toward her. He almost hated posing his question for fear of the answer. "Why is any spare wheel involved?"

"Because I am going to change Mattie's wheel in midair." Vera smiled at him in the same manner she'd employed when she'd offered him a frothy pink cocktail.

"In midair?" He couldn't help it. He crossed his arms. All four women followed his gesture with their eyes. Mattie scowled, her back noticeably straightening several notches.

Vera, however, merely arched an eyebrow. "Well, it wouldn't be very interesting if I changed it on the ground."

"Do you have any idea how dangerous that would be? You'd be dangling on the underbelly of a plane as the earth whizzed below you at fifty miles per hour or faster."

"There are more flying circuses than ever," Mattie pointed out. "We need to do something to stand out, to bring in the crowds, Leo."

He heard the unspoken message, and guilt strafed him as he thought about the debt hanging over both their heads. Leo jammed his fingers into his hair, massaging the crown of his head.

"Why don't we test how close Mattie and I can fly in tandem before we make any decisions?" Carrie asked. "Vera can ride in Mattie's bird so she can experience what it feels like when the planes pass each other. Sadie can ride along with me to pick up more techniques. What do you think?"

Before Leo could object, the women chorused their yeses and quickly raced off. Within minutes, the noses of Carrie's and Mattie's planes lifted into the air. As the two flew side by side executing various maneuvers, the little differences in their flying styles stood out to Leo. Most people wouldn't notice, but he'd been trained to watch each rattle and shake of a plane, each faint dip and lift of a wing as he tried to divine a Fokker's next move. And he'd watched over the new aviators in his squadron, giving them pointers to help keep them alive during the next battle.

Carrie flew with surgical precision: straight, smooth, and crisp. She did not waste a single movement. Mattie's style was more brazen and spontaneous as she rushed into each maneuver with endless exuberance. Although diametrically different, both methods resulted in an aerial grace that was absolutely stunning.

"They're amazing, aren't they?" Alice asked.

Leo grunted.

"It is really true, then, that Mattie taught you to fly?" Aida asked, her voice taking on a sharper quality. He'd felt less scrutinized when standing at attention in front of a commanding officer.

He dipped his chin brusquely. His eyes followed the sunny yellow tips of Mattie's plane as she flew inverted above their heads with Carrie soaring above her.

Aida shifted closer to him. "How would you describe your relationship with Mattie?"

Lily suddenly popped into view as she peered around Aida. A sort of strangled choking sound emerged from Leo's throat. It was not his finest response, but it was the best he could manage.

"It really would help my study if you could clarify your relationship," Aida added.

"And it would just help me. In general." Lily winked, the gesture decidedly naughty.

"Gu-mph." He had no idea what the sound was. For some reason, Aida scribbled it down. He had a feeling she did it just to torment him. Her lips did curve suspiciously upward as her fountain pen scratched across the page.

Alice patted his shoulder, almost making him jump high enough to touch Mattie's JN-4. Luckily, he kept his reflexes in check. He had no idea what Aida would record in her tablet if he suddenly started leaping skyward.

"Don't worry, my husband will be here soon. He tends not to ask personal questions . . ." Alice paused before smiling wickedly and adding, "Unless I ask him to."

Leo was dubiously saved from begging *Please don't ask him to* when Aida said, "This will present an intriguing opportunity."

"What opportunity?" Alice shifted her body so she could look around him to face Aida.

"To observe the difference between an established relationship between two daredevils reared in the circus world and a burgeoning romance between two outsiders who weren't." Aida paused and then addressed him. "You don't come from an aerobatic family, do you?"

Leo didn't come from any family—not that he would reveal *that* to Aida. He could only imagine her questions about life in an orphanage and on the streets. He rubbed the back of his head.

"The papers *never* mention anything about his past," Lily said in a stage whisper. "The articles always say he won't comment. It is all *very* mysterious."

Leo didn't think it would help if he pointed out he could hear Lily. He greatly feared that anything he said would only encourage them further, and further encouragement was the last thing they needed. He wondered for a moment if this was how Mattie felt—always outnumbered, always trying to find her footing when everyone else seemed to balance so naturally.

To his great relief, Mattie and Carrie landed their planes in two simultaneous graceful sweeps. He barely noticed the artistic precision of their mutual descent. Breaking free of the women, he strode directly toward Mattie's Jenny. He didn't care if it looked like he was running, because that was precisely what he *was* doing. Ace aviators stayed alive by knowing when they couldn't beat the odds.

Unfortunately, it took him only seconds to realize he might have made a strategic mistake. Mattie bounced out of her plane and bounded toward him. Vera followed at a more sedate pace.

"Did you see that, Leo? We have to try some similar close maneuvers during our flight duel! We could really make the audience gasp! What do you think?" Mattie looked alight with energy, and it damn near electrified him. No doubt about it; she was more perilous to his health than any enemy antiaircraft shells.

"That could be dangerous, Mattie," Leo cautioned, and this time he didn't just mean physically. Until this moment, he hadn't realized how much he *did* want to fly with Mattie in formation. There was a connection between aviators, a kind of instinctual, silent communication. High in the skies where a wing wiggle or a choreographed maneuver was the only way to pass on messages, pilots needed to be in tune with each other. Part of him, *all* of him, yearned to feel that connection with Mattie. And that frightened him.

"Worried you can't control your plane when you're close to me? Afraid of a little proximity?" Mattie broke her tough stance to move toward him, a cocky swagger to her step that sent his heart thudding even faster.

He swallowed, feeling the tightened muscles of his throat slide roughly past each other. Her words struck hard, but not for the reason she'd intended. Right now, especially with Aida's questions, he wasn't thinking so much about airspace as he was about physical nearness. A flare of heat shot through him, and to his embarrassment, a good portion seemed to land directly underneath his cheeks. His suntanned skin could hide some of his blushes but not one this intense.

By the way Vera quirked a knowing eyebrow, she'd immediately detected his flush. Mattie hadn't any more than she'd realized how closely her words had skirted innuendo.

"Darling," Vera drawled out, one side of her lips rising, as if in unison with her amused brow, "you're flustering the poor man with all your talk of *proximity*."

Cocking her head in confusion, Mattie directed her attention toward her partner in crime. "Pardon?"

"Look at him. He's as red as a maraschino cherry." Vera swung her arms in Leo's direction.

Leo feared that his face had brightened even more. Mattie peered at him, her mouth forming an O of surprise as she finally registered the pink spreading over every blasted inch of his countenance. Although he tried to stop himself, he couldn't refrain from rubbing his forehead, as if he could scrub off the tint.

Mattie, thankfully, just folded her arms over her chest once more. "Leo, are you willing to try out close formations with me?"

"I'll consider it," Leo ground out. "We can run some maneuvers in the air. Give it a trial run. No guarantees, though."

A light sparked in Mattie's eyes—gold, bright, and effervescent. A thrill shot through him as he realized he'd caused it.

"You're not just buying yourself time to try to persuade me otherwise?" Mattie asked suspiciously.

He rubbed the back of his head vigorously. "I'm giving us both a chance to convince each other. I promise I won't dismiss the idea outright. If our practice shows that we can pull off the tricks without putting any of us in unnecessary danger, then I'll do it."

"So you're giving me a chance?" Mattie asked. "A real, honest-to-goodness chance?"

"Yes."

A huge grin spread over Mattie's face. And if that wasn't shock enough, Mattie suddenly embraced him, her lithe arms wrapping securely around his neck. Although the McAdamses were demonstrative, Mattie was more likely to affectionately punch one of her brothers on the arm or slap him on his back. This hug, however, was inherently feminine, and its simple sweetness sank into Leo, reaching his core. If she'd slugged him instead, it would have come as less of a shock.

He'd just begun to ease into the gesture when she pulled back. His fingers, which had been slowly unfurling, snapped back against his palms, his blunt nails digging into his calluses. He barely stopped himself from squeezing his eyes shut, as if he could push the unwelcome yearning from his body. But such a reaction would do nothing other than alert the forever-eagle-eyed Vera or Aida to his helpless want.

Mattie cleared her throat, appearing a little unsettled herself. Obviously, she hadn't planned for the impromptu hug any more than he had. And Leo didn't want Mattie feeling off balance. So he reached forward and patted her arm. Awkwardly. He thought he heard a truncated snicker from Vera, but when he glanced in her direction, she looked as sober as a military judge at a court-martial, although perhaps a tad too somber. Otherwise ignoring the bemused heiress, he turned his attention back to Mattie and gave her arm another light brush.

It felt odd touching Mattie . . . and wonderful. It didn't matter that the pads of his fingers grazed her long-sleeved cotton work shirt instead of flesh or even that *he* knew he wasn't doing this quite right. It felt intimate to him. Given the way Mattie's eyes widened ever so slightly, the gold hues almost subsuming the blue-green flecks, she understood the significance of the gesture.

Almost terrified by that thought, Leo dropped his hand, as if he'd placed it directly in the path of steam escaping from a boiler. He flexed his fingers, almost feeling the scalding pain.

"Well," Vera said, breaking the uncomfortable silence weighing down on Leo and Mattie, "I think I will leave you two to figure out how your routine will look. All this talk of maraschinos and flying has made me thirsty for an aviation cocktail."

Vera whirled around to the rest of the group. "Girls, are you thirsty?"

Ignoring the chorus of responses, Mattie gave Leo one of her wide grins that showed she'd discovered her equilibrium again. "Perhaps we should go somewhere quieter than the practice field? Maybe down by the lake?"

A white beach, blue water, a fairy-tale pink castle . . . they all spelled romance. He should refuse. But this was Mattie—practical, *sensible* Mattie. She'd only offered the most logical place. They could even draw loops and maneuvers in the sand. Unlike him, she didn't harbor secret romantic feelings. If Mattie felt any stirrings of longing, she wouldn't hide them. She'd act on them. Openly. Honestly. Boldly. Just like she did everything in life.

But heaven help him if Mattie ever did develop a liking for him. Because if she set her sights on him, he doubted he could withstand her fiery assault. He could dodge German Albatroses and their incendiary bullets, but he very much feared that he lacked the skills to outmaneuver a determined Mattie McAdams.

The warble of a loon wafted across the blue water, punctuated by the sharp call of a gull circling overhead in its never-ending quest for food. A more fortunate osprey dived gracefully into the water, reemerging with a silvery fish flopping in its talons. Avian beauty had never failed to entrance Mattie, and she'd always known that she would join the feathered creatures in the sky. But what Mattie hadn't realized was that it wouldn't just be physics holding her back but also her gender—*especially* her gender.

"We should zoom toward each other when we begin our competition," Mattie suggested as she rested her back against a sun-warmed rock. Leaning forward, she drew the maneuver in the sand. It wasn't a particularly complicated one, but she didn't like to sit still. Plus, sketching with a stick brought to mind childhood and gave her a blissful reprieve from her worries over her family's financial troubles.

"Like a mock dogfight?" Leo asked. Unlike her, he sat stiffly in the sand, his shoes still on, as if part of him rebelled at the very notion of unwinding.

Mattie drew two matching circles. "But with more theatrics. I thought we could charge at each other, then flip backward into identical impressive loops."

Leo leaned forward, the movement stretching his white cable-knit jersey over his shoulder blades. The sight distracted Mattie, and for one mad moment she wondered what would happen if he gave in to the hot summer day and removed his shirt.

Heat that had nothing to do with the overhead sun flooded Mattie. Thankfully, Leo remained oblivious. Instead, he reached for her stick, the gesture hesitant, almost shy. It reminded her keenly of the thin, scrawny adolescent he'd been, so eager to fly but reserved all at the same time. His fingers, warm and calloused, brushed against hers. The slight roughness made her want to shiver. Somehow, she managed to suppress the shake but not the odd awareness swirling through her like a dust devil over parched land.

Leo cleared his throat, as if he, too, had felt the wild madness and was trying to expel it. He rolled his shoulders before he began scribbling his own pattern in the white sand. "We could try this. It's something I saw a lot in the war when each pilot was jockeying for the advantage of a higher ceiling. I could come up behind you, like I was about to strafe your tail with bullets. You pull up and loop backward so you're now the one chasing me."

For the second time that day Mattie found herself wanting to throw her arms around Leo. She didn't understand this sudden need to pull him close.

"How about when I am upside down over you, I drop something. A flower or something," Mattie suggested. "A twist on the man being the one to shower a woman with posies."

"Red rose petals—not real ones but paper," Leo said. "They'd show up in the sky. Most will probably just blow away, but the visual effect would still impress."

"Vera will *love* it, especially since red is her signature color."

Leo groaned. "I hope she won't want you to dump a bunch of cherries on my head."

"Just pray they aren't maraschinos. That would definitely get sticky."

Leo chuckled, low and faint. The rare sound seemed to seep straight into Mattie's heart and fill each chamber near to bursting. She hadn't heard him laugh since Alfred's death.

"Please don't give Vera any ideas." Leo shook his head. "Or you'll need to figure out a gadget that can mechanically wipe red food dye from my goggles."

Mattie stretched back against the rock, enjoying both the external and internal heat spreading through her. She wanted to stay here, in this cove, where her old friendship with Leo was magically reemerging like not one but two fabled phoenixes ready to soar together.

"It's nice." Mattie dug her hand into the hot sand until her fingers scraped the coolness below. She kept it there, loving the contrast between the two layers, thinking how it brought to mind her personality and Leo's. One all flame, and one all ice.

"What's nice?" Leo stretched out his feet ever so slightly.

"Sitting here with you, not arguing." Mattie tilted her head back and traced one of the fluffy clouds with her eyes. "Working together again after all these years."

Leo grunted and fiddled with the tie on his shoe. She twisted her head to watch him instead of the sky.

"You know, you can take off your oxfords," she suggested.

He hesitated for a moment and then shrugged one white-clad shoulder. He removed the left shoe first, then the right. When he kept his white socks on, Mattie had to suppress a grin. It was so much like Leo to stay buttoned up, even in a place where most people took their pleasure.

"It's okay to strip to your bare feet." She wiggled her own gritty toes and then waggled her eyebrows suggestively. He rewarded her with one of his true sheepish grins. He pulled off the cotton material, then folded them neatly and carefully placed them in his shoes.

"Let's make a sandcastle," Mattie suggested. It was a wonderfully youthful notion, creating something so grand out of something so insubstantial.

Leo made a soft surprised exhale that hovered between a chuckle and a grunt. "I wouldn't begin to know how."

His quiet words reverberated through Mattie. Their stark honesty sounded almost like a confession. Knowing how much Leo valued his privacy, she simply began to mold sand into a pile.

"You need a good base first." She paused her work on the foundation to brush away an errant red curl that had blown into her face. His blue eyes followed the motion, and something in his gaze made her feel peculiar—a wonderful, giddy peculiar. He leaned forward, and for one heart-clenching moment, she thought he would tuck the lock behind her ear. He didn't reach for her, though, but rather for the sand. He pushed a heap against hers, nearly doubling the size.

"Now pat it down." Mattie demonstrated. "Make sure it is solid."

They both reached down at the same time, and his larger hand half covered hers. For a moment, his fingers curled around hers, trapping them between the coolness of the overturned sand and the heat of his flesh. Between the sand and his calluses, a delicious friction scraped against her skin. She inhaled, sharp and poignant.

"Like this?" he asked, his voice as rough as the grit between their interlaced fingers. She nodded, squeezing his hand.

"Like this."

He leaned forward, his brown bangs brushing against her forehead. She could feel his breath, warm and pleasant against her cheeks. Her eyes began to flutter closed, but before they could completely shut, the call of the loon rent the air. The eerie warble sliced through the gossamer strands pulling Mattie and Leo together. Suddenly he jerked, yanking his hand away so fast puffs of sand flew. An odd sense of loss filled Mattie as Leo's brilliant blue gaze left hers. With fast, economical motions, he molded the sand as carefully as a stone mason laying rock for a real fortress.

Mattie fought the urge to use her right hand to touch where his fingers had held her left. Her skin still felt tingly and oddly alive. Curiously, she regarded Leo, who seemed to be gathering enough building material to erect a life-size monument.

"What kind of castle should we build?" She kept her voice cheerful and light.

Leo eased back on his haunches and regarded the large lump with more scrutiny than necessary. He wiped his brow with his forearm, the weave of his jersey easily picking up the fine particles.

"I had a château in mind."

Surprise rushed through Mattie. She'd had that pegged wrong. She'd thought he would want to build a tough, no-nonsense fortress, especially after his confession last night about his unease over staying in Vera's house. Leo pressed the sand into a rounded turret. When it started to collapse, Mattie moved to help shore up the crumbling structure. Their hands brushed together again, warmth meeting warmth. Mattie expected Leo to quickly withdraw.

He didn't.

Instead he spoke, low and deep and more earnest than she'd ever heard before. "I flew over a lot of châteaus in France. It was different than staying in one. I could see the history instead of the luxury."

Mattie studiously kept her attention on the pale-white castle emerging from under their fingertips. She was afraid if she hazarded a glance in Leo's direction, he might freeze up.

Leo shifted on his haunches as he worked on a sloped roof. "There was so much destruction. Shells had torn up roads, fields, entire villages. Places that had stood for centuries. I saw refugees who'd lost their homes where their families had lived for generations. The war blew up so much tradition, so many connections and ties. But then I'd see one of the old châteaus rising from the ground, and there was a sort of strength in that. A promise of continuity."

Mattie didn't speak for a moment, wanting to make sure she wasn't interrupting. She had so many questions, but she didn't want to make him relive anything he didn't want to about the war. Instead, she made an observation that gave him the choice to alter the direction of the conversation. "I didn't know you liked old buildings."

"I find a certain peace in a structure that's stood for year after year, no matter the changes around it."

Mattie placed a blade of grass above one of the windows like a lintel. "Not a fan of the modern skyscraper?"

“They have their purposes.”

“I love tall buildings,” Mattie admitted.

“Old stone structures are solid.” Leo was situated between Mattie and the sun, so she had to squint to make out his features in the brilliant light. He looked so sober, not at all like a man creating a whimsical sandcastle. She wondered, for a moment, if he'd positioned himself purposely in the glare.

“I didn't know you felt so strongly about the past,” Mattie admitted.

“I like order.” Leo tilted his head to inspect the rear of the castle, effectively putting a barricade between them. “The past is a known entity. The future is not.”

“That's precisely what I like about the future.” Mattie added some decorative dribbles to the castle. They landed haphazardly but in a rather delightfully wild way. “Ever since the end of the war—the horrible, horrible, life-altering war—there's a . . . I don't know . . . a *change* in the air, like spring's rebirth after winter's devastation.”

“There was a château that was my favorite. It was one of my landmarks when I was over German-occupied territory.” Leo suddenly shifted back to their previous conversation, and Mattie wondered if she'd made a mistake mentioning the Great War again. “It got hit by shells, maybe even from the Allies, since it happened during one of the last drives of the campaign. I don't know if they'll ever rebuild it.”

“Maybe they'll erect something better, stronger even?” Mattie suggested softly. “Maybe it'll even be designed by an architect like Mary Colter.”

“The Santa Fe Railroad architect? Her ideas wouldn't make much sense in the French countryside.”

Mattie peered over the castle. “I didn't mean her precisely—just that a female might create the new structure. We're not just shortening our skirts and bobbing our hair; we're trying to do so much more.”

Leo didn't snort like her brothers would have done. Instead, he shifted so he could regard her fully, the sun no longer blocking his face. "Maybe some traditions need changing, but that doesn't mean we discard everything, does it? Cautious change is good."

"I'm all for a little revolution. We women have waited too long for incremental advances."

Leo rocked back on his heels. An odd whisper of excitement shot through Mattie as his blue eyes bored into hers. She didn't know if he'd ever held her gaze this long. Certainly, he'd never done so without talking. Part of her wanted to squirm, but she remained still, allowing both the inspection and the burgeoning awareness growing inside her.

The sound of the lapping water and the cries of the birds cocooned them, holding them in this moment and safeguarding them from the interruptions of the world. Mattie had never felt so conscious of another human being before. An odd connection seemed to shimmer between them, not visible, certainly not tangible, but palpable all the same.

Leo opened his mouth to speak, but Vera's voice called out from the knoll above them. "So this is where you two disappeared to! I can't wait to hear what you've dreamed up. I hope you haven't been too much of a bluenose, Leo."

Mattie shaded her eyes and caught sight of Vera silhouetted against the clear blue sky. The wind caught the bottom of her green skirt, ruffling the fabric around her knees. Vera lifted her cocktail glass, and Mattie could just make out the maraschino cherry cheerfully floating on top.

"Come rejoin us. Aida and Alice just devised the most outrageous stunt. It involves a motorcycle. Leo, I don't suppose you rode any during the war?" Vera must have meant the question rhetorically, because she had already turned, her drink still held high in the air as she picked her way through the tall grass.

Mattie exchanged a look with Leo and tipped her lips up into a smile. "Revolution?"

He jammed his hand into his hair as he stared after Vera. "Chaos. Pure chaos."

Chapter Seven

"What is *that*?" Vera pointed one rose-colored nail in the direction of a watermelon stuck to a stick in the middle of the training field. The white half-moon tip stabbed in the direction of the offending fruit.

Alice left Mattie's side to link her arm with her cousin's. "That represents you, dear. Isn't it clever? I came up with it."

"I need a target to aim at when I practice buzzing the ground for the stunt where you grab onto a ladder extending from my wing," Mattie explained.

"Mattie and I calculated how high you would be when standing in the Duesenberg," Carrie said. "The twig that we lashed to the stick is perfectly aligned with where your hand would be as you reach up."

"It looks nothing like me." Vera cocked her head and studied the melon disapprovingly as it slowly dripped red juice down the pole.

"It's supposed to be a generalized representation, not an accurate model," Aida pointed out. "You typically possess an extraordinarily healthy and active imagination, Vera. Picture it as you."

Vera tapped her finger against her chin as she studied the speared fruit from all angles. "It needs a hat."

"A hat?" Leo, who had been standing on the fringe of their group, choked out the words.

"Yes." Vera gave a sharp nod of patent satisfaction. "One of my cloches. I know just the one."

Vera waggled her fingers without even looking back at the group as she headed toward her Duesenberg and climbed in. When a Model T came puttering up the road from the castle, Vera tootled the horn merrily.

"I believe that is my family," Alice said, shielding her eyes. Sure enough, when the black motorcar stopped, three children poured out, followed by a tall ginger-haired man.

A chorus of *Mamas* rang through the air as the little trio dashed toward the aerialist. The youngest, a little moppet with a wild mane of strawberry-blonde hair, did her best to keep up with her older siblings, who looked to be about seven and ten. She did an admirable job, her sturdy little legs pumping furiously as she clutched a blue toy plane in her hand.

Alice crouched down to enfold her offspring in her outstretched arms. A chorus of high-pitched voices rang through the sedges.

"I found a bug, Mama."

"We saw three airplanes on our way here!"

"I have a cut on my finger."

"I just finished *Anne of Green Gables*, and Papa bought me *Anne of Avonlea*."

"I'm reading *The Story of Doctor Dolittle*. He can *talk* to animals."

With surprising adroitness, Alice parsed through the cacophony of voices and addressed each comment solemnly. "Oh my, Milly, that *is* a big caterpillar and so fuzzy . . . do you know that you're going to get to ride in some airplanes? Let me see that scrape. It looks like it's healing nicely, but I'll still give it a kiss . . . that is wonderful, Ruthie. Anne Shirley is such a lovely character . . . how fascinating, Eddie. He communicates with animals! And what do they have to say?"

Standing up with her daughters and son still dancing around her, Alice turned toward her husband, who was standing slightly to the side of the little throng, his mossy-green eyes warm and a smile below his thin, barely there mustache.

A faded recollection flashed to life in Mattie's mind, like a water-damaged movie reel. She did not have many memories of her mother. Most were flickers of sensations. The warmth of a hug. The faint smell of the lilacs her mother had loved. A cool hand in the midst of a fever.

But suddenly—although the image still remained slightly out of focus—Mattie could see her father come up behind her mother as she sat in her favorite armchair. He placed his hand on her shoulder, and she lifted her fingers to cover his. Then she tilted her head, and their gazes met in a quiet rush of mutual love.

Mattie witnessed that same look now as Alice and her husband regarded each other over the heads of their children. To Mattie's surprise, a deep longing seeped into her. She wondered what it would be like to have a partner—someone who supported her with a wordless glance full of strength and affection.

"Planey wants to see the big air-o-planes." The little girl had a high, lilting voice, but she spoke without a speck of hesitation. The child held her toy aloft and made buzzing sounds as she whirled around, her brightly patterned gingham skirt a swirl of color. As her offspring danced around the field, Alice made the introductions. When she reached Leo, John flashed a set of white teeth, looking every inch the performer that he was.

But unlike with Leo's press face, John's smile seemed genuine and not just manufactured to please the crowd. "You're the Flying Lion, one of America's greatest aces! I thought I recognized you."

"What's an ace?" Milly asked as she swung her plane around her father's knees.

"A fighter pilot," John explained.

The movement of the toy stopped. Milly scrunched up one side of her face. "Pilots don't fight. They fly."

"Remember how Papa fought in the Great War?" John said. "So did Mr. Ward here, but he did so in the skies, not in the trenches."

Milly sucked in her bottom lip and began to chew it. "Did the planes get hurt?"

"We took care of them the best we could." Leo's blue eyes had deepened as he regarded the little girl with the seriousness that he'd show an adult. "We had mechanics who watched over our birds and patched up any scrapes."

"Did you kiss the scrapes?" Milly's moss-green eyes had grown even wider.

Mattie watched Leo curiously as he hesitated, a bit of red spreading to his cheeks. He coughed and slid a glance first in her direction and then in John's. "Uh, no, but I might have patted my old Nieuport and then my SPAD once or twice."

A warmth crept through Mattie as she watched the tinge of scarlet on Leo's face deepen into the color of a ripe strawberry after his confession. Although she and her brothers openly showed affection for their machines, she hadn't suspected that Leo ever did the same.

"What were their names?" Milly asked, seemingly satisfied that Leo had adequately cared for his wartime fighters.

The red seemed burned into every inch of Leo's face now. He reached up and rubbed the back of his head. Almost surreptitiously, he slanted Mattie a look. She couldn't completely read it, but she knew two things for certain. He *had* named those machines, and for some reason, he didn't want to admit what those monikers were in her presence.

Before anyone could question Leo further, the crunch of the Duesy's wheels on the gravel heralded Vera's return. She'd brought Ruby with her, and the spaniel sported a ridiculous brown aviator's helmet on her domed head and matching goggles. The latest accoutrements had arrived yesterday, a custom order straight from a Paris fashion house.

"Cousin Vera! Cousin Vera!" All three children ran like aircraft in a formation to the heiress. She gave each child a hug and spun Milly around, who giggled uncontrollably as her cotton skirt once again formed a large puff around her white ankle socks and canvas shoes.

"What *did* you call your planes?" Mattie asked Leo softly as soon as everyone else was focused on helping Vera decorate the makeshift mannequin.

Leo's gaze shifted away from hers, and before he either answered or further evaded her question, Vera called out, "Mattie, are you ready to prove you're not going to bodily injure me when you dive to collect me? Be aware that I do like my head firmly attached to my shoulders or, in this case, the representative stick. I've grown surprisingly attached to that melon after dressing it up."

"The breeze might knock off the cloche," Mattie said, "but I won't touch a hair or vine on either of your heads."

"Perfect!" Vera blew Mattie a kiss, her gold snake bracelet glinting in the overhead sun.

"Want to come?" Mattie asked Leo almost spontaneously. It had been a long time since they'd gone up in the air together in the same plane, and she suddenly missed it.

A slow smile crept over Leo's face. "Yeah. I'd like that. A lot."

"Race you to the plane!" she shouted. It was an old, almost forgotten game of theirs.

He beat her like he always did, but he let her climb in first. As soon as Mattie tipped the nose of her Jenny upward, she felt the shift in her own body. When she gained enough altitude, she executed several barrel rolls, spinning like a lathe straight over the airfield. Flying next in the inverted position, she skimmed at a low altitude over their group several times. Aida lifted her Kodak camera to capture a picture. Little Milly dipped her plane in perfect unison with Mattie's.

"She'll be an amazing pilot someday," Mattie shouted as she righted the Jenny.

"What?" Leo called, clearly not hearing her voice over the thunder of the motor. He turned around.

"Milly." Mattie raised her voice even more. "She'll be an amazing fly girl."

"One day!" Leo yelled back. The two of them shared a quick smile before Mattie returned her attention to the stick and pedals.

Vera wanted Mattie to swoop in from high in the heavens, her engine at full speed. In this trial run, Mattie was supposed to hook a large ring onto the twig representing Vera's outstretched hand.

"Don't come down too sharply," Leo advised. She glowered at him as she focused on tilting the nose of her plane toward the ground.

"I'm the one who taught you."

"I did a lot of strafing during the war, including observation balloons." Leo didn't say the words boastfully but as a matter-of-fact statement. It was the closest he had ever come to acknowledging his war record in Mattie's presence.

"Would you say the same to my brothers? That they were diving too quickly?" Mattie asked.

"Absolutely," Leo shouted, the wind carrying his words past her ears in a roaring rush.

She eased back on the descent. He grinned then. Not cocky. Not self-satisfied. But sweetly shy.

She buzzed over the melon-Vera. Although she had no way of actually seeing how close she'd come to the cloche-wearing fruit, she *knew* she'd nailed the trick. Zipping into the air, she swerved the plane back around in a sharp turn and executed a barrel roll. Skimming inverted over the path she'd just come, she caught sight of the melon with the peacock hat still proudly perched on its bulbous crown. A matching scarf tied around the center of the fruit flapped in the wind, as if cheering Mattie too. Even better, the brass hoop seemed to wink in the sun as it hung around the outstretched twig like an oversize bangle.

"Good job!" Leo turned back in her direction to yell to her. His voice wasn't exactly brimming with exuberance, but that was just Leo.

Those two words coming from him were high praise, and she could hear the faintest rumble of excitement in his deep tone.

"Thanks," Mattie called. She started to let out a whoop, but it died in her throat as she spotted a figure in the woods, a camera in his hands. *Benji Pringle.* There was going to be a new photograph and article in the *Chicago Advance Leader*, and it most assuredly *wouldn't* be about her successful stunt.

Chapter Eight

> The photographic evidence has only confirmed that any performance by Vera Jones's Flying Flappers will be certain to disappoint even the least discerning of airplane enthusiasts. By all appearances, it seems that the girls believe banal displays of hilarity, such as dressing up a melon as a vamp or a toy dog as an aviatrix, will entertain audiences. Unless one is amused by such lowbrow tricks, it may be best to stay home and listen to the radio instead of attending the gals' inaugural show in nearby Platt, Michigan, in three days' time.
>
> —Benjamin Pringle, *Chicago Advance Leader*

"What do you mean, the loan is due by late November?" Mattie whispered urgently into the mouthpiece, not wanting anyone in Vera's household to overhear her. "You originally said we had until May of next year to make the final payment."

"I thought I'd be able to get an extension from the bank, Swift," her father said wearily. Although she couldn't see him, she knew he was rubbing his chin. Mattie herself began to march back and forth like a mechanical toy on a short track.

"You didn't mention this before," Mattie breathed out, trying to douse the anger rising inside her. Her pa was worried—she could hear it in his voice—and part of her didn't want to make it worse.

"We thought it best—"

"Not to worry me," Mattie finished for him, unable to keep the hurt and betrayal from her voice. "What happened to us, Pa? We always leaned on each other during the war. Now you're keeping secrets, trying to protect me. I'm tough. I've always been."

"I . . ." Her father's voice faltered for a minute. "I wish you didn't have to be. I should've done better by you, looked after you more, not placed so much on your shoulders."

Mattie felt tears prick the backs of her eyes, but they didn't fall. They rarely did. It seemed like she'd poured out all her reserves sobbing over Alfred's death all those years ago.

"You're hurting me more by shutting me out," Mattie said quietly.

Her father swallowed hard. "I'm sorry about that, Swift. I thought that I had this handled. You should be thinking about your own future, not worrying about my financial troubles."

Mattie squeezed her eyes shut. "It's the family business, Pa. Of course I'm a part of it. I *should* be a part of it."

"I know. I know."

Mattie straightened, trying to push aside the frenzy of emotions to concentrate on what needed to be done. "We were going to be short before, even with all our earnings pooled. But now with the earlier due date . . ."

"Swift, you might just need to resign yourself to the fact that we might have to shut down the school. We all have to face the truth."

"No." She shook her head for emphasis, even though no one could see her. "I'll figure out a way. I have to."

"Mattie, sometimes it's all right to fail. It's how you pick yourself up afterward that matters."

"No, we can't lose the flight school." Mattie was now whipping her head back and forth. Some of her hair caught in her mouth, but she barely paid attention. "Alfred wouldn't want it to leave the family, any more than he'd allow the circus to shut down permanently."

"Mattie, what your brother would *want* is for you to live your life," her father said. "He wouldn't wish for you to be tied down to any place—any job. You know that, don't you?"

Mattie ignored her father's question. The school and the circus were the two things that kept Alfred's memory alive. "I don't know if there will be time now for me to create a marketable design and sell it for enough money, but I'll keep trying. And I'll figure out other ways to make money."

"Now don't go risking yourself or Leo," her father warned.

"Leo? I wouldn't ask him to take any risks," Mattie said, confused as to why he'd been brought into the discussion.

"If you barrel headlong into danger, he'll be racing to head it off before it can touch you," her father warned.

"Well, then Leo should just let me stand my own ground. He doesn't need to play the knight-errant. I'm perfectly capable of fighting myself."

Her pa was quiet for a moment, and when he finally did speak, he changed the subject. "Is Leo nearby? I should tell him the news too."

Mattie ran her finger down the cord as she gazed up the stairs and down the hallway to the circular steps that led to the turret where she and Leo were staying. "He went to bed a little early. We have our first show coming up, and I don't think he's been sleeping well. You know Leo; he doesn't say anything, but the skin under his eyes looked a tad dark."

"Hmm," her father said, as if he understood something about Leo's insomnia that Mattie did not. "Well, don't wake him. You can let him know tomorrow."

"I will," Mattie promised. "I need to talk to him anyway about me adding some elements to our act."

"What elements?" her father asked, his tone cautious but not outright dismissive.

"I don't know yet," she admitted as she gazed up at the bronze sculpture of the trapeze artist dangling high above her head. "Something big. Something that will attract attention. Leo and the boys have made some decent money with endorsement deals. Maybe it's time I got one of those myself."

"Mattie, don't go getting yourself killed."

Had her father—*her father*—just chided her about being *killed*? They all knew the dangers of aviation and had secret, unspoken fears of dying, especially in a fiery crash. Yet it seemed her family only voiced this hidden concern when it pertained to *her*, as if she were somehow more vulnerable to gravity and flames.

"Have you just turned into one of my brothers?"

"Mattie, I'm just asking you to exercise some caution, just as I would them." Her father sighed, his voice sounding *reasonable*. Mattie hated reasonable.

"Pa, I can't afford to hold back. We need me to perform better than I ever have before. I also have to soar for the Flying Flappers. We've had so many negative articles written about us, including one today, that we have no choice but to take even more risks than a male circus does."

"Chasing glory often leads you to the opposite place that you thought you were going to go," her father said sagely. But Mattie was in no mood for advice—sage or otherwise.

"Pa, I am tired, and it has been a long day. Good night." It was the closest she'd ever come to hanging up on him. Unlike with Jake, she couldn't click the receiver down on her father, no matter how mad he'd made her. Taking a deep, steadying breath, she slowly hung up the telephone. She took another gulp of air before she marched up the grand staircase. By the time she reached the circular steps leading into the tower, she was almost running. Tearing up the narrow passage, she'd just reached the landing by Leo's door when a hoarse, rasping moan stopped her.

Leo's nightmare began as they all did.

With him alone.

It was a bitter winter in New York, and the cold seeped into the small closet-like space where he'd been locked up for some transgression or another by the head of the orphanage. The Reflecting Room, it was called, a dark, unpleasant place. He'd been forgotten again, left inside the blackness. He knocked, but no one came. A sense of urgency filled him. He was missing something. Not something. *Someone.* He had to find this person. He had to get free.

And then suddenly he was. But he still wasn't safe. He was in a poorly lit alley, sleet hitting him—or maybe it was hail. Whatever it was, ice bit into his skin. He was trying to get somewhere. Trying to reach that same person. Angry footsteps thundered toward him, and Leo pressed into an alcove, making himself as small as possible.

Then the dream shifted again. It was dusk now, heading toward twilight. Yet despite the additional illumination, the sense of danger and loss had only intensified. Bullets whooshed by him. The red-nosed airplanes of the elite Jagdgeschwader seemed to surround him. He'd blundered into a trap. Leo turned in the cockpit, trying to find *him,* trying to locate Alfred. But all he saw were more and more Fokkers opening fire. He tried to swerve around them, but he had no choice but to engage. He fought like a madman to reach his friend before it was too late. But for every German he downed, there was another in his way, ready to pounce.

Finally, he broke free, only to spy Alfred's familiar Nieuport zooming in the wrong direction, the plane clearly damaged as it limped awkwardly through the air like a bird with a broken wing. Even though Leo knew Alfred would never hear him, he shouted out his name. Once. Twice. Thrice.

Then the Albatroses appeared like demons bursting from the setting sun. They winged toward Alfred, all fury, vengeance, and death. The bullets ripped through Alfred's fuselage, and his nimble craft burst into flames.

Suddenly, Leo was soaring alongside his friend's airplane. The pilot turned in his direction, but it wasn't Alfred. It was Mattie. Her braid flapped out behind her, her mouth drawn into a wide smile as she whooped.

"Look at this trick, Leo!" she called out, and somehow he could hear each word as clearly as if she sat beside him.

"You're on fire!" he shouted back.

"I know!" She pumped one fist into the air, oblivious to the blaze that inched ever closer to the fuel tank behind the cockpit. "Aren't the flames grand? Just think of how well I'll show up doing night-flying tricks now!"

"Your Jenny is about to explode!" Leo yelled, trying to calculate if they were high enough for her parachute to open in time. But American airmen didn't have that equipment. Were they even at war anymore?

"That would be a spectacular finale! Just think of the press we could get, Leo!" Mattie cried.

"She's right, darling!" Vera suddenly appeared in the passenger seat with Ruby perched on her lap as the plane transformed from a nimble Nieuport fighter to one of the circus's Jennies. The dog wore strips of orange, red, and yellow silk around her neck, the garish colors mirroring the real blaze crawling inexorably forward from the tail of the aircraft. "Think of the tickets we'll sell."

Suddenly Leo's Nieuport turned into a Curtiss too. A man appeared in the passenger seat, his handsome face so much like Leo's own yet so unfamiliar at the same time. "And you'll give all the money to me, son? Won't you?"

"Leo!" Mattie's voice sounded concerned now and muffled but not panicked.

"Mattie?" he called in confusion. A gentle knocking sound caused him to stiffen. Was that her engine? Was it giving her more trouble?

"Leo, it's me, Mattie." Her tone was clearer now. He turned toward it, reaching for her.

"Mattie?" he said again, suddenly plunged back into darkness like he'd been at the beginning. "Where are you?"

"Leo, I think you're having a nightmare. Why don't you open your eyes? You'll see that I'm right here."

Still half-asleep, Leo blinked. Mattie stood by his bedside, her red hair glowing in the light cast by the Tiffany lamp on his nightstand. For one horrible, mad moment, he thought the flames had followed him from the dreamworld into reality.

"I'm sorry I burst in on you like this, but I couldn't wake you up otherwise." Mattie retreated toward the door. "You sounded like you were in pain. I can leave now."

"No," Leo said hoarsely as he sat up. The sheet fell off, revealing his union shirt. Mattie's gaze darted to his exposed upper arms, and he felt his face heat. He'd gone swimming with her and her folks before, and his bathing suit was about the same as his nightclothes, but this felt different. Much different.

Mattie must have noticed his discomfort, for she instantly spun around. "Let me know when you're decent."

He grunted and hurried to dress. This was becoming a habit now—him furtively pulling on clothes in the dead of the night while Mattie waited to talk to him. As he grabbed his trousers, a crumpled letter fell out of them. Quickly, he kicked it noiselessly under the bed before Mattie could see.

"Want to talk about it?" she asked, her back still turned in his direction.

He froze at first, thinking she meant the missive. It took him a moment to realize that she'd meant his nightmare. "Not really."

"Okay," she agreed readily enough.

"Was I—" He paused in pulling the half-buttoned shirt over his head. Licking his suddenly dry bottom lip, he continued. "Was I talking in my sleep?"

The last thing he needed was for someone to know his vulnerabilities. Although he supposed he trusted Mattie more than anyone else, he didn't want his past lying open to her like a massive, festering wound. It would have blunted Walt's sacrifice.

"A little," Mattie admitted, "but it was unintelligible."

Relief flooded Leo as he hastily finished buttoning his fly. Running his hand through his hair in an attempt to smooth the strands, he said, "I'm good now."

Mattie turned around. "Do you think you'll be able to go back to sleep?"

He shook his head. He never could after a dream like that. Luckily, they happened less and less. As the Flying Flapper's first performance drew closer, though, the nightmares had returned a few days ago. The lack of sleep and the vivid dreams had made him as tight as a wire pulled too taut. The letter from his father demanding more money had only made matters worse.

"Nah, I won't be getting much shut-eye tonight," Leo told Mattie.

"I'm not in a fit state to sleep either." Mattie nudged the fibers of the fancy rug with the toe of her shoe.

"Something bothering you?" Leo asked, instantly concerned.

Mattie dipped her chin, and she suddenly looked young, like the willowy slip of an adolescent who'd taught him how to fly. An ache formed in his chest, mixing unevenly with the anxious readiness already pumping through him. He reached forward, his hand almost brushing a tendril of her red hair back behind her ear. But that gesture was too intimate, too forward, so he settled on patting her shoulder. At his touch, she didn't shake him off as he'd thought she might. The fact that she accepted the gentle weight of his palm sent a zip of energy careening through his already volatile emotions.

"Yeah, something is gnawing at me." Mattie tilted her head, her cheek brushing against his knuckles. Leo had no idea if she'd meant to touch him, but it felt both natural and alien.

Her eyes fluttered closed, as if she was gathering a modicum of strength. "I talked to Pa tonight—argued, more like. He was calling to let me know that he didn't get a loan extension."

"What loan extension?" Leo asked, his fingers automatically starting to squeeze Mattie's shoulder before he caught himself. Awkwardly he dropped his hand before she realized how much her words had affected him. He needed to be strong for her, not add to her worries.

Mattie gave a half smile. "I guess he didn't let you in on that particular secret."

"What secret?" Leo kept his voice neutral, a talent he'd learned long ago in the orphanage, even as his heart began to thump.

Mattie kicked a little at the tufts of the rug before she took off pacing. "The final payment is actually due this fall, not next spring like Pa originally said. He thought he could get an extension."

Leo's body instantly tensed. His already exercised heart didn't need an excuse to start thumping madly again. Until he'd met the McAdamses, he'd lived with hunger and the constant thrum of worry that he might never find that next meal. He'd gone barefoot and worn clothes until they were about ready to fall from his skinny frame. He knew how to handle his own precarious financial situation, but not the McAdamses'.

"I'll see if I can rustle up more endorsement deals." Leo rubbed the back of his head. He *loathed* capitalizing on his war-hero status to make dough, but he'd do it for Mattie, Walt, and the boys. He owed it to them.

"I was thinking that it was time I did the same," Mattie said.

That familiar prickle of unease slipped through Leo, giving him another emotion that he didn't want to deal with. "Courting attention isn't as glamorous as it looks from the outside. It can be a darn nuisance."

Like having an unscrupulous parent appear out of the woodwork and then blackmail you.

Mattie flipped her braid over her shoulder. "I don't think I'll mind it as much as you."

No, she probably wouldn't hate the public's interest. Mattie had always been outgoing. She didn't like to retreat into the shadows like he did.

"The crowds can get vicious, turn on you." Leo cleared his throat. "Remember how that one town acted when I couldn't fly due to the fog? We all thought they were going to grab their pitchforks."

Evidently, Mattie wasn't in the mood to hear any of his concerns. He could tell by the way she jutted her jaw. "Then I'll just have to make sure I don't disappoint the audience, won't I?"

The unsettled feeling inside Leo burst into full-blown worry. "Mattie, sometimes I think all the crowd wants to see is a crash. Don't risk your life feeding other people's bloodthirstiness."

Mattie heaved out a huge sigh, so large that he could see the rise and fall of her chest even under her loose hand-me-down shirt. "So we're back to this, are we? You trying to stop me from flying."

"I'm not trying to prevent you altogether, Mattie. I just don't want you hurt; that's all." Leo took another step in her direction. He hadn't intended to, but he wanted her to understand, to see the perils he saw.

Her thin shoulders rose so high they seemed ready to poke through the cotton fabric covering them. "I'm adding more stunts to my routine tomorrow."

Leo's dream came thundering back, as strong and as real as it had seemed during his slumber. *"Aren't the flames grand? Just think of how well I'll show up doing night-flying tricks now!"* Mattie's voice flashed into his mind along with the memory of the fire licking over her fuselage.

"No." The hoarse word tumbled from Leo's lips—harsh and instinctual. He didn't take the time to think of its effect on Mattie. It just ripped from him.

The green glint in Mattie's eyes froze over the warmer golds and browns. She jammed her hands on her hips as she leaned toward him. "I am done with you telling me that."

"Mattie," Leo croaked out, his throat suddenly as dry and scratchy as sandpaper, "you shouldn't make decisions like this when you're emotional."

Mattie's red eyebrows shot into the air as she advanced on him. "When I am emotional? When *I* am emotional? When *I* am *emotional*? What about you? Are your emotions not entering into this? Are you really as cool and logical as you think you are?"

Leo almost blurted out that he was, because he didn't *feel* anything anymore. His finer emotions had always been muted, and the war had dampened even those faint glimmers. But before he could confess his emptiness to Mattie, he stopped. Not just because he wanted to hide his deadness from her—which he most certainly did—but because he realized the truth of what she'd said.

He *did* feel fear. For her. And that worry consumed him—his mind awash with images from his dream blended with memories of Alfred's real crash. He was not acting entirely rational himself.

"Mattie, can we just discuss this?" he asked, wishing they could start the conversation over, hoping that she'd let him.

"No." Mattie shook her head. "Not now. I thought we could talk it over, but it's clear that if I'm going to make a name for myself and save the family business, I need to plan my own tricks. On my own."

Her words seared through him. He felt like he was losing her again, just as he had all those years ago when her brothers had grounded her from Alfred's memorial flight. The pain felt the same—perhaps even harsher because he'd been almost entirely numb in those early days. But as much as it hurt, he couldn't allow Mattie to exchange her life for glory.

"Mattie . . ." Her name came out as a plea—one she clearly didn't want to hear. "Please reconsider."

Mattie shoved her finger into his chest. "I won't, Leo. And when I'm Miss Modernity and you're Mr. Yesteryear, I am going to thrash you just like I said I would when Vera first hired us."

Leo reached for her, but she whirled from his grasp. And then she left him. Alone. With his old memories and new fears.

Chapter Nine

The warm summer sun beat down on the farmer's field in Southern Michigan. The intense rays glinted off the nearby river, making the water look like a molten strand of silver as it cut through the land dotted with grazing cows. Sticky humidity saturated the air, intensifying the cloying smell of cotton candy and popcorn. Not even a single puffy cloud offered relief. Yet instead of seeking the shelter of the trees dotting the bank, a huge throng of over a hundred crowded on the dry, heat-drenched grass. They'd laid blankets on the ground, and more than one family had brought a basketful of cold fried chicken. The greasy odor mixed with the scent of butter and sugar that hung in the atmosphere.

As Mattie's and Carrie's biplanes zoomed overhead, the spectators shielded their eyes, not wanting to miss a single stunt. A few of the younger set had donned round, newfangled sunglasses, the dark lenses giving them a chic appearance as they gazed skyward. In contrast, some of the older women had dug out their broad-brimmed hats from a decade before. The out-of-vogue headgear afforded more protection from the sun than the now-popular tight-fitting cloches. The men in flatcaps and panamas fared better than those in fedoras and straw skimmer hats.

Yet despite the oppressive heat, no one seemed to register their own discomfort, at least as far as Leo could tell. It was as if the audience members had somehow left their sweltering seats on the brown sunbaked grass and joined the female pilots in the cool heights of the air. People always had the same spellbound reactions. It didn't matter whether a flying circus performed in the desert towns of the Southwest, the wide-open sweeping Great Plains, or the quaint little villages of New England. Folks always reacted with the same wonder, even if their excited words were tinged with the hodgepodge of different dialects that made up the States.

Leo didn't often observe the crowds. As the McAdamses' star performer, he'd had the most airtime, and he'd also stayed hidden until it was his turn to burst onto the scene. But Leo found he liked watching the people and their animated, upturned faces. He stood off to the side, shaded by the trees lining the steep gulch that plunged downward to meet the winding river. He wasn't quite part of the throng, but he wasn't thousands of feet above them either.

Vera's sequin-covered head appeared first from Mattie's Jenny. The shiny red slivers of metal caught the light perfectly and made her cap look like a blazing scarlet ball. She leaned far out of her seat, waving to the crowd. Mattie was flying the plane so low that Leo could even make out the brilliant cherry of the flapper's unusual bespoke fingernail polish. The breeze caught the dyed ostrich feathers tucked into the folds of her head covering, and the fuzzy tendrils fluttered madly in the wind, as dramatic and unrestrained as their wearer.

Vera climbed onto the wing of the aircraft like a fairy-tale princess descending from her coach to a plush red carpet. Instead of a long, puffy ball gown, the heiress wore a tight-fitting leotard glittering with cherry-red sequins. Her only wink at propriety was the flounces at the bottom of the garment and her dark stockings. Although circus performers had worn such revealing attire for years, it was another thing to see the long legs of a wealthy society darling. The outfit might have looked garish if Vera hadn't worn it with such brazen boldness, challenging anyone to call her tawdry.

Sharp whistles from the men rent the air as some doffed their caps and waved them over their heads. The younger women clapped and hollered. Leo detected clucks of disapproval from the broad-brimmed-hat-wearing matrons, but he noticed none of them rose to stomp off in a huff. They all wanted a performance, and Vera was going to give them one. Society rules be damned.

In a blazing stream of red, the flapper twirled her body through the wooden struts and wires supporting the wing structure. While the crowd watched Vera's flashy acrobatics, Leo kept his attention on Mattie. She flew with such technical precision that awe swelled in Leo's chest and caught in his throat. Despite the fact that one wing now held over a hundred pounds of extra, always-shifting weight, Mattie kept the old trainer balanced.

She buzzed low enough that every now and again he caught a glimpse of her broad smile. Her engines drowned out any sound, but Leo knew she was laughing and whooping in equal measure.

Another cheer and gasp arose as Alice stepped onto the green wing of Carrie's Jenny. Her sparkling outfit was identical to her cousin's except for its turquoise color and the peacock feathers. She grabbed onto one of the ropes and spun her body around it like a wooden button on a string.

Clapping, yells, and more whistles filled the air, but Leo paid attention to the pilot. Like Mattie, Carrie controlled her craft beautifully. The wing barely even dipped as Alice tumbled and whirled.

With the audience energized, the two pilots withdrew farther across the sky, strategically maneuvering their aircraft to hide the movements of the daredevils on their wings. Leo watched with his arms folded over his chest as the throng collectively leaned forward. Some members even stood up, as if it would garner them a better view.

It didn't. Both aviators knew how to flawlessly position their planes, and they allowed not a single peep of their intrepid passengers. Tension built, so thick it practically rolled from the crowd like a palpable fog.

Without warning, the planes simultaneously swerved so that they flew side by side, their noses pointed straight toward the crowd. Vera and Alice dangled upside down from the sturdy trapeze bars that hung from one wing of each plane.

Their legs draped over the trapeze bars, each cousin reached up and grabbed the metal tube with one hand while releasing a foot. Then, buzzing a thousand feet in the air, they each stretched out their free arm and leg, making their bodies into vertical slashes, heedless of the wind buffeting them. They did not move quickly, but they didn't need kinetic energy to impress.

"They're magnificent, aren't they?"

Leo turned at the deep voice to find Alice's husband, John, standing beside him. Leo had been so focused on the aerial stunts that he hadn't even heard the other man's approach. Leo had begun to bob his head in agreement, but now that he knew the speaker of the question, he froze.

An entirely new wonder now held Leo in its thrall. John was . . . relaxed. His hands were jammed in his trouser pockets and his shoulders were loose as he gazed skyward, where his wife dangled a thousand feet above him by *one hand and a foot*. There was no net to save Alice if she fell.

The cousins proceeded to twist their free legs, wrapping them around their bodies in partial loops. Then they grabbed their feet with *both* hands so that each woman's only contact with the bar was one knee draped over the metal. It made a lovely but lethal shape.

Yet John did not tense. He didn't lurch forward as if he could run and catch his wife in case she fell. His stance was not callous or uninterested either. He was engaged in the performance, his eyes carefully watching each move Alice made.

"How do you do it?" Leo asked before he thought better of it.

"Aerial gymnastics?" John asked absently. He spared a glance at Leo before his chin snapped back in the direction of his wife, as if it were attached to her by an invisible spring. "I suppose it isn't so much different from your flying. You may have an engine and canvas wings, but the important thing, the lack of a safety net, is the same. Of course, that's the mental side. On the physical, we've spent our lives training our bodies to perform."

"I didn't mean acrobatics." Leo shifted his eyes from watching Vera and Alice to where the pilot seat of Mattie's JN-4 was situated. At this angle and with Mattie's head-on approach, he could not actually see her. But war had taught him the exact configuration of planes, and he had an instinct for estimating where each portion of the craft would be positioned over the next few seconds.

John followed his gaze. Although Leo doubted that the man carried the specifications of a JN-4 in his brain, the circus performer seemed to instinctually know exactly where—or rather *who*—Leo was looking at.

"I might not know you and Mattie much, but things seemed pretty stilted between you this morning. I'm assuming it has something to do with the stunts she wants to make and you thinking she's not ready for them." John wasn't asking a question, just stating a fact.

Leo shoved his hand in his hair. Vera and Alice were now hanging with both hands on their respective bars, their arms fully extended, their legs stretched into splits. He had no idea how they managed to cling on when traveling at such a high velocity. But they did. If it had been Mattie dangling in the air like that, he couldn't have handled even a simple conversation, let alone a philosophical one.

"It's not that I doubt Mattie's talents." Leo could feel his back muscles tighten into a ball-like mass. "But I've watched so many excellent pilots crash."

John didn't speak for a moment, and Leo guessed he was trying to figure out if it was his place to talk. Finally, the man said gently, "No one is shooting at her."

"Many of those pilots weren't brought down by bullets—sometimes their machines failed them, or they just made an error in judgment."

An image flashed in Leo's mind of Alfred's Nieuport flying blindly into an ambush.

"The trapeze is part of who my Alice is." John jerked his chin toward his wife, who was swinging her body in order to gather enough momentum to hook her legs around the bar. "I first saw her when her great-uncle, Vera's grandfather, hired me. She was flying through the air toward her partner, and I knew that I wanted to be the man who'd catch her. But I realized something then. To be that person, I also had to be willing to release her too."

Release her. Leo tracked Mattie's position in her two-seater. It sounded so simple, those two words: *release her*. Not even a positive action was required. Just letting go . . . it should be easy for him. He'd had so little in his life. He'd left the orphanage without a single thought. Through the war, he'd lost so many comrades—not just Alfred, but other compatriots: brash ones, quiet ones, pranksters, and scholars. He'd learned how to mourn one moment and fight the next. Leo had never even jealously guarded his own life. It was always something he was prepared to part with.

But this was *Mattie* . . . the woman whom his mind had drifted toward during solo patrols over enemy lines. Thoughts of her had beckoned like the Very lights released by aerodromes to guide aviators home from dangerous night missions.

In the late evening while the other pilots had slept and he couldn't, Leo would lie in the barracks and painstakingly reread one of the cheerful letters that Mattie had sent. He had heard her voice as he'd studied her bold, messy scrawl that somehow was still perfectly legible to a man who hadn't had much book learning. Even after half a decade on the road, he still had all those missives. They were well worn and weak at some of the folds but not wrinkled or bent.

For a man who'd let go of most everything in his life, how could he release the one thing that he'd held on to?

"I've learned to view Alice's choices through a lens of fairness." John rubbed his thumb across his jaw as Alice and Vera sat on top of their trapeze bars, giving one last exuberant wave to their spellbound audience.

"Fairness?" Leo asked.

"I expect Alice to support me jumping off a high platform and releasing one swing to grab the next. Why shouldn't I do the same for her?"

Leo massaged his head, as if he could rub the man's words into his brain. He'd never thought about his relationship with Mattie from that angle. It struck him that he was always looking at it from his perspective, not hers. The thought unnerved him, and he felt more than a little trickle of guilt.

"The Great War . . . it changed things." John shifted as his wife finally climbed back inside Carrie's Jenny. "We were fighting to preserve our way of life, but in all that destruction, it got us thinking about what things mean. Then we also started wondering if the way we did those things made sense. Some women like my wife, Vera, and Mattie have looked and found they wanted something different than what they've been handed. They saw how women drove ambulances, cared for the wounded, and took on factory jobs, especially overseas."

John couldn't have known how much his words echoed Mattie's on the beach when she and Leo had built the sandcastle together. And Leo . . . Leo wanted that halcyon lakeshore moment back, when he and Mattie were finally not at odds but working together. It wasn't that simple, though.

"Mattie takes unnecessary risks." Leo watched as Mattie's yellow-tipped plane landed in concert with Carrie's green Jenny. Vera and Alice jumped from their seats, blowing kisses to the crowd. Carrie and Mattie leaned from their cockpits to wave to the hollering assembly. Although Leo couldn't make out the color of Mattie's eyes from his far-back position, he knew that the gold flecks would have overtaken the blues and greens in her rush of excited pride.

"In my experience, people like Mattie don't take kindly to orders and demands." Now that John's wife was safely on the ground, his full attention was on Leo, a fact that made Leo more than a little uncomfortable. The acrobat's moss-green eyes were dark and serious as he added, "Maybe your job is being her flying partner instead of her flight leader."

Flight leader. It had been Leo's job to protect the men flying under him, but he wasn't at the head of the formation anymore. Maybe he needed to try to work *with* Mattie and not try to act like a commander.

Unfortunately, in less than ten minutes, he needed to stage an argument with her in front of a crowd of over a hundred. People who wanted a performance with sparks and real heat. With one last scrub of his hand against the back of his head, he pulled a fake mustache from his pocket. Rubbing the ridiculous piece against his skin, he, as Mr. Yesteryear, marched toward his appointed rival, Miss Modernity.

As soon as Leo emerged from the sidelines after Vera's introduction, cameras clicked, and the crowd hushed. With his fake press smile plastered across his face, Leo waved. Despite his cartoonish mustache, he looked heroically handsome in his old military flight jacket made from sealskin. The brown hue complemented his neatly trimmed chestnut hair and provided a perfectly neutral foil for his cobalt-blue eyes. A group of vamps sighed lustily and grabbed each other's arms when they caught sight of the famous balloon buster.

Mattie felt her blood rise too.

But from irritation.

At least she *told* herself it was just from annoyance. But part of her couldn't completely deny that Leo's presence was having an increasingly strong effect on her.

The realization frustrated Mattie. Mattie and Leo had come so close to reaching some sort of accord . . . but then he just had to backslide and become so stiflingly protective and overbearingly *male*.

The welcome flicker of rage licked through Mattie again. That turbulence was so much easier and less dangerous than whispers of desire.

"Is anyone bold enough to try to outfly a real-life balloon buster and one of our top American aces who is flying today as Mr. Yesteryear? I heard that the enemy observers used to quake in their overly polished boots when they heard the roar of his SPAD." Vera flung out her arms, punctuating each word with the energy and volume of a ringmaster. She'd cinched a satin robe trimmed with feathers over her red leotard. Although the garment fell well below her knees, it was scandalously reminiscent of a silk dressing gown.

Vera's offer of a challenge was met with a chorus of good-natured laughs. After all, not a single male pilot was in the vicinity, let alone a flyer who was a war veteran. Mattie stepped forward, feeling a rush of stubborn pride as she did so.

"I'm Miss Modernity, and I will." Mattie stuck her chin in the air, trying not to feel self-conscious about her new outfit. Vera had gifted her with new trousers and a shirt this morning. Unlike her old hand-me-downs, these fit snugly to her curves. There was no hiding her natural form in this getup.

"Aww, go make the man a cake instead, sweetheart!" The male voice sounded jovial on the surface, but an ugliness threaded through his laughing snipe.

"Maybe a pie, a nice apple one." The second heckler also aimed for a degree of affability, but he couldn't keep the words from ending in a sneer.

"I can think of better uses for her kisser than for challenging heroes." The last speaker didn't even try to make his voice pleasant as he referred to Mattie's mouth. His tone was hoarse and just plain mean, like that of a troll in a children's story.

Mattie didn't even turn her head to acknowledge the loudmouthed drugstore cowboys. She'd heard similar and worse during her career as a pilot. Rather than argue, Mattie much preferred another method of shutting them up: empirically proving them wrong.

That was when she spied Leo's left hand clenching in response to the last jeer. Although he was generally a reserved man, she knew from her brothers that Leo was as handy with his fists as he was in aerial combat. And Mattie did *not* want the spotlight to move from her and Leo's competition to a brawl between him and the three bozos.

"Well, aren't you going to say something, Mr. Yesteryear?" Mattie marched over to Leo, purposely placing herself between him and the crowd. With her back to the audience, she shot a meaningful glare toward his balled fingers. Leo gave her an almost imperceptible nod as he unfurled them. His ready compliance mollified her a bit, but she wasn't about to release all her frustration.

"He doesn't need to say anything to you, doll," the man with the troll-like voice shouted. "His record proves he's better than you. You really think a dame can beat an ace?"

When she answered the troublemaker's question, she addressed Leo and Leo only. Stabbing a finger at his chest, she said, "Any trick you try, I can improve upon it."

Leo crossed his arms and stared down at Mattie. He only had a few inches on her, but he made the slight difference count. "Let's be sensible, Miss Modernity. This isn't a competition. We're in the same flying circus."

Although Leo's words held a faint echo of his normal arguments, he was definitely adding an arrogant twist to his words. He was playacting, sounding just like one of her brothers. Unfortunately, he sounded stiff and a little too practiced. They *needed* the spark of a real argument.

"How good are you at avoiding obstacles?" Mattie drilled her finger farther into Leo's chest, trying not to notice how his muscles refused to give under the poke.

Mattie heard a few boos, but she ignored them. Leo's eyes narrowed, but not at her . . . at the hecklers. Desperate, Mattie leaned closer and whispered in his ear. "Ignore them. Argue with *me*. Treat me like one of the fellows. Bait me. Don't defend me."

Leo's eyes blazed as he stepped closer, mimicking their old tiffs. This time, with the argument only half in earnest, Mattie registered the heat rising from his body. She could feel the puff of his warm breath against her cheeks, almost like soft caresses. Her already heightened emotions swirled into an intense, heady mix. For one mad moment, she didn't know whether to kiss him or jab him again.

"I was pretty swell at evading the German Albatroses and Fokkers while I was defending freedom." One side of Leo's mouth twisted into a cocky, lopsided grin. Knowing it was for the audience and not a real smirk, Mattie unfortunately found it intriguing instead of irking.

And that thought *did* rile her.

"Well, I can fly under that covered bridge." Mattie jerked her finger toward the quaint, red-painted structure stretching over the gorge. When they had first surveyed the field before the show, Leo had specifically recommended that they avoid using the tempting hurdle for a stunt. Mattie had no intention of listening.

"There's barely enough clearance." Leo's anger blazed, and Mattie could no longer tell how much was real and how much he was feigning. It felt like it had last night. Almost. This time the intense emotions crackling around them didn't just push them apart; they paradoxically drove them together.

"Plenty of room for me." She recurled her extended finger and instead pointed her thumb toward herself.

"It's a fool's errand. We're not doing that stunt." Leo ground out his words, his nose practically brushing against hers.

"Oh, you don't have to, Mr. Yesteryear, but I am. Just try and stop me." Mattie jammed her leather helmet over her head, the edge of her hand brushing against Leo's cheeks. Ignoring the explosive ripple *that* caused, she pivoted and marched straight toward her Jenny. As soon as her back was positioned toward both Leo and the audience, she allowed a triumphant smile to bloom across her face. She wasn't just going to dive under the picturesque roofed bridge. The trick she had in mind was much more diabolically dangerous, and the mere thought triggered a white-hot thrill. She felt like a bare wire arcing with energy.

By the time Mattie strapped herself into the cockpit and snapped her goggles into place, Leo had also assumed his position in his JN-4. Even from several yards away, he appeared terribly grim, his jaw set so tight she was surprised it didn't crack. She wondered for a moment if he'd looked like that before he'd set off on patrol. For the briefest of moments, a flicker of sympathy shimmered through her. It seemed like the joy of flying had all but vanished from Leo, leaving nothing but hardened determination to get the job done.

But she couldn't afford to dissect Leo's deeply hidden emotions right now. She had a plane to fly and a contest—no, a *battle*—to win.

Vera started Mattie's engine, giving her a wink as she yanked down on the propeller with a Herculean flourish. The crowd thundered with excitement. No one sat now. They had all clambered to their feet, ready to follow the path of the JN-4s as they danced and looped their way toward the river.

As Mattie buzzed the ground, she could spy the upturned faces of the crowd. By chance, she caught a glimpse of little Milly clutching her Planey.

The last trick is going to be for you, Milly, and me and all the girls like us who not only want to soar with the men but who can fly even higher. Hopefully by the time you take to the skies, you won't have to constantly prove yourself.

Mattie held back, strategically allowing Leo to zoom under the barnlike covered bridge first. She knew he'd jockey for the forward position. It wasn't that he needed to be a trailblazer. Leo never seemed to mind when she took the lead or even if she beat him. No. What bothered him were the risks that she took. And now he wanted to test the clearance first. It was a move to protect her, not to upstage her. Yet it rankled all the same.

But she had her own reasons for permitting him to take the first pass. It freed her up for her fait accompli.

Sucking in her breath to prepare for a long battle cry, she zipped toward the elongated structure spanning the gulch. The bright-red siding flashed before her eyes like a matador's cape. Going nearly one and a half times faster than Leo had, she whizzed under the lower chord of the wooden truss. The thick stone abutments rose inches away from either side of her yellow tips, like stout sentries guarding the bridge from below. Mattie saw the underside of the crisscross pattern of lateral wooden floor braces above her. The threaded ends of wrought iron tie-rods extended down from it, like the teeth of a great beast. Below her the silvery river rushed, forming white foam eddies around the rocks jutting through its glistening surface. The roar of her motor intensified in this shadowy place of wood, stone, metal, and water.

Then Mattie was through to the other side, zipping once more into the blazing sun. Ahead of her stood the newer railroad bridge, its stone arches glowing nearly white in the harsh light. Several hundred yards downstream from the pretty little wooden one, it crossed the gully at a broader, deeper section. Tall, with narrow repeating barrel arches, it looked like a formidable Roman aqueduct. Although it offered more vertical clearance than the covered bridge, its closely spaced repeating piers presented a tight horizontal squeeze. Mattie knew she couldn't fly her plane straight through the openings. If she did, she'd clip off both wingtips.

Leo had swept over the structure and was doing loops above it. She'd known ahead of time that he wouldn't try to maneuver through the supports of the railroad bridge out of concern she would follow. Mattie grinned. She didn't point the nose of her Curtiss upward. Instead, she dipped a wing. With another yell, she scooted her plane at an angle through one of the barrel arches. Gray, immovable stone surrounded her. And then she was back in the blue sky. Leveling the trusty old trainer, she bolted up and over Leo. Upside down at the apex of a loop, she noticed to her delight that a steam locomotive was chugging straight toward them. Whipping underneath Leo and over the engine's stubby steam dome, she barreled through the cloud of coal smoke and back into the view of the breathless crowd. Mattie ignored the acrid scent and waved down at the train before soaring back over the Southern Michigan fields. Leo joined her, his plane moving in unison with hers. They landed together in formation.

Mattie killed the motor, and the roar of the crowd immediately replaced the engine's loud thunder. She swiveled in the cockpit and waved with both hands, clapping her fingers off her palms. She could hear the higher-pitched chorus of women's voices mixed with the men's. Even some of the older matrons in their broad-brimmed merry widows had forgotten to act prim and proper. One lady, her face wrinkled and browned from the sun, was waving her hat in a circle above her neat, tidy bun.

Mattie had never really been one for girlie gestures, but when she saw Vera clapping, she was suddenly inspired to blow kisses to the crowd. A couple of men pretended to pluck them from the air. Mattie ignored them and instead focused on the ecstatic faces of the women who had just watched one of their own soundly trounce a celebrated male aviator.

As soon as Mattie's feet touched the ground, the women of her troupe stampeded her. Carrie reached her first and enveloped her in a huge hug. "I knew you could fly like that! Just don't get too cocky. You're made of flesh, muscle, and bone, and that plane is just canvas and wood."

Alice and Vera converged next, wrapping their arms around both Mattie and Carrie. The twins followed, jumping onto the pile. Lily giggled vivaciously while Sadie shouted a few whoops that put even some of Mattie's to shame. Aida reached them last, her notebook hanging half out of her tooled-leather purse and thumping against her thigh while she ran toward them.

"This is definitely going into my book!" Aida practically leaped onto the heap that they'd formed. "Maybe a whole chapter."

"That was marvelous, darling. It was even more than I could have dreamed up, and I've been staging spectacles since before I left my bassinet." Vera wormed her way into the center of the group and squeezed Mattie like a boa constrictor.

"You must teach me to fly like that." Sadie slung her arm around Mattie's shoulders before her bubbly twin jostled her out of position.

"Did you see the men capture your kisses from the air?" Lily grabbed both of Mattie's arms. "They practically worship you now. You're like a movie star! Clara Bow better watch out, or you'll be stealing her spotlight. You're going to be an American sweetheart! I just feel it."

But Mattie didn't want to be America's sweetheart. She wanted to be America's aviator.

Then her friends parted, and Mattie found herself face to face with Leo.

He stood, as always, with his legs slightly braced. He still held his helmet and goggles in his hand, the gear hanging limply against his side. His hair stood up in clumps, and he'd clearly made no move to smooth it down despite the hundreds of eyes staring at them. His blue eyes latched on to Mattie's and held. Neither of them spoke for a moment. The hubbub around them seemed to fade away into a distant, almost pleasant hum.

Yet the energy swirling through Mattie didn't recede. It spiked.

She had no idea how eyes so blue could look so molten. But they did. For one mad moment, she didn't know if he was going to shout at her . . . or stride over, gently grab the back of her head, and dip her into a passionate kiss.

Instead Leo did neither. He just stayed where he was. The only thing that changed was his breathing. He'd unzipped his flight jacket, and the knit fabric of his jersey pulled tight across his muscular body. She could see his chest rise and fall, getting deeper and faster with each intake and exhale.

Now Mattie wondered if *she* would be the one to dash to him. She could toss her arms around his neck and tilt her chin up a few scant inches until their mouths met.

The thought made her own breathing tempo double.

"That . . . ," Leo began and then trailed off. His gaze shifted away from hers and suddenly stopped. Mattie followed the tilt of his chin and found he was glancing over at Alice's husband. When Leo faced her again, his jaw seemed a little looser, his shoulders a little less bunched, and his mouth definitely a little more relaxed.

"That—that was some impressive flying." He spoke the words carefully, making sure no one was listening to them.

She steeled herself for the inevitable argument.

"If . . . if you plan on slipping through another narrow spot like that, we should do more measurements beforehand."

Mattie blinked. Hard. Was he actually offering to *help* her?

"You're not going to argue with me again?"

A small half smile touched Leo's lips. "Would it make any difference?"

"No."

"I—I was thinking if you're dead set on this, then maybe you could let me help you work through your stunts beforehand like a team."

Mattie cocked her head and gave him a hard stare. "Why the change of heart? You were dead set against this."

"Something John said to me," Leo admitted.

Another wave of shock rippled through Mattie, but before she could probe further, a gravelly voice shouted loudly from the crowd, "Hey, fly girl! What's your name?"

Mattie turned toward the speaker and found a man standing a few steps in front of the rest of the audience, his fountain pen poised over a steno pad, his fedora tilted back from his eyes. He gave her a grin—a grin she'd seen Leo receive a hundred times, a thousand times. It was the smile of a reporter trying to put his subject at ease. But Mattie didn't need any cajoling.

"It's Mattie," she said firmly, walking in his direction with her heart thumping. "Mattie McAdams."

"Can you put your helmet back on and stand by your machine?" a man with a tripod and a camera asked. He had the look of a newspaperman too.

Mattie lost no time in complying. Pulling the leather over her hair, she left the goggles situated on top of her head. Unable to stop her beam, she sidled up to her Jenny, her eyes trained on the line of reporters. Flash powder sizzled and popped while camera clicks filled the hot air like the buzz of cicadas in the autumn.

For the first time, the large photographic lenses were trained on her. Not Leo. Not one of her brothers. Not her father. But *her*. Mattie McAdams.

And it felt exactly how she had dreamed it would feel.

Chapter Ten

Sweetheart of balloon buster and flying ace Leo Ward led the war hero on a wild chase through the air during the Flying Flappers' debut performance in Platt, Michigan. Miss McAdams's long auburn hair gives hope that this impetuous young lady has not entirely forsaken modesty. With bobbed hair all the rage, it is a relief and a succor to witness such long tresses on a petticoat flyer so determined to abandon all other hallmarks of her sex. It is a pity that most of her companions have elected for the more vulgar styles, which distract from their otherwise feminine proportions. Miss McAdams's attire, however, leaves much to be desired. It is best for women to leave flight jackets and trouser wearing to the men.

—Benjamin Pringle, *Chicago Advance Leader*

That—*that*—was the article about yesterday's show? Mattie was *not* Leo's dame. Even if she was, her relationship would have had no bearing on what she'd accomplished. *She'd* been the one to inch her Jenny between the stone pillars holding up the railway bridge. Leo had just looped prosaically above. Yet the article still managed to be about *him*, as if it had been some sort of a lovers' romp through the air.

Indignation gushed from Mattie like water from an uncapped fire hydrant as she stepped into the pink parlor, where the female members of the Flying Flappers were gathered. When she shook the paper furiously over her head, her friends looked at her in confusion.

"Grr-ahh." Too angry to articulate her rage beyond that single nonsensical sound, Mattie stabbed her finger against the article and accidentally ripped a small hole.

Everyone crowded around, each jostling to see what had upset her. Vera snagged the paper first, her painted lips pursing angrily. She practically flung the periodical at Aida before she reached forward to pat Mattie's arm.

"I was called Packard Jones's daughter for years until I gave the newspapers enough fodder that they started using my full name."

"When Leo downed his first enemy plane, no one reported that the airman instructed by the skilled pilot Mattie McAdams brought down his first enemy plane over the hills of France in a display of her fine teaching skills. Nor should they have done so. Leo earned his victory, just like I've worked for mine." Mattie began to pace. Part of her wanted to stomp from the room and take to the skies in her Jenny. But for the first time, she wasn't alone in her disappointment.

Aida crumpled the paper. "Every society has a way of framing events, and it is through the male lens that much of history has been portrayed."

Mattie rubbed her forehead. She very much wanted to kick something but had no intention of scuffing one of Vera's intricately carved furniture pieces. Vera moved to the bar and quickly whipped up a cocktail. When the heiress handed her a golden-tinged drink, Mattie automatically closed her fingers around the cool glass stem. Unthinkingly, she lifted the concoction to her lips as she sank into the mohair settee. An odd combination of sour and spice exploded in her mouth, echoing her feelings toward the damned article.

Carrie, who had just finished skimming the paper, sank down beside Mattie. "At least there was a picture of you. The only one of me was the very top of my head when we all hugged each other."

"You should have been featured alongside me! If we had been men, they would have been praising how well we steadied the planes so as to keep our lovely lady companions aloft."

Carrie nodded. "But at least the article finally gets around to identifying you. I'm only referred to in passing by the color of my skin and my sex. I know that the reporter had both my first and last names. I spelled them for him. Twice. And 'Carrie Wilcox' is not difficult to remember."

Mattie paused, taking in the enormity of Carrie's words. How often had Mattie railed about the need for equality? But she had never considered that she herself had an automatic advantage.

"I should have considered that, Carrie. Here I was outraged just on my own behalf."

Carrie sighed and straightened her spine. "I've learned that I need to work four times as hard. Double for being a woman. And double that again for being Black. But I am still going to fly, and I am going to love it. I won't let narrow-minded reporters diminish any of my accomplishments or joy, and you shouldn't either."

Mattie was used to people trying to dismiss her contributions as a woman. But she never had to think about being shut out completely because of her race. The realization barreled into her that Carrie was not just fighting for females to be seen and acknowledged, but her efforts were also making a difference for her entire race.

For that, Mattie truly admired Carrie.

"Nor should we allow troll-voiced hecklers to intimidate us." Mattie raised her glass.

Carrie arched an eyebrow. "Troll-voiced hecklers?"

"There was a man who said, in a horrible troll-like tone, that there were better things I could do with my kisser than challenge a war hero."

Carrie lifted her cocktail as well. "Here's to defying narrow-minded reporters and trolls!"

"And parents who think your value is intrinsically tied to your marriageability!" Vera stood, her chest thrust out, her shoulders squared, her posture positively militant.

"And people who say that females shouldn't tinker with machines." Sadie jumped to join Vera, her face flushed and her brown freckles standing out against the red hue.

"And those who say a mother and wife's place is only in the home." Alice bounced to her feet with the power and grace that allowed her to soar under the big tent.

"Or folks who claim that being a woman in show business is the same as being a whore." Lily tossed her blonde curls, sending them bouncing in a surprisingly fierce manner that seemed to echo the rhythm of a beating drum.

"Or sociologists who claim that the only natural pursuits of the gentler sex are domestic ones." Aida put down her notebook and rose, her feet slightly spread apart as she held her cocktail aloft like a flaming torch.

Mattie and Carrie both scrambled to their feet. As all the women's glasses met in one glorious, resounding clink, a wonderful swell rushed through Mattie. It was as if the Flying Flappers had created their own electromagnetic force field, and they'd all become charged by it.

Vera spoke first, her delicate jaw set in a firm, unyielding line. "I shall handle the press better in the future. After all, I've been manipulating journalists since I was in leading strings. I'll ring up one of my reporter friends from Chicago to do a piece on us and insist that we are all properly featured."

Miss McAdams's long auburn hair gives hope that this impetuous young lady has not entirely forsaken modesty.

The words still burned through Mattie. The reporter seemed to want to dissect every aspect of her femininity and judge it. But why should *he*, this virtual stranger, be allowed to define *her*?

Well, she was *not* going to allow Benji Pringle that control.

"Girls," Mattie asked, swinging her gaze about the gathered women, "how does one go about getting a bob?"

"I could cut it," Lily offered. "I used to bob the girls' hair back in Pennsylvania. Our local town only had a barbershop, and the owner absolutely refused to serve a female customer."

Mattie stiffened her lower back. She hadn't expected Lily to be the one to lop off her hair. But then again, Mattie had never before realized how rebellious fashion could be.

Sucking in a deep breath, she moved to the edge of her chair. "Okay. Do it."

"Now?" Lily repeated. "This very instant?"

"Yes," Mattie said resolutely.

"I'll get my scissors and haircutting supplies!" Lily practically bounced from the room, and for once, the blonde's enthusiasm did not set Mattie on edge.

"Let's all head to my bathroom," Vera said as she led the group from the parlor and through the castle until they reached an absolutely massive water closet. Having only seen small functional private bathrooms in the past, Mattie couldn't help but stare at the elegant, cavernous space.

"Aida, are you going to mention this in your book?" Carrie asked.

"Most definitely!" Aida unscrewed the cap of her fountain pen. "The metamorphosis into a visible New Woman."

Mattie took up her position in a chair resting against the sink as Lily joined them and flitted around setting up shop.

"How serious are you about a transformation?" Vera leaned toward Mattie. One of the heiress's tweezed eyebrows dramatically arched as the flapper studied her with a slightly alarming intensity.

Hell's bells and buckets of blood, she really *was* doing this.

"A full metamorphosis," Mattie confirmed decisively.

Lily whipped her scissors out from behind her back. The blonde twin worked surprisingly fast and efficiently, even though she chattered the entire time. The rest of the group all stayed, watching Mattie and Lily as intently as they would a Rudolph Valentino picture show. As clump after clump of hair fell, Mattie experienced a lightness. By the time Lily had finished, Mattie felt positively giddy.

Mattie drew in a sharp breath when she spotted in the gilt-framed mirror a confident woman, her red hair a wavy tumble about her head. She loved the bob immediately. Slowly, gingerly, she reached up to touch it.

"Do you like it?" Lily stood behind her, fiddling nervously with the cord of the hair dryer. In the reflection, Mattie saw Vera reach down and unplug it.

"It's me!" Mattie laughed, tossing her head, loving how her new coiffure moved in a saucy bounce.

"Now for the clothes." Vera steered Mattie and the others into her massive bedchamber. "We're about the same size, and I have more than a department store's worth of outfits. Marshall Field's has nothing on me."

"Clothes?" Mattie repeated cautiously.

"Well, you did say a full metamorphosis." Vera winked at her.

Mattie had, and she was beginning to discover that fashion, especially feminine fashion, could make a statement as bold as a spiraling barrel roll through the sky.

"I did, didn't I? And I don't believe in doing things in half measure." She boldly stepped up to the massive wardrobe and glanced inside. She had never even dressed her dolls in clothes, but when Mattie found herself staring at an ocean of chiffons and silks, excitement rippled through her. Although she couldn't imagine ever wearing the full puffy skirts of the past, the sleek modern styles called to her.

"This. This one." Mattie ran her hands down a sage-green dress.

"Try it on." Vera pulled it off the hanger and handed it to Mattie. The silk floated over Mattie's skin in a way that cotton fabric never did. The uneven hem swirled wonderfully about her calves with the right amount of flounce to give the dress a feminine look but contained enough that it didn't resemble a fairy princess's gown. The bit of beading about the hip caught the light, and the sight made Mattie feel as if she were sparkling too.

Mattie had never even shown off her ankles before. Now most of her calves were visible. But she didn't feel vulnerable or exposed, even though the dress was one of Vera's shortest. Quite the opposite. She felt powerful and daring. It was like shooting into the sky with her throttle fully open.

When Mattie stepped into view, Leo's brain blanked. Utterly and completely blanked.

Surrounded by a kaleidoscope of hues from a massive stained glass window as she stood at the top of Vera's grand staircase, Mattie looked like a royal pixie or some other fair princess from a lushly drawn children's book. Not a maiden in distress but a dragon slayer herself. Her short locks blazed in a wild nimbus about her head, bringing to mind a fiery sunrise.

And there was the dress . . . the green, flowy slip of a dress. Despite the fact that she stood three stories above him, Leo swore he could feel the delicate fabric of her skirt rustle against his borrowed dark-blue dress pants.

"What do you think? Do I look ritzy enough for my first speakeasy?" Mattie, still being Mattie, hung over the banister as she called down to him, heedless of the more-than-three-story drop. She might be wearing a society darling's clothes, but she was still the intrepid pilot who'd taught him how to fly.

"You look like a daring aviator ready to take the town by storm."

She rewarded him with a huge grin. "I clean up good, don't I?"

"Not bad." Leo was very proud that he didn't choke on his words. His voice remained remarkably steady despite the bolt of need searing through him. He was fairly certain he flushed, but luckily Mattie didn't seem to notice as she raced down the steps.

"What do you think of the new Mattie?" Vera appeared next, flanked by the other women, all dressed in their glad rags.

Leo held Mattie's gaze as he answered Vera's question. "I wouldn't say *new*. Mattie's always bold no matter what she wears, but I think she looks swell."

"Why, Leo, darling, you may have an unexpected honeyed tongue," Vera teased.

"I think it is just Mattie who inspires it," Alice chimed in.

Leo knew for certain this time that his face brightened into an uncontrollable scarlet. Luckily, the women turned their attention from him as they discussed who would ride with whom into Chicago. Wisely, he and John did not offer their opinions. After a five-minute debate that involved as much strategizing as an entire military campaign, Leo found himself wedged into the passenger seat of Vera's Duesenberg with Mattie crammed next to him in the center and Vera at the wheel.

"I've never been to a speakeasy." Mattie lifted her hands in the air, much as Vera had done when Mattie had first driven the Duesy.

"You will absolutely adore it, darling." Vera turned the wheel to whiz past a farm truck lumbering down the road. Leo clutched the dashboard and earned a reproving look from both women.

Despite her speed, Vera was a skilled driver, and the countryside eventually gave way to the outskirts of Chicago and then to the city itself. Imposing skyscrapers rose like bold monoliths from the western shore of Lake Michigan. Traffic had noticeably thickened—and not just with Fords, Dodges, and Studebakers, but with horse-drawn vehicles as well. The motorcar might have started to take over the American road system, but the clip-clop of the past still echoed through the streets.

Vera pulled up to the front of a swanky hotel, the Bolton. After climbing out of the vehicles, the women linked their arms to form a brilliant line of finery as they crossed the boldly lit threshold into the equally bright lobby with Leo and John taking up the rear. Several sparkling Murano glass chandeliers hung high over the black-and-white diamond-patterned marble floor. Part of Leo wanted to turn heel at the opulence and head to the dingiest establishment he could find, but he wouldn't leave Mattie.

"My usual table, Claude." Vera bussed the maître d's cheek when they arrived at the grand dining room. "The one out of the draft. You know how I detest getting a chill."

Claude inclined his head and guided them behind a beautifully painted screen surrounded by a profusion of tropical foliage. On the other side of the gilded artwork was a surprisingly utilitarian hallway. Waiters hurried by, their trays laden with food arranged in fussy displays. Claude opened a door that looked like the entrance to a storage closet but instead revealed narrow, plain steps.

When their party reached the top, there was another unembellished door made remarkable only by its sturdy metal construction. A sign on it read **Employees Only**. The maître d' knocked in a distinct pattern. A muffled voice responded, and their guide said, "The usual guests." The heavy steel door swung open, revealing a hulking bruiser of a man. Although all the hotel's employees wore impeccably tailored uniforms, the bouncer's fit a tad too snugly, showcasing his rather impressive set of bulging muscles. He was the type of man who ruled the boxing ring and was clearly the first line of defense in any raids.

"Miss Jones!" The man's pale, craggy face burst into an incongruously wide smile. "It's good to see you. You haven't stopped in for a long time."

"I've been busy starting a flying circus, Harold." Vera winked at the man. "You should see one of our performances. I walk on the wing of a plane. It is quite thrilling."

"I'll be sure to see that!" The man's brown eyes had grown wide.

"I'll send you tickets for you and your wife," Vera promised before she strode into the room, her graceful steps like those of an empress. Taking up the rear, Leo entered last and found himself in the middle of the most subversive tea party ever.

Gaily dressed patrons sat around round tables and sipped from elegant teacups. Waiters suspiciously shook elongated chrome teapots. Not only did the metal not burn their hands, but when they tipped over the device to deliver the contents into the awaiting china, the liquid that poured forth decidedly did not look at all like tea. Still, the scene was peaceful enough that a policeman, especially one encouraged with a bit of dough, could accept the illusion presented to him. Yet even as the diners ate their beautifully plated five-course dinners and sipped their special brew, raucous sounds occasionally invaded the faux peace.

"Welcome to your first speakeasy, the Gilded Secret," Vera told Mattie, Sadie, and Lily. "This entire floor of the hotel is dedicated to the most delightful debauchery."

"But it's an entire city block!" Sadie gazed around the initial room, clearly calculating how much speakeasy was still left, which by Leo's estimate was quite a bit.

"And the police don't know about this?" Lily whispered the words, her voice sounding just as awestruck as her starry-eyed expression.

"They're paid not to know," Carrie explained.

"The subculture that Prohibition is creating is immensely fascinating." Aida nodded to the scene around them. "Many of these people never would have considered encouraging lawbreaking, yet here they are, Chicago's wealthiest, sipping contraband from priceless porcelain. After the flying circus research, I might do a study on speakeasies."

"Subculture?" Mattie asked.

"It's a rather new word," Aida explained. "It is used to describe pockets of society existing within a broader population."

"Which is a terribly academic explanation of such freewheeling fun." Vera linked arms with Aida and gently pulled her along the pathway leading away from the dining area, waving for the others to follow. "Come on. This is the dullest room. We have so much more to explore. If you want to start building your reputation in high society, this is the best place to start doing it. You never know who you'll be rubbing shoulders with. Could be a businessman in need of a pretty face to help hawk his newest brand of detergent. And don't forget, whatever happens tonight, any press is good press when you're a bear cat."

The sounds of people laughing grew progressively louder and the lighting moodier. Vera expertly wound their troupe through the spiffily dressed throng. Bright, tinkling laughter mixed with loud guffaws. Soulful strains of music drifted through the noise along with the enchanting notes of a powerful female contralto. Some groups seemed divided by gender. Young women giggled, their sequined headbands glittering as they pressed their heads close together before fluttering long mascara-blackened lashes toward men. The playboys lounged against tall tables, the bar, or even the walls, trying to look casual and bored by the proceedings. But their half-lidded eyes didn't fool Leo. The males were here to flirt as much as the females.

Leo's own party wove its way into another section of the club. Black Carrara glass covered the walls, rising in repeating onyx columns. Between each shiny panel were gilded floor-to-ceiling murals of stylized cranes stepping out from behind clumps of papyrus reeds. Continuing the architect's wildly fanciful and inaccurate interpretation of ancient Egyptian art, the equally golden ceiling also boasted a Nile theme. A sparkling river flowed above their heads, surrounded by marshes and various birds taking flight.

It wasn't the architecture that impressed Leo, though, but the singer crooning onstage. Her rich voice filled the room in defiance of the chatter and surrounding chaos. Leo had always appreciated music, although he'd had little exposure to it growing up. The blues, especially, resonated with him.

"My goodness!" Carrie clutched Vera's arm, her voice vibrating with pure excitement. "That's Thelma Stanton! *The* Thelma Stanton! I have all her records."

"I know," Vera said. "When I heard she was going to be singing here tonight, I knew I had to bring you."

"She has her own train car." Carrie's eyes remained glued to the woman commanding the entire room with her powerful contralto. "She, a Black woman from rural southern Alabama, who started with nothing and fought her own way to fame no matter how many times prejudice has tried to pull her down."

Letting go of Vera, Carrie drifted closer and closer to the stage. Leo figured it was only the instincts of an amazing pilot that allowed her to navigate around the dancing couples. She was clearly lost to the music. He would have been, too, if he hadn't wanted to stay sharp to watch over Mattie and the rest of the women. He didn't consider himself or John their chaperones. The gals could do as they wished. But if any of them required his assistance, he could help in an instant.

Vera waved cheerily to someone in the crowd, and a tall, dashing fellow in a dinner jacket and white gloves stepped forward. Leo could tell instantly the man originated from money—old money. He had the kind of polish that came from a good education, a carefully prescribed childhood, and scads of ever-present wealth. In his youth, Leo might not have been able to distinguish one dapper gentleman from the next, but he had served with enough aviators from privileged backgrounds—solid men with guts and determination such as Quentin Roosevelt and Douglas Campbell.

This man with his square jaw and neatly groomed blond hair seemed affable enough. When he was introduced to Mattie, he leveled his full charm on her. Leo didn't blame him. Mattie just carried this brightness with her, and why wouldn't a fellow want to bask in some of her warmth, even if only for a little bit?

"A girl flyer, huh?" The fellow grinned down at Mattie, his teeth a white gleam against his lightly tanned skin. To Leo's disgust, a dimple appeared in the interloper's cheek. The gentleman could outshine even the suave leading man Douglas Fairbanks.

Although Leo understood the aristocrat's interest, he couldn't quite stamp out the curl of jealousy slipping through him like a poisonous serpent. But what Leo could do, and did do, was ignore it. It wasn't his place, his right, to feel such emotions.

Mattie blessedly did not melt under the rays of the gentleman's male beauty. Instead she gave her normal impish grin. "We prefer *fly girl*."

"Fly girl, huh?" The man cocked his hip and leaned against one of the tables. "Sounds exciting."

"Oh, it is." Mattie winked. Clearly, she was enjoying the attention, and more importantly, she could hold her own. Realizing that Mattie didn't need him hovering behind her like some sort of antiquated chaperone, Leo slipped away. He didn't leave the room, though.

Instead, he took up a seat by the bar and ordered tonic water with lime. From here, he could establish a good vantage point from which to observe the room. Carrie had found a table near the stage, and Sadie and Aida had joined her. John and Alice had taken to the dance floor while Vera and Lily flirted their way around the room. And Mattie . . . Mattie was still talking to the aristocrat. But her eyes kept flitting about, drawn to the band, the swaying couples, and the laughter bubbling up all over the gilded room.

Relief crept through Leo, and he wished it weren't so powerful. One day Mattie would find a man worthy of her, and this fellow, with his fancy clothes and highly polished dress shoes, could offer her a lot more than Leo could even dream of giving her. Annoyed with his own reaction, Leo glanced away. By the time Mattie and her companion came into his field of vision again, she was leading him over to Lily and Vera. The two women gladly chatted with the handsome devil while Mattie slipped away. She seemed to be intent on joining Carrie and the others at the table, but another pretty-faced man intercepted her.

Earl Crenshaw. The bastard whose dangerous pranks had almost gotten Alfred killed on the front.

Chapter Eleven

"Where's your alarm clock?" The gruff voice was oddly soft around the edges, like a half-sanded surface. Mattie debated whether she should just keep on walking. She probably should, but the man's assumption that she would or should have a chaperone irritated her.

"Where's yours?" she shot back as she spun on her heel. Her borrowed dress flared out around her legs, drawing the attention of the man standing before her. As he stared down at her gams, shocked recognition slammed into Mattie.

She *knew* that face.

After all, for the past few years, it had stared back at her from every can of Rockol machine oil that she'd used to maintain her Jenny. Since it was her favorite brand, she'd seen a lot of his smiling, debonair mug. She'd never, however, actually met the famed ace of the Great War, even though he'd served in the same squadron as her brother and Leo.

Earl Crenshaw finally lifted his eyes to her face and smiled. Wolfishly. Mattie did not like wolfish. It irritated her.

"You've got a smart mouth on you, don't you?" He leaned a little closer, and a distinctive floral and antiseptic scent slammed into Mattie. The aviator had recently consumed gin—and a lot of it, judging by the intensity of the odor.

"I like to think so," Mattie retorted, trying not to destroy her imperious tone by gagging at the overbearing aroma of alcohol.

She started to turn, but he caught her arm. Hard. Her brothers had taught her how to unman a brute like him with a knee to the groin, but she didn't want to employ that trick, not just yet. It might not even be necessary. She'd rather extricate herself from the situation. Although she wasn't above causing a scene, she had a feeling that starting a brawl in a speakeasy, even an upscale one, was akin to throwing a match in a vat of nitroglycerin.

"You're that petticoat flyer? Alfred McAdams's lil sis." The man peered at her, his nose almost touching hers. His pale-blue eyes were glassy from drinking, and Mattie found herself suppressing a shiver. But that wasn't the only sensation she felt. There was a prickle of awareness, and she knew at once Leo was watching her.

Leaning back to avoid smacking the edge of her nostrils against Crenshaw's, she caught Leo's gaze. He'd already started moving toward her, but she shook her head. She didn't exactly have the situation *under* control, but it wasn't out of control yet either. If, however, Leo charged forward with his quick fists flying, trouble would definitely start.

Leo instantly paused, understanding her signal immediately. His hands still clenched at his sides, he stood like a sentry, ready to be called into action should the need arise.

"You outflew the Reverend." The oaf reached up and touched Mattie's bob. "You cut your pretty hair, though. It's a shame. Men like long locks."

Dunderheaded, ossified bastard.

"Well, it is a good thing that I wasn't trying to impress you, then," Mattie said sweetly before she reached up and grabbed his wrist with her hand. She gave a little twist like her siblings had shown her, and the aviator's eyes narrowed.

"Hey, I wasn't doing any harm." He started to reach for her again, but suddenly Vera materialized at Mattie's side.

"Darling, I do believe my friend is being very clear that she is not interested in your rather clumsy pursuit." Vera linked her elbow with Mattie's.

"I don't see how this conversation is any concern to you." He crossed his arms, his muscles flexing underneath the black material.

Carrie also hooked her arm with Mattie's in a show of solidarity. "Since she is our friend, it is more of our concern than it is yours."

"Agreed." Alice appeared on Carrie's other side. Soon all the female members of their troupe were standing together, forming a linked chain. Crenshaw's face turned a curious shade of purple. One of his hands balled into a fist. Mattie tensed her leg, readying to jam her knee into a certain vulnerable appendage if necessary. Out of the corner of her eye, she saw Leo move forward. Crenshaw's knuckles started moving in a downward trajectory.

And then the music stopped. Crenshaw jerked back on his heels. When he gazed around the room with a stupefied expression on his handsome, chiseled mug, Mattie took the opportunity to do the same. But even as she turned her head, she still made sure to maintain her awareness of the buffoon's position. The entire gathering had stopped to stare in unabashed interest. Since Mattie rather enjoyed the spotlight, she didn't mind. After all, Vera had said any press tonight would be good press. But clearly Crenshaw didn't appreciate the attention. He uncurled his fingers . . . slowly. Although he sent Mattie a rather menacing look, he didn't move any closer. Instead he rolled his shoulders and made a great show of casually walking away.

Not about to allow the boozy bore to ruin her first speakeasy experience, Mattie swung their fierce chorus line in the direction of the table that Carrie, Sadie, and Aida had just vacated. "What do you say, girls? Should we sit down and listen to some fine singing?"

Several people began to clap, and then the whole room erupted into good cheer. When the noise settled slightly, Thelma Stanton once again commanded the room as she extended one silk-covered hand in their direction. "What a lovely compliment! And I have just the song to thank you with."

After sending a signal to her band, Thelma swiveled back to face the crowd once more. The lights above her head caught the net of fine beads covering her gold dress. The garment complemented the warm hue of her brown skin and sparkled almost as much as the legendary performer herself. Once more, Miss Stanton held the room in her thrall.

She began to sing low and deep about failed Casanovas and the headaches caused by unwanted male suitors. Soon the whole room was laughing, but no one louder than the group of young men near Crenshaw. Although Mattie took care not to stare in his direction, she did covertly keep watch. An unusual sliver of unease snaked through her when she noticed Benji Pringle was among Crenshaw's cronies. The two men seemed to grow increasingly agitated, their hands making angry slashing movements. Their comrades' expressions shifted from mirth to something darker.

"I have a feeling that trouble is about to drift our way." Carrie spoke the words lightly, but all the women understood the seriousness of her observation.

"Drat," Aida hissed. "He seems to have formed some sort of male pack—typical social behavior for characters of his ilk and Pringle's. I wonder if Pringle didn't put Crenshaw up to approaching Mattie in the first place. Maybe he was hoping to snap another embarrassing photo."

"Perhaps we'd better leave." Lily's hand fluttered to her neck.

Vera tossed back her curls. "Oh, piffle. I have no intention of letting ill-mannered brutes chase me from my favorite club. Arrogant fools who think they have some claim over you just because you're in the papers are the downside to fame. I've learned it's best to ignore them."

Mattie exchanged a look with Alice. Both of them had noticed Leo and John moving surreptitiously in their direction. For once, Vera's boldness and wealth wouldn't necessarily provide a buffer. Although the women might emerge unscathed, their two male companions could not defend against eight alcohol-soaked imbeciles.

"Lily is right." Mattie began to rise, with Alice following her. The acrobat shifted her eyes meaningfully toward her husband and Leo, and finally Vera seemed to understand.

She sighed and placed her drink on the table with a resigned plop. "Men and their constant need to defend us. This is one of the main reasons I have no desire to marry."

They had just begun to move toward the exit when Mattie felt a sharp yank on her elbow. She was spun rather roughly into the arms of Crenshaw. He leered at her. "I heard you ladybirds like a bit of adventure. I promise to show you one that'll really send you soaring."

He started to dip his head to kiss Mattie, but she was faster. She jammed her knee into his groin and then stabbed his instep with her heel. His eyes squeezed shut as he grabbed himself and tottered on one foot. Already unbalanced from liquor, he toppled into an undignified heap. Moaning and caterwauling like a lovesick bobcat, he rolled on the floor.

Mattie felt a strong arm on her back, and she started to stab with her elbow. Luckily, she realized just in time that it was Leo. He started to whisk her away from the scene, but before he could, one of Crenshaw's friends charged them. Leo didn't even raise his fist. He just tucked his body and let the man barrel into his bent form. This launched their attacker into the air. He landed with a rather dramatic crash on a nearby table filled with fedora-wearing men. Teacups crunched, and liquor flowed everywhere. Not pleased to have their drinks destroyed, the men jumped to their feet. One pulled the human projectile off the table and slugged him in the face.

Leo and John moved around Mattie and her friends, trying vainly to transform their bodies into a fortress. Mattie balled up her fists, getting ready to fight.

"Carrie Wilcox!" The calm, confident voice cut through the din the way only a professional vocalist could manage. At the sound of her friend's name, Mattie swiveled to the stage. The legendary singer stood on the edge, beckoning Carrie's group to join her. They moved without hesitation, Carrie leading and the men taking up the rear. The platform didn't have any steps leading up to it, but that didn't stop them from easily catapulting their bodies up the four-foot rise.

"This way." Thelma pulled back the curtain leading to the backstage. Before anyone could notice their escape, they pounded over the floorboards and ducked behind the thick black velveteen fabric. To Mattie's surprise, Thelma crouched down and lifted up a rug that had concealed a trapdoor. Yanking upward on the brass ring, she hefted open the hatch, revealing a steep set of steps that looked more like a ship's ladder than stairs. She climbed down them backward, only pausing briefly to gesture for them to still follow.

The nine of them didn't hesitate. One by one, they clambered down the surprisingly sturdy escape route. Leo went last, firmly pulling the wooden covering shut.

"There's two bolts on the right and left side. Secure them," Thelma instructed crisply as she stood at the base of the steps. Leo immediately complied. They were now situated under the stage. The floor was slightly sunken, but they still needed to duck. Once again, Thelma guided them. With their backs bent, they followed her through the wooden supports. Although the stage muffled the noise from the fight, it seemed as if the volume had only grown. Grunts, growls, and the sound of fists smashing against flesh echoed through the air. A few ladies screamed, but none of the cries seemed filled with pain. In fact, more than a few of the shrill shrieks had a downright theatrical quality to them.

Thelma slid back another piece of paneling. They crawled through the opening and emerged in a long hallway with no other apparent exit. A man, even bigger and broader than the bouncer guarding the door to the speakeasy, stood at the other end. He started to slip his hand under the lapel of his dinner jacket, but when he saw Thelma, his white, pasty face split into a wide, welcoming grin.

"Hello, Miss Stanton." He placed his arms behind his back, and Mattie wondered for a moment if a button on his white shirt would pop under the pressure of his flexed muscles. "What's the trouble now? Full-scale invasion or run-of-the-mill fracas?"

"Run-of-the-mill fracas, Henry. Run of the mill," Thelma said conversationally with an easy grin. "My friends here got into a spot of trouble definitely not of their own making. Would you be so kind as to escort them safely to the back exit?"

"Of course, Miss Stanton."

As the singer turned to leave, Carrie said, "Thank you so much for coming to our rescue."

"Don't think anything of it." Thelma waved her gloved hand, the gesture just as graceful as her voice. "Anything for Carrie Wilcox."

"You've heard of me?" Carrie, who generally was unflappable, had widened her brown eyes in surprise.

"You're the Flying Angel, friend to Brave Bessie. I've read all about you in the papers. Maybe someday I'll see you soar."

"You can do better than that," Carrie said. "If you're interested, I can take you up for a ride."

"I'd love that!"

Carrie extended her gloved palm. "It's a deal."

The two women shook hands. When they separated, Carrie added, "I've been listening to your records for three years now and reading all about you too."

Thelma laughed. "Imagine that. Us following each other in the papers. I'm glad we met."

"So am I."

"Well, I have a brawl to settle down. I am turning into a regular Orpheus with this gig."

With one final elegant wave, Thelma ducked back into the secret passage. A few seconds later, her rich voice wove through the cacophony.

"Will she be safe up there?" Leo, ever the worrier, asked.

"Yes, sir. All the bouncers at the club will make sure to protect her if things get out of hand." Henry nodded as he pressed the button to an elevator that Mattie had overlooked in her excitement. Even with the turmoil, she had no idea how she had missed the doors, since they were shiny chrome with a copper-inlay starburst pattern.

Henry entered with them and served as a rather overmuscled operator. The well-engineered contraption whooshed downward and opened into a concrete, subterranean tunnel. It was narrow, poorly lit, and damp, but it served its purpose. Their group quickly breezed through the passageway and reached a set of stairs that led to the back of a storage room. Henry shut the escape-route door behind them, revealing that the corridor was hidden behind a false shelf. They snaked through towers of stacked dining room chairs, discarded lamps, and wobbly tables. Finally, Henry pushed open the exit, and they all spilled out into a moonlit alley.

Henry made his goodbyes and then quickly disappeared to resume his post. John heaved a sigh, the sound heavily laden with relief. Leo shifted his body, his shoulders uncoiling. Carrie shook her head, as if still in disbelief over what had transpired. Alice, Aida, and Sadie also relaxed their taut forms, and Mattie could feel herself doing the same. Even Lily seemed remarkably subdued.

Vera, however, laughed—bright, happy, and triumphant. "That," she declared, tossing her arms toward the inky night sky, "was a thrilling adventure. I've never started a brawl before. If any of the papers pick it up, it will definitely cement our image as daredevils—or she-devils, even."

"Technically," Aida said, straightening her light-blue dress, "Mattie began it. Very impressively too."

"Four brothers." Mattie was feeling enough like herself again that she could accompany the words with a smile.

Sadie sighed. "My brothers would never show Lily and me how to fight."

"That's because you had a tendency to always win." Lily fluffed her hair and then paused for dramatic effect. "She is very scrappy."

"I prefer *determined*." Sadie shrugged. "But even I don't know if I could have managed that brute so handily."

A swell of pride rushed through Mattie. "I did dispatch him rather quickly."

"Maybe he'll think twice before pawing another woman." Lily reached into her beaded bag to retrieve a small compact mirror.

"Doubtful." Aida sighed. "He seemed rather thickheaded."

"Leo, you were very impressive as well." Alice patted his arm. "The way you sent that man sailing with such little effort was quite remarkable."

With his free hand, Leo rubbed the back of his head. Alice's compliment clearly not only embarrassed him but made him almost palpably uncomfortable.

"Where did you learn to fight like that?" John asked.

Leo scratched harder as he lifted his shoulders in a quick shrug. "Here and there."

Mattie had only watched Leo scrap a few times, mostly to break up her brothers. But each time, he'd moved with a wicked proficiency. She wondered why she had never questioned it. But with so much of Leo a mystery, at some point, she had started accepting his quirks automatically.

Yet now something . . . something was changing. During their conversation in Vera's garden and then on her beach, Mattie had caught a glimpse of the part Leo kept tucked away like an engine hidden under a steel covering. And she suddenly wanted to pop that hood open—not to tinker but to understand how he worked.

"The night is still as young as unaged whiskey." Vera's declaration interrupted Mattie's thoughts. The flapper twirled, her cherry-red skirts swaying about her silk stockings, the beads catching the light of the nearby streetlamp. "There is another little place just a few doors down. That way our poor feet will only get sore from dancing and not walking."

"Haven't we had enough excitement tonight?" Aida asked.

Vera simply began to twirl and trip away, presumably in the direction of the other establishment. "Darling, you know me better than that! We are just getting started. I promised a night on the town, didn't I? A little ole brawl is hardly sufficient entertainment."

"It is a wonder I survived boarding school." Aida rolled her eyes, but no one could miss the affection in her voice. She headed after her cavorting chum, and the rest of their group followed. Mattie was about to when she felt a gentle touch on her upper arm, so different from the drunken dunderhead's grip earlier. This was questioning, light. Asking permission, not taking it. From the familiar warmth, she knew at once it was Leo touching her.

"We can borrow John's Ford if you want to return to Vera's," Leo offered in a low voice.

Mattie slowed. Leo hadn't spoken the words like an order, but she wasn't sure if he was being overprotective again.

"Are you saying we should go back to the castle?" she asked carefully.

"Not necessarily. I just thought you might have been a little shaken after what happened back there. Most folks would be, men or women."

"It's not that you think I shouldn't frequent speakeasies?" Mattie asked.

Leo didn't answer right away. Instead he looked down at his polished shoes, and Mattie wondered what he was thinking.

"It's not the place I'd choose to go with you," he finally answered, lifting his chin to shoot her one of his slow, shy smiles, "but you certainly showed you can hold your own in one."

"I was pretty impressive, wasn't I?" She tossed her head back in mock dramatic pride, but the real reason for the gesture was a lot simpler . . . and much more complicated. Leo's words had caused a sweet arc of energy to burst through her, and she had to make some sort of gesture to release the raw giddiness.

"I wouldn't have minded having you at my back when I was a boy; that's for sure."

Mattie might not have thought much of the offhanded statement if she hadn't just been wondering how he'd learned to fight so proficiently. "Did you get into a lot of tussles when you were younger?"

His pace faltered ever so slightly, and he glanced away from her again. This time he trained his eyes on the brick walls surrounding them. Of course, he gave as cryptic an answer as possible. "Something like that."

Vera's voice broke into their conversation. "And we are here!"

"The back of a button factory?" Sadie asked.

"Clearly it is a front for a club," Lily said in a dramatic stage whisper.

"You are both right." Vera knocked twice on a door that Mattie had almost overlooked. It had been painted to resemble the rest of the redbrick facade. Vera waited several beats and then gave three short raps followed by a thud. A small crack appeared in the wall.

"What's the matter?" a rough voice croaked.

"I'm here to complain about my last shipment. It was pink. I wanted green."

The two inches became several feet. Vera breezed inside the dark hole first, while Mattie and Leo were the last to enter what appeared to be the bowels of a factory. Crates rose above their heads, while odds and ends from bits of rope to broken pieces of machinery cluttered the floor. It made the other storeroom look practically neat and tidy in comparison. Vera, however, did not need the doorman to guide her. She wound her way through the warren of buttons, wood, and even seashells with the confidence of someone keenly familiar with the potential death trap.

The guard at the door tipped his hat to the rest of the Flying Flappers as they hurried to keep up with Vera. The bouncer's face was surprisingly as smooth and refined as his voice had been coarse and rough. He gave Mattie a particularly devilish wink. Unlike the dreadful Crenshaw, he exuded a kindhearted charm despite his job as an enforcer. She responded with a bright smile but nothing more. She hadn't come to the speakeasies for meaningless flirtations, although she supposed it was part of the experience. But she would much rather talk to Leo than a handsome stranger, no matter how chiseled his jaw or jade green his eyes.

Vera's cherry-red dress sparkled in the dull, dusty room as she ducked behind a rather large coil of rope and opened another obscured door. Within moments, they all found themselves in the low-lit interior of a bar. This didn't have the opulence of the first speakeasy. Cigarette smoke, dense and thick, hung in the air. People were jammed into the small space, especially near the stage, where a band played. The tin ceiling seemed to trap and amplify every sound, making it hard to hear the bluesy music. Mattie's head swam from the press of bodies, the jumble of raised conversations, the smell of alcohol, and the heat of the hidden room.

Vera, however, plunged into the swarming crowd. She was soon swallowed up in a sea of colors, followed by John and the rest of Mattie's friends. But Mattie stayed back with Leo.

"You can go on." He jerked with his head in the approximate direction of the stage. "I'll stay back here."

And observe, Mattie thought, *like Leo always does. On the edge but not really part of things.*

"I'll stay with you." Mattie looked around and found a table tucked into a corner.

"You don't need to on my account. I'm fine by myself."

"Crowds this thick make me feel like a caged swallow," Mattie said, relaying half the truth. She also simply found herself wanting to be with Leo.

"All right," he said. "I'll get us some drinks, and I'll meet you back here. What do you want?"

"A mint julep."

"I'll be back in a jiff," Leo promised before he, too, disappeared into the ever-shifting wall of human beings. He hadn't been gone too long when a rough voice spoke near Mattie.

"I'd hoped to see you on my break."

She turned to find the bouncer standing there. Unlike Crenshaw, he didn't encroach into her space but stood back like Vera's aristocratic friend Edward. The two fellows might have been of different social classes, but they were both gentlemen.

"Do you mind if I chat with you?" His gravelly voice carried such an incongruous strain of earnestness that Mattie didn't have the heart to dismiss him outright.

"Until my friend returns with some drinks."

The fellow grinned. It should have been devastating. So should have Edward's charming smile. But neither of the men's handsome expressions had affected her, not like one of Leo's slow, shy looks.

"Are you the same dame who flew that airplane yesterday?" the man asked. "I was there. Your hair is different, though."

"I had it cut today." Mattie couldn't help but reach up and touch her wild curls. They felt so different. Light. Buoyant. Free.

"It's nice. I like it."

His words were pleasant, but they didn't explode inside her like Leo's had. *"Mattie's always bold no matter what she wears, but I think she looks swell."*

The bouncer and she slipped into small talk. Mattie learned his name was George and that he originally hailed from Indiana. She found him interesting enough, just as she had Edward, but she was distracted . . . and not just by the speakeasy's raucous atmosphere. She wondered where Leo was. He'd been gone longer than she'd supposed, but then it would take a while just to navigate through the crowd.

When the aviator finally reappeared, he faltered. He stood still, and then he started to turn, not angry or blustery but courteous. He was giving Mattie a chance to get to know this stranger better if she desired.

"Leo!" She waved at him, just like she'd seen Vera do when hailing an acquaintance. He shot her a questioning look, and she beckoned again. Slowly, as if letting her have the opportunity to change her mind, he stepped forward.

"Your friend?" George's voice held a twinge of disappointment. Mattie could have assured the bouncer that nothing romantic lay between her and Leo. But she didn't.

Instead, she nodded her assent and introduced the two men as Leo drew closer. George stayed for a bit, but the conversation had grown stilted. Finally, the bouncer excused himself, saying he had to return to his post.

"Sorry. I didn't mean to chase him off." Leo eased into a chair and slid her drink toward her. A sprig of mint cheerfully peeked from the glass.

But as much as Mattie wanted to try the drink Vera had called "simply the berries," she didn't reach for it. She had something to say. Something that suddenly felt critically, overwhelmingly important.

"He was sweet, but I didn't want to get to know him better. I want to be with *you*."

As soon as the words fell from her lips, Mattie realized the startling truth of her statement. This . . . *this* was what she had been feeling the whole evening. She *wanted* Leo. Handsome, boyish, quiet, protective, wonderful Leo.

And when Mattie wanted something, *really* wanted something, she never hesitated and always raced toward it, throttle open, caution be damned.

⁂

"I want to be with you." The words threatened to ignite Leo into a ball of burning hydrogen. But he knew all too well the danger inherent in an explosion. How it burst out of control. How it became a force of its own. How once triggered, it became unstoppable.

Surely Mattie did not mean the words romantically. She only meant that she preferred his company. And the cautious part of him, the part that had kept him safe through a life of peril, hoped it was true. Because if she did desire him . . . then he was truly lost to her.

"You know," Mattie said, leaning over her sweet-smelling drink, her eyes a molten gold, "I realized something tonight."

Leo should have glanced away, excused himself, found some reason to flee. Instead, he sat rooted to his chair like one of the ancient gnarled yews he'd seen on leave in France.

"What?" The word sounded hoarse to his own ears, and a strange prickly sensation spread over his body.

"If someone asked me to describe my perfect man, he'd end up sounding a lot like you."

Her confession was just the oxygen needed to feed the spark that her first statement had triggered. His control erupted in a burst of orange fire. His fingers gripped the cool glass holding his tonic water, as if somehow the substance could cool him down.

It didn't.

Instead, he was afraid he would crack the cheap crystal.

Mattie reached over, her fingers so close to his that he swore he could feel their heat. But she didn't touch him. Not yet. But he wanted her to. Wanted it with his entire body. He thrummed with need, need that he had repressed for over half a decade. Need that he'd never expected to tempt, let alone to fill.

"We were friends so long ago." Mattie's words teased him like a physical touch, and energy skittered along his flesh. "And then we were always fighting. Do you think there was something there all the time? Something we've been overlooking?"

He'd never overlooked it. Not once. He'd buried it. But not deep enough. Never deep enough. It wasn't possible.

"I don't have a lot to offer, Mattie. I don't own a single piece of property other than an aging biplane that was built to train pilots, not to set records."

Her lips curled up . . . dangerously. The muscles in his throat closed, holding further protests at bay. The tip of her finger touched his. He should have withdrawn. He should have scrambled backward quickly enough to upset his chair. But he didn't. He stayed.

"I had a millionaire's son flirt with me tonight. He was nice. Charming. Affable. And he bored me. What would I do with a big mansion and heaps of bric-a-brac anyway? You can't fly them."

Leo choked, his first words coming in a splutter. He hadn't expected her to say that. For some women, it might just be sentimental bluster. But not Mattie. She'd never cared much about material possessions. She enjoyed looking at them, for sure. She appreciated them. But she didn't need them. Didn't desire them. Not like she did excitement.

"I'm not adventurous enough for you either, Mattie." He couldn't keep the desperate tone from his voice, but whether he was desperate to convince her of his unsuitability or desperate for her to deny his objections . . . he didn't know. But it seemed that she did.

Her finger slid up to his knuckle. He swallowed at the burst of sweetness that cascaded through him. How was she managing to seduce him with the most innocent of touches?

"I had a bouncer at a speakeasy flirt with me tonight. He has connections to the underworld. He knows bootleggers and gangsters, and maybe he even is one. But he was still nice and courteous and seemed like a generally good man. But he isn't right for me any more than the wealthy aristocrat."

"And you're saying that I am?" The words squeezed out of him. He actually hurt from trying to physically hold them back. He shouldn't have said them, shouldn't have encouraged her to rush into this like she did everything else. But he couldn't stop her . . . or even himself.

Her hand closed over his. It was smaller, more delicate, but no less capable than his larger one. Her warmth, her confidence, her unshaken belief in them seeped through him. His heart seemed to swell like a hydrogen-filled balloon and threatened to lift straight from his chest. His inhibitions certainly did.

"You're honest, and you're steady, and you're completely devoid of unnecessary flash."

Leo grinned. Mattie's words weren't those that a lover would typically utter, but he liked them. Liked their sturdiness. Liked that they weren't sweet nothings but something blessedly logical. Something real.

This was happening fast. But then Mattie never did like to apply the brakes.

"Are you saying that you are attracted to me because I am boring?" Leo didn't know if he had ever teased a woman in his life, but it suddenly came naturally.

Mattie's fingers now grazed his wrist. Her eyes blazed with golden fire. "Because you're solid, Leo. Sensible. Sometimes I chafe when you try to stop me from doing a stunt, but there is an unwavering strength in you that I cannot deny. We complement each other, like two opposite ends of a magnet. I just don't know why it took me so long to notice the pull."

Because he'd been fighting it for the both of them.

"It came to me in a brilliant flash tonight," Mattie continued, "but I think part of me has been thinking about us since we built the sandcastle."

He shifted his palm until it pressed against hers. Their fingers closed around each other's hand, tight and firm. Her thumb danced along his flesh.

"You were right before." Mattie paused her caress as she spoke the words.

Leo froze, sharp little shards of pain like shrapnel ripping through him. "I was?" Did she know how he'd struggled against his feelings for her? Was she changing her mind about blazing forward with her newly discovered attraction for him? He should be reassured she was being uncharacteristically wary, especially when he'd lost his own caution . . . but he wasn't relieved. Quite the opposite.

"Let's blouse." Mattie winked at him, indicating they should leave the speakeasy. "I've always wondered what a beach looks like in moonlight."

What she was offering was probably the most dangerous challenge Leo had ever faced. But with her hand snug against his, he didn't balk . . . he *couldn't* balk. In fact, he felt a glimmer of fresh excitement, a light, buoyant, springy feeling that he hadn't experienced since his first days in the skies.

"I'll ask John if we can take his Ford." Leo stood up. He almost bent over their still-joined hands and pressed a kiss against her knuckles. But he wasn't a knight or even a military man anymore. And sweeping emotive gestures weren't him.

So instead, he just gave her a light squeeze before letting go. And she smiled. Warm. Bright. And entirely Mattie.

He'd just stepped back from the table when Vera appeared from the middle of the crowd, glass in one hand. This time her cocktail was a frothy green substance, unlike her normal drinks, which tended toward pinker hues.

"Is this where you two have secreted yourselves? Why, you can't even hear the band from here! It's a shame there's so much noise tonight. They're really the bee's knees."

"Actually, Vera," Mattie said as she slid from her chair, "Leo and I were just thinking about finding John and seeing if we could borrow his car. We're a bit tired and thought we'd call it a night."

"You were?" Vera asked in surprise and then glanced between them. Suddenly, she blinked her violet-blue eyes. "Oooh." She paused as a knowing gleam leaped into her gaze. "Oooooooh."

Mattie didn't try to dissuade the heiress. Instead, she smiled smugly and boldly reached for Leo's hand. Leo knew he blushed. He was afraid that even his neck colored, but he didn't avoid the symbolic declaration. In fact, he felt warmed that Mattie was so openly announcing that she'd chosen him.

"Finally!" Vera clapped her hands before reaching into her white-sequin-and-pearl clutch and withdrew a calling card. "I hardly use these anymore, but I keep them for occasions just like this."

"Are you writing us a congratulatory greeting?" Mattie arched one of her auburn eyebrows as Vera began to scribble a missive on the back of the scrap of paper.

"Heavens no. I'm not *that* eccentric." Vera laughed. "What I am doing is letting the hotel know that you can have my Duesenberg. I'm not fit to drive back tonight, and you might as well travel home in style. It will be so much more romantic to ride under the stars rather than beneath the roof of John's old Model T."

With a flourish, she handed the perfumed cardstock to Mattie. Leaning close to her, Vera spoke in a lower voice that still managed to carry to Leo's ears, too, despite the noise buffeting them. "Have fun, and don't take things too seriously. That is the quickest way to ruin a delightful affair." Then, stepping back, she cried to both of them, "Enjoy the Duesy, darlings!" before disappearing into the crowd.

"I enjoy having a wealthy chum." Mattie smiled impishly up at Leo. He wanted to kiss her then and press his lips against the wide mouth that had fascinated him for years. But he'd waited this long, and he certainly wasn't going to have their first embrace in a speakeasy that reeked of bootlegged booze, imported cigars, and cheap cigarettes.

"Being friends with Vera has its perks," Leo admitted, although he wondered a little about her cavalier approach to romance. But then, unlike the heiress, he rarely did anything lightly.

"Who's going to drive?" Mattie asked.

"How is that even a question? Obviously you." Leo chuckled as he gently rested his arm on Mattie's shoulders, something he'd imagined doing more times than he could ever count. He'd underestimated how *good* it would feel. His hand brushed against the soft skin of her upper arm. He'd never felt something so smooth and inviting.

"You don't mind giving me the wheel, then?" she asked as they left the establishment together and started picking their way through the warehouse.

"As long as you don't break our necks."

She smiled at him. "I can manage that."

Mattie reached up and laid her hand over his as they stepped into the street. A city with its narrow alleys, glaring streetlights, and pungent odors had never seemed so beautiful to Leo or filled with such potential.

"I like this." Mattie tipped her head up at him, her skin somehow still glowing despite the unforgiving glare of the artificial lights. She had the amazing ability to take any harshness and transform it into softness.

"What?" Leo asked, leaning his head closer to hers as they walked along. A motorcar or two passed, but otherwise it was quiet, peaceful even.

"Us getting along. Not fighting. Walking together. *Working* together."

"I like it too." More than anything. He traced his fingers over her skin. She shivered despite the humid night air. His touch had done that. Inspired the pleasure. And he wanted to give Mattie more. He wanted to give her everything.

"I feel so wonderfully alive—so energized!" Mattie snuggled her body against his. "I never thought mere emotions could do this. Did you?"

They'd rounded the corner now, and Leo could see the brilliant lights of the hotel's marquee, big and bold as it declared the establishment's presence to the world. It, like the woman in his arms, shrank from nothing.

"Yeah," Leo admitted. "I did."

"How—" Mattie began to ask, but he was spared from answering by the doorman, who snapped to attention at the sight of them. The older gentleman clearly recognized Leo and her as Miss Jones's friends. With the efficiency of a butler on an old English estate, he arranged for one of the bellhops to pick up the Duesy. The exchange, blessedly, had distracted Mattie, but it hadn't Leo.

He knew the powerful effect of emotions because he'd battled them for so long. Unlike Mattie, he didn't have many feelings bouncing inside him. He didn't often have little spurts of joy or whispers of affection. He couldn't find inanimate objects cute like she did, and he'd never sobbed over a sad picture show, although he'd watched her bawl during *Something to Think About*. But on the rare occasion when Leo did feel, it roared through him.

The sleek Duesenberg pulled up to the curb, and the bellhop jumped out. Mattie slid into the driver's seat. After stripping off the white gloves she'd borrowed from Vera, she caressed the steering wheel and emitted a little breathy sigh. Leo hadn't thought he had any space left in him to burn, but clearly, he did.

He wanted her hands on him like that, her lips parted in the pleasure he'd given her. Drawing in air, he quickly pulled open the passenger door and sat down in his seat, glad that the style of men's trousers had grown roomier in recent years.

Mattie pressed on the accelerator, and they sped off. At this time in the evening, traffic in Chicago was thinner but still thick enough that Mattie couldn't race the machine. They didn't talk as the Duesy rumbled through the city lit by streetlamps and the glow from apartments, hotels, restaurants, and clubs. It was as if they'd agreed to take this time for each of them to adjust to the monumental change.

When they reached the open road and the moon provided the only illumination other than the automobile's headlamps, Mattie reached for his hand once again. It felt so natural, weaving his fingers through hers, yet Leo had never done this before. Not with Mattie. Not with anybody.

He liked it . . . but that didn't mean it was necessarily safe.

"Shouldn't you have two hands on the wheel?" Leo asked as casually as he could. He really should have released her, but he couldn't. Not yet.

She shot him a quick look before returning her eyes to the hard-packed dirt road. "How about a compromise? I won't increase my speed, and we keep touching each other."

She was driving at a sensible pace, so Leo settled back in the leather-upholstered seat. The evening air gently buffeted his face, a cool contrast to the orange-colored inferno still raging inside him.

"What are you thinking about?" Mattie asked.

"You," he admitted. It was surprisingly easy to confess his internal thoughts. After all the years he'd kept them hidden, he would have thought he would face some sort of barrier. But they just seemed to flow, and not even in some released-dam sort of way.

Mattie smiled in the moonlight, the air ruffling her short curls. Her hair looked like dark shadows, but he didn't need the sun to show him that her locks glowed with fiery redness.

"I like that," Mattie said, and even her words sounded like a grin.

"Me thinking of you?" He rubbed his thumb against her palm, drawing circles on it with slow precision.

"Yep. It makes me feel all gooey inside, like a melted caramel."

He barked out one of his rare bursts of laughter at her turn of phrase. "I'm glad, because I'm planning on doing plenty of it."

"Thinking of me?" Mattie asked, her voice rising almost girlishly at the end. He liked hearing the giddiness, knowing he'd caused it.

"Constantly."

"I'm going to be a giant puddle all the time, aren't I?" The wind caught Mattie's happy laughter, carrying the lilting melody into the night.

"Maybe." Leo's voice had taken on a flirtatious tone that even he didn't recognize. He didn't know when he'd last felt this carefree—maybe never. "You'll get used to it."

"I suppose so . . . ," Mattie said airily before she trailed off. Suddenly, she whirled in his direction. Her eyes glittered in the silvery light, the myriad of color lost in the darkness but not the intensity. "Wait! Do *I* make you a puddle?"

He hesitated. Should he reveal this weakness to her? Should he confess how much power she wielded over him, had *always* wielded over him?

His momentary pause evidently confirmed her suspicions.

"I do. I do!" She paused and then added suspiciously, "How exactly are you a puddle when you're constantly arguing with me?"

"Hard-coated exterior," Leo admitted.

"You know I'm going to keep on penetrating it." Mattie quickly sent him one of her cockiest grins.

"That's exactly what I'm afraid of," he said dryly.

They fell into another silence, this one a happy, contented one. It reminded Leo of the days before the war when he, Alfred, and Mattie would lie on their backs for hours, watching the clouds and talking about flying. Well, talking and listening. Mattie and Alfred had done most of the chatting and he the contemplating. But tonight, it was just the two of them, and they were both enjoying the quiet.

About ten minutes later, they arrived at Vera's castle. Somehow, even bathed in moonlight, it looked fairy tale–like instead of foreboding. Leo still couldn't believe he was living in such whimsy. Climbing out of the Duesenberg, he stared up at the spires stabbing the star-studded sky. Mattie snagged his fingers once more.

"Come on." She gave a tug as she slipped off her high heels with her other hand. "We have a beach to explore."

They ran like carefree schoolchildren. The full moon provided ample light, but they still slowed when they reached the edge of the bluff. Although it wasn't a sharp cliff, the trail was still steep enough that they couldn't barrel down it. As soon as they had picked their way to the bottom, Mattie turned toward him and smiled. "Shoes off, Mister!"

"Is it a requirement?" Leo laughed.

"At beaches? It sort of is. Don't you want to feel the sand between your toes again? It's soft and sinky."

"Sinky?" Leo repeated with a chuckle.

"You know what I mean."

Still holding on to her, he untied his shoes. It was a little more difficult for him to remove his oxfords than it had been for Mattie to undo the buckle on her pumps, but he was managing without too much undignified hopping.

"You know, it would be easier to do that with two hands," Mattie observed, but Leo noticed she made no move to release him.

"I'm not ready to let go of you just yet." Now that he was finally touching her, he had no idea how he'd had the strength to keep his distance all these years.

Her fingers squeezed his. "To tell the truth, I'm not either."

Emotion gushed through Leo, rushing into every hollow, every deep, chiseled place that he'd never hoped to fill. At last, his second shoe popped off. Leaving it in the sand beside its mate, he pulled off his socks and then straightened. Mattie's light laughter mixed with his deeper, rustier chuckle, and together they dashed along the sandy stretch. The water lapped lazily against the shore, the sound rhythmic and soothing. Pearly light danced along the surface, giving a pleasant, magical glow.

Mattie suddenly skidded to a stop, her neck craned upward. "Isn't the sky beautiful tonight?"

She grabbed Leo's other hand and twirled them in a mad circle, her chin pointed toward the heavens. He, however, watched her face and the wondrous emotions that flitted across it.

"Yes, it is," he said.

"The stars are a bit overshadowed by the moon, but altogether it is breathtaking. Don't you just want to jump into our Jennies and dance among the constellations?"

"Night flying is dangerous," Leo pointed out, thinking of how Alfred had gotten so twisted during his final battle as the twilight had crept in upon them. "It's easy to get disoriented and lose your way, and you can't see to land."

"It's what happened to Alfred." Mattie echoed his thoughts as she stopped their mad whirl. "If only there had been some way for him to know where he was headed."

"During the war," he admitted, "I volunteered to perform reconnaissance months after Alfred's death. It was near the end of the fighting, and a group of doughboys were pinned down under heavy fire. Headquarters wanted to make sure that more German troops weren't being sent to wipe them out."

"I didn't know that," Mattie said softly.

"By then, I'd grown to be calm in the air—maybe preternaturally so. But it was unnerving being up there in the darkness with nothing to guide you, no landmarks below, your maps useless. Any signal, any hint of my direction other than my less-than-reliable compass would have helped."

"But you never thought about turning back, did you?" Mattie asked.

"Our boys on the ground needed me. I wouldn't abandon my mission until I had the information. I was never so glad, though, as I was when I saw the spotlights from my own aerodrome."

"Home," Mattie said softly, as if she understood, but then Mattie had always seen his inner thoughts so easily. That is, all the ones except his affection for her.

Leo cleared his throat, the old memories pressing down on him, deflating his elation. He'd never spoken much about the war, not even to Mattie's brothers nor to other fellow veterans. He supposed it was like any other part of his past. Something he either swept away or hid deep inside.

Yet here with Mattie, on this magical stretch of beach, he found himself able to talk.

"Sometimes when a pilot didn't return after dusk, we would shoot Very lights into the sky. They would burst in the air, sort of like fireworks or shooting stars. We were all trying to bring lost aviators home, as if those little streaks of brilliance would somehow produce a miracle."

"I can see why you don't want to go night flying," Mattie said softly.

"Mattie, you don't have to go sailing off into the stars to find excitement." He stood before her, their hands still clasped in each other's from their wild spin. Instead of turning their bodies again, Leo gently pulled Mattie close. She could break his grip at any time and stop her forward momentum, but she didn't.

"Exactly what adventure are you proposing?" Mattie asked impishly, clearly taking his cue to change the mood back to lighthearted. She collided gently with his chest, her chin now tilted up at him instead of the firmament.

"I'm thinking that the best way to soar without ever leaving the ground is to do this . . ." He dipped his head and pressed his mouth against hers. Having lived as a nomad most of his life, he hadn't had too much experience in the kissing department. He figured Mattie really hadn't either. But it didn't matter. Their lips might have slid over each other's a little awkwardly at first, but his heart still pounded from the thrill of it all.

He hadn't felt this alive, this *good*, since before the war. It was like flying for the first time, only better because he was still grounded. There was a rightness at the core of this, a marvelous, wonderful steadiness in all the swirling madness.

Mattie's lips felt soft and cool, and the gentle friction triggered glorious sparks. Mattie's body sank against his. They didn't have too much difference in height, and he loved that fact. Loved how they fit together so neatly, her softness against his hardness. Yet she possessed undeniable strength too. Her arms were strong against the back of his neck. He could feel her muscles, earned from years of fixing engines and hauling parts. This was his Mattie, unique and utterly perfect for him.

His hand touched her curls, and he marveled at their smooth, soft resilience as they bounced back into shape as soon as his fingers brushed over them. They didn't feel like fire, but they affected him just the same. Warm heat zinged through him, like a thousand incendiary bullets finding their marks. He made a sound, a low groan that seemed to reverberate through him. Mattie rewarded him with a little moan of her own. Her fingers dug into his shoulders, the pressure echoing his own tumbling need.

Leo's lips moved from her mouth, exploring her cheeks. If it had been daylight, he might have taken the time to kiss each individual freckle. But he swore he knew where most of them were from memory. She shuddered in his arms, her breaths growing shorter and shorter. The sound galvanized him. He traced his lips over her temple and then drew them over her jaw. She uttered another marvelous sound as she allowed him to explore.

Then she lifted her head. The silvery strands of moonlight illuminated her pale skin. He recognized her expression instantly—the thrill and utter glee. Mattie looked this way when she whipped her Jenny through the sky, letting the machine swoop and dance more gracefully than a majestic hawk. Her lips pressed against his mouth with the same focus and passion she exhibited in the cockpit. He felt like he did when in free fall, spinning, whirling, his mind utterly dazed. But for once he didn't worry about the landing.

He just let himself feel, giving himself over to Mattie and her wild joy.

⁂

Mattie had never thought she could soar on the ground.

She'd been wrong.

Her body felt like it did during takeoff. Primed. Ready. Energized.

It fascinated her how many sensations Leo could evoke. She had stolen kisses from boys before, meaningless moments, all but forgotten. An embrace had never felt like *this*. Monumental. Marvelous. And above all *memorable*.

It wasn't that Leo was a Casanova. Mattie had been embraced by men with more finesse, more practice. They'd been smooth talkers who'd pictured themselves as suave Valentinos. But their slick kisses had never inspired her, let alone devastated her.

Not like Leo's.

She'd heard the expression of knees growing weak. She'd always dismissed it as overromanticized ridiculousness. Even if it were true, she'd had no desire to feel *swoony*, especially over something so silly as a mere embrace.

But her legs *did* feel very much like a newfangled Jell-O salad, all wobbly and unsteady. But somehow, despite currently having gelatin for joints, she wouldn't have called herself *weak*, not with all this amazing power rippling through her.

Mattie ran her fingers down Leo's back, freely exploring his body with her hands as she plumbed the depths of his mouth with her tongue. Even with his dinner jacket and cotton shirt, she could feel the ridges of his muscles as they stretched and bunched the fabric. Leo had never shied away from manual labor. Even with Vera employing several mechanics to maintain their planes, he still did more than just tinker with the engines. He was always hoisting the heavy parts, always in the middle of any major repair. That work had shaped his entire body into something glorious.

Mattie was a woman who marveled over machines instead of men. But something about Leo fascinated her even more than Vera's sleek cherry-red Duesenberg. Yet it made sense. After all, he had the same strength and steadiness as one of those finely crafted mechanical masterpieces.

Leo's lips left hers again, making those naughty, delicious patterns over her skin. He smelled slightly of engine oil, like he always did. Although it wasn't the world's most pleasant aroma, it was a solid one, like him, and Mattie had always associated the scent with flying.

Sounds emerged from Mattie, low and throaty. She'd never thought she would ever make such needy moans, but they felt right. Even better, they seemed to encourage Leo to do more wonderful things with his mouth. He gently sucked the skin between the crook of her neck and her shoulder, and glorious shivers danced through her until she positively reverberated.

Just then the sky lit up. Mattie thought at first it was her imagination, but a bright light filled the atmosphere, causing the lake to glow. She and Leo pulled apart, breathless, as they stared at the horizon. Suddenly, another burst of energy illuminated the water.

"Heat lightning." Leo's voice sounded ragged, and its coarseness caused Mattie to shiver.

"I firmly believe we caused that."

He chuckled as he drew her close. "I don't think that's scientifically accurate, but I like the explanation."

Mattie leaned her head against his shoulder as they watched another flare in the distance far across the lake. "You act pragmatic, but I think you might be hiding a romantic side. After all, you're the one who wanted to make a sand château instead of a fortress."

She could feel the curve of Leo's lips against her forehead, and the intimacy thrilled Mattie. He didn't argue, but he didn't agree either. Instead, he just sucked in a deep breath and pulled her even more tightly against him.

"Do you think it is still there?" Mattie asked.

"The sandcastle we built?"

She nodded. It had been several weeks, so she doubted it. But they had built it far from the water and on private land. And Lake Michigan, as huge and mighty as it was, was not the ocean with its thundering, demanding tides. But there had been rainfall and wind. Still, Mattie liked the notion of it standing in defiance to the odds.

"It's mostly gone," Leo said, "but there's still a bit of a raised mound."

Mattie shifted so she could get a better look at him. He kept his eyes trained ahead, and in the low light, she couldn't tell if he was blushing. Curiously, she pressed her fingertips against his strong cheekbone. Yup, his skin definitely felt overly warm.

He shrugged a little helplessly. "It happens to be on my flight path when I'm out practicing alone."

"You've been checking up on it!" Mattie was delighted by the thought. Leave it to Leo to be so secretly sweet.

"Maybe," he admitted and then glanced at her. "Or maybe not."

He had been, no question. But Mattie didn't push him. Instead, she tugged on his arm.

"Let's go rebuild it."

"The castle? But it's dark," Leo protested, digging his heels in slightly.

"Come on. It will be fun." She pulled a little harder.

"How would we even find it?" But he gave in and allowed her to guide him farther down the shore.

"Because I bet you know exactly where it is," Mattie said.

"And why would you think that?" he asked.

"Alfred always said you had the instincts of a homing pigeon."

He barked out a surprised laugh. "You certainly know how to flatter a man, comparing him to a pigeon."

"Well, they might not be the most noble of birds, but it is certainly a useful trait."

Leo turned, walking backward so he could face her, their fingers now laced. "Is this more about me being a steady sort of a fellow?"

Mattie leaned forward and pretended to knock on his bicep. "Yup. Rock solid, I tell you. Rock solid."

He stopped short. She could have done the same, but she chose to crash gently into his chest. His arms swept around her as he dipped her. The gesture made her so giddy that she gave an uncharacteristic giggle.

His warm mouth closed over her laughing one. Mattie gasped at the intense jolt of pleasure that surged through her. His strong hand cradled her spine, supporting her as her knees turned into gelatin again. Sensations like iridescent sparks from a roman candle cascaded through her. Her whole being seemed to tingle as his lips brushed against hers.

When Leo finally gave her a moment to breathe, she beamed up at him. "I take it you liked that description."

He tucked his chin in slightly, the gesture at once shy and adorable. "Yes, and, well, we're here."

"Here?"

Leo jerked his head in the direction of a small heap of sand. Tiny mounds rose a little taller than the rest where their turrets had stood. Bits of driftwood and other pieces she'd used for decoration littered the ground.

"Our château!"

"What remains of it, at least."

Mattie laughed and leaned against Leo's arm, squeezing it against her. "It's amazing how there can be something right in front of us, and we don't notice."

Leo's voice was gruff. "I always saw you."

She lifted her lips to his, and when their mouths touched, she swore her body fairly buzzed with electricity at the connection. When they pulled apart, she reached up and cupped his dear face—familiar yet suddenly new. "I don't know how I could have overlooked such powerful currents."

"Interference?" Leo suggested, his voice light again. She'd never heard him sound so . . . so bright as he did this evening.

"Maybe," Mattie said, but she didn't want to think right now of all the old pain between them. Instead, she walked them over to what was left of their castle's foundation. Bending down, she started scooping sand, and he quickly joined her in the rebuilding.

"Perhaps it is more like a radio signal." Mattie started mounding more material onto an old, mostly worn-down tower.

"In what way?" Leo asked, pausing to look up from the main section of their château.

"In the way that a loop antenna doesn't pick up a signal when it is pointing directly toward the source."

Leo chuckled. "I love how your mind works, Mattie. Only you can go from kissing and building a sandcastle to talking about—"

Mattie gripped Leo's shoulders as an idea bolted through her. "That's it, Leo! That's it!"

"What's *it*?" Leo asked, his voice confused but reflecting her excitement.

"How I can use radio to improve navigation!" Mattie planted an emphatic kiss on Leo's cheek. Their talk of night flying and of radios had mixed in her brain to produce a most glorious, wonderful solution. "You know how the government just began parceling out specific frequencies to different radio stations so they don't have to share just one?"

"Yeah," Leo said. "The switchover just happened in the last two months."

Mattie nodded, making sure not to break eye contact with Leo in her utter excitement. "That means if you program a radio on the airplane to a public radio station . . ."

Leo cupped her elbows as understanding flashed across his moonlit face. "Then you know your antenna is pointing directly toward or away from that city when the radio goes silent."

"Precisely, and it's reliable data. More accurate than a compass."

Leo sank down in the sand. "That's brilliant, Mattie!"

"Sadie told me to start simple. To think about the existing technology. I won't need to create anything new for this to work."

"Are you considering using two or more radio stations to triangulate the point?" Leo asked.

Mattie shook her head. "That would work with a navigator on board, but it would be too hard for a single person to do while flying a plane. It's not just the math but fiddling with the radio itself."

Leo pushed more sand toward the center of their structure. "It always takes me several attempts to tune in to a station."

"The best method would be if the aviator could adjust the radio before takeoff." Mattie paused in her selection of shells to consider this.

"You wouldn't be able to determine an exact location with just one point," Leo said.

"No." Mattie tapped two smooth pebbles together. "But it *could* indicate the right bearing."

"Well, when the radio went silent, you'd know if you were winging straight toward the station or straight away from it but not much more than that." Leo eased back on his haunches as he considered it.

"Not if I connected it to some sort of a light system on the console." Mattie clicked the rocks faster and faster as her mind churned through idea after idea.

"An indicator?" Leo asked.

"Exactly." Mattie rubbed a stone between each thumb and forefinger. Then she dropped them and launched herself at Leo for a second time. Wrapping her arms around his neck, she gazed up at him. "It may have taken me weeks, but I did it! I finally figured it out!"

"No shock there." Leo's grin was surprisingly easy as his white teeth flashed in the pale light. "You always do."

"The antenna could rotate slowly, and a light could flash on for the duration of radio silence as the antenna is pointed directly at the source of the signal. I could set up twelve lights to reflect the bearing. Twelve o'clock, one o'clock, two o'clock . . . general directions, just like you fighter pilots love. Then, every rotation, pilots could see the direction of the radio station relative to the heading of the aircraft. Before they took off, the pilots could map out their course and calculate the bearings and time intervals so they could double-check to make sure they were on track."

"And since we do that anyway, it is no added work. It will just be more reliable and precise. Pilots won't get lost trying to find a city through darkness or under a cloud or while trying to figure out which town the blob of light ahead of them actually *is*," Leo said with uncharacteristic excitement. "Mattie, you're a genius!"

He kissed her then, and she tasted his jubilant celebration of her success, his thrill for *her*. It was intoxicating, his support for her. But even as they stood there in the shadow of a fairy-tale castle, a part of her wondered how long this euphoria would last. She'd trusted Leo before, cared deeply for him as a friend all those years ago, but it had all gone sideways once before. When she'd needed his faith in her the most, needed *him* the most, he'd not only withdrawn from her, but he'd betrayed her flight plans to her brothers on the eve of Alfred's memorial service.

Chapter Twelve

> A hero both in the air and on the ground, Mr. Leo Ward, the Flying Lion, defended his lady love's honor at a local Chicago club. Witnesses say that he pitched another man into a nearby table while shielding Miss Mattie McAdams. It is rumored that another ace from the Great War, Earl "Quick" Crenshaw, was fighting in the opposing group and was at one point unmanned. It is unknown what could have caused the bad blood between the two former squadron comrades.
>
> —Harvey Weston, *Lake Michigan Times*

"I wish I had better news to report," Jake said, his voice uncharacteristically soft.

Mattie squeezed her eyes shut, as if she could will her older brother's next words away. It didn't work.

"I mentioned that I had a sister who was coming up with some brilliant use of radio to help with navigation." Jake spoke slower than usual, as if he was picking out each word in an attempt to soften his message.

"And?" Mattie asked. She dug her nails into the palm of her free hand. "Don't mince words. It's easier if I know the truth."

"You want me to tell you exactly what my bosses at the Airmail Service said?" Jake asked skeptically.

Mattie swallowed. Most of her didn't, but she needed to understand what she would be fighting against in order to sell and profit from her idea. "Yes."

"Let me just say that I don't agree with their reaction," Jake hedged.

This time Mattie clenched her teeth. "I know you're trying to sugar-coat what they said to protect me, but you're only making it worse by dragging it out."

"They didn't take it seriously, Mattie—at least they didn't when I mentioned it was my sister who came up with the idea. I don't think the newspaper articles about the Flying Flappers have helped either." Jake spoke so fast now Mattie was surprised his tongue wasn't as tangled as her guts currently were.

"What were their precise words?" Mattie asked, even though she dreaded the response. The fact it involved the horrible articles about Vera's circus only made it worse. She needed to know the truth, though. Needed her brother to stop mollycoddling her. Needed to face the height and breadth of the obstacles before her.

"That, um, dames can't even tune a radio to save their lives, so there's no way a doll could come up with a useful application involving the actual signal. Also there was some ribbing that my sister should stick to dressing up watermelons and toy dogs and stop trying to play with things best left to a man."

"That's absurd!" Mattie burst out as ire blazed through her. Furiously, she beat the sole of her shoe against the marble floor of Vera's entrance hall and wished it were a certain reporter and his drunken friend instead. "I'm the one in the family who knows the most about radio!"

"I know that, Mattie." Jake sighed, and she could just imagine him rubbing his forehead. "But they don't, and I can't convince them otherwise."

"What if I had a functioning prototype? Would that convince them?" Mattie's heart contracted almost painfully in anticipation. She'd planned to start building a working model this afternoon. Carrie was even bringing Mattie parts from Chicago today.

"Maybe?" Jake drew out the word dubiously. "But it would have to work perfectly. And even then, I don't want to get your hopes up."

"If I were a man, they'd be interested, wouldn't they?" Mattie asked.

Jake sighed. "More so, but they'd still be skeptical, Mattie. It's a new way of doing things."

"You'd think aviators would be more open to change!" Mattie grabbed the entire candlestick telephone and marched as far as the cord allowed her, and then circled back. "After all, flying itself was considered impossible less than twenty years ago."

"I agree, Mattie. But you know how things are. I wish I could tell you something different, but you wanted the truth."

She had. And it was a fact she'd faced all too often. As much as a shiny, new future beckoned, the past always reached out to hold her back.

"What are we going to do about the flight school?" She felt like she had to press the question through a sieve, it was so hard to get out.

"Pa, Otto, Will, Leo, and I will figure it out, Mattie. We'll make sure you're provided for, no matter what."

"Why is it that we *all* are in financial trouble, but *I'm* the one who needs saving?" Mattie asked.

"You're our little sister, Mattie. We're always going to watch out for you," Jake said, his tone matter of fact and eminently reasonable, as if his perspective were the only possible way of looking at things.

"Maybe I also take care of the family," Mattie shot back, not exactly wanting to get in an argument on top of her current disappointment. But she was also *not* going to allow Jake's statement to pass unchallenged.

"Of course you're important to us, Mattie." Jake misunderstood the extent of what she meant, seeing it only in domestic terms. "That's why you need to be careful. Let Leo look after you when we can't, and stop going to speakeasies."

Of course he'd think Leo was more capable of protecting her than she was herself.

"You do realize that the article in the *Lake Michigan Times* failed to mention that *I* was the one who unmanned Crenshaw."

Jake sounded not impressed but exasperated. "Then also stop punching former scout pilots."

"I didn't slug him. I kneed him in the groin."

That got a good chuckle out of Jake at least. "Of course you did."

"He had it coming."

Jake sobered. "I'm sure he did, Mattie, and that's why we worry about you. You're our heart, little sis, especially now. Don't forget that. Don't try anything crazy in an attempt to earn more cash. You just stay safe."

With that parting advice, Jake hung up, but Mattie didn't.

She spoke into the disconnected line the words she so desperately wanted her brother to understand. "I don't want to just be the heart of our family. I want to be part of its strength too."

Suddenly, a great weariness rushed through her as she gently replaced the earpiece. *"But you know how things are."* Jake's statement seemed to embody the inertia dragging her down. She was so, so tired of fighting against what everyone perceived as irrefutable.

"Oh good, you're here!" Carrie's cheerful voice broke through Mattie's glumness. "I was afraid I'd have to go searching through this giant house."

Mattie turned to find her friend pushing open one of the massive front doors with her shoulder, her hands full of packages. Mattie immediately started forward to help, but a male servant materialized to hold open the door.

"May I assist you with your packages, ma'am?" the young man asked politely as Carrie bustled inside. Although he was in his early twenties, the smattering of freckles across his pale cheeks and nose made him look like an adolescent. Despite his youth, he was as prompt and courteous as the rest of Vera's well-trained staff.

"That would be exceedingly helpful," Carrie said as she handed over the parcels. "We're heading directly to the basement workshop. I *know* I can't wait to start tinkering!"

Carrie directed the last statement at Mattie with a broad smile that Mattie just couldn't return in equal force. With what she feared was a rather poor facsimile of one, she asked, "How are your parents?"

"Wonderful." Carrie linked her arm with Mattie's. "It's always great to see them, and I'm glad I squeezed in a visit before the Flying Flappers take off on our western tour. Dad was especially excited when I told him about the power generator at Fete Castle. He is extremely curious about all the radio equipment I asked him to purchase, but don't worry. I didn't spill the beans, even though I generally tell my parents everything."

"Thanks," Mattie said, and despite her melancholy, she meant it. It was odd, working with others on this project. But Sadie had helped direct her thoughts, and Carrie, who'd grown up working in her father's bicycle enterprise, could use a lathe better than Mattie. And she would rather rely on these women, who had stood up for her in the speakeasy, than on one of the various machinists that Vera employed to maintain her vehicles and the estate's equipment.

"I normally like flying better than I do working in the back of a shop," Carrie said as they wound down the stairs to the lower level, "but I can't wait to get started on this project of yours. It is brilliant in its elegant simplicity."

"You can thank Sadie for that. My original plans were much, much more complicated until she gave me advice to try a more straightforward approach." Mattie really wanted to confide her latest conversation with her brother to Carrie, but not when the servant carrying the packages was still within earshot. It was a discussion that required privacy.

"We'll have to let Sadie know that I've returned. She'll want to join us."

"Of course," Mattie said, although she wasn't completely sure if she wanted to start the project immediately. Maybe she should beg off and go flying instead.

Carrie shot her a questioning look, clearly realizing something wasn't quite right. She didn't say anything, though. Instead she switched the conversation back to her parents. "My mother was fascinated by the business end of the Flying Flappers. She does my dad's books and handles the customers, and she has no idea how Vera intends to make a profit."

"I don't think she expects to actually earn money," Mattie said, trying not to sound too absent.

"Oh, it's clear she doesn't." Carrie waved her hand. "That is what really fascinated my mother."

"I'm just thankful for the opportunity to be part of the Flying Flappers." After all, Mattie's generous salary might be the only way for her to contribute to saving the flight school, since it was looking doubtful that she'd be able to sell her invention.

"So am I," Carrie agreed as they finally reached the machine shop, which was tucked in next to the power station and the battery room. The servant left the collection of boxes on the well-worn worktable. It was past hours, so the maintenance staff had left for the day. Mattie appreciated not having to fight over work space . . . or endure the half-amused, half-displeased eyes of the machinists.

After Carrie had given the young fellow instructions to let Sadie know they were about to begin work, the servant left. As soon as he softly shut the door behind him, Carrie turned in Mattie's direction, her expression no nonsense.

"What's eating at you, Mattie?" Carrie asked. "I thought you'd be tearing into the parcels by now."

Mattie sighed and scrubbed her face. "I had a discouraging phone call with my oldest brother."

Frowning, Carrie leaned her back against the wooden workbench and folded her arms over her chest. "He's the one who's a mechanic for the US Airmail Service?"

"Yup." Mattie kicked a little at the basement floor in frustration. "He was supposed to be testing the reaction of his bosses to a new means of navigation."

"And they're not taking too kindly to the notion?" Understanding threaded through Carrie's voice.

"Not when they found out who is coming up with the idea." Mattie scuffed the back of her heel, feeling trapped, as she so often did. Living at Vera's had been freeing—a mad whirl of adventure in a fairy-tale world where women soared—but reality had returned, harsh and unyielding.

"Do you know what the greatest lesson my parents taught me was?" Carrie asked, and when Mattie shook her head, she continued. "That each time someone says *no*, you just have to tell yourself *yes* and keep repeating it until you believe it body and soul."

"And you and your parents have wrongly been told *no* a lot," Mattie said, thinking of all the places that displayed signs forbidding entrance to Black folks or how in the South it was common to have different train cars depending on the color of a person's skin, with the ones for whites invariably newer and more nicely appointed. The Supreme Court had come down with an unfair decision about "separate but equal," but nothing was equal or just about it.

"When my dad set out his shingle on the edge of where mostly white people shopped, everyone thought he was crazy except my mother. Committees full of 'good-hearted, civic-minded' crusaders tried time and again to force his business out, but he stayed on. He offered better products and better service than anybody else, and my mother is like Vera when it comes to advertising. My parents made a good life for themselves and for me, and they've built a solid enterprise, with Dad adding new products like radios and now starting to offer auto repair services. They still hear *no* all the time, but they haven't let it stop them."

"And there's you and Brave Bessie," Mattie said.

"If it weren't for my mentor leaving the racial prejudice in America and traveling to Europe to get her pilot's license, I probably would not have had the opportunity to obtain one myself. That's why you can't let a few men force you into thinking that you're defeated. What you have in mind isn't just a brilliant convenience. It can actually save lives. Don't let naysayers stop you from pursuing it."

"My twin brother died after flying deeper into German territory when he thought he was on his way back to our side of the lines during the war. His plane was badly damaged, and we don't think his compass was working properly." The words rushed out of Mattie, something she'd never said aloud to anyone apart from her family and Leo.

Carrie's entire face softened as she straightened from her leaning position. "Oh, Mattie, that's why you feel so strongly about making planes safer!"

"It was getting dark, and that probably contributed to him losing his way," Mattie admitted. "I know I can't save him, but my other brothers are flying mail routes, and they'll be going through all sorts of weather and facing poor visibility."

"Then you *have* to make this prototype," Carrie said. "For them. For yourself. For all of us. You don't need your brother's bosses to tell you it's a good or bad idea. You *know* it is a great one. I know it. Sadie knows it. And all of us Flying Flappers will cheer you on every step."

Mattie was so accustomed to pushing alone to make space for herself—it was amazing to have someone on her side, heaving against the obstacles with her. A renewed determination rushed through her, fierce and focused. This thrill was even better and definitely more durable than the one she got from flying. "I'll make a prototype to prove that my design will work, and I'll convince someone to buy it—be it the military, a manufacturer, or even the shortsighted airmail organizers."

Carrie turned and pushed the largest box in her direction. "That's the Mattie McAdams I've come to know. And you will have Vera's backing, and I don't mean just financially. Not to discount that she paid for our 'new toys,' but she can sell anything, including this idea of yours. And if she can't, there's always my mother."

Resolutely, Mattie cracked open the wooden crate. There, nestled inside the straw, was a beautiful vacuum-tube radio. Relatively small, sleek, and compact, it was, above all, tough and ready to face the rigors Mattie would put it through.

A sharp whistle drew Mattie's and Carrie's attention to the now-open door, where Sadie stood admiring the new equipment. "Well, isn't he a beaut!"

Mattie laughed. "I thought machines were usually referred to as *she*s."

"That's because it's mostly men doing the talking," Sadie pointed out. "Are you ready to start creating this antenna of yours?"

Carrie glanced at Mattie, her look questioning. Mattie nodded to indicate to the other aviatrix that she'd put all those worries behind her and that she was ready to soar.

"I'll work on the worm gear." Carrie headed over to the lathe and ran her eyes across it appreciatively. "Even Vera's machinery is ritzy. Many factories don't even have something of this quality."

"I'll throw together a wooden box to hold the motor and drivetrain that will spin the loop antenna." Mattie headed over to the scrap pile of wood to find suitable pieces. "I need to whack something anyway."

"Brother troubles again?" Sadie asked.

"Actually, this time Jake was mostly being supportive," Mattie admitted. "I'm just vexed at how we fly girls are always having to prove ourselves over and over again, whether inside the cockpit or outside of it."

"I understand that." Sadie headed over to the stores of wire. "I'll work on making the loop antenna."

As Mattie sawed and hammered away her lingering frustrations, she found a surprising peace underneath it all. She felt . . . comfortable, at home even, surrounded by these women who didn't let wood, metal, or radio waves intimidate them any more than they did the constraints of gravity.

Connection. It was something she'd been unconsciously searching for, especially after Alfred's death, and she wondered if she'd finally found it with both Leo and the Flying Flappers.

"Swanky place you're staying in."

Leo froze in the middle of the hotel lobby. He'd only heard the deep voice once before in his adult life, but he wasn't apt to forget it.

"I told you not to approach me again, Clive." Leo kept his voice cold and steady, his only weapon in this particular skirmish.

His father stepped from a dark corner, his overcoat tattered and worn. With all the dough showered on the bastard from Walt and Leo, he could have afforded better. Much better. But it appeared all the money was immediately transferred into liquid form and then literally pissed away.

"You haven't answered my letters." The ragged man didn't move any farther from the shadows, probably because the hotel staff would have booted him from the spiffy premises. But Clive was good at sneaking into places where he didn't belong.

"The well is dry. You've drained Mr. McAdams, and you've drained me."

A smile slipped across Clive's features. Hard living had cut deep grooves into his leathery skin, but he still maintained vestiges of handsomeness . . . and features that Leo recognized from the mirror. It wouldn't be hard for folks to see the relationship—something the cowardly snake used to his advantage.

"That rich Miss Jones must pay a pretty penny. She ain't too hard on the eyes either. Maybe you could persuade her to give you a little extra."

Leo spread his legs apart and stiffened his back. "I don't seduce women to get my way."

"Must not take after me, then." This time the man's grin showed a broken tooth.

Clive wasn't just shameless; he *reveled* in his lack of a moral code. And Mattie would be walking into this room in mere minutes.

Leo dug into his pocket and pulled out his billfold. He yanked out the money and thrust every buck in his old man's direction. "Here, take it. It's all I have right now."

Clive's fingers closed around the thin stack. "Mighty obliged."

Leo didn't respond.

His father tipped his battered cap. "Be seeing you around."

The bastard melted away, somehow making himself unobtrusive despite the contrast between his old-fashioned rags and the sleek minimalist interior of the Prairie School–style hotel, which was located between Iowa City and Cedar Rapids. Leo swallowed, suddenly yearning for a shower. A long one.

"Leo!"

The sound of Mattie's cheerful call sent twin bolts of pleasure and guilt through him. She walked as she always did, with a bounce in her step that he swore he could feel echoing in his heart. Vera had insisted on buying Mattie new cotton shirts and trousers. Tailored for the female form, no longer did her clothes hang loosely about her. The better-fitting clothes made her seem bolder than ever, and the sight of her looking so comfortable and confident made something inside him turn over.

When she reached him, her grin faltered. "What's wrong?"

Damn. He never could hide from her. But he wasn't ready to tell her this particular secret. Maybe he never would. He didn't know if that made his guilt worsen or lessen.

"Nothing," he lied. "You just caught me thinking. That's all."

She cocked her head as they moved toward the private room Vera had booked for all of them to use to try out Mattie's prototype for the first time. "Are you certain? It's not like before?"

He knew, without her saying more, that she was referring to his unease at bunking down in Vera's castle.

"It's getting better, especially since I'm with you. You've always had a way of setting me at ease, Mattie." He realized as he spoke the words how true they were. Already he was feeling less trapped by his old man.

Mattie led him to the private lounge. When they walked onto the balcony, she spread her arms wide, reminding Leo of an airplane about to lift off. "I'm glad this hotel isn't in the center of town but the edge. I've missed the country air. The sky is beautiful tonight."

Leo scanned the pink sky and fields of corn, alfalfa, and oats that seemed to stretch on forever in the rosy, gold-tinged glow. "It sure is."

"What do you smell?" Mattie asked. It had become kind of a game for them since the night in Vera's garden—Mattie pushing him to notice something about their surroundings. And playing it had become easier.

Leo sucked in his breath, too, and the smell of freshly cut alfalfa filled him. The sweet scent helped force away some of the lingering chill his father's unexpected appearance had caused. Instead light, almost frothy emotions tripped through Leo's heart. Being with Mattie felt like spring—an awakening of sorts with little buds of emotions unfurling.

"A farmer must have just harvested the field." Leo leaned next to Mattie, letting his shoulder brush against hers.

Her eyes looked as golden as the sun dipping below the horizon as she reached for him. Their lips met, wonderfully hungry and urgent. Emotion swelled through Leo, deep and sure. He drank in the sensation, letting the sense of happiness simply absorb into him and chase away the last remaining darkness that his father's visit had left.

They broke apart slowly, like two people emerging from deep, blissful slumber. Mattie's pink lips tipped upward. "I do like this new development in our relationship."

"So do I," he admitted.

"In the spirit of it, would you help me with my newest stunt? I've convinced Vera to let me soar through Sunset Rock Canyon before our show in Troy, Wyoming. I'll be flying just in time for the ten o'clock train. I wanted to know more about the topography so I can really stun my audience."

Leo's first instinct was to stiffen. He'd flown through the perilous, twisting gash in the rocks when the McAdams Family Flying Circus had performed in Troy. Mattie had always wanted to buzz through the gorge, too, but her brothers had always refused.

"To be that person, I also had to be willing to release her too." John Kunkle's words during the Flying Flappers' first performance in Platt, Michigan, flashed into Leo's head.

Leo swallowed. "Do you want me to help you time your stunts so they're most visible from the passenger cars?"

"I was hoping you'd offer." Mattie reached into her back trouser pocket and unfolded a well-worn United States Geological Survey map.

Leo bent over her shoulder and jabbed his finger at a bend in the canyon. "Right here the railroad tracks go through a tunnel. If you time it right, you can be in position so that your plane is the first thing that the rail passengers see when they reach the other side."

Mattie turned and kissed him. Rather enthusiastically.

"Good thing I rented the entire balcony and lounge for a private party!" Vera announced as she bounced into the room, holding Ruby.

Leo leaped from Mattie, his face burning. Even Mattie pinkened as she ignored Vera's observation.

"Why are you dressed in glad rags?" Mattie asked in an obvious attempt to change the subject. "You're not going out on the town, are you?"

"And miss the demonstration of your RadioNavigator? Heavens no. This is a celebration of your success, so I chose party clothes." Not only had Vera donned a blue-and-green dress with a beaded design of peacock feathers, but she wore a glittering headpiece of rhinestones.

"You did? For me?" Mattie's voice rose a little higher than normal.

"Of course, darling." Vera settled in a chair with Ruby on her lap. "I've even ordered the hotel's 'special tea' for us all to drink."

"But you don't know if it will even work. I've run a few tests, but . . ."

"It will," Vera said with the utmost confidence.

Just then the rest of the women arrived, their voices bright. When Mattie caught sight of their finery, she pressed her hand to her lips and emitted a happy sound. It was a feminine gesture, and Leo had noticed that Mattie had been making more and more of them since joining the Flying Flappers.

Just then, one of the men who helped maintain the planes and Vera's vehicles appeared, hefting several crates. Mattie's prototype.

Mattie, Carrie, and Sadie immediately jumped up and began assembling it. First, there was the circular antenna perched on its wooden gearbox. It was connected to a switch, which allowed the operator to choose between it and the radio's original whip antenna. From there, a wire led into the compact receiver in its sturdy wooden chassis. Sitting behind it all, with thicker wires joining everything together, was a bank of lead-acid batteries. But the true masterpiece was Mattie's circuit board with twelve light bulbs arranged in a circle, like numbers on a clock, that would indicate the general bearing.

"We're ready to start!" Mattie announced, her voice sounding just like it did during takeoff.

Nervousness fluttered through Mattie. Although she loved flying for an audience, she'd never demonstrated one of her designs to anyone except Leo and her family before.

Huffing out a breath, she found herself searching for Leo. He stood off to the side, letting her female friends crowd around her.

Pride for *her* suffused his features. Belief in her. Joy for her.

Drawing strength from Leo's conviction, she lifted both hands and said in a booming ringmaster-like voice, "Are you ready to witness the latest advance in air-travel safety?"

Sadie whooped loudly. Vera lifted her flask while the rest of the women clapped.

"Do we have the map ready to confirm that my bearings are correct?"

Lily lifted it into the air. "Sadie has put me in charge."

"Although she'd never admit it, my sister is actually a wizard when it comes to mathematics," Sadie said.

Lily? A mathematical genius? Really?

Lily rolled her eyes. "I thought you weren't going to tell them."

"Well, you have the map, don't you? They're all a rather intelligent lot. They're bound to figure it out," Sadie said.

Lily sighed. "I wish you would have just done it yourself. You're almost as quick as me."

Sadie walked over to her sister and slung her arm around her. "Lily, this isn't like what happened at the schoolhouse all those years ago when Rose Thomas and Willy Lewis made fun of you for being the teacher's pet. The Flying Flappers are going to love your ability to do complex problems in your head."

Mattie straightened. Could silly, fashion-obsessed, dramatic Lily Lenhart actually share a similar past with her? "How complex? Can you triangulate in your head?"

Lily shrugged almost helplessly, looking more girlish than movie-star glamorous at the moment. "Yes."

Carrie stared at her. "Do you realize how invaluable you would be as a navigator, especially during long night flights?"

"You don't think it a bit odd?" Lily chewed her lip.

A bolt of empathy crackled through Mattie. She'd always felt out of place in the classroom. If it hadn't been for Alfred, she didn't know if she would have had a single close friend. While Mattie had entrenched herself in her uniqueness, it appeared that Lily had done the opposite.

"I find it refreshing," Vera said. "You are quite the Renaissance woman, aren't you? Acting? Haircutting? Dancing? Barnstorming? Mathematical computation?"

"I believe *Renaissance man* is the only expression used," Lily said, and her normal brightness had started to creep back into her voice.

Vera could do that, Mattie realized. She had a way of bolstering people, making them feel stronger, more powerful.

"From a sociological standpoint, women, who are most often charged with childcare and domestic tasks, have always been challenged to handle multiple duties at one time. It is nonsense to assume that our minds aren't capable of the same degree of flexibility as a man's," Aida pointed out.

"Lily, I wish I had known about your mathematical ability," Mattie said as a twinge of remorse pricked her for mentally dismissing her fellow Flying Flapper. "I definitely would have strong-armed you into helping me figure out the light board. It would have saved me a lot of paper."

Lily's already round baby-blue eyes grew even larger as she swept her gaze around the room. Like an actress being showered with roses and applause, she clasped her hands to her bosom. "You are all so wonderful."

"As are you, Lily," Sadie said.

"Well, enough about me." Lily unfolded the map with a grand flourish. "This is Mattie's moment, along with Sadie's and Carrie's."

"This moment is for all of us," Mattie added, her prior nervousness replaced with a swell of love for these women. She turned to Sadie, who would be calling out the frequencies. "What radio station should I tune to?"

"940!"

Mattie fiddled with the radio until a man's voice crackled to life. "The Pittsburgh Pirates beat the Brooklyn Robins three to two in Ebbets Field in front of a crowd of fifteen thousand. In other sports news, American Bobby Jones won his first US Open at Inwood Country Club in New York, edging out Scotland's Bobby Cruickshank."

With the flick of a switch, the box containing the electric motor emitted a steady hum, and the loop antenna began to pirouette atop its casing with the slow grace of a music box ballerina.

Lily groaned. "It would be sports. I was all ready to start dancing."

"Don't underestimate the glory of going to a game and watching fine young specimens of males stealing home or strutting across the green. There is something about those golf knickers that catches my eye each time." Vera winked.

The sportscast suddenly faded, and a light on Mattie's board flickered to life. Excitement burst in Mattie's chest like a firecracker on the Fourth of July. "The radio station is at four o'clock, east southeast."

"Correct!" Lily pumped one arm.

Mattie's heart didn't need a tune for her heart to start dancing in her chest. It was working! Her brainchild was *working*! She *had* her prototype.

"1010," Carrie called out.

This time opera music crinkled out of the speakers.

"There's some music for you, Lily," Alice joked.

Lily groaned theatrically. "I can't very well dance to *that*."

"Eleven o'clock. Just west of north," Mattie cried out.

"Perfect!" Lily clapped but *not* in tune to the increasingly melancholy notes.

And it was perfect, Mattie thought. Her device wasn't just working; it was reliable! Although a pilot would still need multiple ways to check and confirm the bearing, this—this would be invaluable. Although Mattie did not know if it would have saved Alfred, he would have been better equipped. And that *meant* something. She could never rescue him, but she could and *would* stop other preventable deaths.

Just then the bellhop arrived with a tray of tall silver teapots and porcelain teacups. Vera handed the lad a tip and announced, "Gather around, gals. The celebrating can begin!"

"Your RadioNavigator is marvelous, Mattie. You should be very proud of yourself." Leo's voice was a balmy caress.

Mattie trailed her finger over the light board. "Thank you."

"Alfred . . ." Leo paused and then swallowed hard. "Alfred would have loved it. He would have crowed to everyone who'd listen that his sister had figured out a new navigation system."

It was the best thing Leo could have said. The fact that he had—at cost to himself—showed how much he understood her. And that . . . that frightened Mattie almost as much as it thrilled her.

If they weren't in a crowded room, she would have hugged Leo to reassure herself. But she settled for laying her hand over his.

"That . . . that was all right of me to say?" Leo asked.

"It was absolutely perfect, Leo. I *like* talking about Alfred. It makes him feel less far away."

"He'd be right there with Lily wanting music to dance to," Leo added, a little halting at first and then more easily.

"They'd be quite the pair, and he would definitely appreciate Vera's 'special tea,'" Mattie said with a wistful laugh.

Leo's gentle chuckle joined hers. Then a companionable silence fell over them as they stood staring down at her prototype and thinking about her dauntless, charismatic twin.

"Tonic water for you, Leo?" Vera called out.

He shook his head as he slowly withdrew his hand from Mattie. "I was thinking about heading out and keeping John company."

"He and the children would appreciate that," Alice said with a smile.

Leo turned back to Mattie, his eyes searching hers. "Are you okay with me leaving? I'd stay, but I thought you and the gals might like to have some time without any male company. I sure did like seeing your prototype work, though."

"I enjoyed you being here," Mattie told him and wished she could embrace him, but they had decided to keep their new relationship quiet for now—at least from everyone but the eagle-eyed Vera.

"I'd kiss you, Mattie, but not with an audience—not yet. So I'll just tell you toodle-oo."

"Toodle-oo?" She almost giggled at the ridiculous words.

"My way of secretly embracing you when I can't physically," Leo said, his explanation causing her heart to swell like a hot-air balloon.

"Toodle-oo, then, Leo."

With a nod of his head to the others, Leo slipped from the room. Still feeling bubbly inside from his words, Mattie accepted the teacup that Vera handed to her.

"What's in here?" Mattie sniffed at the liquid, smelling gin and honey.

"A bee's knees," the flapper told her as she rejoined Ruby on their chair, "because that's what your invention is. The bee's knees."

"680." Carrie called out the next station.

James Scott's "Broadway Rag" came blaring out over the speaker. Lily squealed and began to two-step around the room with an imaginary partner.

"There's no need to dance alone, darling," said Vera as she assumed the role of the man. Mattie was so intent on watching the whirling women in their glittering gowns that she entirely forgot to look at the signal. She had to wait until it came back around the second time. "Three o'clock!"

At that precise moment, Vera dipped Lily. With her golden curls pointed toward the floor, Lily cried out, "Correct once again!"

In lieu of her twin, Sadie checked the bearings, and the RadioNavigator successfully indicated each one. The rest of the Flying Flappers danced as the music turned from ragtime to jazz back to ragtime to some fast-tempo Broadway. Finally, one by one, the women dropped back into their chairs. It was Vera, not Lily, who was the last one dancing, with Ruby in her arms. She probably would have continued, but the dog twisted her head to give Vera a rather mournful expression just as Mattie flipped to a station broadcasting a gothic drama about a young bride trapped in a sea-cliff mansion.

"Oooooh," Lily cried out. "Let's listen to this!"

Mattie, who was now seeing the blonde twin in an entirely new light, complied. The actors were good, and it didn't take long until all the Flying Flappers were thoroughly engrossed. When the segment drew to a sudden end, they all gasped.

"And so, listeners, as the young Mrs. Langton hangs perilously above the abyss, we must bid you adieu. Will the mysterious figure save her? Is the man her husband or his evil look-alike? Tune in tomorrow to see what happens."

"And that is why I am never going to get married," Vera announced to no one in particular as she dumped the remainder of her hip flask into her teacup.

"Because your husband may either be mad or have a mad twin who will attempt to throw you off a cliff face?" Lily asked with a little hiccup at the end of her question. They were all a little pie eyed from the cocktails, but Lily was the most ossified.

"Vera views all marriage as a metaphorical leap off a precipice." Aida waved her fountain pen haphazardly.

"If your parents all had a marriage like mine do, you'd know why walking down the center aisle is my version of a living nightmare." Vera tossed back her tequila and then gave a sharp shake of her head against the sting. "And to make matters worse, they keep trying to foist an equally horrid union on me."

"At least you have your own funds," Aida pointed out.

"Yes." Vera eyed her empty glass. "Thank goodness for my grandparents and Great-Aunt Opal. Between those three, I am blessed to be free of my parents' plans to trade me off to the man with the best title and who will happily squander my family's cash on mistresses, horseflesh, and crumbly houses."

"Not all marriages are like that," Alice said gently as she cast her cousin a concerned look. "Look at my union or your grandparents'."

Vera snorted, sounding rather like her dog. It was the first ungraceful sound that Mattie had ever heard from her. Even her *sneezes* generally sounded fashionable. "Those are as rare as finding two identical snowflakes. I'm afraid I have no desire to risk my independence on such a gamble. If I'm going to take a risk, I prefer it to be at two thousand feet with my head dangling toward the ground."

"Marriage is just another social construct." Aida tapped her chin. "You are not bound to have one like your parents any more than you are bound by the social mores you currently reject. Although I do not believe a woman should feel a need to marry, neither do I think she should feel an obligation not to. I think a union like Alice and John's could be quite rewarding."

Mattie shifted in her seat, wishing she hadn't started on her third teacup. Vera's and Aida's views on marriage felt *critical* to Mattie, even as they twisted her stomach.

"It is funny how men have recently begun to refer to their wife as a *ball and chain*, when it is the female who is more tied down by marriage," Vera sighed. "Society is not yelling at *him* to keep house and care for his offspring. Yes, there is a sense that he must provide for his family, but he has so many ways to fulfill that duty. If a woman has the audacity of pursuing a career outside of the home, she is wrongfully perceived as abandoning her family."

"Is that why you are always warning me to not take my relationship with Leo too seriously?" Mattie asked before she realized what her question had revealed. The women, however, seemed to understand that this was not a time to ooh and aah.

Vera ran her finger around the rim of her empty teacup, causing a slight squeaking sound as she considered her words. "Leo seems like a nice enough fellow. Decent even. But are his plans for the future the same as yours? Do not trade your freedom for the illusion of security. I understand that as an independently wealthy woman, it is easy for me to make such statements. But you . . ." Vera paused and waved her hand in the direction of the RadioNavigator. "You are brilliant, Mattie. You are going to sell that idea and make a mint. Even without your genius, you could support yourself as an aviatrix. That's why I've started the Flying Flappers, to show that women—all women—can work and hold careers. So that each and every one of us has opportunities beyond the marriage bed."

Mattie realized she had barely thought about a future with Leo or what their relationship even meant. But it was so new. To her. To him. She could barely define who they were now, let alone who they would be years from now. Did she want permanence? Did Leo?

Chapter Thirteen

> The brand-new barnstorming group, the Flying Flappers, is making its way west to Troy, Wyoming. Led by none other than the incomparable Vera Jones, the primarily female troupe has been charming audiences with their smiles and spunk. The famous Flying Lion also soars with the ladybirds. Still displaying the same derring-do that he demonstrated in the Great War, he's always sure to be an audience favorite.
>
> —Chester Anderson, *Troy Star*

When the ten o'clock train chugged out of the second tunnel in Sunset Rock Canyon, Mattie and her Jenny were there to meet it and herald the arrival of Vera Jones's Flying Flappers. Soaring inverted beside the track cut high in the cliff face, Mattie waved at the excited passengers. Then she dipped low into the valley, skimming over the scrubby lodgepole pines and buzzing a grove of quaking aspens. With a parting whoop, a wave, and one corkscrew of a barrel roll, Mattie left behind the twisting canyon and headed toward the town of Troy, Wyoming.

Although Troy didn't have as many geothermal features as nearby Yellowstone National Park, it boasted a huge hot spring that formed a breathtaking cyan lake. Mattie flew low over the blue-green water as she wove in and out of the rising plumes of steam that smelled like rotten eggs. Some people called it a hellscape. She didn't. It was more like a fierce fairyland—bold, uncompromising, and utterly magical.

After aiming her Jenny for the town of Troy, Mattie landed her plane in an open stretch of land not too far from the grand hotel. Although the Flying Flappers weren't scheduled to start their performance for a few hours, people had already started milling about. When they cheered, she waggled both her hands and blew kisses. As always some of the men pretended to catch them, but she paid them no mind.

She had her fellow already.

And there Leo was, heading straight toward her, no doubt intent on checking over her aircraft. His mere presence caused a spike of excitement inside her. With him waiting for her on the ground, landing had become almost as exhilarating as takeoff.

"It went well?" he asked.

"Like a charm. Thanks for the advice. I was able to time every stunt perfectly." Mattie pulled off the leather helmet and goggles.

"Anything I should be aware of when I check over the Curtiss?" Leo focused on her when he asked the question instead of immediately starting to scan the biplane.

"She didn't give me any trouble." She shook out her short curls, enjoying the feel of the slight breeze.

"Good." Leo nodded. "Vera asked if I could tell you to head over to the dining area in about thirty minutes. There are two people who she wants you to meet. She told me that if you wanted to put on makeup, it might be a good idea."

Mattie paused in fluffing her bob. "More press?"

Leo shrugged. "I'm not sure. She said it was a surprise. You know Vera."

"Did you dig for more details?"

Leo shrugged. "I'm not you, but I figured you'd want some, so I did try."

"And?"

"I got a very Vera smile." Leo bent slightly to check under her Jenny's nose.

"The mischievous I've-got-a-secret-plan-you're-going-to-adore one?"

"That would be the one." Leo pulled over the ladder to inspect the propeller blades.

"Well, thanks for trying," Mattie said and then paused to add, "Toodle-oo."

Leo shifted around the propeller to deliver his new grin—the broad, wide one that had nothing to do with the press and everything to do with her. "Toodle-oo."

It was still a silly-sounding word, but it never failed to give Mattie a happy rush. Walking briskly to obscure her sudden desire to put an extra-cheerful spring into her step, she headed toward the white wooden building. Imbued with rustic charm, it boasted a huge wraparound porch offering sweeping vistas of the wild countryside. But the true pride of the Geyser View Inn was its numerous recreational pools fed from the large hot spring. Some were oversize, some midsize, and some private . . . very private. Mattie had plans for the latter type. Plans that definitely involved Leo. Plans that were currently making her hotter than the geothermal water feature itself. Plans that she needed to really stop thinking about if she wanted to focus on the mystery meeting ahead of her.

Stopping by the luxurious room the hotel had provided free of charge, Mattie quickly opened the supply of cosmetics that Vera had given her from the heiress's own collection. Mattie didn't know much about powders and paints, but she had a feeling Vera had spent a small fortune on them.

Mattie preferred a subtler application, except for the lipstick. She liked that bold. The old Mattie never would have believed that one day she'd have so much fun applying paint to her mouth or powder to her face.

Pleased with her coral lips and a slight smudging of eye shadow, Mattie headed down to the hotel's dining room. She didn't bother to change into one of the frilly frocks Vera had lent her. There wouldn't be enough time to change back into her trousers before the performance. Besides, not only did she feel comfortable in the khakis and simple white shirt, but it had become part of what Vera called Mattie's *image*.

Walking through the groupings of white-cloth-covered tables, Mattie heard a few whispers. Women nodded their cloche hats in her direction while men nudged their companions. It wasn't the rush of low sound that Mattie heard when she entered a room with Vera, but it was something. People were beginning to know her. *Recognize* her. And not just as Mattie McAdams but as Mattie McAdams, aviatrix.

Vera caught sight of her and waved enthusiastically. She wore a light-orange dress of chiffon silk that seemed to float around her willowy frame. The gossamer capped sleeves made the dress look even more whimsically delicate. Beside her sat two men in well-tailored suits and expensive-looking silk ties. They didn't have the appearance of newspapermen but instead carried a whiff of the business world.

Mattie froze.

She'd grown up in the sphere of daredevils. Reporters, she could understand. Men in fancy clothes who stayed inside offices all day and played with numbers were another thing altogether. But if she was going to get endorsements and license her RadioNavigator design, she needed to learn how to conduct herself in meetings. If soaring through the sky didn't intimidate her, she wouldn't let these two fellows bother her either. She'd think of them just like any other obstacle to fly around . . . or through.

"Mattie!" Vera gestured for her to sit as the two men stood up to greet her. They were both middle aged, one balding slightly and attempting to use a comb-over to hide his receding hairline. The other was carefully groomed in an austere, no-nonsense fashion.

"This is Mr. Monroe and Mr. Lewis from Rockol Company." Vera moved her gloved, upturned palm in the direction of the first man and then the second.

Both men had perfectly polished, perfectly polite smiles, the corners of their lips turning upward to exude some degree of warmth but not far enough to feel obsequious or overly familiar. Despite their pleasant demeanor, Mattie experienced another hint of unease. Resolutely, she straightened her neck and responded with a similarly congenial but unremarkable expression.

"I don't suppose you've heard of us before, but we sell motor oil for both cars and airplanes." Mr. Lewis spoke, his voice tinged with a congeniality that felt practiced rather than genuine.

Now *this* was a world Mattie knew. She could talk grease and machines and parts all day long. Sitting down with the rest of the group, she felt a bit more comfortable. "I've been seeing your company's name on cans in my father's garage since before I could even read the words. I'd recognize your blue-and-white-striped design anywhere. Why, I might recognize the smell even if you blindfolded me first!"

Mr. Monroe's slightly round cheeks glowed with pleasure. He spoke in a pleasant southern drawl as he addressed Vera. "My goodness, Miss Jones, you *are* right. She is mighty perfect for the position. Mighty perfect."

Mr. Lewis, however, eyed Mattie suspiciously. "Did Miss Jones instruct you to say that, Miss McAdams?"

"I still have no idea what this meeting is about, so no," Mattie answered honestly. "But my family has always trusted Rockol. You can talk to my mechanic and check my supply trailer. You'll find cans of it there."

"I couldn't script her any better." Mr. Monroe stared at Mattie as if she were the next Clara Bow.

"Script me?" Mattie asked in confusion, glancing at Vera for an explanation. The flapper looked thoroughly pleased. But before she could answer Mattie's question, Mr. Monroe spoke again.

"Would you be interested in flying with our lovely Rockol brand painted on your Jenny? We'd pay a pretty penny for the chance to advertise."

Mattie was very glad the server hadn't taken her drink order yet. If she had been sipping any liquid, she would have choked on it and likely spewed it all over Mr. Lewis's flawlessly cut jacket.

"What—what exactly are you asking?" Raw excitement flickered through Mattie, and she was almost hesitant to believe it.

"Miss Jones contacted us a few weeks ago and sent us a bunch of newspaper clippings about your exploits. We generally liked what we saw, and we started following the news reports ourselves." Mr. Lewis sprawled in his chair, making his body relaxed. Deceptively so. Mattie recognized a con when she saw one. This man might be a professional instead of a grifter, but he wanted to give her the impression of friendliness, false as it might be. Well, if all pitfalls in business deals were so obvious, she could easily navigate around them.

"They were quite impressed," Vera added.

"Now, Miss Jones," Mr. Monroe drawled as he leaned back in his chair too, "we haven't rightly said that exactly."

Vera's painted lips stretched into her trademark smile. Wild. Mischievous. And downright flirty. "You are here in Troy, Wyoming, hundreds of miles from company headquarters, to see Miss McAdams fly. That does tend to flatter a woman."

The men laughed, the sound only a little forced. Vera's expression never changed. She only arched one delicate, sculpted brow. "Were you not just telling me how delighted you were when she flew by your train car?"

Realization flickered through Mattie. Vera had specifically asked her to impress occupants of the first-class cars. She hadn't thought much of the request at the time, but clearly, Vera had been planning this.

The men exchanged looks. Mr. Monroe appeared a little sheepish. Mr. Lewis remained stony faced.

"We still want to see her perform." Mr. Monroe's southern charm was in place, but Mattie could detect steel underpinnings.

"Naturally," Vera said. "But Miss McAdams's flying will once again leave you breathless. You can't find a better spokeswoman for your product."

"Spokeswoman?" Mattie repeated. She had thought they would just pay her and Vera for permission to advertise on her JN-4. But an actual, honest-to-goodness spokeswoman? To become part of their marketing strategy beyond just decorating her airplane with their trademarks? And not just any company's branding, but Rockol's, the motor oil she'd been using since she could barely reach the pistons? Could this help save the flight school?

"The very face of Rockol." Vera smiled, raising her glass of lemonade. Even the flapper didn't risk consuming any alcohol before a performance.

"But isn't Earl Crenshaw your spokesman?" Mattie asked. "Would we both be representing your company?"

Because she really didn't want to work alongside that drunken oaf.

The two men exchanged a look. They glanced back at Mattie. It was Mr. Monroe who spoke. Mattie was beginning to get the impression that the honey-toned southerner was the boss, maybe even the owner of the operation.

"We're considering a fresh face for Rockol."

Fresh face. The words settled uncomfortably in Mattie's stomach like an overripe peach. Was this the reason they had selected her? Not for her flying skills but for her looks? Although she wouldn't mind knocking the arrogant Crenshaw from his plum position, she didn't want it to be because the Rockol executives found her attractive.

Mr. Lewis was blunter. "Our customers are male. They'll pay more attention to our advertisements if they feature a pretty young woman."

Pretty. Young. Woman. Mattie didn't want to lose out on opportunities because she was female, but she didn't want to get them because of sex appeal either.

"A pretty young woman who flies like no other," Vera added. The perpetual grin had fled from her face, and she regarded Mattie solemnly. The message was clear. She did not want Mattie to damage the deal without listening to more.

"Yes indeed." Mr. Monroe shot Mr. Lewis an irritated look. "We want a woman who can show off the performance of our motor oil with stunts of her own. Even better, you have a natural ability to sing its praises."

"Better than Mr. Crenshaw." Mr. Lewis muttered the words under his breath. Mattie didn't think she was supposed to hear him, but just like her uncanny eyesight, she'd always had unusually keen hearing.

The words mollified her . . . mostly.

The conversation floated away from business terms. By the time the oysters Rockefeller arrived, Mattie found herself regaling the men with more of her childhood memories of Rockol. Even Mr. Lewis seemed pleased. Vera took over most of the talking when the main course was served, for which Mattie was grateful. While she loved to talk, chitchatting was a different skill altogether. Besides, it gave her more time to focus on the absolutely divine chicken à la king.

She noticed Mr. Lewis glancing at her as if taken aback by her lusty consumption of her lunch. After dabbing her mouth with her napkin, she shot him a grin. "I believe in enjoying the fine things in life, Mr. Lewis, like the sound of a motor freshly lubricated with Rockol."

Mr. Monroe laughed heartily. "Provided you put on a show to remember today, you are definitely our girl."

"I promise to deliver an unforgettable circus," Mattie promised. She actually appreciated the fact that her hiring was contingent upon her performance.

The men excused themselves after the delightfully moist pineapple upside-down cake, but Mattie and Vera lingered. Vera reached across the table and gently placed her gloved hand over Mattie's.

"If you don't feel comfortable, you don't need to accept the offer that they make." Once again, the heiress looked uncharacteristically solemn. Her violet-blue eyes had lost their mischievous twinkle, making them even darker and more fathomless. "I am not going to ask for a percentage of your earnings, so please do not think you are obligated to do this for my sake or for the Flying Flappers."

"You would let me fly with Rockol's brand on my plane during your circus without any compensation?"

"I don't ask Carrie or Leo for a cut from their endorsement deals," Vera pointed out.

"But you arranged this," Mattie said.

Vera waved her gloved hand dismissively. "It is easy to conduct business when you already have the money and the connections. I did this for *you*. Because you're talented, and you deserve it. That is why it is completely *your* decision on how to proceed. And I encourage you to talk everything over with my attorneys. I've already arranged for you to have a meeting with them to discuss protecting your rights to the RadioNavigator."

"Do you think my looks are part of the reason Mr. Monroe and Mr. Lewis chose me?"

Vera cocked her head. "How would you describe Mr. Crenshaw? Physically, I mean. Inwardly, he's certainly proven himself to be a toad."

"Well . . . handsome," Mattie admitted.

"Square jaw, dimple in his chin, cheekbones that could cut butter?" Vera batted her eyes and gave a dreamy sigh worthy of the screen star Norma Talmadge.

"Is your point that perhaps it wasn't just his flying skills that got Earl Crenshaw his job at Rockol?" Mattie asked.

"That is precisely what I am saying."

"It doesn't seem very fair, does it?" Mattie sighed. "Endorsements should be based on talent alone."

"Life is more complicated than that and is rarely equitable," Vera said. "Although I do hold the highest opinion of myself and my abilities, I would be a fool to believe that my wealth and family ancestry hasn't helped me. Goodness, I could never begin to afford this circus otherwise."

Mattie tapped her finger against the table as she thought. "They partially chose me because I am a woman."

Vera shrugged. "I hardly see how that matters. They've been picking men for jobs based on their sex for years. It is about time women have their chance. You are more qualified than Crenshaw anyway."

"How do you know that?" Mattie asked.

Vera tossed her hand into the air. "Because you are *you*. I've never met anyone more driven or daring. You are a bear cat, Mattie, and you wouldn't let a drugstore cowboy like Earl Crenshaw be better than you."

Her eyes almost as deep purple as the fresh irises in the centerpiece, Vera sobered again and leaned forward across the white tablecloth. "Do you know what I dream of? That someday a woman can be unabashedly who she is and still taken seriously. Enjoy this opportunity to be admired both as a female and as a pilot. Perhaps seeing you marketed as a fly girl will make girls realize that they can do what they want and they don't have to sacrifice parts of themselves to get it."

"You aren't who the press thinks you are, are you?" Mattie asked.

Vera laughed, the sound as bright as always. But in all the lightness, a somber chord rang. "I'm who the press wants me to be so that I can use their attention to become who I desire to be."

"That's very convoluted." Mattie frowned, pushing some of the leftover pineapple syrup to the side of her plate. "Aren't you ever afraid you might get lost in who they wish you to be and forget the goals that drove you in the first place?"

"It's a risk," Vera answered as she shrugged, causing the thin silk of her orange dress to flutter, "but I am not afraid of losing any bit of myself that I don't wish to shed, nor do I shy away from positive change. Although self-reflection sounds like a terrible bore, it really isn't. It's good to check in on yourself from time to time and confirm you like what you see."

Mattie went back to drumming her fingers against the table. Could she do what Vera proposed? Could she be the flirty fly girl whom Rockol wanted and still be herself? But why not? Why couldn't she be feminine and tough all at the same time?

"I'll do it," Mattie said. Then she pushed her chair back from the table and bobbed her head. "I'll do it."

Vera winked. "Well, then we have an amazing stunt to perform, don't we?"

Mattie jerked her chin in a way she hoped conveyed steely determination. She knew exactly what trick Vera wanted her to perform. "Should I warn Leo?"

Vera raised her thin eyebrow and delivered a rather penetrating look. "Wouldn't you wish to know ahead of time if Leo was going to try something like this?"

Yes, Mattie would, but unlike Leo she wouldn't try to stop him.

But that was the thing. Leo was no longer trying to prevent her from performing. He didn't patronize her but instead gave good suggestions like he would to a male pilot.

A few weeks ago, Mattie would have hidden this from him. But not anymore. Besides, if she caught Leo by the supply trailer, they might have time to slip inside for a kiss. Or two. Or three.

"I'll go find him," Mattie said as she started to rise, but Vera laid her hand on Mattie's arm.

"Mattie?" Vera sounded serious and perhaps cautious even. Mattie had never heard her bold, irreverent friend sound quite like this, and she instantly sank back into her wooden chair.

"Is something wrong?" Mattie asked.

"Not precisely. I am not sure if this is exactly my place to say this. Goodness knows that I'm the last person who should ever give relationship advice beyond how to embark on jolly good affairs."

"Is there something about Leo and me that's concerning you?" Mattie asked. Her heart seemed to slip sickly around her chest.

"No. Not in particular." Vera rubbed her forehead. "I was ossified that night in Iowa when we tested your prototype, but I still meant what I said. Marriage can be a ball and chain for women."

"Do you think Leo would try to restrict me?" Mattie asked, feeling her old unease roar through her. He *had* stopped fretting over her constantly, but had Vera noticed something that Mattie had been blinded to?

Vera rubbed her temples. "This was much easier to say drunk. Leo appears to be a rather lovely man, but any marriage—any long-term partnership—will cost you some degree of independence. If you were not something to Leo, then you would have no need to tell him that you're about to perform a new stunt. Small things like that are necessary when two people form a connection and are not necessarily bad. But you need to consider how much freedom you are willing to part with and how much Leo expects you to. My parents never had that discussion. Most couples never do. But it is imperative that you have it, especially as the man rarely if ever considers what a woman sacrifices. Society has never informed him that she loses more autonomy than he."

"Do you think I've become too serious with Leo?" Mattie asked, not exactly sure what to think. She did not want to consider these questions. Not now. Not when things were so new and wonderful. Not when she wasn't sure of the answers. Not when she didn't know if she'd *like* her answers.

"No." Vera drew in a sigh, as if returning to her normal self. "I wouldn't have arranged for you two to have a private steam bath this evening if I had. I just don't want you going too far down a path you might not wish to take."

"I've just started down this particular one. I am still getting my bearings," Mattie said, feeling as if she'd been given a reprieve.

"Well then," Vera said as she began to rise, "it is good that you are an expert at figuring out methods to chart your own way."

Mattie jumped to her feet. "I'd better go find Leo and give him fair warning about our stunt."

"And I'll tell my driver to gas up the Duesenberg."

"We're really doing this?" Mattie asked, letting the thrill of what she and Vera planned to accomplish push out the spiderwebs of doubt that Vera's words had inspired.

"We're really doing this." Vera's lips curved into a resolute grin.

"Now, it's very dangerous for a pilot to fly this close to the ground." Carrie spoke with authority to the reporters gathered around her and Leo, but he barely registered her words.

His focus, his entire focus, was on Mattie's yellow-tipped plane as she dipped perilously close to the dusty earth, a ladder trailing from her wheels. Over and over, he told himself that they'd practiced this move.

But Vera wasn't a melon on a stick any longer.

She crouched in the passenger seat of her Duesenberg, the hot western sun catching the sequins of her cherry-red leotard. She looked like a red diamond, but neither she, Mattie, nor the male driver were as durable as those gemstones. One miscalculation, one wrong move . . . and they all could be lost.

Now that Leo had truly found Mattie.

But John was right. Leo couldn't stop her from flying, but he *could* help Mattie do it as safely as possible.

"Is that true, Mr. Ward?" Benji Pringle spoke sharply to him.

Just then Mattie whizzed over Vera. With impressive skill, Mattie kept the speeding airplane perfectly steady and perilously low. Vera grabbed for the rope ladder, snagged it with her hand, but didn't have a good enough grip to pull herself up. Mattie pointed the nose of her plane skyward. When she'd gained enough altitude, she dipped her left wing and banked hard to turn the plane around. Clearly, she intended another pass.

"What Miss Wilcox said was correct." Leo tried his best not to speak absently. He didn't need to hear Carrie's words to know whatever she'd described was right. For weeks now, he'd been listening to her give explanations when Mattie took to the skies and he was on the ground. It had been Vera's idea for the nonperforming pilots to explain the maneuvers to the press. Since the mostly male reporters had a tendency to quote Leo more than the women, Leo let Carrie and Mattie do the talking.

It suited him just fine. He'd never liked the glare of flash powder. But it meant he often found himself muttering "What she said" whenever a journalist inevitably asked him to confirm Mattie's or Carrie's perfectly sufficient explanations. Carrie—who faced dual prejudice due to her race and sex—experienced the worst of the dismissiveness despite her patently obvious competence. Often Leo wanted to shake the dunderheaded reporters who failed to notice either her or Mattie's brilliance, but he admired Carrie's resilience as she continued to fight to be heard as a Black woman.

Never, though, had Leo been more grateful for her presence. He felt as tightly stretched as a loaded slingshot. Words sounded like distant buzzes as he watched Mattie dip the nose of the JN-4 toward the scrub once again. As she plunged, he tried not to let images of her brother's last flight cloud his vision. Alfred had shredded his wings in a sharp descent like this, a tragedy due not entirely to enemy fire but to the failings of his own Nieuport. More than one American aviator had crashed after the canvas had disintegrated during a race toward the ground. For Alfred, it had left him helpless against the enemies' bullets, which had pierced his fuselage and caused his plane to erupt in flames.

"It is true, then? That when flying low, a pilot has to maintain a fast speed to make it easier to pull up?" Pringle spoke almost directly in Leo's face now. Leo craned his body to the side so that he could see around the man's wide fedora.

"Uh-huh." This time Leo didn't care if he sounded distracted.

Mattie controlled her craft brilliantly as she skimmed near the ground. The wind stirred up by her plane blew off the dogged reporter's hat. The ladder in perfect position, she passed over Vera. In a streak of brilliant scarlet, the flapper snagged the rung and sprang from her perch on the seat of the Duesenberg.

Despite the sudden, almost violent addition of weight, Mattie's Jenny didn't even bob. Flawlessly she adjusted the elevators and increased the power as Vera clung to the bouncing ladder.

With incredible strength and even more tenacity, Vera maintained her grip. As Mattie steadily ascended, Vera began her own climb. Except for the roar of Mattie's Curtiss, the sunbaked field was utterly devoid of sound. Vera safely reached the support structure of the biplane's wings, and the audience erupted into a mighty shout.

"What happened?" Pringle asked, his gray eyes wide as he swiveled his head back and forth like a turnstile at the state fair.

Several of his fellow reporters laughed. "Only the biggest stunt of the day."

"You mean Miss Jones actually jumped from a speeding Duesenberg onto a moving plane, and I missed it!" Benji bent to pick up his hat and beat it in disgust against his leg.

"I did say she'd be moving fast." Carrie did a remarkable job of keeping her expression and voice pleasant, but the reporter caught her underlying message. Huffing out an annoyed breath, he smacked his fedora again, this time releasing a cloud of dust.

Ignoring Carrie once more, Pringle glared at Leo, as if he were to blame for the man's lack of attention. "Can you explain to me what just happened? I traveled from Chicago to see this event."

Benji's gripe was only met with more snickers from the rest of the press. Leo barely noticed. He was too intent on watching Vera enter the front seat of the trainer. Mattie executed a perfect stall turn, engaging full rudder at the perfect moment. Her airplane hung in the atmosphere for a second before it dipped toward the ground. Mattie righted the craft and pulled back on the throttle. Another cheer rose up.

"Gosh dang it. Now what did I miss!" Pringle ground out.

Leo stepped around the journalist as Mattie headed into a landing as planned. He couldn't wait to greet her, to congratulate her. She'd just pulled off something he'd never even tried, let alone her brothers. And he was going to do something equally bold, at least bold for him. He was going to allow himself to celebrate with her.

The newsman grabbed Leo's arm, tugging on it. "Hey. Don't walk away. I need my story."

Leo easily pulled his elbow from Pringle's grip. "Ask Miss Wilcox."

"But—"

"You want details on what you missed?" Leo asked as he finally brushed past the burr of a man. "Talk to Miss Wilcox."

Leo strode across the open field, the sun so hot it seemed to burn straight through him. But even the dry heat of the West couldn't compare with the inferno raging inside him. Mattie's gaze lit upon his, the golden flecks in her irises making her eyes that wonderful molten color.

He wanted to run toward her and pick her up in his arms. Every instinct ordered him to whirl her in an arc befitting her aerial skills. He yearned to press his lips against hers, to capture some of her wonderful, wild joy.

But he didn't.

Couldn't.

Not with the press watching. Not with the photographers waiting to snap photographs. Not with the audience's eyes fixed on her.

This was her triumph. Her success. Not his.

So he stood off to the side as she posed for the lenses trained on her. Unlike him, Mattie seemed to absorb energy from the camera clicks and the flurry of questions. She relished the spotlight, and he loved watching her enjoy it. She grinned naturally, waving and winking. This was Mattie amplified. Leo had never seen her so free, so confident, so utterly comfortable with herself.

When Mattie finished posing by her Jenny, she walked his way. She stopped a few feet from him—close enough for colleagues but far enough not to raise suspicions.

"You stopped my heart several times, Mattie," Leo admitted. "But you were right. You had the skills to pull it off magnificently. If I ever need to jump on a moving plane, I want you piloting it."

Mattie glanced surreptitiously around. She must have decided that they were far back enough from the crowd to speak freely. "I really, really want to kiss you right now."

He laughed. Truly laughed. "Tonight."

"Tonight," Mattie said, her words a promise.

Chapter Fourteen

"I cannot believe that Vera arranged this for us. It feels positively decadent." Mattie leaned back against the whitewashed walls of the cave. The hot vapor from the bubbling natural spring in the center of the small cavern had plastered her short red curls to her forehead. Her brilliant locks had always reminded Leo of a sunrise, but they positively glowed in the small vapor-filled room—a splash of vibrant color in an otherwise muted space.

"Vera's a generous person," Leo said, "and more of a romantic than she'll ever admit."

"Mmm." Mattie's eyes fluttered shut. Blindly, she reached out and captured Leo's hand in hers.

He also pressed his back against the rough stone wall. The coolness contrasted with the humid warmth enveloping them like layers and layers of wool blankets. The owners of the Geyser View Sanitarium had blasted out a small alcove in the mountainside, creating an intimate space. A fountain of hot water gurgled pleasantly. Wrought iron fencing had been placed around the source, but white mineral deposits had formed on the leafy-patterned metals. The whole thing looked a bit like an otherworldly garden grown from rocks instead of plants.

Languid pleasure seeped through Leo, but unlike Mattie he didn't allow his eyelids to drift shut. If he did, he wouldn't be able to watch her. The humidity had caused not only her curls to cling but her ribbed bathing suit as well. The wet navy-blue fabric melded to every curve, every swell . . . every dip. He'd mostly seen Mattie in loose-fitting clothing, often her brothers' castoffs, which had been cut for male bodies. Even the evening dresses she'd borrowed from Vera had either no waist or a dropped one, creating a drape-like effect that fluttered around her calves. Leo loved her in all those clothes—the boyish ones, the girlish ones; it didn't matter. Because Mattie was Mattie. But he sure was enjoying the tight little swimming outfit.

The bottom of her suit ended midthigh. It was like a combination of cutoff pants that seemed painted to her skin and a very *small* and very *tight* skirt. The deep-blue fabric contrasted with the pale, creamy smoothness of her complexion. A thin sheen of sweat covered her body, giving her skin an almost pearly luminescence under the electric lights of the cave.

And Leo wanted to touch . . . and taste every tantalizing part.

"You can." Her closed eyelids hadn't even flickered, yet somehow it appeared that she had divined his thoughts. A teasing smile curled the edges of her lips. "I can sense your gaze on me, Leo. As much as I like it, I'd rather feel your hands."

She paused, and one brilliant gold-green eye popped open. "And your mouth and tongue. I wouldn't mind a scrape or two of your teeth, either, as long as you're gentle."

He swallowed, the sound so audible that he swore it echoed off the curved stone walls. When he spoke, his voice spluttered like a flooded engine.

"After those words, I'm not sure if I can manage gentle."

She shut her eyes again and tilted her neck invitingly. "I'll risk it."

"I feel like a male version of Alice Eis's monster in the 'Vampire Dance.'"

"Hmm. I'm all for the seduction part, but the bloodletting, not so much."

"I promise not to drain you," Leo teased. Then he brushed the lightest of kisses against her neck.

"Hmm." She sighed, adjusting her body to allow more access. "I've always found it irritating that women are portrayed as oversexed vamps who are financially and emotionally draining to men. A woman who is confident in her own sexuality is far from villainous."

Leo eased a few inches back from Mattie. What he was about to say was important—*very* important. As much as he was looking forward to nibbling on her neck, he wanted to look into her eyes when he said this.

"Your boldness, your kindness, your incredibly wonderful spirit—they all fuel me, Mattie. Being near you is like being hooked up to a dynamo. I've never felt more alive, more filled with life. I would never call you a vamp. If anything, you are an amp, a bolt of raw energy. You charge me, Mattie McAdams."

Her eyes flashed gold before she planted an unforgettable kiss on his mouth. Current surged through him, electrifying every inch of his already primed body. Her hands dug into his hair, and he loved the feel of her fingers pressing against his scalp—the demand in them, the explosive need. Their tongues tangled. Their breathing deepened. Their already sweat-slicked bodies pressed closer.

Leo caught on fire like a long-dried-out piece of driftwood. He kissed his way toward Mattie's ear, taking time to thoroughly explore her cheek and temple. Then he whispered, low and soft, "I'm going to take you up on your offer of touching you now."

He licked the delicate shell of her ear and gently nipped her earlobe. She gasped, her back arching enticingly. The already clingy, wet fabric of her bathing suit seemed to stretch even tighter across her bosom. He sucked in his breath, yearning to touch.

One of Mattie's hands moved from the back of his head, her fingers drifting down the bare skin of his arm. Like her, Leo wore a ribbed suit with straps over his shoulders. Yet it felt like no fabric separated them as they clung together, their heat combining with the already intense humidity of the cave.

Mattie's fingers closed around his. As he watched with tensed muscles, she guided his hands to her breasts. When he cupped the soft weight, Mattie threw her head back, her lips parting with the most wonderful, guttural sound. He kissed along her delicate neck, feeling her throat muscles shift and slide as another of her moans bounced off the rock walls. The cave seemed to catch and amplify not just the sounds they generated but their emotions too.

Arousal. The perfection of the word struck him. Never before had he felt so awakened. Every bit, every *fiber* of him burst with kinetic energy like a machine at full throttle. After years of feeling grounded, rooted to the earth, Leo soared.

Mattie gasped, her fingers now spread against his back, some of them on his suit, some touching his bare flesh. His mouth skimmed over her body, his hand touching where his lips did not. Their already labored breathing grew shallower. Mattie's skin tasted salty against his tongue, cool yet also burning up. His hand slid over her chest, and Leo could feel the frantic fluttering of her heart echoing his own desperate beats.

He pulled back. Mattie made a mewling sound of protest at the sudden loss of physical contact. Gently, Leo framed her face with his hands. Her skin had flushed rosy, and her hair stood up in a wild mass of flames.

"We'd better move to the private cooling room next door that Vera arranged for us." Leo brushed his thumbs against Mattie's temples, not able to keep from touching her.

Mattie coyly traced the scooped neck of his swimsuit, leaving a blaze of fire in her wake. "I like the heat."

"So do I." The words came out in a groan.

Mattie's mouth moved less than a quarter of an inch away from his. "Then let's generate more."

Now it was his turn to rasp out a deep moan. Her lips captured the sound, her hands sweeping across his chest. But her forehead felt clammy against his, and he knew they had to move to a lower temperature.

"Wouldn't it be more of a challenge to create fire in cool water?" Leo asked.

Mattie leaned slightly back, her golden-green eyes intrigued. "Well, when you put it that way . . ."

"Vera did tell us to give each other massages."

"Hmm. That does sound tempting." Mattie's hand moved from the top of the swimsuit to dance over his chest and upper torso. "I'm eager to explore your muscles."

"Given how I feel about your curves, I completely understand." Leo swore his voice sounded like it was being squeezed through a mechanical grinder.

"The touching will continue?" Mattie asked, her tone almost impish.

"Oh yeah."

"Then I accept your dare."

Carefully, the two of them slid around the stone seat that encircled the natural spring water. When they burst into the cooler private room built outside the cave, Leo saw Mattie shiver. He wrapped his arm around her trembling shoulders and held her close as they made their way to the pool of water in the center of the small room with a ceiling made of rough-hewn pine logs. He had never been in a bathhouse back East, and he supposed that this sanitarium was more rustic than those in the big cities. But to him, the place was classy. The small pool, just big enough for two people to dip in, was sunk into the floor and lined with cobalt-blue tiles. After the steam of the cave, the water beckoned, promising a bastion of welcoming coolness.

"My teeth are going to chatter." Mattie regarded the octagon-shaped depression with a hint of suspicion.

"You like a challenge," Leo pointed out.

Mattie laughed. Although the cooling room didn't echo as much as the rock alcove, it still was mostly hard tile, with little softness to absorb the sound. Her mirth, light and airy, sang through the enclosed space. "I do indeed."

With no more hesitation, Mattie tugged Leo toward the water. She didn't even test the temperature. Instead, gripping his fingers tighter, she slipped into the coolness, bringing him with her. The cold shocked his system—but in a wonderful, refreshing way. The pool had a bench they could rest on, and Leo took full advantage of the seat. He stretched out his legs, enjoying the gentle slosh against his calves and thighs.

Mattie's teeth did click together, but she made no move to climb out. Leo pulled her onto his lap. When she wiggled closer, he sucked in his breath, closing his eyes against the sweet delight that stabbed him.

After crossing his arms around Mattie's torso, Leo rubbed his hands vigorously over her biceps. Her soft flesh had risen into goose bumps, but under his administration, he could feel her relax.

"Hmm," she murmured, her breasts shifting against his forearms as she sighed. "I could get accustomed to being warmed this way."

He kissed the curve of her ear. "I fully recommend it."

"Based on how good this feels, I cannot wait for my massage. Vera says they feel absolutely divine."

"Vera definitely knows her divine," Leo joked, but he had a feeling he would agree with Vera this time, even if he never would have chosen that word.

"She definitely does." Mattie sighed. In this light, surrounded by a background of cobalt, her eyes looked more green blue than golden. They made him think of seas and ocean breezes, which of course turned his mind immediately to sandcastles and moonlight embraces.

"Are you ready to be toweled off?" His voice, almost of its own accord, had turned low and husky. Mattie must have noticed it, because she gave a little shiver, even though she no longer appeared cold.

"As long as you're doing the toweling." Mattie quirked her pink lips into a decidedly come-hither expression.

He brushed a kiss against her cheek, keeping his mouth near her ear as he whispered, "At your service."

She rose first, holding out her hand to help him up. Together they climbed from the pool, the water running off them in rivulets. Mattie shivered again, but they moved slowly toward the white cushioned benches. Their wet feet made the terra-cotta floor slick, and neither of them wanted to fall.

Leo bent to reach into the basket of fresh towels and pulled out an extremely large fluffy one. Mattie's eyes went wide. Pinching it between her index finger and thumb, she sighed. "It's so soft and thick. It is even bigger than the ones at Vera's castle."

"I never realized how luxurious terry cloth could be until I entered her world," Leo admitted as he draped the absorbent fabric over Mattie's shoulders. She pulled the towel tight and rested her chin on her fists. She looked so charming he leaned forward and brushed his mouth over hers. Her lips opened, and he couldn't resist exploring the warm heat. Through the wonderful haze buzzing through him, Leo realized that his body was making her previously warm swath of terry cloth soaking wet. After stepping back, he bent once more to retrieve a towel for himself. Before he could begin to wipe his arms, Mattie gently grabbed his wrist.

"Let me."

Those two words—so short, so simple—blasted through him. He nearly dropped the towel. His numb fingers eagerly released it into her hands. She started with his arms, her eyes following the path of the terry cloth with golden intensity. He burned hotter than a blast furnace in a steel mill. It was a wonder he didn't dry himself from the inside out.

But Leo was very glad he didn't. No one had ever taken care of him like this—seen to his needs. He loved the feel of Mattie's hands on him. Her fingers were delicate, but they had calluses, testaments to a life of working around machines and engines. Just like when she tightened a bolt or twisted a wire onto a contact, Mattie approached the task of drying him with the utmost thoroughness.

His knees felt peculiar, shaky even. He eased onto the cushioned bench. Mattie nudged his knees, and he spread his legs apart, allowing her to step closer. She focused on his chest, using just a corner of the massive towel. Sparks spiraled through him, as if someone had released a thousand Very lights. He felt vulnerable and strangely exposed.

He didn't fight it, though. He would've with anyone else, but this was Mattie. He trusted her. For her, he'd permit himself to feel.

As she leaned over to dry his back, her breasts brushed against his chest. He gripped the edge of the bench, squishing the cushion down. Lust and need shot through him like a shell from one of the Archies. But it didn't obliterate him. It powered him.

Leo could smell her scent—the mixture of sweat and the lavender soap that she used in her hair. He gently stroked her red curls, watching the delicate fiery strands wrap around his fingers. They didn't burn, but they seared him all the same.

Their lips tangled together—hot, eager, and demanding. Their normal positions were reversed with his head tilted back, her body bent over his. Mattie drove the kiss like she flew a plane. Boldly. Without hesitation. Fiercely.

When she lifted her lips from his to catch a breath, he gasped out, "I thought we were supposed to be cooling down."

Mattie shook her head, causing a spray of droplets to rain down on him. "You did dare me to create steam."

"That I did." A laugh bubbled up in Leo, strong and real. He'd never chuckled so much in his life.

"Did I succeed?"

"Admirably."

"Good." She smiled broadly and stepped back. "I do believe it is time for my massage, if you don't mind me going first."

"Not at all," he said truthfully, standing up so she could lie down.

With her typical abandon, she flopped onto the cushions with gusto. Leo knew the smile spreading across his face was a silly one, but he didn't care. Mattie couldn't have seduced him more if she had sensually slid onto the couch while stroking the cushions suggestively.

Starting with Mattie's shoulders, Leo kneaded her muscles. The feel of her flesh nearly undid him. Then she emitted a groan . . . a satisfied, deep, undeniably sexual *groan*. And that pushed him over the precipice. He'd had a lifetime of controlling his inner emotions. But it seemed that nothing could have prepared him for touching Mattie.

He needed a distraction, and he needed one *immediately*.

Mattie moaned again.

If she released another . . .

"You were going to tell me more about your endorsement," Leo said quickly. He thought he might have spit out the words too swiftly, but Mattie didn't seem to notice his tommy gun–like delivery.

"Oh yes." Mattie shifted slightly. Both her eyes were closed, and she wore a little smile on her lips. "I was. Something, or rather *someone*, distracted me."

"What company is it?"

"Rockol." Excited pride thrummed through Mattie's voice, and Leo loved the sound.

"Rockol!" he repeated, feeling his own swell of delight. "You've been singing their praises for years! I remember when you were showing me how to oil an engine—you told me always to use their brand."

"Precisely!" Mattie managed a little bounce despite being prone.

"It couldn't be more perfect for you."

"Even though it isn't a girlie product?" Mattie opened one of her eyes to watch him.

"Hey, *I* use it because of your expertise."

"Not because you were sweet on me?" Mattie teased.

He hesitated.

Mattie raised her chin, astonished. "You *were* sweet on me? Even back then?"

Leo wanted to rub his head, but that would mean removing one of his hands from Mattie's back. Instead he focused on kneading the muscles around her shoulder blades.

"You weren't like any other girl I'd ever met," Leo admitted slowly. "When I first saw you, you were fixing a lead wire."

"You developed a crush on me because I was repairing my plane?" Delight spread across Mattie's face.

Leo focused on his hands pressing against the navy-blue fabric of her swimsuit. "Yes."

Mattie flopped back down with a huge sigh, and her eyelids drifted closed once more. "That is just about the most romantic thing anyone has ever said to me."

Mattie looked serious, utterly serious, and a pleased thrill shot through Leo. "Yeah?"

"Yeah."

"But, Mattie," Leo said, knowing this would be important to her, "I would have used Rockol even if I hadn't been sweet on you. You were, are, an excellent pilot and mechanic. I've always known that."

One of Mattie's eyes popped open again. "Really?"

"Really."

"Do you think men will buy Rockol because of how I fly or because of how I look?" Mattie asked, her voice soft and unusually unsure. His heart twanged. He wanted to reassure her, but he didn't want to lie either.

"You want the truth?" he asked.

"The truth."

"Both," Leo admitted. "You're adventurous, and that's what Rockol is aiming to sell. They're trying to convince men that if a fellow uses their brand of motor oil, then he can attract a gal with your spirit."

"And there's nothing wrong with that?" Mattie asked.

"No more than men buying the stuff that I endorse because they want to be as brave and daring as an ace pilot," Leo pointed out.

"Rockol's former spokesman was an ace too," Mattie said thoughtfully. "I guess Rockol *is* trying to market adventure. I like the idea of representing female derring-do."

Leo paused in the massage as cold realization slithered through him. "Wasn't Rockol's last spokesman Earl Crenshaw?"

"Yes. It might be petty of me, but it makes the deal even more delicious after how Crenshaw treated me at the Gilded Secret."

"You should be careful." Leo worked to keep his voice even. He didn't trust his old comrade, and he worried how the man might react once he discovered that his former rival's sister, a female, had "stolen" his endorsement deal.

"Careful?" Mattie asked. "Why in heaven's name would I need to be careful? It's not likely that I'll ever see Crenshaw again."

"There's a nastiness deep inside Crenshaw, and I don't want it touching you."

"You didn't like him even when you served together?" Mattie asked.

Leo hated talking about the war, especially the memories tied up with Alfred. But this was important for Mattie to hear, to understand . . . for her own safety.

"No," Leo said shortly.

Mattie didn't ask another question like she normally would. She must have sensed this was difficult for him. And that was Mattie. Always understanding him when no one else did.

"He wasn't like the rest of the pilots." Leo forced himself to continue. "It wasn't just that he was brash. A lot were. But he had a meanness, a competitiveness, that went beyond rivalry. He gloried in death. He'd shoot at a pilot even after it was clear that the enemy's plane was crippled badly enough that the German fighter would need to land within our lines and be captured."

Mattie opened both eyes now. They looked softer, the blues and greens predominating. "Did you have many interactions with him?"

"Not as many as he had with Alfred." It hurt even saying his old friend's name. Leo swallowed and focused for a moment on just rubbing the muscles near Mattie's delicate spine. "They were competitors, Alfred and Crenshaw, each vying to be America's Ace of Aces. Plus, you know how Alfred could never tolerate a bully."

"No, he couldn't," Mattie said softly.

"Alfred was a favorite of the other aviators. Crenshaw resented that almost as much as Alfred's talent. Even if Crenshaw had taken down more planes during a battle, everyone always talked about Alfred's escapades instead. Your brother also was just a better pilot. Someone played a series of nasty pranks on Alfred, including removing the firing pins from the guns on his fighter. We could never prove it, but we always suspected Crenshaw."

"I promise to maintain a healthy distance from Earl Crenshaw," Mattie told him, "but I doubt he'll ever pop up again. Meeting him in Chicago was just a coincidence."

"And you'll tell me if you do encounter him again?" Leo asked.

"I will."

Even with Mattie's assurances, Leo couldn't stop the chill of foreboding. He hadn't experienced a metallic taste in his mouth like this since the Great War. He felt like he had on an evening before a major mission. And now, he didn't have as many layers of numbness to wrap his concerns in. Slowly but surely, Mattie had been stripping away that protective padding, leaving him raw to the world.

Mattie shifted and sat up. Yawning, she reached her arms toward the ceiling and moved her head from side to side. Her stretches weren't meant to entice, but her sinuous movements entranced him all the same.

"It's your turn for the massage." Mattie gave him a mischievous smile as she stood up and patted the cushions she'd just vacated.

Gingerly, Leo stretched out on the bench. To his surprise, Mattie straddled his back. She placed one knee on either side of his rib cage as she kneeled above him. When her fingers brushed against him, his muscles all simultaneously contracted.

"I believe a massage is supposed to make you less tense, not more," Mattie teased as she kneaded the tops of his shoulders.

"I'm sorry." His apology came out muffled. "I'm not used to anyone tending to me."

Mattie pressed her thumb into a particularly tight knot. Pain and pleasure mixed, and he groaned helplessly and audibly.

"Why are you so stubborn about accepting help when you so freely give it?" Mattie asked, her voice slightly distracted as she worked his flesh.

"I've had to be self-reliant, I suppose," Leo admitted as the kink in his shoulder finally unfurled. "It's habit now."

"When flying against the Germans?" Mattie asked.

"Long before that." Leo didn't know why he allowed the words. Perhaps it was the effect of sweltering in the vapor-filled cave and then plunging into the icy water. Maybe it was Mattie's hands, so firm yet still gentle as they touched him. It might have even been her voice, soft and sweet. Or it could have been the fact that he yearned for a connection with Mattie, and he knew he'd never achieve one if he didn't give something of himself.

"You've never talked about your childhood."

Leo tensed again, and Mattie immediately stopped pressing against his skin. He had a choice. He could relax his guard and finally open fully to her . . . or he could keep everything closed off. He knew how to make his inner self impregnable. He'd done it for decades. What he didn't know was how to set down the armor he'd spent so many years carefully crafting.

But he needed to try.

Mattie leaned back. Perhaps she had pushed Leo too far. But as they had grown closer, she had found herself longing to understand more about his past. She had always been attuned to Leo, always felt a link. But despite those unspoken ties, she did not know many basic facts about his personal history. She did not know where he'd grown up, how many siblings he had, or whether he'd had any pets.

"Could . . ." Leo trailed off for a moment before continuing. "Could you touch me again? Like you were? It makes this all easier somehow."

Mattie's heart flipped in her chest. She leaned forward and quietly began kneading his strong, corded muscles. He had so much strength, her Leo, both internal and external. But what had forged it?

Neither of them spoke for several long minutes. She could hear the bubbling of the fountain from the cave echoing through the pristine stillness of the cooling room. The rhythmic sound soothed, and Leo's deltoids went practically pliant beneath her fingertips.

When he finally spoke, his voice sounded even deeper than normal and heartbreakingly hollow. "I don't talk about my childhood because I didn't have one. Not in the normal sense of the word."

Mattie's heart shuddered like a stalled-out engine, but somehow she managed to keep on massaging his back without faltering. He needed her to stay the course and keep them both steady.

"I . . . I think I have some memories of my mother, but they're like an old, cracked, and overexposed tintype. Not very clear. The head administrator at the orphanage, Mr. Knight, said that both my parents were drunkards. When my mother tired of me, she dropped me off on the doorstep of the foundling home. She wouldn't even give her last name, so Mr. Knight just used Ward for mine."

"Is that why you never drink alcohol?" Mattie asked the easier question, the less personal one, the least painful.

"We were taught at the orphanage that it was worse than the devil's brew and that most of us were there because of its ruinous properties. I never wanted to be like my parents—choosing liquor over family. Seemed like it was best if I avoided something with power like that."

"You could never be like them, Leo." Mattie pressed a kiss to his shoulder as she worked his lower back. His eyes squeezed shut at the contact, and she noticed that his hands clenched the cushions so hard that the fabric and stuffing both bunched up.

"It was cold there," Leo said. "Everything about it was cold. The cracked walls. The rotten windowpanes. The lessons. The food. The people in charge of us boys. But in the summer, we sweltered. And we never lived up to Mr. Knight's standards. He had a veneer of morality that he donned when the donors or the trustees visited, and he imposed so many exacting standards that we could never hope to meet. When I got older, I tried to protect the younger ones from his punishments. But finally I couldn't endure it any longer. I left when I had the chance. I never went back. I shoved it all from my mind."

Mattie's heart ached, and she longed to embrace him. But she didn't want to upset the delicate balance they'd found. It was as if the consistent pressure of her hands and fingers somehow steadied him. She'd waited for years to hear Leo's story, and now that he had begun to tell it, she needed to listen.

"The streets were freezing, too, but I found a degree of peace as long as I kept to myself. I scrounged, wangled odd jobs, scraped by. When I got older, I left New York and traveled west, picking up work here and there until your father hired me to help out around the flight school."

And he still kept to himself, Mattie thought. But she didn't say those words aloud. Didn't want to hurt Leo or for him to think she judged him. She remembered, though, all the moments when he would stand off to the side observing the family but never really participating. He was a master at keeping his distance, but she'd never stopped to really contemplate why. She should've. Leo would've. Quiet, observant Leo, who'd learned to be that way to survive.

"Even when you frustrated me by trying to curb my flying, I've always admired you," Mattie admitted. "You have such quiet strength. I've told you before, Leo, that you're solid. And now . . . now I find myself in a bit of awe over you."

Leo shifted, one shoulder rising, then the other. Clearly, she'd made him uncomfortable, but that didn't mean that what she had said hadn't needed to be verbalized.

"I admire you too, Mattie. You're all brightness, passion, and fearlessness."

After all these years at odds with Leo, it felt good, so good, for him to acknowledge her like that.

"You're an incredibly decent man, Leo Ward. You've made something of yourself when the world gave you nothing to build with. And you did it honestly. Thank you, Leo, for sharing your past with me. I know it wasn't easy, but it meant a lot to me to hear it."

"It meant a lot to me to say it," he admitted gruffly. "Someday, I'll tell you more."

"Whenever you're ready, I'll listen." She kissed the part of his spine between his shoulders. She knew Leo had left much unsaid. Some she could fill in; other parts she could only imagine. But in time, he would tell her at his own pace. Mattie was accustomed to flying toward every obstacle with an open throttle, but Leo wasn't like that. His revelations were not hers to control but *his* to share.

Leo shifted then, and she sensed he wanted to rise. She eased back and slipped to one side of the bench. When he sat up, she plopped down beside him. He gathered her against his side and wrapped one of his strong, capable arms around her. She leaned against his shoulder and listened to him breathe, slow and steady. He sounded contented, and she realized how simply *right* this moment felt.

Years ago, they had been good friends. Even when they had been at odds, there'd been some vestiges of that old connection. Now they were sweethearts.

And this evening, away from both flying circuses, their relationship had deepened even more. It had developed into companionship.

It felt strong to Mattie. Durable.

But then again, so had their old comradery before it had fractured. And what did she desire from their connection? Why did she have such trouble imagining what she wanted in the future?

Chapter Fifteen

In a world-gone-mad moment, Rockol has made the dubious decision of replacing its spokesperson Mr. Earl "Quick" Crenshaw with a ladybird flyer. Previously known only for her relationship with Mr. Leo "the Flying Lion" Ward and her membership in Vera Jones's attempt at a flying circus, Miss Mattie McAdams is an odd choice. Perhaps Rockol thinks scandal will sell more motor oil than good old-fashioned flying.

—Benjamin Pringle, *Chicago Advance Leader*

"We're not holding up the test of your device, are we?" Guadalupe Espinosa-Diaz, Aida's mother, asked as she and her husband, Amando Sanchez-Teneiya, hurried out from the U-shaped courtyard in the center of their sprawling white-stucco hacienda. The two had become fascinated with Mattie's RadioNavigator during dinner last night. The Flying Flappers were beginning a series of shows that Vera had scheduled down the California coast, and the Sanchez family had invited them all to stay in their luxurious compound for a few days. Aida's parents had welcomed their daughter's friends with a meal featuring much of their own produce, from figs to almonds.

"Not at all," Mattie called back. "We're still just getting set up."

"Bien," Amando said. "My business call with the canning company went longer than expected, and I was afraid I had delayed things."

"Goodness no," Vera said. "It always takes us forever to get our troupe moving, and you're right on time."

Mattie felt a rush of pride as she saw the grouping of motor vehicles gathered like a parade. Even John and the children were going to tag along.

As the rest of the group chatted among themselves, Mattie, Carrie, Sadie, and Leo mounted the rotating antenna to the strip of metal skin between the front bench and the rumble seat of the Duesenberg. When that was secured, they placed the radio unit up front in the passenger seat with Vera. Mattie and Leo squashed into the bumpy back seat. There was barely enough room for them and the control panel, but the cockpit of a plane would be crammed too.

"All ready?" Vera asked, pausing before she climbed behind the steering wheel.

"As soon as Carrie and Sadie tune the station, we can take off," Mattie said. Since her friends couldn't join her in the Duesy, she wanted them to be part of the critical test somehow. When the words and music to "The World Is Waiting for the Sunrise" became clear enough, Carrie and Sadie wished Mattie good luck before they joined Aida and her parents in the Rolls.

Mattie glanced down at the control board. "Redding is at one o'clock."

"Right!" Leo said, his index finger on the map they'd marked with the bearings that Lily had calculated.

"It's working! Let's hit the road!" Vera hollered, and all the drivers started their automobiles.

"Miss the motorcycle?" Vera asked Leo as she pulled the Duesy away from the hacienda and pointed it toward the rows of vines stretching over the rolling hills. She'd added a Harley-Davidson to her collection a few towns back. She was planning on learning to ride it for a stunt, but she let Leo use it for the most part.

"In this rumble seat, it feels about the same," Leo said as they hit a particularly big bump. If Mattie hadn't been wedged next to Leo, she probably would have popped up a few inches from her seat. Holding on to the control board, she called out as the indicator moved from the one o'clock position to two o'clock.

"Right on time." Leo smiled at her, the grin so warm and natural that Mattie almost forgot to look back at her prototype.

"Eyes on the lights!" Vera cheerfully sang out. Ruby, who was sitting on her mistress's lap, poked her little nose over the heiress's shoulder, as if echoing the command.

Mattie obeyed, but she couldn't resist responding, "Eyes on the road!"

"Typically, I would have a hard time looking away from the snow-capped Mount Shasta, but you and Leo can be quite fascinating."

"You sound like Aida." Leo rubbed the back of his head, but he only turned a light pink under his tan rather than a full red.

"Well, she did ask that I report back to her. She finds your and Mattie's interactions over mechanical matters an interesting case study."

"Case study?" Leo repeated, sounding more than a little discomforted by the thought of being analyzed. Mattie agreed with him but perhaps not for the same reasons. It seemed like everyone had given more thought to her relationship with Leo than she had. Every time she tried to consider the future, she shied away from it, almost as if in a panic. Since she normally faced problems head-on, her reaction was more than a little unnerving.

"Three o'clock!" Mattie cried out. She was so glad for the interruption she wanted to kiss the control board.

"Perfect," Leo confirmed, checking the map and his watch.

"This is remarkable, Mattie." Vera turned her head to regard them. "You are brilliant. Simply brilliant."

Leo reached over and squeezed her hand. "You truly are, Mattie."

He looked like he had that night in the cooling room, his blue eyes earnest, his expression relaxed, open even. She felt so close to him, so connected, yet Vera's words had once again pricked at the fears Mattie still couldn't completely define.

Leo held Mattie's hand as they stepped into the courtyard on the Sanchez estate. After the ride, everyone had gone back to their rooms to freshen up. They were planning to regroup over wine, cheese, and crackers to celebrate Mattie's latest success. It appeared that Mattie and Leo were the first to arrive.

Drawing in a deep breath, Leo consciously glanced around the garden paradise. He knew Mattie would ask him questions about their surroundings again, and he wanted to surprise her with an unprompted observation.

Over the red terra-cotta shingles, he could spy Mount Shasta in the distance, its snowy cap a burst of white against the darkness of the other visible peaks. The open side of the courtyard looked out upon the vineyards and showed a flash of blue water beyond. Manicured lemon, orange, and lime trees grew inside the courtyard along with a variety of succulents. Around the center fountain, birds-of-paradise bloomed. But the sensation that gripped Leo the most was the sweet scent from the ripening figs.

"It smells wonderful," Leo said, and Mattie rewarded him with a smile. She sucked in her own breath, drawing back her shoulders. The motion pulled at the delicate fabric of her royal-blue dress, causing it to tighten over her breasts. She looked wonderful with her short hair ablaze and the greens in her eyes bolder than normal.

"It's magical here," Mattie agreed.

"Every place that Vera has taken us has been that way," Leo admitted. It was as if he'd entered a new world entirely.

"It's like a fairy tale with her," Mattie said, echoing his thoughts.

"Yeah," Leo agreed, but a whisper of disquiet crept through him . . . for all stories ended. He did not want his time with Mattie to draw to a close. He had never spent much time thinking about the future. But for the first time, Leo had begun to consider making plans . . . plans that involved Mattie. But did he dare ask her to join him permanently, this brilliant, passionate woman who was on the brink of accomplishing so much? Although she had every right to leave him behind, what would it do to him if she did?

"Hello," Guadalupe called as she and Amando appeared, also hand in hand, interrupting Leo's suddenly dismal thoughts. It gave him some measure of hope when Mattie's fingers tightened around his instead of releasing them. She obviously did not mind claiming him as hers in front of these people whom she respected.

"Hello," Mattie called back as the four of them met by the table set up near the three-tiered fountain.

"Amando and I were so thrilled by how well your RadioNavigator worked," Guadalupe said as she took her seat next to Mattie. "I've never had a chance to watch a new technology in its first trial—not like Amando, who tours factories and buys new machinery all the time."

"What are your next plans?" Amando asked as he began to pour wine for all of them. "I assume you have taken steps to protect your intellectual property."

Mattie nodded, looking a bit nervous to be entering into a business discussion without Vera at her side. Leo, however, had no concerns about her ability to handle it. He squeezed her hand supportively.

At his touch, Mattie straightened, and when she spoke, her voice sounded confident. "Yes. I am working with Vera's lawyers, and they are handling the legal matters."

"Good. Bueno." Amando inclined his head. "Vera always employs the best. Have you given any thoughts about how to market the RadioNavigator?"

"Vera and her lawyers suggested that I try to license the idea rather than build it myself. I don't have the funds to set up my own manufacturing company, and the value is mostly in the idea." Mattie spoke with authority now, and Leo liked hearing the conviction.

"Who are some of your potential customers?" Amando asked. "Do you have a list?"

"The beginnings of one," Mattie admitted. "The US Airmail Service, the army, and the navy for starters."

"What about Fabin Flyer?" Guadalupe asked. "That new airplane manufacturer in the southern part of the state? Aren't you planning a show near their headquarters in Oceanbreeze in a week or so?"

"Yes," Mattie confirmed. "In fact, they're the reason Vera scheduled our performance there. Fabin Flyer is holding a flying derby the day before, but they've only invited ex–war pilots to race in their pylon course. Since we couldn't join the main attraction, we decided to create our own event."

"Sounds like they want to attract the attention of the US military and make a deal to supply them with planes," Amando said thoughtfully, giving Mattie a significant look. When she stiffened, Leo immediately knew she'd had an epiphany.

"And if they could advertise their planes as being safer with my navigation system, that would be sure to interest the navy *and* the army," Mattie said excitedly.

"You should set up a meeting when you're down there." Guadalupe nodded. "Just make sure that Fabin signs something to protect your idea. Men have been stealing credit from us women for years."

Amando sighed and shook his head. "You've been talking too much to Aida."

Guadalupe arched one eyebrow imperiously. "Are you saying that businessmen are never underhanded? How many times have you complained to me about unfair practices, especially when people think they can quote you a ridiculously low price for our products because of your race?"

Amando turned to Mattie. "Guadalupe is right. The value of your invention is in the design. Make sure that you have an executed confidentiality agreement before you discuss anything with Fabin Flyer or any other company."

"Vera's lawyers mentioned something like that to me." Mattie's voice had grown a little soft again, and Leo could sense her nervousness. "I wonder if Fabin Flyer will take me seriously, but I'll see if I can arrange to talk to their purchasing department when I'm in the area."

"You're going to convince someone to accept your design." Leo spoke up. "It is too good, and you're too passionate about it. You'll make the right person listen. I know you."

Mattie beamed, and her smile meant everything to him. Even if he could not see his own future, he'd always known hers. Mattie was destined for greatness with or without him.

Chapter Sixteen

"To another successful show!" Carrie raised her bright-red Mary Pickford cocktail above her head. Since Vera's Flying Flappers were in Southern California, home to stars and starlets alike, they had decided to all order the drink named after the famed actress. Even the men had tried it . . . well, Leo was drinking club soda mixed with pineapple juice and a touch of grenadine. Mattie doubted he was enjoying the almost sickly-sweet combination, but he gamely downed a healthy sip.

"I cannot believe it is the beginning of autumn." Mattie practically had to shout to be heard over the roar of the other patrons. The basement room of the seaside Victorian inn where they were staying wasn't exactly spacious, and it seemed as if everyone in the surrounding area knew about the Lost Tide Pool Lounge and had crowded inside. Mattie had yet to find a speakeasy where folks actually "spoke easy." Fortunately, the thick stone walls set deep into the earth blocked out the roar. Mattie also assumed that most of the local police were already aware of the illicit bar and, more importantly, were well paid to ignore occasional bursts of sounds that might drift their way.

"We'll do the southern circuit this fall." Vera leaned her left arm against the back of her chair to strike one of her classically dramatic poses. Her red drink matched the bold cherry hue of her lipstick. "We can winter in Sarasota. My grandparents left me another house there. It is wonderfully eccentric and definitely big enough for all of us."

Aida shook her head. "It's back to graduate school for me, but perhaps I can take the train and visit you during winter break."

"Do you have enough fodder for your book?" Carrie asked.

"Scads of it." Aida gave her ever-present notebook a fond pat.

"How many of those did you fill?" Lily asked, reaching for it.

Aida lightly swatted her curious fingers away. "Six point five."

Lily's eyes widened. "My goodness, I don't think I've ever written down that much in my life."

Sadie rolled her eyes. "She's always starting diaries, but I don't think she's gotten past three entries."

Lily poked her twin. "Someday I will be a famous actress, and someone will want to read the account of my life."

"Do you really believe you'd want to sit down and write an autobiography?" Sadie asked.

"Hmm." Lily tapped her chin. "Perhaps I shall hire a ghostwriter."

"Personally, I enjoy writing," Aida said as she folded her hand over the edge of her notebook, "but not typing—at least when it comes to formatting and finalizing a manuscript. I'll hire someone for those details."

"Will you join us next summer?" Vera asked. "I will miss you dreadfully, darling, but we all must make sacrifices for the advancement of science. And the world definitely needs a glimpse into that wonderful mind of yours."

"I might." Aida reached over and slung her arm around Vera in an impromptu hug. "It has been a fun and grand adventure, just like you promised."

"What about the rest of you?" Vera asked.

"Sadie and I will definitely join you." Lily took a sip from her glass.

"It will be nice to be in a place where you can actually see the sun in the winter," Sadie added. "Western Pennsylvania always seems to be in a permanent overcast gloom starting in the fall."

"Knowing how much the children love the beach, John and I will come." Alice rested her head against her husband's shoulder and looked up at him. "Won't we, darling?"

"As long as Vera doesn't mind the not-so-quiet thunder of little feet," John said.

"Oh, I adore your children," Vera said, "and I absolutely love spoiling them."

"And us." Alice gave her cousin a nod. "Thank you again for arranging for a nanny to watch them tonight."

"I'll want to check what Bessie's plans are for the winter months and if I can help her out. If not, I'm more than happy to spend time by the water," Carrie said.

"What say the two of you?" Vera swung her gaze toward where Mattie and Leo sat together, their hands clasped under the table. Mattie felt Leo's grip tighten around her fingers as she instinctually did the same. They hadn't spoken of the future, hadn't discussed what they would do once their current stint ended, hadn't shared with each other what they desired out of life.

"We . . . we haven't discussed it," Mattie said, feeling an alien sense of hesitation. What did it say about her and Leo that they hadn't talked about even the immediate future?

Leo watched her, his expression stoic and practically impenetrable. Yet she sensed in him the same unease and uncertainty that she felt.

"There's no need to give me an answer straightaway." Vera's hand fluttered carelessly in the air, and Mattie knew the flapper had detected her and Leo's discomfort.

A commotion on the small stage provided, at first, a welcome distraction. The band members were taking a break, and two men ascended to the stage. A cold chill raced through Mattie as she recognized Earl Crenshaw and Benji Pringle.

"Miss McAdams, don't be shy now." Crenshaw's deep baritone boomed through the room, drawing the attention of all the patrons. "You come right up here and join Mr. Pringle and me for our big announcement."

Leo's grip on Mattie's hand grew hard. She barely stopped herself from swiveling her head to look around the room, as if another Miss McAdams would suddenly manifest. What in heaven's name was happening?

"Now, you can't tell me that the Rockol Mattie who has challenged the Flying Lion is intimidated by a little audience like this." Crenshaw's voice sounded jovial, if a tad patronizing, but Mattie could detect the meanness in it like a clink in an otherwise perfectly operating motor.

Everyone in the room except for Mattie's table laughed. She readily recognized the tone of the guffaws. It was snide amusement at the idea that a mere woman was foolish enough to believe not only that she could shed her innate frail femininity and boldly take to the skies but that she could fly better than a man.

Mattie started to stand, but Leo gave her a gentle tug. He leaned over and whispered so softly that only she could hear, "Don't go up there. It's a trap."

"You all might be wondering what an aviator and a reporter are doing on the stage tonight at the Lost Tide Pool. Well, we are here in case you didn't see this evening's edition of the *Oceanbreeze Chronicle*."

Mattie stiffened at the name of the town where Fabin Flyer had just held its derby. Mattie had tried calling the company several times since her discussion with Guadalupe and Amando. She'd left the number of Vera's attorneys since she was on the road, but the law office had not received any communications.

With a dramatic flourish, Crenshaw unfurled a broadsheet. The room had grown so quiet Mattie swore she could hear the rustle of each individual page even from her seat in the back. Leaning forward, she squinted. When she caught a flash of her own face in newsprint, her blood froze. But Crenshaw's next words made it burst into unstoppable flames.

"You see, *Rockol* . . ." Crenshaw paused, obviously trying both to drum up more tension and to cast doubt on the legitimacy of Mattie's endorsement deal. His lips curved into a decidedly oily grin when he continued, "*Mattie* has agreed to fly the Fabin air course against me. I was able to persuade the company to allow us to use their planes so no one can say we were unevenly matched in the way of aircraft."

Mattie bounced to her feet like a daredevil shot from P. T. Barnum's legendary human cannon. "I—"

At the sight of Crenshaw's triumphant face, Mattie choked back her denial. The odious charmer *wanted* her to appear cowardly. Leo had warned her that her brother's rival might come after her. She'd thought it was just another product of Leo's tendency to worry. Clearly, she'd been wrong.

"Having second thoughts, *Rockol* Mattie?" Crenshaw sneered out the words. "Afraid you can't win in a *real* race against a *real* man who isn't sweet on you?"

Mattie bristled at the patent insinuation that Leo had allowed her to beat him. "Mr. Ward is twice the aviator and four times the man that you'll ever be. And I won those competitions fair and square!"

"Then prove it." Crenshaw bent forward slightly, his voice booming through the room, causing a murmur to rise through the entranced crowd. The man had the charisma of Vera but none of her kindness.

Mattie felt a nudge against her foot. She glanced down to find Leo watching her. For once, he didn't try to mask his emotions. She understood his silent message immediately. He was trying to tell her that she didn't need to do this. She had no obligation to take Crenshaw's bait.

But Leo was wrong.

She did have a duty. To herself. To female aviators. To little girls like Alice's daughter who wanted to take to the skies themselves.

Until now, the press had been relatively kind to her, but there were still those comments about her "womanhood" and "femininity" that pervaded almost every article. Even in the most flattering pieces lurked barely veiled hints that Mattie's flying was more than just unconventional; it was perversely abnormal. She faced so many probing questions about her personal life and her wardrobe choices—inquiries Leo never received.

"Miss McAdams?" Crenshaw's voice had gone as smooth and as thick as a Walgreens malted milkshake. "We are all very interested in whether you'll keep your promise, especially Mr. Pringle here, who covers sports for the *Oceanbreeze Chronicle*'s parent newspaper."

Mattie turned away from Leo and headed toward the stage. She made certain neither to stalk nor to flounce. Instead, she walked with utter confidence, a broad grin on her face. She acknowledged the crowd, strolling among them, not through them. Earl Crenshaw wasn't the only aviator in the room who could play to the audience.

"Why, Mr. Crenshaw," Mattie said loud and clear as she stepped onto the wooden stage, "I would never do something so unwomanly as to renege on a commitment. That would make my words mere fabrications, and I believe a body should be nothing but honorable."

Crenshaw's self-satisfied sneer drooped for a shadow of a second before he covered it with greasy obsequiousness. "We'll see you bright and early at the racecourse tomorrow, then?"

Mattie refused to allow him to shake her any more than he'd already done. "Yes indeed. I'll be there at . . . ?"

She arched her eyebrow as imperiously as Vera did. Crenshaw didn't squirm much, but he twitched just a little. Unfortunately, his next words drained her slight satisfaction.

"Six a.m. with a start time at six thirty a.m."

That was a little over five hours away. Although pilots often rose that early, especially when attempting distance flying, it wasn't necessary for a closed course. It would cut down on the spectators too.

But clearly Crenshaw didn't want to give Mattie a chance to study the setup of the pylons or test-fly the unfamiliar Fabin. For all his bluster and confidence, the man was doing his utmost to make sure she couldn't beat him.

But she *would.* Soundly. Mattie did her best when faced with low expectations and no support.

"Afraid of too many people watching me trounce you?" Mattie asked, keeping her voice light and airy when she wanted to haul back and slug the man in the kisser.

"But, Miss McAdams"—Crenshaw's pearly whites flashed, and his perfectly sculpted lips tilted upward into a sickening smile—"you were the one to request that time. I told both the *Chronicle* and Fabin Flyer that you specifically wanted to begin at the crack of daylight to show the world you were ushering in the dawn of female aviation. But we'll see whether it is you or me who greets the sunrise with success."

As soon as he tossed the verbal gauntlet, the room exploded with noise. She could hear illegal bets taking place. Odds were *not* in her favor.

Mattie seethed, but she would unleash her anger on the field tomorrow. If she did so on this stage, she would look like the unhinged fool—and Crenshaw the sane, calm one. She might have allowed the odious reprobate to maneuver her into this particular skirmish, but she wouldn't let him win the campaign.

"How do you think the *Chronicle* and Fabin Flyer would react if they knew you made this all up?" Mattie hissed under her breath as she waved to the crowd like a beauty pageant contestant on the beach.

"Fabin Flyer would never believe it, especially since they said that their secretary had been receiving calls from you when I mentioned your name. I have no idea why you were actually contacting the company, but they think it was because of this competition between us." Crenshaw waggled his hands like a returning war hero at a parade held in his honor. "If you try to call me a liar, everyone will just blame it on fickle female nerves."

"How *did* you get Fabin Flyer to agree?" she asked through gritted teeth, although she somehow still managed to form her lips into a winning smile. Not only was the bastard putting her endorsement with Rockol in jeopardy, but he might have just ruined her opportunity to pitch the RadioNavigator to Fabin.

"You've made quite a name for yourself, *Miss* Rockol." Crenshaw flashed his deep dimples as one of the women winked at him. "At first Fabin Flyer wasn't happy about having a dame at the controls of one of their birds. Then I pointed out the attention they'd get. What really sold them, though, was the fact that they could market their planes as being so safe that a doll could operate them."

"Oh, *did* they?" Mattie wanted to smash something. Instead, she gave a flirtatious tilt of her head.

"You know, Miss Rockol, you haven't asked me how I knew you'd agree." Crenshaw slipped his hand around her waist, as if they were best of chums. Mr. Pringle, who must have gotten permission to take a photograph inside the speakeasy as long as he didn't show any illegal activity, snapped a picture.

"Obviously, you realized that I was more courageous than you." Mattie tossed her head just as Lily and Vera had taught her when the flash powder ignited.

"Hardly." Crenshaw scoffed. "Your brother was a hothead, and I knew any twin of his would be an unholy terror of a wildcat."

Mattie paused for a moment at the mention of Alfred, barely keeping her anger from exploding. But the best way to honor her twin was a well-placed quip worthy of his quick wit.

"Then I guess you won't be surprised when you fall victim to my sharp claws." Mattie quietly tossed the words back at Crenshaw before she descended from the platform, her back rigid, a wide grin pasted on her face.

Immediately, her friends surrounded her as they spoke all at once.

"What an utter scoundrel!"

"The nerve of him to lie like that!"

"Do you mean to actually fly tomorrow?"

Carrie grabbed Mattie's hand. "If you want to review your flight strategy tonight, I'll stay up with you. I'll give you whatever pointers I can."

Vera laid her fingers on Mattie's other arm. "I am so sorry, darling, that I couldn't think of a way to intercede without making matters worse."

"That's okay," Mattie said. "It was my battle to fight."

She looked for Leo, and he stood at the edge of the Flying Flappers. Worry etched across his normally stoic mien. A new unease slipped through Mattie. Leo might have suppressed his protective instincts to allow her to handle the situation as she saw fit, but she had a feeling his support might not last.

"It's clear that the annoying troll of a man doesn't like you disrupting what he incorrectly believes is a preordained social order." Aida drew Mattie's attention back to the conversation. "He clearly has an agenda that he thinks will bring the world back into *his* sense of balance."

"If you don't want to fly tomorrow, don't let Crenshaw force you into this," Sadie said. "But if you do choose to get in that cockpit, know that we'll all be cheering you on."

"With gusto!" Lily added, giving a little bounce to punctuate her words.

"We know you can beat him in a fair race," Alice said, "but he doesn't seem willing to give you one."

"If you want, I can make some calls, although it *is* dreadfully late," Vera offered. "I'll do my best to try to salvage the situation."

"There's no time." Mattie rubbed the bridge of her nose and then stopped. If Crenshaw was watching her, she didn't want to give the impression that he'd rattled her. "If I withdraw or protest, it will be used as an example of why women shouldn't fly: we don't have the constitution for it; we're too sensitive to assume the terrible risk; we're meant for gentler pursuits."

"Mattie is right." Aida sighed. "When women step beyond the role of domesticity, it threatens to disrupt the established mores, and there will always be resistance."

"He has put you in a difficult position," Carrie agreed.

"There is no real choice," Mattie said. "If I try to withdraw, I'll have to say goodbye to any chance of securing a meeting with Fabin Flyer and probably my Rockol deal too. I won't let Crenshaw ruin my reputation or the reputation of female aviators. I am going to fly tomorrow, and I *am* going to win."

"And you'll do it with aplomb!" Lily clapped her hands. "Your flight will just be applesauce!"

Sadie slung her arm around Mattie's shoulders. "We'll be with you in spirit in that cockpit—all of us gals who dream of taking to the skies."

A chorus of yeses filled the air as Mattie found herself enveloped in a group hug. The arms around her were all slender, but each of them carried undeniable strength. They bolstered her. She wasn't alone in this fight. She had a whole phalanx of women rooting for her.

When they broke apart, Leo stepped close, his jaw clenched, his blue eyes dark with gathering clouds of worry. "We need to talk. Alone."

Mattie dreaded the conversation, but she could not avoid it. She gave a crisp nod. "Fine, but not immediately. I don't want Crenshaw to think that he chased me away."

Leo jerked his head just as sharply as he shoved his fingers deep into his chestnut locks. Clearly, he didn't want to wait, but he didn't fight her decision.

Her friends all tried to distract Mattie, but she couldn't focus on their funny stories. When half an hour had dragged by, she finally nodded to Leo. Together, they slipped from the Lost Tide Pool. Instead of heading toward one of their rooms in the inn above, they stepped out onto the hotel's beachside veranda. A breeze fluttered over them, a cool respite from the stifling heat of the packed room.

Moonlight spilled onto the white sands, a bittersweet reminder of when she and Leo had raced hand in hand along the shore of Lake Michigan. This evening, she feared, would end much differently than that one.

"Should we walk near the waves?" she asked. "Then there's no chance of someone overhearing us."

Leo bobbed his head, his shoulders hunched as if against a bitter wind. He obviously dreaded this discussion as much as she did. She didn't know if that realization was a balm or salt upon the rawness forming inside her. Perhaps both.

They didn't entwine their fingers together or rush with headlong abandon. Instead, they trudged slowly through the thick, shifting sand. The water sounded different here. No longer did it lap, but it burst shoreward with a loud crescendo and then a whooshing retreat. The rhythmic sound, soothing yet whispering of alluring adventure, normally called to some instinctive part of Mattie. Tonight, she felt as if the sea just crashed against the hollowness forming inside her chest.

Mattie and Leo walked through the wet sand, their footprints almost immediately swept away by the tide. The lights from the hotel grew to mere pinpricks, and finally Leo spoke.

"Earl Crenshaw is trying to lure you into a snare."

"I know." Mattie rolled her shoulders and threw her head back to stare into the endless night sky.

"Then why are you agreeing to it?" Leo's voice sounded as deep as the sea swirling against their feet.

"Because if I don't, then he's already won along with everyone else who thinks like him. All of what I've gained will be swept away."

"Even if you lose your Rockol endorsement, there'll be others. It's just one event, Mattie, and not even a real one. It's just something Crenshaw is trying to make a lot of noise over."

"But it's not just one event, Leo." Mattie spun on her heels to face him, churning up the wet sand as she did so. "Not for me. When a male pilot fails, he's seen as daring and courageous for even trying. When a woman does . . . well, it just proves the overwhelming sentiment that women aren't meant to fly. Not even that we *shouldn't* fly but that we're not *meant* to. Why can't you understand that?"

Leo shoved his hand into his hair so roughly his chin jerked back just a little. "You, Carrie, and Vera have done a brilliant job managing the press. Yes, this might be a setback, but—"

"A setback!" Mattie jammed her hands onto her hips. "People will be arriving at that field tomorrow wanting me to fail, hoping for me to fail, wishing for me to fail. And you want me to just hand it to them, to prove them right, to not even show!"

"Crenshaw has it arranged so you can't win!" Leo's normally calm voice broke into an urgent rush, his hurried tone matching the rapid beat of Mattie's own heart.

"It is *always* arranged so that I can't win." Mattie thumped her fist on her sternum, as if she could pound the truth into both of them. "It is the playing field that *I'm* accustomed to. And I'll manage to come out on top. I always do."

"Mattie." Her name sounded like a hoarse plea on his lips. "You don't know what you're dealing with. Earl Crenshaw isn't like the opposition you normally face."

"You mean like the people who are supposed to have my best interests in mind?" Mattie couldn't stop the flow of words spewing from her lips. Years of being told *no* welled up inside her and bubbled over like the scalding, sulfuric steam she'd flown over weeks ago in Wyoming. "People like my brothers . . . or you?"

Leo closed his eyes, and the wind gently ruffled his hair. If it weren't for his strained facial muscles, he'd look like a man preparing to give his lover a kiss in the silvery moonlight.

When his eyelids flickered open, his gaze appeared even more haunted than before, his face almost gaunt in its intensity. "Mattie, I am trying my best to support you."

"Then support me!" she snapped. "My female friends have no difficulty doing so."

"Because they don't know Crenshaw either." Leo spoke carefully . . . too carefully. His tone reminded Mattie of every time a man tried to "patiently" explain to her a concept she already knew too well. Anger burned through her caution.

"Oh, they know Crenshaw. We all know *a* Crenshaw." Mattie gripped her hands into fists like a pugilist getting ready to pummel her opponent—only her competitor was hard to define and even harder to defeat. She wasn't fighting just a person but thousands of years of expectations.

"Even if I trusted Crenshaw not to pull another underhanded trick, everything is stacked against you!" Leo started to step forward, as if to touch her, but he stopped. "You've never even looked at Fabin's designs. Do you know how dangerous it is to just jump into an unknown aircraft and start speed racing?"

"How much practice time did you log in the SPAD before you took it instead of your Nieuport into battle?" Mattie was tired, so tired, of being judged by a different standard just because of her sex.

"That was completely different. That was war, Mattie. This isn't."

"Oh, it isn't?" Mattie stepped forward this time, advancing on Leo. "You know, when I stood on that stage, I thought of Crenshaw's manipulations in war terms. Skirmishes. Campaigns."

"Mattie, he's not even giving you a chance to inspect the aircraft. If you want to use military terms, you hopping into the cockpit is like leading a forlorn hope."

"How many times did you get into a plane and not expect to survive?"

"I was fighting to protect something I cared about!"

"So am I!" Mattie clasped her right hand back over her heart. "I am not just flying for myself but all female aviators. If I fail to show, this will make national news—empirical proof of a female flyer's innate fickleness. I'll be a laughingstock with no reputation left to help save the flight school. Who would buy a RadioNavigator from a silly female braggart who can't back up her outlandish boasts?"

"Is it worth your life, Mattie?" Leo asked. Mattie knew he meant the question earnestly, but it stung nonetheless. She had no idea how she could make him understand the importance of what she was doing.

"When you and Alfred left for the war, I didn't want to lose you—either of you. But I not only let you both go—I wrote to you every week with words of encouragement. Can't you do the same now? For me? Support me even if you are worried?"

"Mattie, I don't want to help you fly to your death. Something isn't right about this competition. We have no way of even checking if the plane is safe."

The fight drained out of Mattie with a whoosh, like a hot-air balloon snagged on a power line. Leo would never understand. Never see her side. She rubbed her forehead wearily. "Yes, air races are inherently dangerous. I know that, but even if Crenshaw engineered this race to my disadvantage, Fabin Flyer won't give me a shoddy aircraft. Me dying in one of their creations is not the press they want."

"But Crenshaw—"

"Is not the bogeyman, Leo," Mattie interrupted him with a sigh. "You said this isn't war. That might not be accurate, but it is true that this isn't like any battle that you're accustomed to fighting. There are no blatant hostilities. It's more subtle than that. It's words and newspaper articles and even sideways glances."

"Mattie—" Once again, Leo made her name sound like a prayer, but she wasn't about to answer his plea.

"I'm flying tomorrow, Leo. Nothing will change my mind on the matter. Now I am going to go and eke out what little sleep I can manage to cobble together."

She turned and prepared to sweep back into the hotel in a flutter of silk and sequins. However, a large sandcastle foiled her dramatic exit. Instead of making a graceful departure, she pitched forward into the mound. She took out two turrets before she managed to catch herself with her hands. Leo, being Leo, immediately rushed to her side. He reached down, but she clambered to her feet.

"Thank you, Leo," she told him crisply, "but I won't be needing your assistance. I can stand on my own."

Then, with a painful ripping in the vicinity of her heart, she marched toward the glowing lights of the inn.

Leo stood in the ruins of the sandcastle, watching Mattie's retreating figure. The dark always seemed on the verge of swallowing her up, but somehow between the moon and the lights of the hotel, he could still track her shadow moving ever farther away.

He'd handled the discussion poorly, but then again words had never come easily to him. Mattie seemed convinced that she was caught up in some grand metaphysical battle between the sexes. But it wasn't some amorphous danger that he was worried about.

Although Leo doubted Crenshaw believed that women should fly, he wasn't goading Mattie into a race just to prove gals belonged at home rather than in the air. This was personal to him. Mattie had publicly rejected him, unmanned him, stolen his job, and again made him the fool. Crenshaw didn't just want her grounded; he wanted her destroyed. This was about payback—and not just for Mattie's own triumphs but for her brother's as well. Even though Alfred had died months before the war had ended, his record still outshone Crenshaw's. So did Leo's, but he hadn't lorded it over Crenshaw like Alfred had.

With the fanciful turrets of the sandcastle still crumbling around his feet, Leo glanced out toward the inky waves. A cloud partially hid the moon now, and the scene had plunged even further into darkness. The salty tang of sea air rushed past him, as if in a hurry to join the breezes across the ocean. With the sounds of the speakeasy muffled by walls of stone and piles of sand, he heard nothing but the sea pummeling the sandy ground.

Leo was the methodical one. He needed to push aside the throbbing ache, move past the gnawing worry, and concentrate on keeping Mattie safe. Although he agreed that Fabin Flyer would not provide Mattie with an inferior plane, he didn't trust Crenshaw not to tamper with it. The man might be thoroughly unpleasant, but he was a wiz when it came to mechanics.

Leo needed, somehow, to ensure Mattie's plane wasn't sabotaged. He owed it to Alfred, to himself, and to Mattie. Checking his wristwatch, he saw it was already nearing two in the morning. Unlike Mattie, he doubted he'd sleep. Leaving behind the shore and the crushed sandcastle, he headed toward the parking lot where the flying circus's trailers were. Inside he found the motorcycle.

Keeping his body low over the handlebars, Leo concentrated on moving as quickly as possible to Oceanbreeze. He barely noticed the moonlit water to his right or the flash of lights from the seaside towns on his left. No other vehicles traveled in the darkness, although he thought he'd caught the faint but rich sound of jazz floating out from one or two of the establishments. With his blood heated, Leo only faintly registered the cool wind slapping against his cheeks. He ignored everything but his need to reach the plane Mattie planned on flying in just a few short hours.

Unfortunately, when Leo arrived at the airplane hangar, he found a burly, barrel-shaped security guard at the fenced entrance. Clearly, Fabin

Flyer was taking no chances with outsiders tampering with their aircraft, but were they as vigilant with the pilots operating their machines?

"What's your business here?" The night watchman barked out the words in a loud growl that matched his enormous physique.

"I'm a mechanic for Mattie McAdams."

"Who?" The man seemed decidedly grumpy at being forced to handle Leo's unexpected arrival in the wee hours of the morning.

"Mattie McAdams. She's the pilot who will be racing Earl Crenshaw tomorrow. I'm here to check over the aircraft she'll be flying."

"My job isn't to play butler or to host events. My shift ends at five thirty a.m., so I am not privy to what's happening tomorrow. I only know who is allowed to be on the grounds tonight, and a mechanic for Mattie McAdams isn't on the list."

"My name is Leo Ward. I'm a pilot too. You might have heard of me." He hoped the guard followed aviation enough to recognize his name.

Leo's last attempt at persuasion was met with a decidedly cross glower. "I don't pay attention to flyboys any more than I do to petticoat flyers."

"Is there someone else I could talk to?" Leo asked, realizing the man wouldn't relent.

"At this hour?"

"Please. It's vital that I look over the plane Miss McAdams is going to fly. There could be sabotage."

That was evidently the wrong thing to say. The night watchman appeared to miraculously double in size, muscles bulging in places that seemed rather superfluous. "Are you insinuating that I haven't done my job properly?"

"No." Leo shook his head quickly. "It's just—"

"Do you take me for the gullible sort? You show up in the middle of the night and bandy about the word *sabotage*, thinking you'll scare or fool me into letting you enter?" The man's ire wasn't just a performance.

"Fine, sir. I'll just come back in the morning." Leo made a show of backing away.

"You do that, and don't even think about creeping in here. All the planes are locked up inside the hangar, and the only door is right behind me."

"I wouldn't dream of sneaking around," Leo lied. He had been contemplating slipping onto the grounds, but he didn't want to risk getting caught and spending the night and morning in the pen. Then he would never have the chance to inspect Mattie's aircraft.

After he left the bulldog of a guard, Leo parked his motorcycle and walked around the perimeter of the airfield. The pylons stood out as black pillars against the faint glow from the moon, their tall, narrow forms blocking out patches of the now-star-carpeted sky. A fence ran the whole way along the field, although Leo could have easily scaled it *if* he had noticed any planes. But he didn't. The night watchman had been telling the truth about the Fabins being housed indoors.

Even if Leo could sneak into the building undetected, which he sorely doubted, he did not know which aircraft Mattie would be assigned. He'd have to check each one, and he had no idea how many he would find tucked away in the sizable hangar.

Battling down frustration, Leo returned to his bike. He couldn't allow his irritation to affect his thinking. He needed to remain methodical. His first plan had failed, but he had time to devise another.

After starting the motor, he tore up the road. There were even fewer lights burning on his trip north, and he swore the sea sounded angrier, as if intent on beating the beach into submission. When he reached the inn, he had barely an hour before they had all agreed to gather before leaving for Oceanbreeze.

Leo didn't even attempt to sleep, but he didn't pace in his room, either, or go out for a walk. That would have been a waste of energy. Instead Leo lay in bed and stared unseeingly at the high ceiling, concentrating on how he would try to slip away from the group once they arrived at the airfield. Hopefully, he could manage to inspect the Fabin's engine with no one noticing, especially Mattie herself. She'd made it patently obvious that she didn't desire his assistance, but he couldn't let her soar into danger, no matter the cost to their relationship . . . or to him.

He stayed on his back, thinking and planning, until the time came to join the others downstairs. Quietly, he slipped from his room and padded down the grand wooden Victorian staircase that led to the quaint lobby. Outside on the front porch, Leo heard the murmur of low voices. When he stepped through the inn's entranceway, he found Mattie and Carrie in conference. Carrie was doing most of the talking and Mattie most of the listening. Leo was glad Mattie had another even-tempered pilot to strategize with, since she clearly wouldn't take his advice at the moment.

At the tread of his shoes, the women looked up. Carrie waved cheerfully, and Mattie sent him a polite but decidedly not-welcoming smile. Shoving his hands into his pockets, he stayed on the other end of the veranda. Mattie didn't need another argument, and he knew if he tried speaking with her, their conversation would almost immediately devolve into one. She needed to focus on her flying, and he—he needed to continue fine-tuning his own plans.

Soon the others joined them. When they piled into the vehicles, Leo chose Vera's motorcycle. He didn't want any distractions—or anyone to guess his intent.

Sunrise was still almost an hour away, so once again he found himself hurtling through blackness, although not quite as thick as before. Even with Vera in the lead, their caravan moved slower than his previous mad dash. Birds that made their homes along the shore had begun to awaken, and Leo was traveling slowly enough that he could catch their songs here and there between the rush of the wind, the whoosh of the now-retreating sea, and the roar of his motor. Normally he found the chirps cheerful, but today they seemed sharp and demanding. He didn't know if the avian calls were urging him onward or scolding him to turn back.

When they arrived at the field, the gray predawn light had rolled in, almost like a thick, unfriendly fog. The pylons looked even more menacing now. Instead of giant shadows, they seemed like black fangs piercing holes in the colorless sky. A few people were milling about, including some who were clearly reporters with their notebooks and ever-present cameras. A handful of spectators had taken their seats in the crude stands that Fabin Flyer must have temporarily erected for their showcase. Representatives from the company strode to greet Mattie's group, their suits perfectly tailored, their shoes shining, their fedoras at rakish angles.

Leo paid no attention to the pleasantries that the men exchanged with the members of Vera's Flying Flappers. Instead he scanned the field, his gaze alighting on two planes sitting near the course. Shifting toward one of the more junior Fabin Flyer men, Leo jerked his head in the direction of the aircrafts.

"Which one will Miss McAdams use?" Leo asked without preamble. Luckily, the man was distracted enough by the conversations swirling about them that he didn't seem to notice the abruptness of the inquiry.

The fellow pointed to the Fabin on the right. "That one, sir. The one with the red nose."

Of course Crenshaw would have somehow wrangled for Mattie to fly a plane with a pattern associated with Germany's Ace of Aces, the Red Baron, Manfred von Richthofen, and his squadron, the Jagdgeschwader I. It was clear how the former American fighter pilot envisaged himself as the hero and Mattie the villain. Given how mercilessly Crenshaw had pursued their foes on the front, Leo didn't like how the bully had framed Mattie as the opposition.

Crenshaw himself appeared riding a motorcycle at a breakneck speed. He churned up the ground as he skidded to a stop. But even with his theatrics, he didn't come close to upstaging Mattie's arrival in a Duesenberg. Still, his presence prompted a flurry of activity. Sleepy reporters snapped to attention. Pringle in particular hurried to his crony's side.

Questions pelted both Crenshaw and Mattie. Leo noted ruefully that the ones directed at Crenshaw seemed related to his flying technique, while Mattie's were about whether she was terrified and if she had a sweetheart, and if so, how did he feel about her flying?

"Oh, I don't get into personal details." Mattie's voice sounded light, but he recognized the diamond-hard undercurrent in her tone. "But whenever I fly, it is on my terms alone."

Alone. Mattie had sought her whole life for independence, while he'd sought for interdependence on a family. Perhaps their relationship had always been headed for a tumultuous landing on rough terrain.

But regardless of what Mattie wanted from life and what he'd always dreamed of, he couldn't watch Crenshaw lure her into a dangerous booby trap.

With the attention focused on the competitors, Leo took the opportunity to slip away. No one tried to stop him as he moved silently across the field. He stayed in the shadows of the buildings and kept his posture and pace casual. A few Fabin Flyer maintenance workers were drifting around the airfield, and he wanted to blend in.

Forcing himself to maintain his unhurried walk when he yearned to jog straight toward the red-nosed airplane, Leo finally crossed over to his goal. Fortunately, someone had left a ladder not too far from the aircrafts, probably for some final inspection. Hooking it under his arm while whistling "When My Baby Smiles at Me," Leo never slacked on his slow, steady progress. After setting up the wooden legs near the Fabin, he first checked the shiny, new propeller. There wasn't a single ding, let alone any pitting.

Yet Leo still didn't feel assured. He next ducked under the nose of the Fabin to evaluate the motor. Luckily the plane didn't have cowling on the bottom of the radial engine, which saved him time. He had no idea how long it would be before someone noticed him. Mattie would have his head for this impromptu examination.

Leo scanned his eyes over the mass of piping and wires. Out of the corner of his eye, he thought he noticed something wrong with one of the rubber tubes connected to the oil line. He was just about to study it more closely when a rough hand yanked him backward.

"Hey, what are you doing tinkering with that engine! Only Fabin Flyer personnel are allowed back here before the start of a race." The voice sounded as hard as the fingers digging into Leo's shoulder. Leo awkwardly managed to pivot his body to find a man about four inches taller than him and forty pounds heavier.

"You need help over there, Jimmy?" Another worker began running in their direction, followed by a third. All the shouting had begun to draw the attention of the crowd gathered around Mattie and Crenshaw.

"Someone tampered with the engine," Leo said, but his captor's bruising hold didn't lessen.

"Yeah, well, no one has been around this machine except for you." Jimmy shoved his face close to Leo's, clearly not impressed with his excuse. "The night watchman did say a fellow matching your description was lurking about last night, though."

Leo realized the man wouldn't listen. There was a good chance no one would check over the motor. Frantic, Leo searched for Mattie's face in the group of now-avid onlookers. When his gaze fell on her, his heart plummeted faster than a stalled-out fighter. Her features had crystallized into raw, frozen anger and betrayal, just as they had on the day her brothers had stopped her from flying during Alfred's memorial.

"I think there's something wrong with the oil—" he started to shout, but she squeezed her eyes closed, as if shutting out his words. He knew then that he'd just pushed Mattie into jumping into the cockpit. She wouldn't want his theatrics to cast aspersions on her bravery.

Desperate, Leo turned his thoughts toward his last and final plan, the one he'd sorely hoped he wouldn't need. But he had no time left to try to persuade someone to believe him. The other two men would be upon him in mere moments, and he would forfeit his opportunity to implement his last-ditch effort.

Twisting from Jimmy's iron hold in a move he'd learned as a slight lad on the streets, Leo ducked low and dodged. Jimmy lunged but slipped. After scrambling into the Fabin, Leo hastily prepared it for takeoff, turning on the spark and opening the choke and throttle. Jimmy rose to his feet and stalked toward the cockpit. Leo swung his body outward, striking the bigger man in the chest with just enough force to knock the wind from him but not enough to cause any lasting injury. Jimmy spiraled backward into the dirt while Leo quickly leaped to the ground. More men ran in their direction. After yanking the propeller down with almost violent force, Leo dashed back around the side of the craft. Just as the other two workmen reached the Fabin, Leo catapulted himself into the cockpit. Before anyone could stop him, he shot down the clay runway. Luckily, his path remained clear. He didn't want to put anyone at risk in his quest to save Mattie.

The airplane barreled along the ground without any sign of trouble. The engine sounded strong, with a good healthy roar that would make a lion proud. It was well crafted, much faster than the Jenny. It reminded him of his old SPAD—small, fleet, and easily maneuverable.

Over the last several weeks, little by little, bit by bit, he'd started to feel more emotion when flying. But today those nascent emotions had shriveled up, leaving him once again barren. Emptied of everything but the task before him, he continued to pull back on the stick and opened the throttle until he shot skyward.

He swooped toward the course, determined to confirm that the Fabin could handle the sharp turns and fast speed. The pylons loomed before him. He focused entirely on the engine and the mechanics of flying as he buzzed almost automatically through the impressive towers. He'd been like this during dogfights, his mind and body completely given over to the objective of the mission, whether protecting a British bombing squadron, taking out an enemy observation balloon, or engaging directly with the Jagdstaffeln.

He made it through the course once. Banking the plane, Leo turned the nose back toward the rickety grandstand. He'd just started his dive between the first two pylons when a fine mist of oil sprayed over him, dousing his face. The motor gasped and spluttered to a coughing and decidedly final stop.

Leo had no time to feel even a single sharp, shredding bite of fear. He had returned to the mentality of combat. He assessed the situation with calm fatalism.

He had no power from the engine, but the wind still held the Fabin aloft. With enough distance, he could keep the bird steady and gently bring her downward. The contact with the ground might be a bit rough, but he'd landed with a dead motor more than once, including in the shell-blasted No Man's Land.

But he didn't have enough distance, not with the grandstand stretching before him. If the structure had been empty, Leo would have flown straight for it. He was higher, and by his estimate he could drift over the bleachers. But it would be close. And his calculation could be wrong. The seats weren't a permanent structure but a temporary one. Even if he just clipped it, the whole wooden construct could collapse.

All these thoughts zinged through his head like a stream of machine-gun bullets. Leo had the barest fraction of a moment to make his decision. But war had taught him to make practically instantaneous analyses. And he chose, as he always did, the safety of those he sought to protect over his own.

Turning the plane from its course would cause him to lose the airspeed that was holding him aloft and send him into a spin with no way to recover. It meant an uncontrolled crash but risked no one else. So he dipped his wing and veered away from the crowd.

The Fabin almost instantly began its deadly tumble. Even though Leo had no way of righting the path, his training kept him alert despite the dizzying effects of the whirling plunge. He kept his eyes open, his hands on the controls, but he didn't brace for impact. Instead, he thought of Mattie.

Chapter Seventeen

Mattie had experienced almost suffocating pain when her brother had died. She'd lived with the sorrow of her mother's passing and the bittersweetness of fuzzy, out-of-focus memories of her. As a young flyer, she'd experienced a clench in her heart when she'd executed her first barrel roll and hung upside down over a patchwork of ground far below. She'd lived with worry for all her brothers and Leo as they'd fought in Europe.

But she had never, ever known terror. Until now.

It screamed through her like a projectile shredding the air in a long, extended screech. Her body, her mind, her very soul reverberated with its force.

She lurched forward, as if somehow she could stop the unstoppable. She wanted to reach up and catch Leo, to prevent him from slamming into the unforgiving dirt. He'd been flying low enough for her to see the dark stains covering his face and flight jacket. An engine would fail after losing that much oil. And the silence—the horrible, endless, irrefutable silence—confirmed the horrific truth. The plane's motor had become a useless, heavy weight, dragging the craft downward.

Built for speed and maneuverability, the Fabin wouldn't glide well. But it *would* glide. And a pilot with Leo's skills could carefully bring it earthward. Mattie had no doubts that Leo could have coaxed the aircraft over the bleachers to land in the field beyond. But that would have put others at risk—a proposition intolerable to Leo.

He'd turned the plane, obliterating the lift buoying the craft. For the briefest of moments, the Fabin had responded to the commands Leo had given it. But now it flopped over and began its terrifying fluttering spiral earthward.

Mattie screamed, a guttural, splintering echo of the raw pain tearing through her chest. Picking up speed, she dashed toward the field, toward Leo. A gentle but firm grip held her arm, stopping her forward progression. Mattie tried to yank herself free, but her captor held fast. Before Mattie could put up another struggle, the Fabin smashed into the ground in a hideous rendering of metal and splintering wood. The sound seemed trapped inside her, bouncing back and forth in her skull until she, too, thought she would break from it.

The left wing cracked off first and bounced into the air. It rolled on the ground a few yards before coming to a stop. The right one just dropped while the severed tail shot into the air as if launched by a medieval catapult. The nose slammed into the ground—and the fuselage, the protection around Leo, crumpled.

Mattie cried out again and struggled to break free of the hands preventing her from reaching the wreckage. Vera's voice sounded in her ear, devastating in its soft kindness.

"The gas could explode, Mattie."

"I *know*!" The words ripped from her, grating against her throat. "I need to get to Leo, Vera! I need to see him!"

"Be careful," Vera warned as she released Mattie. At their feet, Ruby whined plaintively.

Not pausing to respond, Mattie tore across the clay runway and then the sandy dirt field. Employees from Fabin Flyer pounded past. They had already begun to toss away ripped pieces of canvas and chunks of plywood to reach Leo when Mattie joined them.

"Miss, get back!" one of the men warned. "It could blow at any second!"

Ignoring the warning, Mattie skidded to a stop in front of the wreckage instead of retreating. Heedless of the hissing coming from the hot engine and the pungent odor of gasoline, she fell to her knees. With surprisingly steady hands, she helped move away the debris.

When her fingers brushed against warm flesh, she cried out for help. With the ever-present threat of fire, the men moved Leo immediately, dragging his limp form without ceremony. Mattie pulled, too, putting all of her strength into bringing him closer to safety.

Then she heard it . . . a sound at once heart lifting and heart wrenching. A low, pain-filled grunt. From *Leo*.

But she had no time to rejoice at the sign of life. An ominous popping sound heralded a new lethal peril. Instantly, Mattie threw her body over Leo's. Only a handful of yards from the wreckage, she could feel the blistering heat from the explosion blast over her skin. Pieces of the plane rained down on her, followed by a shower of sandy dirt and clumps of grass. Cradling Leo's head beneath her chest, she prayed that no smoldering embers would land on any of them.

Suddenly, hands urged her up, and she and the Fabin crewmen all worked to carry Leo. Finally, they moved him out of the range of the fire. After sinking to her knees once again, Mattie gently brushed her fingers against Leo's cheek. Oil and blood mixed, making it impossible for her to examine the extent of his injuries.

Somehow, against all odds, his left hand fluttered upward, trying to grasp at the strap of his goggles. Mattie gently loosened the fabric and eased off the oil-coated lenses. Startling blue irises with a starburst pattern greeted her. His eyes swam with silent pain, and his hand trembled as he cupped her cheek. When he spoke, he could only huff out one agonized word at a time.

"You. Okay?"

Mattie's tears broke loose then. She, the girl who never cried, started to sob uncontrollably. Leo was worried about *her*. She wasn't the one who had just plummeted from the sky . . . although she should have been. Guilt pushed its serrated edges through the terror and agony already ripping through her. *She* was the one who was supposed to have been in the cockpit. *She* was the one who had insisted on flying an unknown aircraft on a moment's notice. *She* was the one who hadn't listened to Leo . . . yet *he* was the one who lay battered upon the ground.

"Mattie?" Her name sounded even fainter on Leo's lips, but still it vibrated with concern.

"I'm fine, Leo," she managed to blubber out. "I owe that to you. Thank you."

A faint smile touched his split lip. Then his eyes—those brilliant, shining eyes—fluttered shut, and his fingers dropped limply to his sides.

A little cry escaped Mattie as she frantically felt for a pulse in his wrist. It was there. Remarkably steady and strong. Just like Leo.

"I love you," Mattie gasped out in case some part of him could make out her words. "I'm so sorry. I should've listened."

He gave no outward response, but somehow Mattie knew he'd heard. And there, sitting in the dirt, clasping Leo's motionless hand, she felt a truth explode in her chest. She had been willing to sacrifice her own life to prove woman aviators could fly as well as any man, but not Leo's life. Never Leo's.

"The ambulance is here." Carrie touched Mattie's shoulder gently.

Mattie glanced up to find Vera leading two men in their direction. The sight of the long black car made bile rise up, and the air was expelled almost violently from her body.

"That . . . that's a hearse." Mattie's lips felt so numb that she had to work to make them cooperate.

"It's a combination vehicle," Carrie assured her. "The town is too small for a separate ambulance service, so the local funeral home provides transportation."

"I don't want him to go into a hearse." Mattie wasn't thinking; she could only feel.

Carrie squeezed her arm. "It is the safest and quickest way to get him to the hospital."

The truth of her friend's calmly spoken words finally sank through Mattie's instinctual reaction. Sucking in her breath, she gave a resolute nod as the men quickly began to put Leo's right leg into a traction splint. When the two morticians lifted Leo into the back of their converted ambulance, Mattie followed.

"May I ride with him?"

"Are you his wife?" one of the men asked, his eyes kind, his smile even more so. Yet still his words sliced. How could Mattie describe her relationship with Leo? They had made no promises, no lasting declarations. She might have even fractured the fragile foundations of their love with her rejection of any assistance from him. They had been sweethearts for certain, but *sweethearts* didn't even begin to describe the depth of their connection, a connection she had overlooked and misunderstood for so long.

"Mattie is Leo's fiancée," Aida declared without hesitation.

"He'd want her by his side," Carrie added firmly.

"Well, climb on in, then, Miss," the sympathetic man told Mattie. "It'll be tight, but we'll find room for you."

As she sat inside the hearse, clinging once again to Leo's hand, she heard Aida instruct the drivers to take Leo to Our Lady Hospital, where Aida's former college classmate worked as a surgeon. The morticians agreed without argument. During their travels through Aida's home state, Mattie had learned that in California, Aida's connections and influence were even greater than Vera's.

The kindly mortician stayed in the back with Mattie and Leo as his partner drove down the straight stretch of highway. Even all the worry and fear she felt couldn't completely stifle Mattie's pilot instincts. A distant part of her noticed how the driver moved the vehicle quickly yet still relatively smoothly. Despite her earlier hesitation about transporting Leo in a hearse, Carrie was right. It was the best option.

When they arrived at the hospital, Leo was whisked away. A nurse quickly checked over Mattie for any injuries that she might have sustained during the explosion. When the woman found only slight bruising on Mattie's back, she ushered Mattie into a simple yet comfortably appointed waiting room. Wooden chairs and benches offered a place to sit, but Mattie couldn't. Luckily, at this hour, no one else occupied the area, giving her the freedom to pace. She had just completed her tenth circuit when her friends hurried through the entrance.

They all enfolded her into a hug, and she clung to them. For a long while, no one spoke. They seemed to understand that Mattie needed their silent support. Talking would come. But not now. Not yet.

Somehow, Mattie found herself on the bench, wedged between Vera and Aida, while the rest of the Flying Flappers gathered around. Alice's husband, John, had gone back to the inn with the children and Ruby, where he was waiting for any news.

"Aida and I will deal with Fabin Flyer and the police," Vera told Mattie softly. "It will be easy enough to convince them that Leo was trying to expose sabotage. Something was clearly wrong with the engine. When no one listened to Leo, he did everything possible to protect the spectators."

Mattie nodded, unable to speak. Her throat had grown so tight a part of her wondered if it was possible for a human trachea to collapse from sheer emotional pain. Vera and then Aida patted her on the back.

"It's okay to cry, Mattie," Aida said softly.

"B-b-b-but I never cry." Tears, however, drowned out her assertion.

Aida shoved a brightly embroidered handkerchief into Mattie's hands. The cheerful orange-red and turquoise flowers only made her sob harder. How could something be so joyful, so *bright*, as her world crumbled? Yet the gesture also touched Mattie. She knew that Aida's grandmother had sewn the beautiful artwork. Aida always carried it with her to remind her of her family, and she was sharing that comfort with Mattie.

Mattie clenched the cloth as she dabbed at her eyes. With her female friends surrounding her, she allowed her emotions to flow.

"Why? Why did he get into that plane?" Mattie asked, even though she knew the answer, knew it all too well. Leo had done it to protect her from her own arrogant belief that she was somehow invincible. She scrubbed her eyes. "It's all my fault."

"It is *not* your fault," Carrie told her sternly. "This is Earl Crenshaw's doing."

"Carrie is right." Vera's voice, normally so light and airy, sounded fierce. "Don't blame yourself."

"Leo tried to warn me." Mattie clenched and unclenched her fists. "He told me Crenshaw was a dangerous man. I should have demanded that the plane be inspected."

Aida reached out and squeezed her hand. "You didn't because the press was there. You know how they would have portrayed it—a nervous female too silly and too stubborn to admit her own fears about flying."

"Leo and I fought." Mattie rubbed the bridge of her nose, wishing she could go back and listen instead of angrily digging her heels into the unsteady sand. "Or at least *I* fought. I thought his reaction to Crenshaw was just another example of his overprotectiveness and that his concerns were overblown because of my sex."

"There's nothing more maddening than a man who thinks he knows more about your business than you do." Sadie leaned around Lily to address Mattie solemnly.

"If fellows spent as much time supporting us as they do trying to hold us back, imagine how far we gals could go," Lily said. Her statement was met with a chorus of agreement. Mattie thought of the Earl Crenshaws of the world, men who had such anger, such rage, toward women who had the audacity to think themselves equal. Crenshaw's anger had become so intense, so irrational, that he had not only tried to kill her but also risked the lives of countless spectators.

Then Mattie considered her older brothers, who believed that their solemn duty was to keep their younger sister from all harm. But if she had been born a little brother, they would have seen it as their obligation to teach her to be a daredevil like they had Alfred.

Yet Leo . . . Leo didn't seem to fit either mold.

"I don't think Leo was trying to hold me back," Mattie confessed. She thought of the fear she'd felt, the *terror* as his plane had hurtled to the earth. Did he experience something similar when she did stunts like purposely stalling in the air without warning him? What thoughts had ripped through him when her engine actually had failed all those months ago in Missouri?

"I don't think Leo wants to limit your flying either," Aida said softly.

Mattie turned toward her in surprise. Aida was normally the first to point out how perceived social constructs guided so many human actions.

"You don't?" Mattie asked.

Aida idly tapped her purse like she normally would her notebook as she entered what Vera termed her *scholarly mode*. "There is a natural human instinct to protect each other that is distinct from society's particular views of the roles each sex should play."

"In what way?" Vera tilted her body forward so she could see Aida around Mattie.

"Think of the ancient hill forts in the British Isles, this need to encircle the village and all the people with jagged rocks. There is this deep desire to keep loved ones safe, which then extends to the community. Consider how we as humans care for our injured and sick. Birds will peck, kill, and stomp out weaker members, even push them from the nest, but we humans, *we* build hospitals. This instinct has propelled us throughout history, from the first evidence of a healed life-threatening fracture to the ancient Incas, who developed brain-surgery techniques."

An image of Leo's spiraling plane whirled into Mattie's mind, coupled with her memory of guarding his body during the blast. She understood now that powerful drive to protect, the need to wrap someone she loved in her arms and try to keep tragedy at bay. After all, she'd wanted to catch a falling aircraft, and if Vera hadn't grabbed her, she likely would have tried.

But Mattie didn't think of Leo as weak. Far from it. He was one of the strongest people she knew. The desire to defend didn't necessarily correlate with the belief that the intended beneficiary was frail.

"Leo seems to possess an extraordinarily powerful urge to protect." Aida's fingers had stopped dancing across her clutch, indicating she had reached a logical conclusion.

"He does," Mattie agreed in a whisper as her mind flashed back to pulling Leo from the wreckage.

"You. Okay?"

Even lying in the dirt, flames roaring around him, his body mangled after a fall from the sky, Leo's first words had been an inquiry about *her* well-being. And it wasn't just her whom he'd sought to save. He'd turned the Fabin, knowing it would most certainly stall, in order to not risk the lives of the people on the bleachers.

"Men are always saying women like to fuss over their partner," Aida said, "but men have similar desires and tendencies. It is one of the things that I find magical about society as a whole—our ability to care for each other."

"I'm not used to anyone tending to me." Leo had confessed those words to Mattie in the cooling room at the Geyser View Sanitarium. He'd grown up alone, in an orphanage that he'd only described as *cold.* Yet he had not become frigid himself. *"When I got older, I tried to protect the younger ones from his punishments."* Leo made up for his lack of receipt of affection by, conversely, devoting himself to the care of others.

Before anyone could say more, a woman in a white lab coat entered the room, her dark-brown eyes solemn.

"Lizbeth?" Aida clambered to her feet, and Mattie followed, realizing this must be Aida's surgeon friend.

"Are you Leo Ward's fiancée?" Lizbeth turned toward Mattie, her expression kind, competent, and thoroughly unreadable.

"She is his partner," Aida confirmed, saving Mattie from speaking a falsehood.

Lizbeth looked intensely at Mattie, her expression frank and honest. She spoke with a straightforward matter-of-factness that made the details somehow easier to bear. "I'm Dr. Carillo-Barrera, and I helped to triage Leo. He is out of surgery. His right leg was broken in several places, but we were able to successfully set it. We did not detect any signs of internal bleeding, but we will still need to monitor him, as it is often difficult to determine the extent of injuries in a situation like this."

"But there's nothing to lead you to think this will be fatal?" Mattie gripped her hands together so tightly her short, blunt nails still managed to slice through her skin.

"He is still sedated, but his pulse is strong, his heart rate is good, and his body has not gone into shock. I cannot offer any guarantees at this juncture, but those are all good signs."

Mattie lifted her clasped hands to her mouth. Leo was going to be all right! The love of her life was going to survive!

"May I see him?" Mattie asked quietly. She needed to sweep her gaze over Leo and ascertain for herself the extent of his wounds. She needed to touch him and to run her fingers gently through his hair. She needed to talk to him, to reassure him of her love even if he lay unconscious.

"Shortly," Dr. Carillo-Barrera said, "when he is moved to a bed in one of the general wards."

"If you have any private rooms available, I shall pay for it." Vera rose to her feet. "I will be covering all of Leo Ward's bills."

Mattie shook her head. "I should be the one. Leo's accident was caused by my choices."

"Nonsense," Vera said. "Like we said earlier, it was Crenshaw's actions that injured Leo. I consider Leo my friend, and I have more than enough means to take care of the hospital expenses."

"We do have a few private rooms," Dr. Carillo-Barrera confirmed. "The money we receive from patients who use them helps keep us funded and able to accept charity cases."

Mattie found she didn't have the strength to fight both women. It would be better for Leo if he was in a quieter place rather than a big open room stacked full of beds. When he awoke, Mattie had so much to say to him and ask him that any degree of privacy would be appreciated.

While Dr. Carillo-Barrera and Aida had a quick chat with each other, Mattie sank back onto the wooden bench. Alice materialized by her side and sat down next to her.

"I did not want to say anything until we knew more about Leo's condition," Alice told her gently, "but Leo talked to John about you during our first exhibition back in Illinois."

"Leo did mention that he'd had a conversation with John, but not what it was about," Mattie said.

Alice nodded. "Leo wanted to know how John does it."

"Does what?"

"Supports, loves, and has a lasting relationship with a woman who chooses a profession that puts her in constant peril."

"Leo asked about that?" Despite all the pain, a thrill shot through Mattie's heart. Leo understood her more than she'd given him credit for.

"He did indeed." Alice folded her hands in her lap in an uncharacteristically solemn gesture. "John told him that Leo should try being more of your flight partner instead of a flight leader."

Leo's attitude toward her flying had changed after that first show. He'd listened more and suggested instead of commanded. He'd tried to be her partner, but had she ever considered him hers? Had not part of her always seen him as her competitor or, at least, as someone trying to hold her back and prevent her from achieving her dreams? Had part of her even been afraid to treat him as a partner? When she'd lost Alfred—her twin, her best friend, her coconspirator in life—she had lost an integral piece of herself. Was part of her afraid of exposing herself to such grief again?

"How do *you* do it?" Mattie asked.

"What do you mean?"

"How do you stay strong and independent while being a wife and a mother? How do you balance your desire to soar on the trapeze with John's need to keep you safe? How do you watch him fly through the air yourself?"

Alice thought for a moment, and then a broad grin broke over her face. "Why, what John said—a partnership. We talk to each other about our stunts, give each other advice. Sometimes I take it; sometimes I don't, but I always consider it. I never dismiss it outright. I listen. John does the same when I'm the one making suggestions. There's a mutual respect and understanding."

Partnership. Mutual respect. Equals. All those words were two sided, connected. They didn't weigh a person down or restrict them. They were supportive, constructive, freeing even. Yes, it opened a person to the potential pain of loss, but the gains were so much greater. Mattie had let these wonderful women into her life, and each lady had made her stronger.

"Thank you for telling me this," Mattie told Alice and then pressed her eyelids tightly closed.

She prayed that Leo would wake up. She prayed that she would be with him when he did. And she prayed that they would remain that way. Together. Side by side.

Leo awoke in a sea of grogginess and pain and an incongruous sense of warm comfort. He focused on the latter despite it being the faintest. He drew strength from the sensation as he battled through the heavy sleepiness that threatened to drag him back down into the dark oblivion. His leg throbbed, and his entire body felt as if it had been tossed around in a human-size saltshaker. The head of the orphanage had firmly believed in corporal punishment, and Leo had learned early to deal with discomfort, but this was greater than he'd ever encountered.

But Leo knew how to fight it. And this time he had that wonderful whisper of warmth. He clung to it, using it to leverage his body out of the morass of agony. His eyelids fluttered open, and an overwhelming sense of white and light struck him. Fuzzy and disoriented, he almost slipped backward past the hurt in order to reach the forgiving blackness. Then he heard her. *Mattie.*

"Leo?" Mattie's voice sounded softer than he'd ever heard before. She was scared, worried, frightened. He had to reassure her, comfort her. He forced his eyes open this time. His mouth felt dry, cottony, and his body curiously heavy.

"Leo?" Mattie's tone was stronger now, and her beautiful green-gold irises appeared in his line of vision. She squeezed his hand, and he realized rather sluggishly that her touch had been the source of his sense of succor.

"Hey." His voice sounded raw and shaky even to him, but the word was audible at least.

"Oh, Leo, I'm so sorry I didn't take your concerns more seriously." Mattie brushed her lips against his cheek, and it felt good, so good. He hadn't lost her after all. He'd feared he had from the minute he'd jumped into that cockpit and prevented her from flying. He'd thought she'd withdraw from him the way she had all those years ago when he'd ratted her out to her brothers and that she'd leave him like everyone else. But she hadn't. She was here, holding his hand . . . apologizing to *him* . . . watching over him.

"S'okay," he breathed out. It took so much energy to talk. He didn't feel like he was dying, though—just fuzzy, so fuzzy. "Hard to think."

"They gave you morphine," Mattie explained, "and something to keep you unconscious during surgery."

"Don't like." He knew he sounded grumpy, but he'd rather face the agony, especially if it meant talking to Mattie more clearly. He wanted to say so much.

Mattie gave him a rather watery smile as she gently brushed back his hair. He would have closed his eyes at the remarkable tenderness of her touch, but he was afraid he would fall asleep immediately.

"The doctors have every hope you won't need strong medicine for long," Mattie said. "By some miracle, the worst injury appears to be to your right leg, and that will heal."

Leo had more time with Mattie, then. He wished he could tell her that, express that, but it would take too many words. Instead he, who had always hidden his emotions, tried to convey his feelings with his eyes alone. He greatly feared, though, that his gaze looked as bleary as he felt. Yet somehow, Mattie read his silent message, and even better, she returned it.

"I love you, Leo." Mattie pressed the lightest of kisses against his lips. *"I love you."* A flicker of memory winked through him. He'd heard her say that before as he'd lain on the ground, his mind drifting away from Mattie when he'd so badly wanted to stay.

He yearned to verbally say the words he'd held inside himself for so long . . . too long. But he didn't have the energy, so he smiled. As he grinned, a gentle, soothing sleep claimed him once more.

When Leo awoke again, the degree of pain had increased, but his mind felt clearer. It took him much less effort to open his eyes. The room had descended into darkness, lit only by a single lamp. Yet still, in his hand, he felt Mattie's. He slowly shifted his head to find her curled in a decidedly uncomfortable-looking chair. Her slight body seemed jammed into several impossible angles, yet somehow, she'd fallen asleep. She snored slightly, and the faint little snorts made him smile. Even in rest, Mattie couldn't stay still. She had to make some noise, some movement.

But he didn't like the light bruising under her eyes. She needed real sleep, not some facsimile in a noisy hospital, her body folded like a lady's fan.

Mattie must have sensed his gaze, for she shifted, stretched the hand not holding his, and blinked. When she spied him awake, she bolted upright.

"How are you feeling? Are you in a lot of pain? Should I call for a nurse? They said to let them know if you needed more medication."

"I've had enough fog for a lifetime," Leo grumbled and then realized that complaining was *not* how he wanted to spend his time with Mattie. Relaxing his scowl, he rubbed his thumb gently over her knuckles. He had never told another being that he loved them, not even in the platonic sense. He huffed out a breath, but when the words finally came, he found them surprisingly and wonderfully easy to say.

"I love you, Mattie McAdams."

He'd always found Mattie beautiful. It didn't matter if she had a smudge of grease on her face or diamonds hanging from her ears. But the *look* she gave him, the utter *glow* shining from her golden eyes, the sheer *love* in her smile as her pink lips tilted upward . . .

It undid him. It was as if everything inside him unspooled so it could wrap up in her.

"You told me you were sorry for not listening to my concerns." Leo swallowed hard. "I wanted to apologize, too, for taking that plane. But once I saw it was tampered with, I knew I couldn't let you climb into the cockpit."

"Why did you fly it? You knew it would crash, yet you still tried to operate it," Mattie asked, her eyes wet again. The sight slayed Leo. Mattie rarely teared up, and he'd never seen her cry until now.

"I couldn't save Alfred." The confession came in a rush, the awful truth that felt like a secret but really wasn't. Everyone knew Leo had returned from the front . . . and the beloved McAdams brother hadn't.

Mattie blinked, clearly not expecting this. Then her entire face softened, not hardened as he'd expected. "Leo, Alfred was brought down by enemy fire. There was nothing you could have done."

"He wasn't brought down by enemy fire, not at first." Leo had told this story only two times before. The first to his commanding officer and the second in a letter—that damned misguided letter. Then he'd never spoken of it again. Not once. He hadn't ever wanted to relive it, but in some ways, by not thinking about it, he'd enshrined it inside himself. And it had become a part of him.

"I know he accidentally flew into an ambush." Mattie's voice wobbled a bit when she spoke, but Leo barely heard the catch as his own guilt roared through him like thunder.

"It wasn't just that," Leo admitted hoarsely, and Mattie's delicate fingers tightened on his. He almost stopped, but he'd already said too much. If he did not continue, her mind would create increasingly worse scenarios, and Mattie possessed a vivid imagination.

Leo swallowed once, then twice, before he could continue. "After he got mixed up, Alfred dived too quickly after an enemy pilot. One of the major weaknesses of our Nieuports was that the canvas would tear off in rapid descents. Alfred knew that—we all knew that—but that didn't stop him from swooping down. You fly so similar to him. Fast. Heedless to danger. Absolutely fearlessly."

"Is . . ." Mattie paused to take her own steadying breath. "Is that why you were always urging me not to fly stunts?"

"Yes," he admitted. "When you dive too sharply or when you free-fall without warning, the images blur, and I think I catch sight of Alfred's plane on that last plummet. It was worse, much worse, when I just returned from the front. That's why when you told me that you planned the stall maneuver during Alfred's memorial service, I . . . I panicked. I ratted you out to your brothers in hopes they could convince you not to try the trick. I didn't realize they'd stop you from flying altogether."

"Oh, Leo." Mattie lifted her other hand and placed it over his, sandwiching his fingers between her two palms. "I never thought, never considered. I should have, but I was just so, so focused on thinking that you wanted to curtail my flying because I am a female."

"That was never the reason, and I should have told you that years ago," Leo admitted, "but I let you believe that because I thought it was easier to keep you safe."

"But why?" Mattie asked. "I might have listened more if I'd understood the truth."

"But you also would have realized how much you meant to me, Mattie," Leo confessed.

"I rather like knowing." Mattie's voice sounded as pleasant as heat from a coal stove on a cold winter's day, and he wanted to warm himself in the glow. She leaned closer to him, as if to impart a secret. "Because I feel the same about you."

Ignoring the protest of his abused body, he lifted himself on his elbows and planted a quick kiss on her lips. Unfortunately, he didn't have the energy for a longer one. He collapsed back down on the bed, feeling not exactly at ease but not as troubled as he'd thought he'd be by the confessions he was making.

"I was afraid that once you understood your power over me, I wouldn't be able to keep you from danger, because you'd see that you could persuade me to agree to anything," Leo admitted. "And I was also afraid of admitting how I felt."

Mattie tenderly brushed back his hair and kissed his cheek. "Says the man who jumped in a sabotaged plane to prevent me from flying it, even after we became sweethearts and argued over whether I'd compete that day."

"I underestimated my own stubbornness." Leo lifted one side of his mouth.

"But not mine," Mattie said softly, "but *that* is going to change."

Leo searched her face, trying to understand what she meant. She looked more solemn than he'd ever seen her. Her determination was there too. Fiery. Intense. *Fierce.*

"I won't always take your advice, and I'll always make up my own mind, but I promise to do a better job of listening. But you have to understand that we'll protect each other. I'll be worrying about you too. You frightened me today in ways that I didn't know that I could be frightened. It made me understand why you worry, and I reserve the right to fret too. You're not the only one with fears about losing someone they love again."

Any other time Leo would have shifted uncomfortably, but he suspected his body wouldn't appreciate the unnecessary movement. Instead, he kept his gaze on Mattie, and the patent affection he saw on her face soothed him more than any amount of fidgeting ever could. This was *Mattie*. Mattie, who had been in his life and in his heart for so long. If he loved her enough to protect her, then he should also love her enough to let her protect *him*, love *him*—in all its manifestations.

It was time for him to share the burden he'd carried for years. The burden he and Walt McAdams had paid over and over to keep buried.

Leo needed to open himself fully to Mattie, to allow her to understand him, maybe even parts of him that he didn't fully comprehend himself. If Leo wanted her to turn toward him, he had to lean on her. He had to stop fearing she would reject him, leave him.

"There was a chance Alfred could have landed his plane. Many pilots did. I have. We were too deep in enemy territory for him to glide to safety, but he was a skilled aviator. He could have coaxed that bird to the ground. He would have become a prisoner of war, but he would have survived. He would have *survived*."

Mattie seemed to sense that Leo needed to speak without interruption. But she still comforted him—supported him—with her tender green-gold gaze, with her butterfly-soft touch, and even with her silence. It wasn't a stony one but a warm one full of empathy and compassion.

"During the first dogfight that day, I was battling an Albatros when out of the corner of my eye I saw a plane with US roundels on its wings heading the wrong direction. The plane seemed like it was moving oddly, like the pilot was having some sort of trouble, but the bird was still mostly operable. Then the German fighting me started shooting, and I turned my attention back to him. By the time I'd freed myself, my comrade's plane was deeper into enemy territory. I was the flight leader, so I took off after him, hoping I could signal for the unlucky fellow to turn around. I'd only been following him for a few seconds when I recognized Alfred's bold flying technique.

"It was awful watching him wing into peril and having no way to stop him." Leo spoke fast now, the words tumbling out one on top of the other. He was afraid if he didn't release them now, he never would. "I spotted the ambush straight off. Alfred didn't. There were five planes surrounding him before I got close enough to engage. That's when your brother dived too fast for how the Nieuport wings were constructed. I saw the bare frame of his plane. The Fokkers who your brother had been chasing had started to loop over your brother to reverse their positions. I went to assist Alfred, but another German plane intercepted me. I took the time to engage him, and by the time I'd finished the skirmish, your brother's Nieuport was in flames."

Leo did not have to tell Mattie that death in a burning plane was the most painful way for an aviator to be killed. All pilots feared it the most, dreaded it the most. In a profession that attracted the intrepid, a fiery crash was the one thing that secretly terrified them all.

"I should've flown around that Albatros," Leo continued. "I should've protected Alfred's rear, guarded him until he could land."

"But you would have died, Leo," Mattie said gently. "There was no guarantee that you could have prevented the shot that caused the leak in his gas tank. You had no way of knowing that the pilot tailing Alfred would even continue shooting. He might have just followed Alfred's plane to the ground to make sure he fell behind German lines."

"I shouldn't have taken that risk." Leo ignored his protesting muscles and shoved his hand into his hair. "Alfred had a family. He had people who would mourn him. He was important."

For the first time since the painful conversation had begun, Mattie's face crumpled, and several tears rolled down her face. "Oh, *Leo*, you are important too! Don't ever think that you're not."

"Your family was the only one I've ever known. You'd given me so much, so very much, and I let one of you die on my watch." The words, laden with half a decade of guilt, ripped from Leo.

Mattie reached up and gently tugged at his wrist, removing his hand from its viselike grip on his hair. She held both of his palms between her own now and applied a gentle, reassuring pressure.

"You are part of our family, Leo." Mattie pulled slightly on his hand when he started to shift his ashamed gaze from her fierce one. He jerked his chin back and allowed himself to accept the intense affection pouring from Mattie. "We would have mourned you as much as Alfred. I would never, *never* want to be forced to choose between your two lives, but I *am* glad you lived through the war. We all are. Father. My brothers. All of us."

Something cracked inside Leo. Not in a bad way but in a good way. It was as if a blockage—old, hard, and formerly impenetrable—had broken off. Mattie's resilient sweetness had been working against the clog for weeks now, weakening it, filing bits of it away, pushing a hole or two through the tough core. Now it burst loose. Messy, sloppy, and chaotic feelings rushed at him, carrying him along in an almost dizzying madness. But he didn't try to dam them back up. He let them wash through him, filling him, changing him.

"That's not all, Mattie." Leo swallowed hard. "A week after Alfred's death, I got a letter. It came from an address I didn't recognize. It started with the man, Clive, congratulating me for becoming an ace and saying that he thought I was his son. I had the right first name, was the right age, came from the right city, and I looked just like him. He'd included his photograph, and I realized it was true. Back then, living in that opulent château, I couldn't escape the grief and the guilt—the horrible, horrible guilt over Alfred. I couldn't tell you or your father about his final flight, so I wrote to this man who claimed he wanted to be my father again. I told him every single detail, said it was all my fault."

"Oh, Leo." Mattie's voice held no condemnation over the fact he'd revealed private information about her brother's death to a stranger when Leo had not told the McAdamses. Instead, her tone vibrated with concern for *him*.

Emotion deepened Leo's voice. "I never heard from my father again until he showed up at the flight school. He'd just gotten out of prison and spotted my face on the soap that I endorsed. He wanted paid, or he was going to publish the letter. I wasn't around, but your pa was. Walt had just handed Clive a check when I walked into the office."

Leo paused as guilt lacerated him. He squeezed his eyes shut, as if he could stop what had happened. "So you see, *I'm* the reason for your family's financial difficulties. Walt didn't make poor decisions. *I* did. He's been protecting Alfred and me."

Two warm hands touched his cheeks. Opening his eyes, he found Mattie watching him with nothing but love on her face. "Leo, you are no more to blame for your father's actions than I am for Crenshaw's."

"You forgive me?" Leo asked, wonder shooting through his agonized remorse.

"There is nothing to forgive. You did nothing wrong."

The conviction in Mattie's voice triggered a relief so strong that it almost hurt. But Leo still wasn't completely sure if he deserved any reprieve.

"But I put your whole family at risk." Leo rubbed the back of his head until Mattie reached up with one hand and stopped him. She swept her fingers over his knuckles, soothing him, quieting the roaring fears.

"You're part of the McAdamses too. And we always protect each other. If Pa had told the boys and me everything, we would have told him to pay off your father too—even if it hadn't involved Alfred and it had just meant defending *you*."

"Walt said something similar." Leo choked out the words as a kernel of belief started to unfurl inside him, taking tenuous root.

"Then you should listen."

"I'm not sure if I know how to step from the sidelines into the heart of a family. I'm used to being the silent, unseen guardian, but I want to be your partner." The confession scraped against Leo's raw, newly released emotions, but it had to be said; *he* needed to say it, and Mattie deserved to hear it.

Mattie smiled through the fall of two more tears. It was her beautiful, confident grin, the one she wore when she soared through the air. She squeezed his hand like she would the stick and throttle of her Jenny, steering them both skyward.

"We'll show each other, Leo." Mattie smiled. "Look at the foundation we've built without even trying. Imagine what we'll accomplish when we're both working together. We're daredevils, Leo. We're used to making the impossible reality. Are you ready to embark on this adventure with me?"

"I'll follow you anywhere you ask me to go, Mattie. If you're willing to take a risk on starting a family with me, I'll get down on one knee as soon as this busted leg heals."

"Leo, I am an expert at risk-taking, and you aren't one. You're surefire."

Her bold assurance boosted him. He'd been a fool to think he wouldn't suit Mattie. They complemented each other, perfectly balanced counterweights.

"I love you, Mattie McAdams."

"I love you too, Leo Ward."

And with those words playing through his soul, Leo let his eyelids finally slide down. He permitted the exhaustion to pull him under, but he had Mattie's confident love to anchor him and prevent him from drifting too far away.

Mattie couldn't help but brush a strand of Leo's hair back as he fell peacefully to sleep. She'd never experienced such an overwhelming tenderness before. It stunned her how such a soft, quiet feeling could be so undeniably fortifying.

She finally understood why Leo had betrayed her confidence all those years ago on the eve of Alfred's memorial. With that knowledge came the rebirth of her trust in him. They had all been hurting then. There'd been so much pain. Not one of them had known how to address it. They'd stumbled along clumsily, hurting each other in the process.

Even after all these years, she and Leo were still healing from the loss of Alfred. A part of them always would be. But it was different now. Because they were grieving together, supporting each other, the way that her twin would have wanted.

Leo's memories of Alfred's death, his guilt at surviving when Alfred had not, his doubts about his own self-worth, his father's betrayal—they had torn through Mattie like shards of glass slicing apart a pneumatic rubber tire. For a moment, it had deflated her to think that he saw himself as expendable. It struck her how many times Leo had performed a dangerous stunt to prevent not only her from doing it but her brothers as well. Leo had been protecting them, safeguarding them *all* for years, and they'd never realized he'd been their guardian angel. He'd never replaced her in dangerous stunts because he thought less of her since she was a woman but because he saw himself as the lesser—the foundling left on the stoop of a cold, austere orphanage.

But that moment in time didn't define him; it had never defined him. Leo was neither the circumstance of his birth nor the consequence of his parents' abandonment. He was a good-hearted hero, a fearless protector, and an amazing adventurer. He had brought so much joy into her life from their earliest days of friendship to their newly deepened relationship. And she would make sure he saw that, understood that.

For it was time that Leo had a guardian angel of his own.

Chapter Eighteen

What was initially meant as a race to determine if a female flyer could possibly outpace national war hero Mr. Earl Crenshaw ended in a nearly fatal crash for another of America's aces, famous balloon buster Mr. Leo Ward. No one is sure why Mr. Ward was in the cockpit of the aircraft designated for Miss Mattie McAdams, but it has been rumored that the famed aviator and the petticoat flyer are sweethearts. There is some speculation that Mr. Ward meant to slip unseen into the airplane and fly in her stead, but the plan went awry, resulting in a nearly deadly tailspin into the ground. At least one expert aviator believes that the curious circumstances cast suspicion on Mr. Ward and Miss McAdams's previous challenges and may indicate that the former balloon buster permitted the girl flyer's alleged wins. At the very least, it appears to once again demonstrate that the dangers of flying make it an unsuitable pursuit for the weaker sex. Mr. Crenshaw is of the firm opinion that had Miss McAdams been in the cockpit rather than the experienced Mr. Ward, the apparent engine trouble would have resulted in not only her tragic passing but those of several spectators in the stands, as the female

> reflexes are biologically not as fast as a man's, especially when it comes to aviation.
>
> —Benjamin Pringle, *Oceanbreeze Chronicle*, *Chicago Advance Leader*

Leo had spent his life watching over others. He was not accustomed to being the one watched. Mattie had stayed by his bedside for over thirty-six hours. It had taken him and all the female members of the flying circus to convince her to depart to eat a proper meal and to rest. She had only agreed to leave when the other Flying Flappers had volunteered to stay with him. In the end, Aida had mentioned that she had something she wished to talk to Leo about, which was how he found himself sitting in awkward silence with her . . . well, awkward silence on his part. Aida seemed entirely at ease as she chatted to him about nothing in particular. He supposed she was trying to make him more comfortable, but he'd never figured out the art of small talk.

She must have sensed this, as she turned to more-direct questions. "How *are* you feeling? Don't worry about putting on a brave face. I promise I won't gab to Mattie."

"Sore," he said, "but fine."

"Are you tired?" Aida prodded.

"Not really," he said, and it was the truth. He'd slept more in the past thirty-six hours than he ever had. Although he still felt the vestiges of the draining effects from the drugs and the surgery, his mind didn't feel muddled. He also wasn't on the verge of drifting off to sleep every time he blinked.

"Would you be up to reading?" Aida asked.

Leo glanced warily at the stack of newspapers perched on her lap. It was a rather intimidating pile with her clutch situated precariously on top. He'd barely had any education, even at the orphanage. He could read, but it was a rather laborious exercise. And he hated doing it with an audience.

"If you are too tired, I can read them to you." Aida kept her voice casual, but Leo suspected she understood the reason for his reluctance. Not only was she classy enough to refrain from calling him out, but she'd given him an excuse to just listen and to avoid chitchat.

"Okay." He eased back onto the pillow, trying to make his stiff, bruised body as comfortable as possible.

"I will warn you that these are about the pylon race," Aida said. "If you are not ready for articles about your accident, I fully understand."

Leo regarded Aida carefully. Like always, she looked perfectly put together, her style more elegant and reserved than Vera's flashier chicness but no less distinctive or compelling. She was a thoughtful, caring woman. If she'd brought the broadsheets with her, she'd done so for a good, logical reason.

"Is this for Mattie's sake?" Leo asked.

A pleased smile touched her lips, painted a dark, muted red. "You are remarkably attuned to her. I find it enormously refreshing."

"Our relationship is definitely going to be in your book, isn't it?" Leo barely, just barely, stopped his groan.

"Only if you both consent. I do think your courtship would make for a very informative study about how a modern love can work between the New Woman and the New Man."

"New Man?"

"It is a term I am planning to coin as a companion to *New Woman*. After all, it wouldn't be fair if only one sex had the fun of going through a remarkable revolution, now would it?"

"Uh . . ." Leo did not exactly know how to reply. He wasn't accustomed to viewing the world in the terms that Mattie, Aida, and their female companions did. But then, he supposed, he never had to. Although he occasionally butted up against class restrictions, he didn't encounter nearly as many unwritten societal regulations. Presumptions generally worked in his favor, not against it.

"Well, you and Mattie can discuss between yourselves whether you wish to be featured in a chapter. I won't ask again, so if I hear nothing, I shall simply assume that you wish for privacy," Aida told him.

Mattie would likely want to, especially if she thought it would help other women achieve independence. But she had always been remarkably cognizant of his unspoken feelings, more so than himself sometimes. She wouldn't force him to permit Aida to write about their personal lives if it made him uncomfortable.

"May I ask why you are so keen to study society?" Leo asked.

"Do you think it an odd choice for a woman?" Aida's lips quirked into a challenge that reminded him of Mattie.

"I haven't put too much thought into sociology," Leo admitted. "I'd never even heard about it until you mentioned it. I'm curious to understand more."

Satisfied with his answer, Aida folded her hands. "I suppose the influence of culture and societal norms has always fascinated me. I've been fortunate to experience so many. I have great-grandparents who are Miwok, Mexican, and Spanish, and I spent my formative years speaking French and German in a Swiss boarding school. It has made me naturally curious to explore the roles and beliefs that form us."

When Aida finished, she unwrapped her fingers and carefully placed her purse on the chair beside her. Selecting the top broadsheet, she unfolded it. "This is Pringle's article that is being run in all of the *Chicago Advance Leader*'s affiliate papers. The headline reads, 'Crash Raises Questions of Legitimacy of Flying Flappers.'"

"Does Mattie know?" Leo asked, his stomach plummeting faster than it had when he'd parachuted from a JN-4 for the McAdams Family Flying Circus. Mattie had been right about how the press would perceive any failure related to her race against Crenshaw.

"No," Aida said. "We're planning to tell her after she's had a chance to rest."

Leo squeezed his eyes shut at the enormity of what Aida had just revealed. For Mattie not to check or even ask about the coverage of the accident showed how much she was worried about him. She did truly love him, something he'd never even dreamed possible before the night on the Lake Michigan beach.

"How bad is the rest of the article?" Leo asked.

"It is not good," Aida admitted with her normal straightforwardness, but she gentled her voice. "Unfortunately, we were all distracted and not able to ensure that the reporters knew the truth. Earl Crenshaw has clearly been manipulating the perceptions of the event. He is rather diabolically cunning at taking advantage of common prejudices to twist events to benefit him. Fortunately, he has not encountered *us* before. Vera and I are both using our connections, and Carrie and Sadie are helping us make the technical arguments in your defense. Crenshaw has already fled town now that an investigation into the crash has started. Fabin Flyer has agreed not to press charges against you, although they do wish to meet with you and Mattie."

"I owe you an additional thanks, then." Leo knew that Mattie had mentioned that he wouldn't face any jail time over his stunt, but he hadn't had the energy to fully consider what the women were doing to protect him. Their defense both warmed and humbled Leo.

Aida waved her gloved hand. "It is nothing. You saved Mattie's life and potentially those of countless spectators. And you exposed Crenshaw's sabotage. You did nothing wrong, Leo, and we were glad to make sure you weren't unfairly prosecuted. And you *are* a famous, handsome Anglo-American war hero. It wasn't very difficult to convince the authorities that you meant no harm, and it won't be hard to change the mind of the press either."

Leo slowly eased his sore body into a sitting position. He shoved his hand into his hair at the back of his head. "I'd better hear what they're saying about Mattie and me."

Aida cleared her throat and rattled the pages before she commenced reading, her voice becoming professorial. Guilt strafed Leo like a barrage from an enemy Archie battery. Mattie had apologized for not taking his concerns seriously, but apparently he hadn't fully accounted for hers either. The news coverage of the accident was exactly what she'd feared. Worse, it put everything she'd worked for in jeopardy. If her reputation was irreversibly tattered, she'd likely not only lose the Rockol endorsement but find no other business offers, including for her RadioNavigator.

"I am not just flying for myself but all female aviators. If I fail to show, this will make national news—empirical proof of a female flyer's innate fickleness." The words Mattie had spoken during their argument on the Southern California beach blazed through his mind. She'd called the race a battle for a cause that she believed in. She'd been right.

"What do the other articles say?" Leo dreaded the answer, but he needed to know.

"Variations of the same," Aida said, confirming his suspicions. "Pringle isn't alone in crowing about the superiority of male aviators and questioning Mattie's previous successes."

Leo exhaled. "Mattie's instinct will be to challenge Crenshaw to a rematch."

"Yes," Aida agreed.

Leo scrubbed the back of his head even harder. "That's why you suggested that I listen to the articles? You wanted me to be prepared?"

"Society is not yet kind to women who wish to pursue careers generally perceived as belonging to the realm of men. Mattie will always face resistance, and some of the opposition will be dangerous. She threatens deeply held beliefs that some will defend even with violence."

Leo thought about how each of the women in their troupe regarded their aerial stunts in a broader, more sweeping sense than mere personal achievements. During the Great War, Leo had flown for Alfred and his squadron, for the Allies, for his country, for his belief in freedom. But since then he had taken to the skies not to defend a cause but only to support himself and protect the McAdamses. In contrast, Vera had formed an entire flying circus to challenge the meek roles prescribed to her sex. All the women had joined for similar reasons, with Carrie also fighting to dismantle racial prejudice. Aida was recording their experiences to write an academic thesis on the emergence of the New Woman.

"There will always be Crenshaws to battle." Leo echoed Mattie's words.

"And Mattie will always want to stand against them. The variable is you. Will you be by her side when she does?"

Once again, Mattie's words burst into Leo's mind, as strong and as forceful as when she'd first spoken them: *"When you and Alfred left for the war, I didn't want to lose you—either of you. But I not only let you both go—I wrote to you every week with words of encouragement. Can't you do the same now? For me? Support me even if you are worried?"*

And there was only one answer to the questions that both Aida and Mattie had put forward.

When Mattie returned to Leo's private room, she found him sleeping restfully, with Aida quietly writing in her notebook. Aida glanced up at her entrance. She gave a nod and began to pack up her belongings. Unfortunately, even after surgery and strong medication Leo was a light sleeper. His blue eyes blinked open, and he fixed Mattie with the shy grin that she loved. His drowsiness made the smile even sweeter, and her heart gave a delightful trill like a sparrow's airy call.

"Should I leave the stack of broadsheets?" Aida asked, nodding to a pile of newspapers. A jarring sensation struck Mattie as she realized she had utterly forgotten about the press in her worry for Leo. In whatever manner the reporters had chosen to report the crash, she knew it would not flatter her or female aviators.

Leo gave a firm, sharp nod. "Yes."

A silent message passed between Aida and Leo. Mattie would have thought more of it if she hadn't found herself battling a resurgence of unease about the coverage of the event. But she tried to force those thoughts away. She could not control what had been printed, and now was not the time to fix it. That would come later, for at this moment Leo needed her attention.

Aida left the room and pulled the door shut softly behind her, leaving Mattie and Leo in relative silence. Sunlight once again washed over the white room. Stirring the curtains, a morning breeze blew through the large open window. The air carried the salty scent of the ocean, although they could not see the water from this vantage point. Despite the fear of the past forty-eight hours, the smell made Mattie think of beckoning adventure.

"You can look at them," Leo said.

"Look at what?" Mattie asked.

"The news rags."

With a start, Mattie brushed her fingers over her fresh pair of trousers. "That can wait."

"Aida read them to me," Leo explained. "You'll want to know what was written about the race so you can come up with a plan."

Mattie didn't need any more encouragement. She crossed the small room in two strides. With a now-trembling hand, she skimmed the first article. Outrage flamed through her, almost destroying her caution and better sense. But not completely. Not again. She would not allow Crenshaw to bait her—or Leo—into another trap.

Breathing deeply, she turned to find Leo watching her, his expression a new one, and for once, she couldn't read it. Her body filled with electrified anticipation, just as it did when she dived down to zoom her plane under a bridge. This moment would be a defining one. For them. For their confessed love. For their future.

"If I wasn't lying here in a hospital bed, what would your next maneuver be?"

Mattie suddenly understood why Leo shoved his hand in his hair so often, because she found herself wanting to do the same. Instead she clenched her hand, letting her fingers dig into her flesh.

"I'd demand a rematch."

"And now?" Leo asked.

"I still want to challenge Crenshaw, but I don't want to put you or Vera's Flying Flappers in harm's way." Mattie knew she'd be getting a call from Rockol after this coverage, and if she had a plan to defend her good name, she might convince them not to drop her. A rematch would also go a long way in securing other sponsors, and the positive press would help make her more well known as she tried to market her RadioNavigator. But as much as she wanted to protect her family's business and her own career, she wouldn't jeopardize the safety of those she loved. Not again.

"Then we'd better be especially cautious in how we organize the event. I assume Vera will have some foolproof ideas, including how to announce the contest in a way that prevents even Crenshaw from slithering out of it."

A swell of love burst through Mattie, along with a sense of incredible relief. Perhaps there was a way to safeguard Leo and her friends while still pursuing her dreams. "You'd help me arrange a race?"

Leo nodded, his certainty reigniting her confidence. "You apologized for not taking my concerns about Crenshaw seriously, but I didn't say I was sorry for dismissing yours. You were clearly right too. Crenshaw manipulated the reporters into denouncing female aviators."

"It didn't take that much manipulating." Mattie tapped her foot in frustration. She wanted to pace, but the small confines of the room didn't allow for a lot of movement.

"No, it didn't," Leo agreed. "I should have listened more to you and tried better to understand what flying means to you—how you see it as a mission, a cause, a battle even. You said you'll start considering my advice more, and I need to learn how to support you even better."

Mattie yearned to fling her arms around Leo and squeeze him tightly, but she didn't want to reinjure him. Instead, she leaned down and kissed him gently but thoroughly. Joy and deep contentment mixed in a wonderful, ecstatic swirl that zipped through her like a bunch of barrel rolls, one glorious twist after another.

When they broke apart, they just grinned at each other, happy, silly smiles that despite their goofy giddiness were anchored by something strong, lasting . . . and solid just like Leo himself. This mutual respect—this was the foundation for a future. White picket fences and a neat little house on a quiet street weren't for Mattie, but a lifetime with Leo? It gifted her with something as broad and unlimited as the skies themselves.

"Knowing you and your meticulous planning, I assume you already have some ideas for making sure Crenshaw can't sabotage this competition." Mattie sat on the edge of the bed so she could be closer to Leo as they strategized.

He dipped his chin, looking more relaxed than she'd ever seen him. There was a casual looseness about all his muscles, including his facial ones. He looked boyish and utterly content.

"I may have a couple plans of attack," he admitted. "But do you want to come up with some of your own first?"

"My only goal at the moment is to firmly trounce Crenshaw. The details are more your expertise."

Sinking deeper into his pillows, Leo reached for her hand. "Do you remember the Canyon of the Bridges?"

Mattie rolled her eyes. "Another place where my brothers refused to let me fly."

Despite her old exasperation, a burst of excitement rollicked through Mattie at the mention of the series of impressive natural bridges carved into the sandstone rocks by a long-gone river. The tight, twisty canyon was located close to the main line of the Santa Fe Railroad and attracted a healthy share of tourists. She'd wanted so keenly to swoop under the massive slabs of rock stretching over the top of the deep gorge. The middle bridge in the set of five required the pilot to fly diagonally through the narrow opening. That and the sharp turns made it potentially perilous but nothing that Mattie couldn't handle. It was the perfect setting to ensure Crenshaw couldn't tamper with the course and put anyone else in danger.

"I was thinking we could use the Fabins," Leo said. "Aida and Vera both have been talking to the owners, and they believe our story of sabotage. My guess is that they'll be happy to provide the planes to prove their machines are safe. And they will be double- and triple-checking the engines. We can arrange for you to have time to fly one of their machines before the meet so you're comfortable with its quirks."

"If we're using a fast plane like a Fabin Flyer rather than a slow trainer like a Jenny, are you thinking more along the lines of a speed competition rather than the aerobatic ones that you and I do?"

"Both. We'll come up with a specific course for you and Crenshaw to follow when you fly through the bridges. The choreography will be included in the newspaper article so Earl can't change it. I figured that you'd want a contest where you can show off your maneuvering skills. You're top notch at aerobatics."

Leo pressed their fingers together briefly, and a jolt shot through Mattie at his compliment. This . . . *this* was the partnership she'd dreamed of: a man who worked with her.

"We could use white smoke to show how close we fly to the formations!" Mattie added excitedly, referring to the white vapors employed by aviators to "write" messages in the air. Vera had been talking about purchasing some of the smoke-generating machines anyway.

Leo paused, considering. Mattie knew he was thinking about how the use of the smoke might encourage her to take unnecessary risks, driving her closer and closer to the unforgiving sandstone walls.

"I won't get overly cocky. I promise. If I start feeling invincible, I'll think about how I felt watching your Fabin tumble earthward."

"Okay," Leo agreed, his voice calm and resolute, without a hint of doubt. "We'll use the white smoke. Crenshaw won't be able to manipulate the obstacles, since they're rock structures that have been around for centuries."

"I figured that's why you chose Canyon of the Bridges—very cleverly done."

Leo's lips quirked up into a shy but proud smile. As much as Mattie enjoyed sparring with him, collaborating was just as thrilling and twice the fun.

"This time, you and I will be able to keep a close eye on your Fabin and make sure that neither Crenshaw nor any of his hired thugs tamper with it."

"That makes sense." Mattie bobbed her head, sending her short red curls flying, as if even her mop of hair wanted to join in the affirmation.

Crenshaw might be underhanded and diabolical, but he was no match for Mattie and Leo. They made an unbeatable team when they finally stopped arguing and started listening to each other.

Which made her think of another villain they needed to defeat. Leo's father.

"Leo?" she asked, and he immediately glanced at her in concern, sensing the change in her tone. "Your father? Has he contacted you since he blackmailed my father? Has he asked for more payments?"

Leo only hesitated for an instant. "Yes. He mostly just sends letters, but he showed up in Iowa at the hotel lobby. That's why I was acting so strangely when you found me."

Mattie understood the trust Leo had just placed in her. Only that knowledge prevented her ire toward Clive from consuming her. She needed to stay calm, rational, for Leo's sake. This wasn't a problem to charge at. She reached over and brushed her hand over his cheek.

"I have an idea of how to stop him, if you want to hear it." Mattie had suspected that Leo's poor excuse for a father hadn't stopped at one attempt to gather money.

Leo's eyes fluttered shut, and he shifted to kiss her hand gently. "I can't see any way that *won't* drag your family and Alfred into the press. I can't make you all go through that."

"It's time we celebrated my brother. It would do us all good to talk about him. We write the article about what happened the day of his death. We tell the tale and frame it how it should be rightfully presented. Pa, my brothers, you, and I will all approve what it says. Once it is published, your father will have no hold over any of us." The more Mattie had considered this plan last night, the more she had realized it would free all of them.

"I wouldn't want to ask you and your family to do that." Leo's eyes fluttered open, and she could see the worry still there.

"You *are* part of the family. It will be healing for all of us to tell Alfred's story. And you better believe that Alfred would demand we do it!"

A soft, affectionate smile, full of fond memory, stretched across Leo's face. "Alfred would, right after he'd punched my old man in the kisser and told him to blouse."

"We'll tell his story and your story."

"Together." Leo reached for her other hand and squeezed it.

Together. Solid yet fierce. Thoughtful but daring. Cautious, though bold.

The perfect combination.

Chapter Nineteen

This is an account of two heroes. One intrepid, one quiet. One who died, one who lived. One who came from a famous family of aviators, the other who grew up in a foundling home and in the streets of New York City.

Many reporters have asked for the story of my past and the details of my days as an ace during the Great War. But it is not my tale alone. It is the story of the McAdams family, who taught me first to soar, and it is the legacy of my best friend, Alfred McAdams. I did not write this article on my own but had the assistance of Alfred's twin sister, Mattie McAdams, and the rest of their family. It is in memory of Alfred—an indomitable spirit whose sense of adventure and love of flying lives on through us, the survivors.

Alfred was the one who first wanted to join the Lafayette Escadrille . . .

—Leo Ward (coauthored by the family of Alfred McAdams), *Aviators' Gazette*

Clive adjusted the collar on his ratty overcoat with a self-important air as Vera's driver escorted him into Leo's hospital room. His steps faltered when he caught sight of Mattie. Clearly, the bastard had thought he'd be meeting his son alone. Instantly, Clive smoothed his lips into a charming smile.

For a moment, Leo wondered if that was what his own "press face" looked like, but then he realized it didn't matter. His features were *his* alone and had nothing to do with this man before him, no matter how much they resembled each other.

"Didn't expect to get picked up in a fancy car, son. You've come up in the world."

No thanks to you. Leo didn't say the words, nor did Mattie, although he knew she was thinking them too. They hadn't set up this meeting to argue with the reprobate but to banish him. And Mattie was letting Leo handle the dismissal, just as he silently supported her during her battles.

"I wanted to make it clear that you are never to contact me or any of the McAdams family—*my* family—ever again." The words brought Leo a sense of freedom he'd never had. Despite not really knowing his parents, he'd felt tied down by them and their choices—as if their decision to abandon him had created him. But it hadn't. It never had. They had no part in the true making of him.

Clive's veneer of charm dropped away to reveal the snarl underneath. "Do you want your precious sweetheart to know the truth about that day?"

Leo glanced over to Mattie. Their eyes met, and he could see her admiration for him.

"She already knows," Leo said, not even bothering to turn back to his old man.

"That I do," Mattie added cheerfully, also looking not at Clive but at Leo.

"Who's going to think you're a war hero after the whole story is known how you saved your own hide instead of your best friend's?"

Clive's words were clearly calculated for maximum damage, but they didn't even graze Leo's heart. He would always carry Alfred's death with him, but he was done with giving this shadow of a human the ability to twist his own memories and grief.

Leo reached over to the periodical that lay beside his hospital bed and held it out toward Clive. "I've told my story, and it seems both Alfred and I are judged to be the heroes. We were different types of fighters, but we both did our duty toward each other and for the Allies. It was never your story. It was ours. And I've told it the way the McAdamses and I wanted it said."

His father made no move to grab the newspaper. He just stared at it like it was an incendiary device.

"If you want, I can read it to you," Leo offered. He wouldn't even need to pick through the sentences. Even though it wasn't a short article, he had each word memorized.

Clive didn't say anything. He glared at the broadsheet a second longer before he seemed to shrink in upon himself. Every tenuous link between them had been permanently severed, if any had ever existed in the first place. Without a parting word, the man slunk away, back to the murky world where he dwelled, a phantom who could no longer haunt Leo or those he loved.

Mattie pressed her warm fingers against his forearm. "How do you feel?"

"Unburdened." The word tumbled from Leo's lips automatically, and the beautiful truth of it filled him.

"I'm so glad." Mattie brushed her lips against his, and he tasted a quiet peace he'd never experienced before.

"Is he gone?" Vera popped her head into the open doorway, her voice sounding . . . off, almost like an engine with a bad carburetor.

"Yes, why? Is something wrong?" Mattie sounded as concerned as Leo was.

Vera rubbed the bridge of her nose with her gloved hand, suddenly looking impossibly young. She exuded such a prepossessing command it was easy to forget that she was only in her midtwenties.

"I . . . I think I may find myself in rare need of advice. Normally, I am the one dispensing it, but I find myself a bit at a loss. And given how you've handled Clive with such aplomb, I was wondering if you could help me come to terms with my own parents' sabotage."

The words were not spoken melodramatically but with a heart-breaking matter-of-factness. Mattie instantly rose and embraced her friend. To Leo's shock, the indomitable heiress broke into tears.

"Benji Pringle told the police this afternoon that he had nothing to do with Crenshaw's tampering with the plane, but he confessed that he had been purposely trying to bankrupt my circus with bad press. My . . . my parents, who are friends with the owners of the *Chicago Advance Leader*, have been paying, *paying*, him to pen negative articles."

"Oh, Vera!" Mattie gasped. "I'm so sorry."

Vera pulled back and gave a watery, self-depreciating smile. Despite her smudged mascara and eyeliner, she still managed to look stunningly beautiful. "They want me to marry, you see. To get them a title. It's the only thing they've ever agreed upon. And I am ruining their plan with my independence. They want my dream broken so they can instead offer the fairy tale that all good little girls are supposed to desire: wedded bliss with a rich, landed man. A damn modern princess."

Vera's violet-blue eyes were huge and glistening as she turned them on Leo. "How do you deal with such betrayal by a parent?"

He should have felt cornered by the question. After all, he wasn't one for emotion. But the answer came to him so naturally, so automatically, he didn't have time for discomfort.

"You rely on your family, Vera. The one you've made. For me, it's the McAdamses. For you, it's the Flying Flappers. You've created a solid unit, Vera. Now, it's time for you to lean on us."

"It's hard to say no to you ladies." Mr. Fabin, the founder of Fabin Flyer, smiled jovially as his gaze swept around the Flying Flappers, who were gathered in Leo's hospital room. When the businessman's gaze met the war hero's, his expression solidified into something more serious. "And gentleman."

"So is that a yes to Fabin Flyer sponsoring and providing the planes for a rematch between Miss McAdams and Mr. Crenshaw at Canyon of the Bridges? And that the winner gets his or her very own Fabin?" Vera asked, her voice both gracious and no nonsense at the same time. As far as Mattie could tell, her friend had buried all hints of her vulnerability over her parents' machinations under her heavily armored flapper persona.

Mr. Fabin, a handsome man in his early forties, nodded at Vera and gave a rueful grin. "I might regret it, but my company will agree to your proposal."

"You won't have any cause for regret." Mattie spoke up, her heart thudding against her chest. "It will salvage all of our reputations." And it had better. Rockol had called her last night and had agreed to keep her as spokeswoman only if she could improve the press coverage.

Mr. Fabin exhaled. "I certainly hope so, Miss McAdams. Our status as an impeccable engineering firm has taken quite a hit due to Mr. Crenshaw's dangerous games. It was one of the main selling points of our planes. Even if we can drum up publicity with this second race, I'm not sure if we'll convince the army or the navy that our aircrafts have the best safety features in the world."

"I know a way to guarantee that they will." Mattie's body felt like it did right before takeoff—her muscles tensed, her mind focused, her limbs ready for action.

"Do you now, little lady?" Mr. Fabin seemed amused, but Mattie refused to allow that to irk her. Instead, she gave him the kind of smile that Vera would deliver. Bold. Assured. In control.

"Yes, and I'll tell you, but you'll need to sign this first." Mattie filled her chest with air as she reached in the hand-tooled satchel Aida had given her this morning for this very purpose. Inside it was all the paperwork prepared by Vera's attorneys—no, *Mattie's* attorneys. The heiress had told her it was high time for Mattie to start considering that the lawyers weren't on loan but were representing Mattie herself.

Mr. Fabin's brown eyes widened in surprise as he stared at the sheets of paper extended in his direction. Then he laughed. "Are you serious? You won't tell me what it is unless I sign a contract?"

Nervousness fluttered through Mattie, along with a sense of hopelessness. How would she ever convince businessmen to accept her and her ideas as genuine if they viewed her attempts to negotiate as a jolly joke? Her hand shook just a little, and the legal document fluttered. She almost drew her hand back, but then she felt it. The wonderful feeling of silent support.

She turned to find all the women of the Flying Flappers nodding at her. She knew even without looking that Leo was doing the same. The papers in her hand stopped rustling as Mattie decided it was high time to stop letting Mr. Fabin pilot this particular conversation.

"It is a confidentiality agreement," Mattie told him crisply. "You will find that when it comes to safety and airplanes, I am *always* serious. My twin brother died during the Great War, and if he'd had the equipment that I am proposing to license to you, he might not have flown further into enemy territory and been ambushed."

The man's mirth died but not his skepticism. "What exactly do you think you have dreamed up?"

"If I am clever enough to develop a technology that will improve airplane safety, don't you think I am also intelligent enough to make sure my design is protected? I will not disclose any more until you have signed a document acknowledging that the idea is mine and that you will not appropriate it." Mattie was very proud that she did not stumble on the words *disclose* or *appropriate*. She had discussed the concepts thoroughly with her attorneys so that she understood how the paper in her hand worked.

Mr. Fabin scratched his cheek. "You're an odd sort of gal, aren't you?"

Hell's bells and buckets of blood. She was so tired of being called a *gal* in that tone.

"I am a businesswoman, and I protect what is mine."

He twisted his sculpted lips as the room plunged into silence. No one spoke, but Mattie could feel the tension of her friends as they all waited for his response. Finally, Mr. Fabin grunted and reached for the agreement.

"My lawyers will have my head for signing this without their review, but you've got me too darn curious. You drive a hard bargain."

"This isn't the bargain." Mattie lifted her chin. "This is just the document we need before we can even begin that step."

This time Mr. Fabin's shock seemed tinged with a hint of respect. "Touché, Miss McAdams, touché."

He patted the front pocket of his tailored suit for a writing implement, but Aida silently handed him her fountain pen. Quickly, he scanned the three-page agreement and then signed it. Handing it back to Mattie, he said, "Now tell me about this design of yours."

Mattie found that talking about her RadioNavigator was a lot easier than arguing over legal terms. She didn't go into the technical details. She only told enough to pique Mr. Fabin's interest. Despite his earlier doubts, she could see a glint in his eyes. He liked what she was telling him, even if it was coming from a female.

"I'll tell you what, Miss McAdams," Mr. Fabin said when she'd finished. "Have your attorneys send over the proposed license agreement to mine, and I'll talk to my engineers. If you manage to save all of our reputations at the rematch, we'll discuss whether my company is interested in your design."

"I have a nonexclusive license already drafted." Mattie dug into the satchel and took out the contract. This time the stack of papers remained completely steady as she extended it to Mr. Fabin. He accepted it immediately and then put on his fedora.

After tipping the brim, he headed toward the door. "Until Canyon of the Bridges, Mr. Ward and ladies."

For at least a minute after the man left, no one spoke. Then, when they were sure Mr. Fabin could not hear them, they all simultaneously broke into excited shouts, cheers, and squeals. Even Leo let out a little whoop. But though Mattie celebrated, she couldn't quite escape a weight pressing down on her.

Everything, it appeared, rode on the outcome of her rematch with Earl Crenshaw.

Chapter Twenty

The day of the competition at the Canyon of the Bridges dawned hot, bright, and cloudless, with nary a puff of breeze. With the exception of the oppressive heat, it was generally ideal conditions for writing messages in the sky. It was not, however, good weather for calming nerves. Mattie felt like a piece of kindling being rubbed back and forth under the glare of the intense autumn sun. The landscape itself matched her fiery anticipation. The red, orange, and white canyon walls swirled below them in a dazzling dance of color. Spectators had lined up along the rim, eager to see what Vera had dubbed the *Aviator's Duel* in the press.

The heiress had used her connections to churn up a flurry of newspaper articles breathlessly extolling the event. It had become a coast-to-coast sensation. Everyone had an opinion about who was going to win. Bookies were set to make a mint. Even Mattie had money on the race: for herself as the winner, of course. With the intense coverage, a man with Earl Crenshaw's ego had no choice but to show, even if the authorities back in California had deemed the crash suspicious and were investigating his potential involvement.

Crenshaw had shown up yesterday, his slick grin replaced with a permanent sneer. Mattie had, at Leo's prudent request, avoided him entirely. She had no need to exchange words with the odious reprobate.

She would prove her superior piloting skills in the air, not on the ground.

"Swift!" Her father's familiar voice pierced through the noise of the gathered crowd milling near the makeshift airstrip.

Surprised, Mattie turned to find him standing with her three brothers. To her shock, smiles wreathed their faces. Not one of her siblings wore a scowl at the idea of their little sister swooping through a canyon they'd all deemed too dangerous for her. Despite their open expressions, she proceeded cautiously, even though she just wanted to run into her father's outstretched arms. She didn't know why they'd come, and she hoped it wasn't to stop her. Not that she would let them, but she didn't want to fight, especially when an uncharacteristic nervousness gripped her. Ever since she had watched Leo plummet from the sky, some of her old feelings of invincibility had been shaved away, leaving her more attuned to the risks she took and the possibility of failure.

"I'm so proud of you, Swift. Just think! All these people are here to watch you fly!" Her father's arms folded around her, tight and strong.

She pulled back and tilted her head up. "A lot are here hoping to see me fail."

"But you're going to prove them wrong, aren't you, sis?" Jake spoke, his hands shoved into the pockets of his khaki trousers, his cap dipped over one eye, his expression . . . contrite.

Mattie didn't answer immediately as she replayed the words in her head. No, she was right. He had actually uttered something supportive. She'd been preparing herself to deal with her siblings' resistance, not their backing.

"Of course!" Mattie tried to speak enthusiastically, but her brothers must have detected her questioning tone. They all shifted and glanced at each other sheepishly.

"What is going on?" Mattie finally asked, sticking her hands on her hips. "Why are all of you acting so oddly?"

None of them spoke. Mattie arched her eyebrow and continued to stare.

"Your clothes look good." Will, her youngest brother, attempted to compliment her. "Guess you're finally not wearing my old castoffs anymore."

Mattie straightened her spine at the reminder. She *was* sporting new trousers and a cotton shirt tailored for the female body. They didn't sag and droop and pool about her ankles. She wasn't dressed in hand-me-downs anymore. She wore something that fit.

"Charm does not work on me, Will. You ought to know that. Now, one of you better fess up. I haven't got all day. I have a race to win. Now, what has gotten into you all?"

She stared at them. They stared back. She just stared harder and leaned slightly forward at the waist. They shuffled their feet. She did not. She remained firm and unwavering.

Otto broke first. "Leo."

At the coughed-out single word, Jake lightly smacked Otto on the back of his head, causing his cap to flop over his eyes.

"Hey!" Otto protested.

"You weren't supposed to say anything." Will nudged the middle brother with his elbow.

"Leo what?" Mattie ground out, ready to lose patience with her siblings. She had been away from their chaos for too long, and she found that her tolerance for it had diminished.

"Leo called them," her father supplied.

"Leo?" Mattie asked. He didn't like to speak in person, let alone on the telephone.

"Read us the riot act, he did," Will said.

"Not you too!" Jake knocked Will's hat forward as well.

"Otto already gabbed!" Will protested.

"Would someone please calmly and rationally explain what happened?" Mattie's voice broke through their bickering.

Jake gave a defeated sigh. "Leo has been sending all of us news clippings of your accomplishments."

Mattie's heart took off like a scout plane—strong, fast, and sure. "He has?"

Will nodded as he carefully adjusted his hat. If there had been a mirror available, he definitely would have looked into it. "Like clockwork."

"I posted the articles on a pegboard in my office," her father told her proudly. "I've read every word. When I talked to your brothers on the phone, I made sure that they had too."

"After Leo's crash in California, he telephoned all of us." Otto's pale skin flushed a bit at the memory. "He told us we'd better come out here—"

"And threatened us with our lives if we didn't support you," Will added.

"And you're listening to him?" Mattie asked, disbelief warring with the warmth filling her at the images of Leo secretly mailing the news pieces to her family and of her father proudly tacking the articles up.

"Well, he might have admitted that he took on the more dangerous stunts so we wouldn't get hurt." Looking surprisingly embarrassed, Jake rubbed his jaw. "Something about a vow he made to Alfred after his death."

Mattie hadn't thought her insides could get softer, but they did. Leo really had become her champion—and in the best way possible. He was allowing her to live her dream.

"We all got as mad as heck." Will tugged his forelock, messing up both his carefully arranged hat and greased-back hair.

"Until Leo pointed out we were doing the same to you. He said that all the frustration we were feeling, you had to deal with fourfold." Jake twisted his lips ruefully.

"It got us all to thinking," Otto said. "Then Pa gave us a lecture."

"Which they finally listened to." Her father made a weary production of sighing, but he sent her a cheerful wink.

"So none of you are going to try to talk me out of this?" Mattie glanced among her three siblings and her father. They all shook their heads in affirmation, their expressions surprisingly solemn.

"We're just here to cheer you on," Jake promised, and then he exchanged a significant look with his brothers, "and to give you something."

"What something?" Mattie asked suspiciously as Otto began to root around in a knapsack.

"We realized that part of the reason we were stopping you from flying is because we all felt like we couldn't lose you after what happened to Alfred," Otto answered as he pulled out a familiar leather helmet and goggles. At the sight of her twin's old gear, Mattie pressed her hand to her mouth.

"And that made us all think about how we'd frozen everything in time," Will explained. "That we thought we were all memorializing Alfred, but what we were really doing was burying his memory along with the pain. We need to honor him by remembering him, talking about him, like you and Leo did in that article for the *Aviator's Gazette*."

"He'd want you to wear these today," Jake said, his hazel eyes shiny with emotion as he lifted Alfred's helmet and goggles from Otto's hands and placed them in Mattie's. "And he'd want you to fly."

It seemed like Mattie had turned into a watering pot. A few tears splashed from her eyes as she pulled her brother's old safety equipment over her head. Then she stepped forward and gave her father and each of her siblings another hug. They all held her fast and tight, and she could feel the love in each embrace. When she'd gone down the line, she stepped back, and they all stood there, bleary eyed and awkward, as if not completely sure what to do with all the emotion they'd stirred up.

Her father finally cleared his throat, his tone more gravelly than ever. "You'd better get going, Swift. You've a race to win."

She breathed in deeply, collecting herself and gathering the strength and support her family was offering. "That I do!"

This time when she hugged her brothers, there was joy too. She started with Will and worked her way up to her father. He held her the longest and said softly, for her ears only, "Thank you for your weekly letters, Swift, even after we argued. I'm glad you and Leo finally saw what was right under your noses. He's a good man, Mattie. A good choice."

Mattie pulled back, startled. Had Leo told him? Her father must have read the question in her eyes, because he gave a slight negative shake of his head.

He'd known. Her dear quiet, observant pa had known, but he'd let her find her own path on her own time schedule. She leaned forward and kissed his cheek.

"Thanks." Her whispered word to him was for more than just his approval of Leo or even his insight. It also was for teaching her to fly in the first place and then giving her the freedom to really soar.

After saying goodbye to her family, she headed straight toward the Fabin Flyer designated as hers for the race. In order to promote the upcoming event, the company had allowed her to fly the new bird in several performances by Vera's Flying Flappers.

As Mattie neared her aircraft, she caught sight of Leo seated in a chair beside the Fabin. Despite the plaster cast encasing his right leg, Leo had insisted on spending the night camped out, his head under the engine bay, his feet pointed toward the cockpit. He'd assigned Vera to watch over Mattie's meals in case Crenshaw tried to lace it with something to make her mildly ill. Mattie had eaten prepackaged food instead of dinner from the lodge's dining room. She would have thought Leo's precautions excessive if Crenshaw hadn't nearly succeeded in creating a literal death trap in California.

Although Leo had probably not slept the entire night, he looked not only awake but alert. His blue eyes softened as he caught sight of Mattie. The rest of the Flying Flappers were crowded around the aircraft too. John and Alice had brought their children. Little Milly perched on her father's shoulders as Carrie and Sadie explained the Fabin's design advances. Oblivious to the excitement, Ruby had fallen asleep in Vera's arms, and her rather loud snores occasionally punctuated the women's descriptions of the plane.

"Other aircraft have radiators that stick out, which cause the plane to slow down." Carrie waved her hand in the air, tracing the Fabin Flyer's sleek torpedo shape. "The smoother the surface is, then the more smoothly the air flows around it. Less drag is produced, and the machine's aerodynamics are improved."

"The body is a monocoque, which means that there's no frame," Sadie explained. "The wooden skin creates the strength of the plane. That's why it's a tube instead of a box. The shape also helps with the aerodynamics that Carrie is talking about."

Mattie ran her eyes over the efficient little Fabin. With stubbier wings than the Jenny and a powerful motor, it could zip and dive through the sky. Sometimes when Mattie did tricks in the JN-4, she felt like she was coaxing the aging trainer like she would a tired old mare. But the Fabin skipped along, frolicking with the ease of a new filly.

Mattie headed over to Leo and placed her hand on his shoulder. Since the news rags seemed intent on labeling them as sweethearts no matter what they did, they had begun to show a degree of affection toward each other in public.

Leo glanced up at the touch and laid his hand on top of hers. He searched her face, his lips flat with concern. "Did you sleep last night?"

"Enough," she said truthfully. "I tossed and turned some, but I cobbled together enough to be clearheaded. I bet you didn't sleep a wink."

His muscular shoulder moved up and down under her palm as he shrugged. "I'm not the one racing."

Neither of them mentioned Mattie's nervousness, but they both knew that the competition weighed on her. Instead, she lifted her finger and lightly tapped Leo's clavicle. "Thank you for the extra cheerleaders. I feel like a varsity athlete now."

He craned his neck back to regard her curiously. "Cheerleaders?"

"I ran into my family," Mattie explained.

Leo frowned, a new worry drifting across his already tense features. "Your brothers weren't supposed to rat me out."

"Otto blabbed."

Leo groaned. "I should've come up with a special threat for him. He always squeals."

"If you want to keep something secret, it's safest not to tell him."

Leo stretched his head back even farther to study her closely. "You're not mad?"

"Not at all." After glancing around to make sure no one was watching them, especially a newsman with a camera, Mattie brushed the quickest of kisses on his lips. "I like having my own personal yell leaders. Do you think I should get Vera to buy them matching boater hats and uniforms?"

"It would have to be in a bold color—puce, perhaps, or maybe fuchsia? There's also bright yellow or orange." Leo's lips quirked, and the sight of his smile caused a gush of hot liquid pleasure to bubble through Mattie. She loved how his spirits had lightened over the past few weeks.

"Vera would probably insist on cherry-red uniforms." Mattie laughed at the image of her brothers dressed in gaudy, matching outfits, but she sobered quickly. "It was very sweet what you did, Leo. Thank you for sending them those articles."

Although Leo had grown better at accepting compliments, she could feel him stiffen under the hand still resting on his shoulder. He jerked his head. "It was time they recognized your talents."

The roaring start of a three-hundred-horsepower motor broke into their conversation. Mattie shielded her eyes and turned in the direction of the makeshift runway. In a slow trundle, Crenshaw maneuvered his plane to the far end of the strip, its fuselage painted a deep forest green. Mattie glanced at the watch Vera had lent her. The odious reprobate was right on time.

She and Leo had arranged that Crenshaw would race first. It gave her the slight advantage of knowing his maneuvers and what time she had to beat. Considering that the unscrupulous man had sabotaged her previous plane, she'd felt no compunction at telling the papers that he would be the first one to fly.

The Fabin shot down the runway, picking up speed until its wheels lifted off the dusty, dry ground and its nose shot skyward. Crenshaw might be a braggart, but he could operate a plane with ease. His style wasn't exactly fluid but an odd mixture of mechanical and brash. He flew as if he could aggressively plow his way through the course, one choppy maneuver at a time. He pounced on each of the stunts, his twists and rolls like powerful swipes of a tiger's paws. His loop over the first bridge could have been tighter, and he lost speed through the narrow center arch.

Racing to the other overlook of the U-shaped canyon, Mattie caught Crenshaw's barrel roll through the last bridge. It seemed a bit hesitant to Mattie, but he'd still zoomed through the entire course in an impressive time.

His performance would be hard to top but was certainly not unbeatable. Still, her nerves started to flare up like a million insect bites—itchy and raw. While walking back to her Fabin, she gave her arms a rub, as if she could ward off the uncomfortable sensation. When she reached the plane, Leo reached up and patted her hand.

"You can do this. I believe in you."

"Thanks." She breathed in the desert air, wishing it were cool and bracing instead of dry and stifling. It did little to calm her.

Her friends formed a line on either side of the cockpit, like a receiving line after a wedding. They all cheered as she walked through their ranks, their words of encouragement helping to make her feel, at least momentarily, lighter than air.

"You can trounce him with one eye closed," Sadie called.

"And you definitely have more style!" Lily's voice, high and clear, rang through the others'.

"Keep your focus," Alice advised, her tone almost parental.

"You know this will be a high point in my book." Aida, who had rejoined the Flying Flappers during her fall break from graduate school, waved her fountain pen like a pendant, squirting a bit of ink into the air.

"He wasted a lot of time by making his loops through the bridges too broad. Tighten them up, and you'll shave off at least a minute from his speed," Carrie coached.

"Darling, you have nothing to fear. You can outfly that silly old drugstore cowboy without even trying." Vera hoisted Ruby in her arms, and the awakened spaniel gave a decidedly emphatic sniff. Her brown eyes were even larger than usual, as if she, too, understood the gravitas of the situation.

Her friends' encouragement blazed through Mattie, but when she touched the side of the cockpit to propel herself into the plane, her fingers still trembled. The enormity of her responsibility pressed uncomfortably down upon her. Vera had mentioned that even one British and two French reporters would be present. So many people wished for her to fail and would ruthlessly use any flop on her part to discredit all female aviators. Yet so many women, young and old, were silently urging her on, some *praying* for her to win. What if she failed?

She felt a small hand tug at hers. Glancing down, she found little Milly, who must have escaped her father's grasp. The girl's round face was ringed with curls as wild as Mattie's own, but her expression was grave.

"Mama said you were worried." Milly's blue eyes were two serious pools of innocent wisdom, the kind that only a child could possess. "You very, very, very much want to win so little girls know they can fly too."

"Yes, Milly dear, that's true." Mattie's voice shook the tiniest bit, but the precocious child didn't notice.

"I want to be a pilot even if mean ole Mr. Crenshaw gets the prize." Milly tilted her tiny chin in an oddly adult expression. Clearly, she wanted to stress the solemnity of her next words. "You don't have to win. You just need to fly. Then we'll all know we can too!"

You just need to fly. The words bounced around Mattie's heart. She could certainly accomplish that. Even better, she could soar!

"Take Planey for luck." Milly shoved her toy into Mattie's other hand. "She also reeeeally wants to be in the air."

Mattie's fingers curled around the well-worn wooden fuselage, and she took the same care she would give to an Imperial Fabergé egg. "I'll make sure Planey has an experience she won't forget."

Milly beamed. "Thank you!" She slipped her hand from Mattie's and skipped over to her parents.

This time, Mattie's hand was completely steady as she launched her body into the cockpit. Before she strapped herself into the seat, she paused and turned her body toward the cameras. When she smiled and waved, she didn't have to fake her confidence as she'd feared. Milly's words had given it back to her in abundance.

Securing Planey so that the toy would not fall out of the open cockpit, Mattie pulled Alfred's goggles over her eyes and waited as Vera stepped forward. The heiress winked and blew a kiss toward the closest photographer. Then, with her cherry-red tube dress swirling about her shins, she yanked down on the propeller with a dramatic flourish.

The powerful motor roared, the pulsating sound sending Mattie's heart beating faster. Vera waved one gloved hand as she stepped safely away from the Fabin.

Letting out one of her trademark whoops, Mattie adjusted the throttle and felt the powerful bird move toward the runway. Staring out from behind her brother's goggles, she realized that a part of him was with her today, cheering her on, being her wingman, urging her to embrace the future, to live her life, to pursue her dreams.

As she angled into position, she didn't hear the cheers or even the jeers. Sound simply drifted away as she concentrated on the bright blue stretching before her. Not even the slightest puff of white or gray marred the monochromatic splendor.

As Mattie pulled back on the throttle, the runway zipped past her, the orange-red of the soil blending with the gray-green of the clumps of sagebrush. She caught occasional flashes of white from the huge blooms of yucca. Soon, though, Mattie could not even detect those snowy hues as she hurtled ever faster. Under her command, the wheels lifted from the ground, and the sleek, aerodynamic bird ascended.

The ticking clock wouldn't allow for her usual dramatic flourish. She lost no time in diving into the canyon. Swirling layers of red, orange, and white rock enveloped her. Vertical, drip-like streaks of black covered the walls. Mattie felt like she was flying through a brand-new impressionist watercolor of the Southwest, the paint still fresh and melding together.

She zipped under the first natural bridge, skimming so close that she swore she could feel the cool dampness of the massive structure's underside. Exploding from the shade, she jerked the nose of the Fabin upward, keeping the loop tight. Below her once more, she spied the silvery glint of sagebrush and the waxy green of piñon pine that thrived on the top of the mesa. Then she plunged down again and zoomed through a sherbet-colored world.

Mattie finished skimming under the first natural bridge again and then banked her plane to maneuver through the constantly twisting canyon. The deep cut in the earth turned back on itself, forming a U shape, so the end of the race was directly opposite the start on the same narrow strip of land that connected the two steep valleys.

Flying over the next bridge, she rolled into an inverted position and then looped back under the rock in a dizzying whirl. The utter freedom of slicing through the magnificent masterpiece of nature blazed through her. The last vestiges of her nervousness fled as she lost herself in the pure joy of the course. Heading around the bend, she reached the trickiest part—a narrow passage right before the sharp curve. Although from a geological perspective it was a natural bridge, it looked more like an arch carved into the thick stone walls. The only way to cross under it was to turn the Fabin practically onto its side. Banking the bird so her right wing pointed toward the dried-up wash below and her left toward the sky above, Mattie sacrificed no speed as she zipped toward the tight opening. She flew low enough to see a blur of light-green cottonwood leaves. Then there was rock so close to her face that if she buzzed any closer, she'd end up giving her own nose a nasty brush burn.

She popped out the other side. Keeping her Fabin in a slanted position, she whipped around the rest of the wicked curve. Hitting an open stretch, she rolled until the wings were horizontal again but with her now in the inverted position. She whizzed over the willows and box elders, daintier vegetation than the tough, scrubbier pine trees that grew on the topside.

Her head pointed downward, Mattie blazed beneath the next bridge. Then she spun in a series of barrel rolls and shot through the canyon like a massive drill. The underbelly of the last bridge blinked in and out of view as she flipped through the air. Then finally, Mattie was through the course. After bursting out of the canyon, she landed deftly back on the mesa and turned off the motor.

Mattie catapulted out of the cockpit as the crowd roared. Her eyes immediately found Leo's. He was leaning on one crutch, a stopwatch in his other hand. Their gazes held, hot and electric. Leo dipped his chin, his lips forming the broadest smile she'd ever seen on his face. This wasn't his press smile or his shy grin. It was pure joy.

She'd won!

Suddenly, Vera wrapped Mattie in a fierce embrace, Ruby smooshed between them. "You won! You won! You won!"

Vera spun the three of them around in a mad circle. Caught in the excitement, the little spaniel licked Mattie's chin. Soon the other female members of the Flying Flappers joined them. But unlike the group hug in the California speakeasy after Crenshaw had challenged her, this wasn't just about support. It was pure jubilation.

By the time they broke apart, they all had tears in their eyes. Mattie was just wiping away hers when she caught sight of Milly jumping up and down, ribbons and curls flying. Drawing in her breath, Mattie climbed back into the Fabin and retrieved Planey.

Milly bounced even higher when she caught sight of her beloved toy. Mattie leaped back to the ground and swooped, banked, and barrel-rolled the small wooden construct over to the young girl. Kneeling down in front of Milly so they were face to face, she started to hand Planey over to the child. Before she could, Milly's strong little arms wrapped fiercely about Mattie's neck in a hug.

"You won!"

"I couldn't have done it without you and Planey," Mattie said, holding out the toy once more.

Milly beamed and snuggled Planey close, then gave it a kiss on its propeller. After ruffling the cherub's hair, Mattie stood and sought Leo.

His joy hadn't diminished one whit. Yards still separated them, and the bellow of the crowd was too great for them to hear each other. But she knew immediately what he mouthed.

You. Did. It.

Pumping both hands into the air, as if she could catch his words, she moved her lips to shout her own silent message back to him.

I did!

Leo watched with warm pride as the press swarmed Mattie, and the reporters finally asked her the type of questions she deserved.

"How did you manage to navigate so quickly through the narrowest bridge?"

"Was there a special technique you used to make your loops so tight?"

"What is it like flying a Fabin versus a Jenny?"

Realizing it would take a while for Mattie to answer all the inquiries, Leo grabbed his crutches and headed to one rim of the canyon. He looked down so that he could compare Crenshaw's faded smoke trail through the course with Mattie's brighter one. The former war pilot had performed passably, but he'd also been sloppy in places—staccato when he should have flown smoothly, loose when he should have been tight. Not Mattie. She'd flown a taut, consistent course, losing no time as she'd spun like an aerial gymnast through the narrow orange-and-white walls.

Hefting his body over to the other side of the U-shaped gorge, Leo saw the same pattern repeated. As he stood looking down at Mattie's triumph, he felt a familiar warm, reassuring hand on his shoulder.

"Our gal did good, didn't she?" Mattie's father asked rhetorically as they both gazed at the evidence of her victory.

"She did indeed," Leo agreed.

Walt McAdams released a low whistle. "I always knew my Swift could fly like the dickens, but never did I think that she could soar like this."

"I did." Leo rested his weight on the crutches, letting the wooden rests dig into his armpits as he kept surveying Mattie's incredible win. She'd beaten Crenshaw, a decorated ace, by a full sixty-one seconds.

"That you did," Walt drawled out, still peering into the canyon as well. Then he turned to face Leo. "That you did."

Leo cleared his throat. It was time he fessed to his relationship with Mattie, and the mere thought of Walt's reaction made his stomach start spluttering like a broken engine. "Sir, I . . ." He trailed off, still not sure how to broach the subject. "Mattie and I, well, we're . . . well, we're . . ."

"Sweethearts like the papers have been saying?" Walt raised one salt-and-pepper eyebrow.

Leo's whole face heated like a radiator in need of water. "I made sure not to send those stories."

"I noticed." Walt chuckled softly and then sobered. "Leo, I didn't need a news rag to tell me what I saw with my own eyes."

"You knew?" Leo asked.

"Of course I knew. Mattie and the boys might have been too thick-headed to notice the looks you gave her, but I've been waiting years for you to finally make your intentions clear. I figured it was no use pushing either of you, even though it was plain as day that you two were meant for each other. Romance works on its own time schedule. That's what my late wife always said, although I only took two years to get around to courting her, not more than half a decade."

Leo shifted his weight to one crutch so he could shove his hand into his hair. He'd spent so many nights the past week trying to figure out how to convince Mattie's father that he was worthy of his daughter. He'd imagined every scenario but this one . . . and it humbled him.

"You don't mind, then?" Leo asked just to be sure.

"Of course I don't mind. Why do you think I was so glad you were accompanying her on this adventure?"

Leo's mind flashed back to the conversation that he'd had with Walt the day that he and Mattie had announced they were joining Vera's circus. Walt had told him, *"Don't try to protect her too much. Be her partner, not her keeper."*

A slow smile spread over Leo's face as he realized how incredibly wise Walt McAdams was. And it touched him to know that such a man thought *him*, Leo Ward, a good fit for his only daughter.

"Thank you, sir."

"You're a good, solid man, Leo. Don't ever doubt that."

Leo barked out a laugh. "Mattie said something very similar to me."

The corners of Walt's eyes crinkled, and his hazel eyes, so much like Mattie's, turned golden. "She's an astute one, my Swift."

A companionable silence fell over Leo and Walt. After turning away from the canyon's edge, they began walking back toward the center of activity.

"How has flying been treating you?" Walt asked, his voice gravelly with a hint of concern. "Are you feeling any joy when you're in the air?"

Leo's eyes fell on Mattie, who was laughing merrily at something one of the reporters had said. He realized he couldn't wait until he could soar with her again and hear her whoop with joy as they spun in a barrel roll.

"It's coming back. Thanks to your daughter."

"Her excitement has always been infectious, even when she was just a wee sprout."

They reentered the crowd, and it took a little longer for Leo to maneuver through the people with his crutches. Eventually, they reached the open swath of scrub where Mattie was being interviewed. A glowering Crenshaw stood on the edge of the throng. The man's flint-gray eyes bored into Mattie, although she stood more than several yards away. Each question seemed to make him fidget a little more, his hands clenching and unclenching.

"Crenshaw's going to be trouble," Leo warned Walt. Mattie's father followed Leo's gaze and nodded somberly.

"I'll gather up the boys in case he tries any funny business." Walt tipped his hat and disappeared into the milling spectators. Leo began swinging his body in the direction of Mattie and their friends. It was best for him to be close in case Crenshaw decided to physically attack. Although the aviator was short tempered, he'd always been sneaky about his maliciousness. Leo hadn't thought that Crenshaw would be so brash as to try to harm Mattie in front of reporters, but he looked like a man on the edge. Sweat slicked back Crenshaw's hair instead of his normal brilliantine. Perhaps the desert heat could explain away the rivulets running down his cheeks but not his eyes, which frenetically flicked back and forth with almost palpable hatred. The man's lanky body appeared to twitch, vibrating with barely suppressed rage. Crenshaw hated being beaten by anyone, and he'd just been publicly trounced by a woman whom he'd sought to humiliate. Worse, the Flying Flappers had forced his hand, and the king of manipulation had become the manipulated.

Leo was almost to Mattie's side when one of the younger reporters turned toward Crenshaw. The journalist cheekily asked, "Hey, Mr. Crenshaw, how does it feel losing to a doll?"

That was the spark needed to light Crenshaw's considerable explosive reserves. Propelled now by sheer anger without any hint of restraining sense, he marched across the dusty landscape. Leo swung his body faster, hopping as quickly as he could manage on his good foot. He needed to get to Mattie. He had to reach her before Crenshaw did. He must intercept . . .

Leo thudded to a halt as he calculated Crenshaw's trajectory, just as he'd predicted the enemy's flight paths during the Great War. The irate aviator wasn't headed toward Mattie but toward *him*. The closer Leo moved to Mattie, the more danger he paradoxically placed her in.

Leo stopped his forward momentum, planting both ends of his crutches as far apart as possible. Normally, Leo would have no trouble handling Crenshaw's forward assault. Although the bully was a few inches taller, Leo was more muscular, and more importantly, he was vastly calmer. The vain man's volatile anger would inevitably cause him to make a mistake—a mistake Leo would normally take full advantage of. But hampered by his cast and crutches, Leo would have a hard time capitalizing on that opportunity.

"You!" Crenshaw shouted at him. "You're nothing but a turncoat, a traitor to real men."

Leo did not rise to Crenshaw's taunts. He just tried to jam the ends of his crutches into the hard-packed soil to give him more leverage. Out of the corner of his eye, he could see the heads of the McAdams brothers as they wove their way through the crowd.

"You're a chump, teaching a broad how to fly in the first place." Crenshaw stalked toward him, his lean chest puffed out.

Now that. That was a comment Leo would not ignore.

"Miss McAdams is the one who taught *me* how to fly, Crenshaw." Leo kept his voice calm, but he made sure to speak loudly enough that the reporters could clearly hear him. He was thoroughly tired of misconceptions about the depth of Mattie's incredible talent.

The revelation caused Crenshaw to explode like a shell fired from one of the Archies on the front line. Leo braced for the blow as best he could, readying to use his left crutch defensively. The McAdams brothers were close but not near enough to reach the fray immediately.

Crenshaw lifted his fist, and Mattie darted toward them. Leo prepared to use his body to protect hers, but Mattie was cleverer than both Crenshaw and him. Instead of placing herself in front of the bully, she simply rose on her tiptoes and tapped the enraged aviator on his shoulder. He jumped like a rodeo bull, kicking up dust as he jerked his body around. He struck brutally but blindly, just as Mattie must have anticipated.

She'd bent her body, neatly avoiding Crenshaw's wildly swinging fists. The undirected force pitched Crenshaw forward, and he stumbled over Mattie. Using her shoulders and her back, just as Leo would have done, she took advantage of the fool's own momentum to send him flipping over. Crenshaw landed on the ground with a hard thump. He lay shocked for a moment and then started gasping for air like a big-mouthed bass. Clearly, the wind had been knocked from him.

By the time Crenshaw was able to lift his head, Mattie's brothers and John had surrounded him. They'd just hauled him from the ground when the rev of a motorcycle rumbled through the crowd, like a faraway thunderclap. Enthused by this additional unexpected drama, the crowd seemed to swivel as a unit to watch the approach of a Harley-Davidson and a Model T. By the looks of the blue uniforms of the rider and driver, they were the police.

"Let go of me!" Crenshaw wiggled his shoulders and jerked his arms, but Jake, Otto, John, and Will held firm.

When a policeman stepped out of the car to join the officer on the bike, Crenshaw made a desperate attempt to change tactics. "Help! These men assaulted me!"

In a resounding roar, the crowd denounced the claim. The atmosphere had returned to a carnival-type feeling. More than one person wore a broad, pleased smile, as if tickled to be part of a spectacle that seemed lifted from the picture shows.

The police ignored the hubbub and strode straight through the throng. The older officer, whose steel-gray hair peeked out from the bottom of his hat, stopped in front of the troublemaker. "Mr. Earl Crenshaw?"

Crenshaw's face purpled in suppressed rage, and his lips squeezed into a tight line. He glared defiantly at the lawman, his body shaking worse than an unbalanced propeller.

"That's him," John said.

"I thought so. I've seen his picture in the paper," the policeman said and then nodded to his backup. As the coppers took over from the McAdams brothers and John, the senior officer addressed Crenshaw. "I am arresting you on a warrant issued by the Oceanbreeze police in California on suspicion of attempted murder, criminal trespass, and vandalism."

Crenshaw twisted and thrashed, but the lawmen resolutely marched him to the awaiting car. They managed to push him inside as he shouted a stream of nearly incoherent obscenities.

When the police vehicles pulled away, the crowd cheered like the audience they were. Amid all the whooping and hollering, Mattie stepped toward Leo, her eyes warm.

"Thanks for saving me," he said, breaking into a grin.

"Thanks for not getting upset that I did," she answered, smiling right back.

"You're tough, Mattie McAdams. I love that about you," Leo said. "And you *did* give me fair warning that you were going to start protecting me too."

"That I did." Mattie's lips curled with pride.

"I'd kiss you right now, but I don't want the newspapers filled with that photo instead of you with your Fabin."

"There's going to be some snapshots of me flipping Crenshaw to the ground." Mattie winked mischievously.

"Does that bother you?" Leo asked, hating the thought of anything taking away from Mattie's triumph, especially when it dealt with that particular scoundrel.

"I kind of like it. It makes it pretty hard to say that I can't play with the big boys, doesn't it? Unlike back in Chicago after the scuffle at the Gilded Secret, there will be no doubt who unmanned Crenshaw."

"Indeed."

Neither of them said anything right away. In lieu of embracing, they just stared at each other, letting their gazes do all the caressing. Leo had no idea how long they would have stood like that if her brother Jake hadn't bounded up, wiping his hands, as if he'd finished a dirty task.

"That should be the last of Earl Crenshaw bothering you. You shouldn't have any trouble now."

Mattie sighed, and Leo knew exactly what she was thinking. Together they swiveled toward Jake and said simultaneously, "There will always be another Crenshaw."

Mattie turned back to Leo, her eyes shining a bold, fearless gold. "But we know how to handle them now, don't we?"

"Absolutely," Leo agreed, and they returned to staring at each other.

Jake cleared his throat. They ignored him. He tried again. Same result.

"Well, I can see when I'm not wanted," Jake finally said, and Leo heard his footsteps retreat until the sound mingled with the rest of the noise from the crowd.

"How about accompanying a gal on her victory lap?" Mattie lifted her eyebrow in a flirty challenge. Although Leo had difficulty getting into the Fabin with his cast, he'd managed it with John's help a few times before. If one of Mattie's brothers also assisted, it would be even easier. Luckily, the craft had a roomier passenger seat than most planes, since Fabin Flyer had left space for a machine-gun mount.

"I'd like that very much." The words seemed to tumble out of Leo, swept along in a rising sea of joy.

Laughing like two goofs, just as they had on that evening on the Lake Michigan shoreline, Leo and Mattie hurried toward her Fabin. The plane was truly Mattie's now, won by her triumphant finish. Leo also had a feeling that she'd just earned herself another lucrative endorsement deal and secured her first license agreement for her RadioNavigator.

When Mattie barreled her craft past the scrubby underbrush, an old familiar sensation stirred within Leo: excitement. It started just as a wisp at first—a faint lightness flickering to life. Yet it seemed to grow in lockstep with the Fabin's acceleration. When the nose popped skyward, Leo's heart lifted too.

He felt the rush of the wind against his exposed cheeks. For so long, he'd overlooked the simple pleasure of experiencing such wonderful power and reveling in the very forces that kept the marvelous machines aloft.

Leo glanced at the ground below, a patchwork of oranges, reds, and whites. It looked like a sunset . . . or more accurately, a sunrise full of new beginnings.

Bursts of dark, light, and even silvery greens flashed here and there, proof of life even in the seemingly barren land. Mattie climbed farther and farther into the cloudless blue, taking advantage of the Fabin's much-higher operating ceiling compared to the Jenny. Leo hadn't been this high since the end of the war, and he allowed himself to feel a roar of freedom.

It didn't matter if he or Mattie was at the controls. This, this was magic, a magic he'd pushed aside because he'd had to focus to survive. But he wasn't at the front anymore. The battle was no longer dogfights above France.

He could enjoy flying again. He should enjoy flying again. He *would* enjoy flying again.

"Are you ready to dive?" Mattie loudly asked.

"Copacetic."

With a whoop, Mattie shot downward into the canyon far below. Like the rumble of dammed-up water finally breaking the levee and whooshing through the dried-up riverbed, his own shout of jubilation thundered from his chest, up his throat, and past his lips. Mattie banked the right wing down and deftly zoomed past the narrow walls. Leo felt as brilliant as the colorful sandstone they shot through.

With a grace that made something superbly difficult appear ridiculously easy, Mattie piloted the Fabin smoothly through the natural bridges. After passing through the fifth, she once again headed into the cool blueness.

"I heard you shouting!" Her words were muffled by the wind the plane produced and the engine itself, but he could still make out her statement.

"I'm having fun!"

"So am I!" Mattie's raised voice vibrated with excitement. "Do you think I should write a message? Show off more of my skills?"

Leo dipped his chin in a deep nod in case she was having trouble hearing him. "Yes!"

"What should I write?"

He paused, contemplating. He considered how Mattie had pursued her dreams, how she'd raced first him and then Crenshaw, how she'd proven that a woman could fly just as well as a man.

"The Aviatrix!"

"Perfect!" Mattie hollered back.

Releasing one of her battle cries, she began to dip, dive, spin, whirl, climb, and twist. Writing with smoke wasn't easy. It required a lot of skill and flying blind, but it wasn't anything that Mattie couldn't handle.

The wild maneuvers energized Leo, and he once again joined Mattie's triumphant shout as she executed one last loop and barrel roll just for the pleasure of it. After she'd landed on the ground and John and Will had helped him exit the Fabin, Mattie and Leo stood together, looking up at her handiwork. She'd written *The Aviatrix* in large flowing letters. It was a distinctively feminine script but no less bold or impressive than a man's.

"Perfect." Leo nudged her shoe with the foot of his crutches, knowing that even if a reporter's camera captured the tap, the snapshot would never be able to convey the sweet import of his gesture.

Mattie shielded her eyes to read the words she'd so artfully scrawled onto the horizon. "I wonder what's next for us?"

"I don't know, but I'm sure it will be another glorious escapade."

"And we'll do it together," Mattie said, her words a statement, not a question.

"Together," he echoed.

They fell into silence then, both appreciating what they had created. The skywriting would fade away, but this—this partnership with Mattie—would not. It was as strong and steady as a well-maintained aircraft climbing ever skyward.

"Here they are!" Lily called out gaily as she rushed up the steps of the lodge while holding a large brown paper satchel in her hands. Her twin,

Sadie, hurried behind her, lugging an even bigger bundle. A dry wind blew behind the women, sending the pungent, piney odors of scrub wafting onto the porch. The sharpness of the scent mirrored the prickles of anticipation crinkling inside Mattie.

In many ways, waiting to read the coverage of the competition was even more nerve racking than the race itself. During the contest, she'd had control. This time, though, she didn't. Reporters—most of them male—steered this particular vehicle.

The Flying Flappers and the McAdamses had all agreed to wait to read any news of the event until they could gather the national papers as well. They'd asked the owner of the little general store near the lodge if he could collect one copy of each of the periodicals that he sold or could easily get his hands on and wrap them in brown paper. Today was the day they would open the collection.

"And," Sadie called out, "we'd stopped at the front desk of the lodge before we left, and there was an envelope for you, Mattie. Do you want me to get it for you?"

"Yup. I might as well read all the news at once," Mattie said, proud that her voice didn't betray any of her anxiousness.

"I'll be back in a jiffy!" Sadie said as she dashed inside.

Mattie beat out a nervous tattoo with her right foot, trying to steady her breathing as she waited for her friend to return. When that failed, she squeezed Leo's hand. He sat beside her on the rustic wooden bench while the other members of Vera's circus and Mattie's family clustered around in rockers and other seats. The sight of her loved ones calmed Mattie more than any action ever could. She owed Vera and her other female comrades so much. Mattie had always known she could fly, but no one else had embraced her true potential quite like these women. They'd nurtured it, nurtured *her*, and helped her come into her own.

When Sadie popped back on the porch, she handed Mattie a large manila envelope addressed from Mattie's lawyers. At the same time, Lily placed the first bundle in Mattie's lap.

"Which are you going to open first?" Lily asked, giving a little bounce.

"I . . . I think the news articles." Mattie glanced down at the bulging stack of periodicals. "The mail from the law office might just be routine."

Inhaling, Mattie tried to undo the string, but her normal dexterity failed her. When she grunted in frustration, every male member of her family thrust a multiuse pocketknife in her direction.

Leo waved them away. "She has Alfred's old one."

It seemed fitting, using her late brother's Swiss Army knife to slice through the string just as she'd worn his helmet and goggles during her flight. Alfred would have been so proud of her and proud of Leo for being by her side. It struck her then that she didn't need his old flying circus or even the flight school to preserve his memory. Every time she took to the skies, he was with her. The best way to honor him was to fully live her life.

Slipping the heirloom back into her pocket, she hoped no one noticed that the blade had trembled in her grip. Then, like plunging into the pool in the spa's cooling room, she ripped open the package. The sound seemed to echo over the vast landscape, reaching the canyon walls and then bouncing back. The brown paper fell away, revealing a well-respected national paper with a huge circulation. Mattie gave her head a sharp tilt and then focused on the headline in one fell swoop.

She cried out . . . in utter delight.

MCADAMS BEATS CRENSHAW IN AERIAL RACE

There were no mentions of petticoat flyers, ladybirds, or even girl flyers. Mattie was identified by her name—not by her sex, not by her relationship to a man, not by a role perceived as womanly. But by her *name*.

Tears sprang into Mattie's eyes, and her hands still shook, not from anticipation now but from pure joy. She lifted her fingers to her mouth and pressed them there as she read the lead. "Miss Mattie McAdams trounced Mr. Earl Crenshaw, beating him by an entire minute in an air race through the famous Canyon of the Bridges. She told gathered reporters, 'I hope this will put to rest the silly notion that women don't belong in the skies.'"

The reporter had chosen to use those words! Her words! The ones she had worked on crafting over and over and over again as she'd lain awake at night.

With a voice as unsteady as her hands, Mattie read the entire article aloud. Mostly the group stayed silent, but occasionally they broke into cheers, whistles, and applause. The entire piece treated Mattie like an aviator—a true aviator, not a silly girl pretending to be one.

When Mattie finished, Vera clasped her hands together. "I don't know about anyone else, but I am dying to see what the lawyers sent. Something tells me it's good news, Mattie, especially based on how Mr. Fabin kept raving about you after you defeated Crenshaw."

Trying hard not to get too excited in case she only ended up disappointing herself, Mattie ripped open the envelope. Out fell a license agreement along with a cover letter. After grabbing the message, Mattie scanned it three times. The blood was rushing through her so fast she was afraid she'd misread the missive.

"Mr. Fabin signed a license agreement for my RadioNavigator!" Mattie waved the document around her head like a team pennant. "I have my first business deal!"

Leo crushed her to him, his fingers wrapped around her shoulder. "Congratulations, Mattie!"

Before he could say more, the Flying Flappers converged on both of them, smashing them even closer together. Everyone's voices were raised in excitement. They were talking so fast that all the felicitations blurred together in a wonderful, uplifting clamor.

When the women shifted back to their seats, Mattie directed her gaze at her father. "The flight school is saved, Pa. Our combined money along with the license fee is more than enough to pay off the debt."

Her father smiled, his hazel eyes warm as they regarded her. "It was never about the flight school for me, Mattie. It was always about my children finding their dreams, their place. And it looks like you have."

Mattie teared up again, and she wondered if she was always going to stay this emotional. But this was from happiness. Sheer happiness. "I believe you're correct."

"Ooooh," Lily suddenly called out as she looked up from a newspaper that she'd grabbed. "You all *must* hear this article!"

After the blonde flapper rattled off a paragraph praising Mattie, everyone took turns rifling through the periodicals and reading aloud phrases and passages that they loved. Mattie spotted mentions of ladybirds, and they laughed over some pompously written pieces that awkwardly tried their darndest not to credit her with the win.

Unfortunately, the prejudice against female aviators wouldn't drift away as easily as smoke written in the sky. One triumph could not overturn centuries of mores and false "truths." But it was a start, a glorious, wonderful start.

"This one is my favorite. It's more than a bit sensational, though," Leo warned. Unlike the others, he hadn't read anything to the group yet. Although he still didn't talk much about his past, he'd started confiding more and more to Mattie, and she'd learned he'd received very little education. To her recollection, he'd never read something aloud before, even to her.

Leo shook out the paper and spoke in a deep, slow baritone. Although he read with slight hesitation, it didn't stop him from plowing right through the paragraph: "Mattie McAdams was crowned 'Empress of the Skies' at Canyon of the Bridges when she resoundingly beat 'Quick' Crenshaw twice. First, she flew faster than the former ace in an aerial race through the Canyon of the Bridges. Then Crenshaw accused Leo 'the Flying Lion' Ward of betraying the bastion of manhood by teaching a woman to fly. Ward, the famous balloon buster, loudly proclaimed that in actuality the Empress of the Skies had taught *him*. Then

Crenshaw tried to attack the Flying Lion, who was on crutches due to Crenshaw's earlier attempts at sabotage. The Empress of the Skies stepped into the fray and neatly flipped Crenshaw to the ground."

Leo placed the broadsheet on his lap and turned his body so his knees touched Mattie's. "What do you think of your new title, Empress of the Skies?"

"It goes splendidly with the Flying Lion." She bent forward and gave Leo a kiss—a *brief* one, given their audience, including her three partially reformed but still overprotective brothers.

"The perfect pair." Leo's voice sounded as smooth as a new engine and just as powerful. His words roared through Mattie. She'd set out to make a name for herself, and along the way, she'd found love and the most-amazing female friends. It was the best journey she'd ever taken.

"A matched set."

"Oooooh!" Lily clapped her hands. "We should get a picture of the Flying Flappers. We can all hold up a newspaper with a clever headline."

"That would be perfect for my book!" Aida immediately put down her notes and straightened.

"I'll take the picture," Mattie's oldest brother, Jake, offered as he stepped off the porch with the rest of her family to make room for the women, Leo, and John. "And I'd like a copy of it so I can show it when I brag about my little sister and convince my boss to license her RadioNavigator."

"Here, use my Kodak." Aida held out her camera.

After a bit of shuffling, the members of Vera's Flying Flappers found the best pose. The women stood at the edge of the porch and linked their arms, forming a solid unit. They each proudly held their favorite article in front of them.

Also clasping a periodical, Leo and John sat on either side of the steps below the women. Ruby sprawled in the middle, her pink tongue drooping out. It was likely just the heat, but she made the most adorable canine grin as she pointed her muzzle toward the camera, the diamond brooch pinned to her cloche hat winking in the sunlight.

Situated between Vera and Carrie, Mattie tossed back her short-bobbed curls. It wasn't the haircut or her new tailored trousers and white cotton shirt that made her a New Woman. It wasn't even just her flying skills. It was these brave women and men who had flown with her, believed in her, and allowed her to truly soar on her own flight path, no matter how many loops, twists, and barrel rolls it took.

Epilogue

The sun had begun to take on a reddish glow as vibrant pink-and-orange fingers of light stretched across the waters of the Gulf of Mexico. The whole sky possessed the golden glow of evening, burnishing every part of the seascape. The hue reminded Leo keenly of Mattie's hazel eyes, especially with the hints of greens from the palms and the gentle waves themselves.

The thought calmed some of the nervousness pumping through Leo. The ring box in his pocket dug into his thigh as he helped Mattie build their latest château of sand. His cast had come off just yesterday, giving him the freedom to finally walk on the beach with Mattie. He'd planned this for weeks. Vera, being Vera, had suspected something. It was good she'd poked at him until he'd caved. After all, he couldn't have arranged the last part of the surprise without the heiress's assistance.

All Leo had to do was ask Mattie *the* question . . . which was proving rather difficult.

He cleared his throat, and Mattie tilted her head to regard him curiously. "Cat got your tongue?"

"Something like that," he muttered.

Mattie smiled and continued patting wet sand into a tower. "Take your time."

And just like that, the silence felt comfortable again. A wonderful sense of harmony had floated between Mattie and Leo for weeks now. Sure, their relationship wouldn't always operate this smoothly—nothing in life did—but they'd forged something strong out in the heat of California and in the sands of the Southwest. The fragile base of their relationship had become sturdy.

Some might have said that Leo hadn't courted Mattie long enough to properly pop the question, but he and she *knew* each other. They'd been friends, then virtual rivals, then friends again, next sweethearts, and finally partners—the true kind.

The past few nights when Leo had closed his eyes, he'd thought about Alfred. Slowly, he had realized that there'd been signs that his best friend had wanted Leo to end up with Mattie. Alfred had always insisted that Leo promise that he'd be there for her. At the time, Leo had thought his friend just wanted him to watch over his sister like a distant guardian angel. But Alfred wouldn't have conscripted Leo to stay in the background as a silent protector, not when he had always been pushing Leo to step from the shadows. Alfred had meant for Leo and Mattie to form a stalwart friendship, a romantic partnership even, just like Walt McAdams had wanted. The trust Alfred had shown humbled Leo, but it also freed him.

Most importantly, there was Mattie herself. She'd called him *solid*, the perfect match for her. If the past few months had taught him anything, it was that he needed to let Mattie make up her own mind and to trust her decisions. It was his choice to ask this potentially life-changing question and her right to accept or reject it.

And Leo very much wanted Mattie to say yes.

Glancing at the sun, he saw it dipping lower. If he waited too long, the second phase of his proposal wouldn't happen. He reached into his pocket, and his fingers closed around the velvet box. Leo brushed his thumb over the softness. Then, with a whoosh of released air, he pulled the ring out. Mattie was so intent on sculpting the peak of the tower that she didn't notice.

He preferred it that way. It gave him time to get into position. He was already down on his knees, so he popped up his right one. He'd had to ask John which one was supposed to be on the ground. Mattie wouldn't care a fig, but Leo wanted to do it right for the both of them.

Carefully he placed the box in his left hand so he could open it with his right. He almost cleared his throat, but he stopped himself just in time. He didn't want her to turn. Not just yet.

"Now that we've got our foundation in place, I was thinking this might make a good addition."

Mattie turned, her body and face relaxed. When she caught sight of his stance, her muscles froze, but her eyes . . . her eyes turned that beautiful molten gold.

"Mattie, would you do me the honor of marrying me and becoming my lifelong partner?"

For once, Mattie was speechless. She brought her hands to her throat and nodded once, then twice, then thrice. Suddenly, she launched herself at Leo and wrapped her arms around his neck.

"Yes! Oh yes! I will!" Her expression reminded him of when she flew . . . pure joy. They both burst into laughter. Leo leaned forward and captured her mirth with his lips. Mattie sank into the kiss, making it long and deep. Luckily, they weren't at a public beach but at a private stretch in front of the massive beach house that Vera owned.

Sweet power roared through Leo, filling him. He'd gotten comfortable with strong emotions. Leo no longer fought them but had learned instead to embrace them. Life with Mattie was simply fuller. It was as if he'd been living in a black-and-white photograph, and Mattie had brought a kaleidoscope of color into his existence. It didn't mean he didn't have bad nights occasionally and that images of Alfred's last flight didn't sometimes flash into his mind. But he'd learned to talk to Mattie about it and to even call up Walt after one of his episodes. And during the good moments, he'd learned to accept joy.

Reluctantly, Leo pulled back from Mattie. He should have budgeted time in his proposal for a rather thorough celebration. Unfortunately, the warm glow of sunset had taken on a smoky tone with hints of blue, gray, and purple.

"I have another surprise." He pushed back a red curl from the center of Mattie's forehead.

Her eyes widened. "Another? I think the last one is going to be hard to top."

"How would you like to fly through the stars?" Leo shifted back on his haunches, and Mattie did the same.

"You mean night flying?" Mattie bounced a little, straightening her spine, looking a bit like one of the prairie dogs they'd encountered out West. Then she sank down on her knees, her expression serious. "Doesn't that bring back difficult memories for you?"

Touched she'd remembered, Leo leaned forward and laid his hand gently on her bent leg. "It's time I created new ones, Mattie. Happy ones. With you."

Mattie remained still as she earnestly searched his face. "Are you certain you're comfortable with the idea? It *is* dangerous."

"Vera is arranging to have the whole airstrip lit up like it's a carnival, and according to the Weather Bureau, the night will be clear." Leo squeezed her knee. "And most importantly, we have *your* RadioNavigator installed on *your* Fabin. It might be best for me if we don't go far, but I want to watch you soar like a nighthawk."

"I'll be at the controls, then?" Mattie asked. "You're the one who's been grounded for weeks with a broken leg."

"I've already piloted a plane in the darkness, but I haven't seen your expression when you're zooming among the constellations."

Mattie leaped forward, her mouth once again finding his. He groaned at the delicious onslaught. His muscles went wonderfully lax as passion spread through him, hot, slow, and downright intoxicating.

Somehow, he managed to find the strength to push through the miasma of pleasure enveloping him.

Breathing hard, Leo lifted his mouth from hers. He could only manage a quarter inch or two, but it was enough. "We need to hurry if you want to fly off into the sunset."

"But we'll kiss later?" Mattie asked, her expression downright impish.

"Count on it." His words came out in a rough growl, and Mattie's smile turned flirtatious. Before he could succumb again to temptation, he stood up. After dusting the sand from his bathing suit first, he offered his hand to Mattie. She took it, and he helped haul her up.

Hand in hand, they ran the few yards to the cabana, where their flight suits awaited them. As Leo slipped into his trousers in his own dressing area, a smile slid across his face as he realized he was looking forward to the night trip with anticipation. Mattie had awoken so much in him. He'd given her his heart, but if it hadn't been for her, he wouldn't have had one to share in the first place. Loving Mattie was his true and very best adventure.

Mattie pressed the side of her face against Leo's back as they sped toward the airstrip on Vera's motorcycle. They were less than five minutes away, and if it weren't for the chance to fly at night, she would have told Leo that they should just zoom along the coast instead. It was the closest thing to soaring without leaving the ground, and Mattie had the added bonus of holding Leo tight . . . and exploring his muscles. She could feel their taut ridges shift under her fingertips while his strong deltoids flexed beneath her cheek. Even cooped up with a broken leg and a cumbersome cast, he'd kept in shape, which wasn't surprising considering all the maintenance work Leo had still managed to do. The stubborn man had insisted on hobbling around and balancing on one crutch.

When they reached the airfield, Leo parked the bike. After reluctantly unwrapping herself from him, Mattie stepped off the motorcycle. Scanning the tarmac, Mattie curled her lips upward when she caught sight of her bright-yellow Fabin looking every inch as shiny as the actual sun. She loved the plane. *Her* plane. The one she'd earned. It wasn't on loan from her brothers or even purchased by Vera. The title was in her name: Mattie McAdams. She'd christened it the *Amazon's Prize* after the famous female warriors of antiquity and had arranged for the name to be scrawled in big orange letters on the torpedo-shaped fuselage.

And she'd be soaring in it with the Flying Flappers. Although Mattie was earning enough cash from endorsement deals and royalties from the RadioNavigator to help her brothers restart the McAdams Family Flying Circus next season, they had collectively made the decision not to reband. Their father was enjoying operating the flight school year round, and Jake had rejoined him now that the money situation had improved. Otto and Will loved their jobs with the Airmail Service, and Mattie and Leo . . . well, they'd found their place in Vera's troupe.

"Did you have the *Amazon's Prize* fueled up?" Mattie asked.

"You bet." Leo finished securing his motorcycle and held out his hand again. She wrapped her fingers around his, and they fell into a momentary silence. As they walked toward her Fabin, a thought struck her.

"You know," she said slowly, "you never did tell me what you called your Nieuport and SPAD during the war."

Leo grinned down at her and swung their entwined fingers. "You haven't figured it out by now?"

"Nope."

"*Mattie's Spirit*, both of them." He flashed an even broader smile. "'Course I never told anybody, but the name meant a lot to me. When I started to feel lost, I'd think of you and your courage . . . and your light. And I got through."

Mattie's heart did five barrel rolls in a row. "I . . . I meant that much to you, even back then?"

"Yup." Leo helped her step onto the wing of the Fabin.

She stopped, carefully turned around, and slowly bent to brush his lips with her own. It wasn't the smartest thing to do when balancing on a wing, but she couldn't allow the moment to pass without touching Leo, without sharing the love bubbling inside her.

"You mean that much to me too," Mattie told him. "It just took me a little longer to figure it out."

He swallowed, his Adam's apple jerking. He no longer hid his emotions from her, and Mattie could easily see how her words had affected him.

Then one side of his lips curled into a teasing grin. "Well, we can't all be fast at everything."

She laughed and lightly bopped his shoulder. After climbing into the cockpit, she waited as he walked around to the front of the plane and yanked on the propeller. She adjusted the choke, absolutely loving the roar of the engine. Leo hopped into the passenger seat behind her. As soon as she'd tuned her RadioNavigator to a nearby station, she took off down the runway. The sun had dipped below the horizon, but the sky still glowed a brilliant red. Now mostly dark, the waves moved like undulating shadows, except for places still lit by the wondrous crimson light.

Flying had always been magical to Mattie but never more than tonight as her Fabin's yellow nose shot into the flood of electric lights. The tip of her plane shone like a replacement sun as they left the ground far behind them. When the craft climbed beyond the reach of the artificial glare, Mattie whooped as they entered a realm of reds, violets, and purples so dark they almost appeared black. Leo hollered, too, and she loved how their voices harmonized.

Mattie danced through the dramatic hues, diving like an osprey one minute and circling like a hawk the next. Yet she did not stray too far from the airstrip, always keeping its yellow-white brightness in sight. Even though she had the RadioNavigator turned on and she'd flown in the area enough to know the bearings, she hadn't charted a flight path, and she didn't want to make Leo nervous if they lost sight of their home destination.

Mattie had learned caution the day that Leo had fallen from the sky. It hadn't clipped her wings, not by any means. It had matured her as a pilot, seasoned her, teaching her a lesson in balance. Stability in the field of aerodynamics was a good thing, a needed thing. It allowed aviators to go faster, farther, and higher every year.

The scarlet finally faded, leaving the faintest line of red-violet on the horizon. Mattie flew directly toward it for a moment, loving how it seemed that she and Leo were trapped together in a timeless, otherworldly place.

"I love it up here," Mattie shouted. "Thank you for arranging this. It is the best engagement present anyone could have ever given me."

"It is peaceful," Leo agreed as Mattie just soared straight—no tricks, no fancy dives, just the beauty of the world before them.

"It isn't bringing back bad memories?" Mattie asked, keeping her voice gentle despite the need to shout over the engine. "Or making you nervous?"

Leo was quiet for a moment. When he spoke, his voice was a deeper timbre. "Mattie, do you remember when I mentioned how we used to fire Very lights into the night sky to try to guide our lost comrades home?"

"Yes." Mattie's own voice sounded thick, even to her. She thought of Alfred and the others who hadn't made it back, and then she thought of Leo and the ones who had.

"I love you, Mattie. You are *my* Very light. As long as I'm with you, I can't ever get lost." Leo's voice had gone hoarse with emotion, and those same feelings swamped Mattie too. But it was a delightful heaviness, like a warm wool blanket to keep away the chill. At the same time, the mood lifted her—a glorious buoyant pressure like the air currents keeping their plane aloft.

"You're *my* Very light too, Leo." Mattie paused and swallowed against the tightness in her throat. "I love you so much."

The purple light blinked out, but in its place rose a million tiny stars. As a child, Mattie used to lie on her back and stare up at the constellations, wondering what it would be like to sail through them.

Now she knew, and it felt absolutely wonderful.

HISTORICAL NOTE

The moment I walked into the Henry Ford Museum's exhibit on barnstormers and spotted a life-size model of a woman hanging upside down from the wing of a Curtiss JN-4 (Jenny) biplane, I was seized by a spine-tingling thrill, and I absolutely *knew* I had to tell this woman's story. With increasing excitement, I read the placards and learned about the intrepid, diverse women who proved that the skies were a woman's domain as much as a man's. There was Katherine Stinson, the Flying Schoolgirl. The white southerner earned her pilot's license in 1912 and became a darling of the press. With her family, she established a flight school in the years preceding World War I.

In the 1920s, more women took to the skies, including the famed Bessie Coleman, Queen Bess or Brave Bessie. An American born of African and Cherokee ancestry, Bessie faced not just sexism but racism in her pursuit to soar. Unlike Stinson, who was white, Bessie could not find a flight school in the United States willing to give her, a Black woman, a license. Undefeated, Bessie learned French and traveled to Europe twice to receive instruction there. She became a media phenomenon despite the obstacles placed in her path due to her race. Bessie was an unceasing activist who refused to speak in places that practiced segregation. Bessie planned on starting her own flight school for Black folks, but this dream was never realized due to the opposition she faced.

Bessie tragically died at the age of thirty-four in an aviation accident due to mechanical trouble.

Mabel Cody, the niece of Buffalo Bill, started her own flying circus. A wing-walker, she fell fifty feet while attempting to jump from a moving car onto a ladder suspended from an airplane. After she recovered, she returned to her daredevil career. Gladys Ingle would leap from biplane to biplane in midair and would even change the tire of one of the aircrafts. Female pilots in the latter half of the 1920s—such as Amelia Earhart, Louise Thaden, and Ruth Elder—also inspired me with their fight to be viewed as serious aviators, especially in the eyes of the press.

Although Mattie, Vera, Carrie, Aida, Sadie, Lily, and Alice are all purely fictional characters, they are each a homage to the indomitable spirit of the fly girls of the 1920s. Leo was loosely inspired by US World War I fighter pilots, including Eddie Rickenbacker, America's Ace of Aces; Frank Luke, the fearless balloon buster; and other war heroes who pioneered aerial combat.

Like my characters, most of the municipalities and places are fictional but were inspired by the towns, parks, and natural wonders that I toured as a child on family vacations with my maternal grandparents, my mother, and my sister. All the newspapers, speakeasies, and establishments are from my imagination but are based on research. The decor of the Gilded Secret in the Chicago, Illinois, speakeasy was particularly modeled off the Urban Room in the William Penn Hotel in Pittsburgh, Pennsylvania. Troy, Wyoming, was inspired by Thermopolis, Wyoming. Natural Bridges National Monument is the real-life Canyon of the Bridges, although it is more remote, and the configuration of the box canyons is different. Carrie and Mattie's visit to the power room in Vera's mansion is based on a similar room in the Biltmore in Asheville, North Carolina, that my husband and I learned about on one of the extended tours offered by the estate. The outside of Fete Castle was inspired by a real Baronial-style fortress, Craigievar Castle, that I saw in Scotland.

The historical detail most personal to me, however, is the mention of couples getting engaged near the McAdamses' flight school. Although it was during the 1940s, my maternal grandfather proposed to my maternal grandmother at the Allegheny County Airport in West Mifflin, Pennsylvania. Even in the thirties and forties, airplanes were still novel enough that young couples like my grandparents would drive to airfields and watch airplanes take off and land. I hope that adding this little family history to *The Aviatrix* helps show modern readers how truly magical and exciting airplanes were in the first half of the twentieth century.

Most of the aircraft in the book are real biplanes. However, the Fabin and its manufacturer are made up, along with the competitions that the company held to attract interest from the US government. Rockol also did not exist. Mattie's RadioNavigator was similar to technology first employed in the late twenties, but which would have been possible in 1923. While radio direction-finding equipment had existed in some form for several decades, they were large, cumbersome units primarily found on ships and had to be used by a trained navigator. Mattie's simplified, scaled-down system allowed a single pilot to easily check their bearings by taking advantage of the brand-new frequency-modulated radio stations that were popping up during the Jazz Age.

The Roaring Twenties was such a fascinating time of old mixed with new, changing social structures and mores, and exciting derring-do. I hope you have enjoyed your visit to this exhilarating period in history as much as I have.

GLOSSARY OF 1920S AND AVIATION TERMS

alarm clock. Chaperone.

Albatros. German World War I fighter plane.

applesauce. Awesome.

bear cat. Fiery, adventurous woman.

bee's knees. Awesome; also a cocktail.

berries. Awesome.

bluenose. Stick-in-the-mud.

chic. Stylish.

cloche. Tight-fitting hat.

copacetic. Okay; cool.

Curtiss. Plane manufacturer and shorthand for airplanes made by the company.

Curtiss JN-4. World War I biplane that was commonly called a Jenny. The US government had a surplus of them at the end of the war, so they sold them cheaply, which led to an explosion of aviation and daredevil stunts.

Duesenberg. Extremely expensive car with cutting-edge technologies.

Duesy. Nickname for a Duesenberg.

fairy floss. Cotton candy.

flash powder. Substance used to create flashes for picture taking before the use of the light bulb.

Fokker. Dutch-built World War I plane flown by German aviators.

glad rags. Fancy evening clothes.

Jagdgeschwader I. Elite group of German fighter pilots; the famous Red Baron was part of this group.

Jenny. Nickname for a Curtiss JN-4.

JN-4. Another nickname for the Curtiss JN-4.

kisser. Mouth.

Lafayette Escadrille. French fighter squadron mainly comprised of US citizen-volunteers; disbanded when the United States entered World War I.

Nieuport. French World War I fighter plane, also flown by Americans.

ossified. Drunk.

peach. To tattle.

pie eyed. Drunk.

Sopwith Camel. British World War I fighter plane, also flown by Americans.

SPAD XIII. French World War I fighter plane, also flown by Americans.

rags. Newspapers.

vamp. Glamorous, seductive woman; a man-eater.

wurp. Stick-in-the-mud.

ACKNOWLEDGMENTS

I want to thank my editor Lauren Plude and the entire team at Montlake. An author always dreams of finding an editor who falls in love with her characters as much as she herself has. Lauren has not only embraced Mattie and her fellow barnstormers but helped me make them fully live on the page. Her comments have prompted me to learn more about these wonderful women and further understand their passions, their dreams, and their fears. Although sometimes this has meant making my heroine and hero face more conflict, they have become stronger and richer for it.

I also want to extend my appreciation to the cultural-review editor who took the time to read *The Aviatrix* and provided me with valuable advice and insight into how I addressed the topic of racism in the 1920s. Mistakes, if any, that I made in the representations of characters of color are my own.

Thank you to the copyeditors and proofreaders who have caught my mistakes and fixed those typos that slyly slipped by me. The art department has created a wonderful cover capturing the spirit of *The Aviatrix*, and marketing and distribution have worked to make sure this book reaches the hands of the readers.

My agent, Jessica Watterson, has been an integral part of *The Aviatrix*. Her excitement when I originally pitched this idea encouraged me to put my heart into this book. She has cheered on my tough, feminist heroines and helps me make sure that their stories are heard.

My critique partners, Sarah Morgenthaler and Suzanne Tierney, have provided invaluable insight and helped me make my writing crisper and more vivid. No matter how busy their own schedules, they have always made time to provide me with incredible feedback. I met both women when our manuscripts reached the finals in the Romance Writers of America®'s 2017 Golden Heart® contest, and we became part of the group of writers called Rebelles. All the Rebelles have been amazingly supportive over the past few years, and I am so thankful I have been able to share this journey with them. They are my Flying Flappers.

I want to give my husband an extra thanks for his support on the technical issues in this book. During our marriage, he has shared his love for all things mechanical with me. Our trip to the National Museum of the United States Air Force near Dayton, Ohio, started me thinking about early aviation, and his joy in viewing the old machines inspired me. When we later traveled to the Henry Ford Museum in Dearborn, Michigan, where he was explaining old steam engines to me for another project, I saw the exhibit on female barnstormers, and my idea for *The Aviatrix* was born. He has very patiently helped provide me technical details when I come to him and say, "Okay, so the plot is *X*, and the characters need to be feeling *Y*, and I want to convey *Z*, so what could go wrong mechanically to enhance the external and internal conflicts?" This makes for some rather interesting conversations over dinner or during car rides.

Although my maternal grandparents passed away before I began work on *The Aviatrix*, they provided me with so much of the foundation that helped produce it. They were the ones who originally took me to the Henry Ford Museum when I was a young girl, which led to the later trip with my husband. Other vacations that I took with my grandparents also helped inspire the scenery throughout *The Aviatrix*, which in some ways is a love letter to them and to the natural beauty of the United States and its national parks.

As always, I want to thank my family for their support during the writing process. In addition to being my go-to source for aviation-related questions, my husband picks up more of the housework when I am on deadline and need to retreat into my writer's cave. During those times, my mother helps by watching my preschool-age daughter, who understands that Mommy needs to work on her "stories." Both my husband and my mother are my first and last beta readers.

Of course, a book would be a static object without readers to open their hearts and imaginations to the characters and allow them to jump from the pages. Whether you are a reader who has followed me from my contemporary romances or one who has taken a chance on a new author, thank you for going on this odyssey with Mattie, Leo, and the Flying Flappers. Your emails, social media shout-outs, and reviews mean so much to me. Thanks again for all your support!

ABOUT THE AUTHOR

Photo © 2018 Skysight Photography

Two-time Golden Heart finalist Violet Marsh is a lawyer who decided it was more fun to write witty banter than contractual terms. A romance enthusiast, she relishes the transformative power of love, especially when a seeming mismatch becomes the perfect pairing.

Marsh also enjoys visiting the past—whether strolling through a castle's ruins, wandering around a stately manor, or researching her family genealogy online (where she discovered at least one alleged pirate, a female tavern owner, and several blacksmiths). She indulges in her love of history by writing period pieces filled with independent-minded women and men smart enough to fall for them.

Marsh lives at home with Prince Handy (a guy who can fix things is definitely sexier than a mere charmer), a whirlwind (her toddler), and a suburban nesting dog (whose cuteness Marsh shamelessly uses to promote her books).

Marsh loves to interact with her readers on social media:
www.facebook.com/violetmarshauthor
www.instagram.com/violetmarshauthor
www.twitter.com/vi_marsh_author